THE LANDLORD'S
BLACK-EYED DAUGHTER

MARY ELLEN DENNIS

THORNDIKE PRESS

An imprint of Thomson Gale, a part of The Thomson Corporation

Detroit • New York • San Francisco • New Haven, Conn. • Waterville, Maine • London

LIBRARY OF CONGRESS CATALOGING-IN-PUBLICATION DATA

Dennis, Mary Ellen.
 The landlord's black-eyed daughter / by Mary Ellen Dennis.
  p. cm.
 ISBN-13: 978-1-4104-0442-8 (hardcover : alk. paper)
 ISBN-10: 1-4104-0442-0 (hardcover : alk. paper)
 1. Brigands and robbers — Fiction. 2. Women authors — Fiction.
3. England — Fiction. 4. Large type books. I. Title.
 PS3604.E58647L36 2008
 813'.6—dc22   2007041148

Published in 2008 by arrangement with Tekno Books.

Printed in the United States of America on permanent paper
10 9 8 7 6 5 4 3 2 1

This book is for Marley Pontius, Jade Manna, Katherine "Katie" Johnson, and Simran Carl

And Loreena McKennitt

6 April 1766

Seated beside the open coffin, the watchers waited. They waited to see whether Barbara Wyndham's body moved. They watched intently while mourners trailed past. Blind belief said that if Barbara's body began to bleed, 'twould identify her murderer.

There was some question as to whether Barbara had suffered a seizure of the heart and fallen and hit her head on a rock. Or had she been struck by some unknown hand?

Seven-year-old Elizabeth Wyndham watched with the watchers, but her mother remained motionless.

"Mama," Elizabeth whispered, "are ye sleeping?"

"Your mother sleeps evermore, my Bess," said Lawrence Wyndham, lifting his daughter up into his arms.

Elizabeth pressed her tear-streaked face against his shoulder. At the same time, she wondered with a twinge of fear how it would feel to sleep evermore.

CHAPTER 1

30 March 1787

"I wonder why Fleet Street calls us Knights of the Road," John Randolph Remington said to his partner. "I'll wager no knight ever spent his days hiding in a copse."

Zak Turnbull swatted his hat at a circling fly. "They call us knights, Rand, 'cause 'tis a snappy title and no one can deny we be a fine pair o' prancers."

Rand gazed north, where the straight highway took an abrupt turn. For the past three hours nothing had passed their way except for a handful of dilapidated coaches and shabbily dressed travelers. While Zak wasn't particular about whom he robbed, Rand agreed with Robin Hood: Proper criminals should take from the rich.

"How much bloody longer is it gonna be?" Zak pulled at his wig. "I'm sweatin' like a bloody barrister 'neath this poll, and I've got so many fleas tormentin' me, ye'd

9

think I was a heap o' dung."

"Patience," said Rand, shifting in his saddle and trying to ease the stiffness in his right leg. "The reason you've spent the last twenty years breaking out of every prison in England is because you grow careless. And then you're caught."

" 'Tis a fine observation, comin' from someone who's been in the business a mere two years. Ye know as well as I that a gagger, though he be rich as King George himself, will dress poor just t' trick us." Zak wiped his sweat-streaked face with his vizard. "And I'm warnin' ye. If a proper gagger don't come along soon, I'll be millin' meself a flat."

Rand mentally translated Zak's cant into something resembling the King's English. Basically, Zak meant you could seldom tell a man's wealth from his attire and he planned to rob the next traveler, no matter what the size of his purse.

"And as far as ever bein' habbled again, it ain't gonna happen," Zak continued. "Ye've brought me good luck, cousin."

"London's poor law enforcement has provided all the luck we need," Rand said with a droll grin.

In truth, London's press had proven to be a far more formidable opponent than the city's decrepit watchmen and underpaid constables. After every robbery, editors of the *Gazeteer* and the *Monitor* and the other daily papers howled for the apprehension of the "Gentleman Giant and his Quiet Companion." But the resultant publicity hadn't brought Zak and Rand any closer to capture. On the contrary, it had turned them into local heroes.

"If I'm gonna have t' wait, I'm gonna spend me time in a more enjoyable fashion." Zak dismounted and stretched his six-foot-five frame upon the grass. He covered his face with his wide-brimmed hat, then clasped his hands across his prodigious belly. "Rouse me if ye see a ratter what meets yer specifications."

Almost immediately Zak's rhythmic snores blended with the buzzing flies and the distant bleats of sheep. Rand tried to ignore his now throbbing leg and his own wig, which was bloody uncomfortable. Generally he wore his thick black hair long and natural, for that was the way the ladies liked it. But disguise was a necessary part of his profession. Today he was dressed as a gentleman. Doeskin riding breeches hugged his thighs and his feet were clad in knee-high, glossy brown boots. His loose-fitting shirt couldn't completely hide his rugged

11

chest, which tapered to a narrow waist, lean hips and a flat belly. In an age where gentlemen prided themselves on their girth, Rand figured his slenderness was the only part of his disguise some observant magistrate might question.

So why did he feel so apprehensive?

He had experienced the same uneasiness before the Battle of Guilford Court House. The night preceding that colonial battle, he had dreamed of war. But the war in his dream belonged to another age, an age of broadswords and chain mail and mace, of armored men clashing on the summit of an emerald green hill. This dream, which had troubled him since childhood, always ended the same way, with the delicate mournful face of a flaxen-haired woman. Over the years he had sought possible interpretations. Eventually, he had stopped probing. It was better to accept the fact that the dream forecast change. Violent change.

The thud of hooves and the squeak of coach springs interrupted Rand's thoughts. He straightened in his saddle. While he couldn't see anything above the distant hedges, a prospective wayfarer was obviously headed their way.

"Zak," he whispered.

A gleaming black carriage, pulled by four

high-stepping greys, came into view.

Zak's snoring continued, undisturbed. Rand maneuvered Prancer, his black stallion, closer. "Cousin, wake up! This is it. Time to earn your keep."

"I'm ready, I'm ready." Rising, Zak secured his hat atop his wig, stumbled toward his horse, and swung up into the saddle. "Who've ye decided we're t' be this time?" he asked, concealing the lower half of his face with his vizard.

"Irishmen," Rand replied. It was necessary to disguise one's voice along with one's appearance.

"And here's me shillelagh, boy-o," Zak quipped, raising his pistol.

Rand lifted his own vizard into place. As the coach rumbled toward them, his muscles tensed. This was the best part of his profession: the anticipation of the chase, never knowing what danger would come within the next few minutes or what surprises waited behind the curtained windows. He scrutinized every inch of the approaching carriage, from the gilded coat of arms on the door to the red plumes topping the heads of the greys, and the brightly polished gold buttons on the liveries of the coachman and footman.

"Now," he breathed.

Bolting from behind the stand of trees, he rushed forward, grabbed the bridle of the nearest grey, brought the carriage to a halt, then trained his pistol on the coachman's chest.

"Stand and deliver!" Zak barked, yanking open the door.

A nervous young whip hastily exited. "My auntie's still inside," he said, his voice cracking. "May I pull down the steps? She suffers from an inflammation of the joints and —"

"Ye need not be deliverin' a sermon, ye chicken-hammed chatterbox. Do it and be quick about it."

The whip scrambled to obey. When his aunt climbed down, she turned out to be a formidable-looking dowager with a jutting jaw and a ramrod straight posture. Smoothing her satin skirt, she eyed Zak. "I'm Lady Avery," she said, "and I was robbed by a footpad only last month. Perhaps you've heard and will think to spare me."

"Prancers, I mean highwaymen, don't rub shoulders with footpads, m'lady, especially *Irish* prancers like we be." Ever mindful of his reputation with the press, Zak kept his voice respectful. "Now, if ye'd be so good as to give me yer bit . . . uh, yer purse . . . and yer rings. And ye, sir . . ." He gestured with his pistol at the whip's feet. "I'll have yer

14

watch, and them be a handsome pair o' shoe buckles."

Lady Avery tapped her first finger against the bridge of her nose. "I know who you are. You're the Gentleman Giant."

Zak dipped from the waist in a half bow. "Aye, 'tis the gospel truth, m'lady."

"I don't recall the *Morning Chronicle* mentioning that you were Irish." Her watery brown eyes turned toward Rand, who still had his pistol trained on the coachman and footman. "Well, no matter what your nationality, you're both impressive specimens." She swiveled her head toward her nephew. "Are they not, Roger?"

"We're being robbed, Aunt Maude." Roger fumbled with the watch and gold fob-seal in his waistcoat pocket. "I'll reserve my opinion for a more propitious time."

Zak pointed to a circle of diamonds nestled in a crevice of Lady Avery's towering coiffure. "I'll have that, m'lady."

"I should never have removed my bonnet, nor my gloves," she murmured, unclasping the circle. But her wedding ring proved a more difficult matter. "It's this damnable arthritis," she said. "I cannot get anything over my joints." In a tone that brooked no argument, she added, "Never grow old, young man. Though in your profession that

15

can't be much of a worry."

"Forget the ring, m'lady, for I'm sure it holds sentimental value. I'll settle for yer earbobs."

"Thank you, Giant. Truthfully, my husband was a poor father and a poorer spouse, and I seldom mourn his passing."

"Aunt Maude!"

"I'm sorry to hear that, m'lady," Zak commiserated, dropping her jewelry into his coin purse. "I'll take that there cameo, if ye please."

"I don't please, but I suppose I have no choice."

"Hurry," Rand urged. Zak was a great one for talking when he should be tending to business. Rand fancied he heard hoofbeats. While Zak assured Lady Avery that she would soon find a more compatible husband, Rand guided Prancer to the carriage door and began retrieving everything within easy reach. The gold and enamel snuffbox would fetch a few coins, and the handsome walking stick was worth at least ten guineas from a good fence. He hesitated when he spied a novel. Entitled *Castles of Doom,* it rested on the velvet seat. The novel had little monetary value, but one of his ladies might enjoy it.

Two riders rounded the ragged hedge.

They were moving slowly and looked like harmless merchants or respectable tradesmen. On the other hand, one never could be too careful, Rand reminded himself. "Time to go, boy-o," he said to Zak.

"Been a pleasure, m'lady." Zak leaned over and kissed the elderly woman's hand. She flushed beneath her rice powder.

"Help, highwaymen!" Roger shouted.

"Don't be such a nincompoop, nephew," said Lady Avery.

The oncoming riders were now only yards away. "Keep yer distance, ye bloody coves!" Zak shouted, and fired into the air.

Glancing over his shoulder, Rand saw both riders scramble for the ditches. The road stretched ahead, deserted save for a peddler who trudged along beneath a huge back pack. Spurring his stallion, Rand chucked the startled man a guinea. Then, shadowed by Zak, he raced toward London's turnpike.

"Hurrah for the Gentleman Giant and his Quiet Companion!" Zak bellowed to the grazing sheep, the freshly plowed fields, and the bright spring sky. "We're a fine pair, ain't we, cousin?"

True to his epithet, Rand merely grinned.

"Are ye certain ye'll not be joinin' us?"

Zak's arms encircled the waists of two pretty bunters.

Tonight Rand wasn't interested. "My leg's bothering me, cousin. I think I'll take a walk, ease the stiffness."

"Ye're not sufferin' one o' yer black moods again, are ye?"

"No. I just need to walk."

But once he was alone, Rand couldn't bring himself to leave their lodgings. While the rooms were clean and graced with quality furnishings, he need only draw aside the lace curtain at the window to look down upon a scene of unimaginable squalor.

Rand and Zak lived in London's Rookery, christened for the thievish disposition of rook birds. Even night watchmen avoided the area, calling it a den of ruffians, cock bawds and beggars, although he and Zak had never been harassed. In fact, the primarily Irish coal-heavers, laborers, porters, and gaunt-faced children who were the recipients of Rand's largesse considered him something of a folk hero. Yet, as he pictured the filthy houses which sold beds for two pence a night and rotgut gin for a penny a quart, he felt the crushing weight of despair. The tiny, windowless, dirt-floored hovels housed up to fifty people each. If Rand robbed every lord from here to Scotland, the Rookery's poverty would not be alleviated one whit.

"I must leave London," he whispered, "for my soul is dying here."

He longed for the gentle hills and stone cottages of his native Gloucestershire, or the vast unpopulated landscapes of America. But he had made his decision following the War with the Colonies and there was no turning back.

Once Rand had admired the rich. As a boy, he had dreamed of emulating the lords driving past in their gilded carriages. Lords attended by liveried footmen who wore scented wigs and supercilious expressions. Lords surrounded by black slaves who wore silver collars round their necks and the marks of the branding iron upon their arms. Someday, Rand thought, he would own a mansion on a hill. Someday he would be wealthy beyond measure.

As an adult, he had nearly achieved his dream. But the War with the Colonies had shattered his fantasies along with his leg. The war had been senseless and stupid, the lives lost on both sides wasted. When he returned to Gloucestershire, he sold his successful cabinetmaking business and did virtually nothing for two years — just walked and brooded. During that time he often asked himself whether England had changed, or was he viewing it through different eyes?

Increasingly, the world reminded Rand of something out of an opium dream, hazy and elusive, a place where reality could change in an instant. Because reality depended on the whims of the rich and powerful, never on truth itself.

"Platitudes," he whispered. During the war he had heard so many platitudes. The rebels declared their independence by founding a nation based on the concept of liberty and justice for all. Which meant, of course, liberty and justice for a few landed white men, not their slaves, nor their women, nor their poor. The war was fought over power and property, rather than principles, no matter how many noble phrases the rebels wrapped themselves in.

But England is far worse, thought Rand. *Here only the lives of the wealthy possess value.*

Now, when he looked at the gilded coaches, he saw carriage-makers toiling for starvation wages. He saw servants working for cast-off clothes and straw mattresses to sleep upon. Parliament prattled on and on about passing laws against the enslavement of the Negro. Paying no heed, ladies treated their blackamoors like trained pets. And the mansion on the hill that Rand had once longed for had been built by men who exploited their workers. "The rich are more deserving," the wealthy justified. "If we weren't, God wouldn't have blessed us with wealth in the first place."

For the upper classes, laws, like women, existed only for men's pleasure. Rand had seen a young fop slit a wigmaker's throat over the price of a wig, while a second ran his sword through a total stranger during a game of cards. Both had received pardons, whereas Rand's fourteen-year-old niece had been hanged for hiding, *on instructions from her employer,* some counterfeit shillings.

Rand had been gone, fighting for England, when the hanging of his niece occurred. Fighting for a country where orphans were sold into servitude to ship captains bound for America or India, and no one raised an objection. Fighting for a country where churchgoers nodded approvingly over sermons advocating that abandoned children should be allowed only enough education to obtain the meanest job. And those same children should learn to read a little so they could decipher the appropriate biblical passages that reinforced their lowly status.

Outside London coffeehouses, ten-year-old whores sold themselves for the price of a loaf of bread. Bucks drank champagne from the slippers of their mistresses while the bastards they spawned off their servant girls were left to die in the streets. Rand never ceased to be amazed, as well as enraged, by the sheer hypocrisy of it all.

With a sigh, he stretched out on the soft feather mattress and tried to sleep. Suddenly, he remembered the novel he had retrieved from Lady Avery. Although Rand was an avid reader, he had never opened a Gothic romance. According to conventional wisdom, such writings required the womanly virtues of imagination and sensibility, but not intellect, so they were a waste of time for serious, meaning male, readers. Not that Rand had ever paid much attention to conventional wisdom. Now, on impulse, he retrieved *Castles of Doom* from his saddlebag.

The novel had been manufactured in three slim volumes. Rand opened the first installment, and a folded piece of paper fell out. It was an invitation to meet the pride of Minerva Press, Miss B. B. Wyndham. Some biological facts followed, concerning the lady, as well as the date of the party: April 1, 1787 — three days hence.

Licking his thumb, Rand flipped to Chapter One. The first sentence read: *That most malevolent of men, Baron Ralf Darkstarre, paced the length of his watchtower, which overlooked the churning waters of the North Sea, and impatiently awaited the arrival of his liege lord, Simon de Montfort.*

Rand felt as if all the heat from the stuffy room had rushed into his body. Simon de Montfort was a familiar name, a very familiar name. Rand had long believed that his recurring dream was connected with Simon de Montfort and his rebellion against King Henry, which had occurred more than five hundred years ago.

His breath uneven, Rand continued reading: *Despite his evil nature, Lord Darkstarre was a comely man of impressive height, and possessed of an arresting countenance. Lord Darkstarre's brow was wide and noble, and it was only after one gazed into his eyes that one could detect a flicker of the madness that would ultimately consume him.*

Swiftly Rand scanned the pages until he found the next mention of Simon de Montfort.

Three hours later, Zak stumbled inside, his waistcoat half buttoned, his voice mangling the strains of a bawdy tavern song.

Rand was still reading.

"Ye bloody flat!" Zak shouted. "What

kinda prancer be ye, spendin' yer nights with books 'stead o' bunters? Damme, lad, what's wrong? Ye look like ye've seen yer own death."

Reluctantly, Rand left the pages of the past and returned to his cousin. How could he possibly explain what was wrong? The whole thing seemed as mad as B. B. Wyndham's antagonist. "I'm going to attend a party," he finally managed. "I do believe I should meet the pride of Minerva Press."

"What the bloody hell are ye talkin' 'bout?" Zak tossed his beaver hat toward a wall peg. "Are ye daft?"

"Yes," said Rand. "Perhaps I am."

CHAPTER 2

Elizabeth Wyndham gazed at her reflection in the mirror above her dressing table. Dispassionately, she scrutinized her ink-black hair, which fell in ringlets on either side of her face, not unlike a spaniel's ears. A scowl caused her delicately arched brows to descend toward her dark brown eyes — so dark that from a distance they looked like lampblack. "You're a fraud," she said to her image. "A cheat."

"What did ye gabble, Mistress?" asked her servant, Grace.

"I wasn't gabbling," Elizabeth fibbed, her lashes thick, dark crescents against her cheekbones. "I coughed."

"It didn't sound like a cough t' me." Grace regarded her mistress with disapproval. While no one could deny that Miss Elizabeth was an attractive woman, Grace wondered how much longer her looks could possibly hold up. After all, she must be close to thirty. And yet she acted as if men would always flock 'round her, like pigeons. Truth be told, Elizabeth Wyndham should have been married for a good decade now, and mother to at least five children.

"What are you staring at? My gown?" Elizabeth allowed a thin smile to tug at the corners of her mouth. "In truth, this gown is so out-of-date, 'tis moss-grown."

"Ye never fret over fashion when we're at home." Grace's gaze touched upon Elizabeth's powdered white shoulders, which contrasted dramatically with the red brocade of her gown — her very low-cut gown. "If ye want the *naked* truth, Mistress, yer bosom's practically fallin' on the table. What would yer mother —"

"Stepmother!"

"— say if she saw such a thing?"

With a shrug, Elizabeth turned back to her reflection. She was aware of her shortcomings and strengths, and considered her beauty her most important asset. But only because of *society's* dictates. Her quick intelligence, which would last far longer than her face and figure, would ultimately serve her better. Until that time, however, she would display her physical attributes, turning a blind eye — and a deaf ear — to the servant, chaperone, or even stepmother

26

who expressed dissatisfaction.

"God blessed me with a generous bosom," she said, "and I see no reason to hide it."

Grace's lantern-jawed face flushed. "Ye're an authoress, Mistress, not a . . . one of them . . . improper ladies."

"Whores, you mean?"

Grace looked as if she were about to faint. "Yer language," she reprimanded. "Wait till I tell your mother —"

"Stepmother!"

"Wait till I tell *somebody*," Grace cried, stomping toward the bed.

"I'm sorry," Elizabeth said. "It's just that I'm so nervous."

It's just that you're a fraud, her reflection silently mocked. How could she face the one hundred and fifty guests gathering even now in the ballroom below? Tonight was supposed to be the crowning moment of a career that, in all modesty, had been enormously successful. And yet Elizabeth felt as if her career replicated the title of her latest book. She felt doomed.

She cradled her face in her hands. Her cheeks were so hot. While she prided herself on her iron constitution, her body was sometimes bothered by a variety of vague aches and pains. She attributed their origin to tension, unhappiness, confusion, and a host of the womanly maladies she had always disdained.

Perhaps I'm coming down with a fever and will die in the next few minutes, she thought hopefully. *Then I won't have to encounter all those smiling faces, and listen to all those compliments, and pretend I'm still the darling of Minerva Press.*

She had already decided that her writing career was over. Pretending otherwise was artifice.

Grace captured two black velvet ribbons and lifted them from the four-poster's gold-threaded counterpane. "What do you want me to do with these, Mistress?"

"Tie them around my neck and wrist, please."

"I'd rather fetch yer shawl."

"No." Elizabeth extended her wrist, but her servant just stood there, holding the ribbons gingerly, as if she'd caught two mice by their tails. "All right, hand over the damnable things. I'll put them on myself."

Grace gasped at the word "damnable." Her thick brows shot up toward her mob cap. Without further comment, she thrust the ribbons at her mistress.

Elizabeth's fingers felt like chips of ice as she fumbled with her accessories. She knew she shouldn't snap at Grace. Her servant wasn't responsible for B. B. Wyndham's inability to finish *Castles of Doom,* and Grace certainly wasn't responsible for Elizabeth Wyndham's related problem, or more precisely, her obsession.

"My obsession," Elizabeth whispered to her reflection.

She squeezed her eyes shut, but it didn't help. Behind her closed eyelids, she conjured up the raven-haired knight whom she hated and feared and loved — the raven-haired knight who existed only in her imagination. His face remained elusive, but the more she wrote, the more frequently she caught flashes of him — the width of his back beneath his surcoat, his thick hair curling over his ears and brushing his nape, the way he held his lithe body so straight and tall. She had fled the Yorkshire Dales in a virtual panic. That way she wouldn't have to confront her knight's forthcoming death. Yet he had followed her here to London, invading her publisher's palatial townhouse. She now knew he would follow her everywhere.

I cannot escape him.

In each of her nine novels she had included the raven-haired knight under various names and guises. In her first work, he had hovered on the fringes as one of the Norman lords who arrived with William the

Bastard. Then, with every subsequent book, he had insinuated himself closer to the core. By *Richard of the Lion's Heart,* he had been the King's most trusted advisor, and, in her last work, one of the barons at Runnymede. Now, as Ralf Darkstarre in *Castles of Doom,* he threatened to take over the entire narrative. Darkstarre had never existed, of course, but he was the book's villain, as well as a rebel, and he must die alongside Simon de Montfort.

How could she kill him?

"I don't like pictures of people," Grace said, as she examined a Gainsborough portrait. "I like huntin' dogs and horses."

"That painting is very expensive. Everything the Beresfords own is very expensive."

"I still like animals better."

Elizabeth rubbed her temples, trying to ease the start of a headache. *Perhaps I could make something up about the rebellion,* she thought. Gothic novels were not required to be factual, yet when it came to historical events she had always striven for accuracy.

I know what I'll do, she mused, wrapping a curl around her index finger. *I'll return to the Dales and fake my own death. That way I won't have to finish the book and nobody will blame me.*

"I hope ye'll act like a lady tonight." Grace

30

shifted her gaze to the console table where a set of porcelain ladies perched. "No talk 'bout free love, whatever that's supposed to mean, or education, or jobs and laws. Yer papa's right. He says ye'd be a dangerous woman if anyone paid attention to ye."

"For once I agree," Elizabeth said, her voice wry.

She could do as she pleased at home, thank goodness. Locals expected her to be eccentric. After all, she was a novelist, an occupation that was considered, if not disreputable, at least unusual for a woman. Elizabeth often imagined regulars at her father's establishment, the Inn of the White Hart, pointing her out to strangers, as if she were some slightly suspect landmark. "There goes Bess, the landlord's black-eyed daughter," they would say. "She writes Gothic romances." But perhaps they were simply saying: "I wonder if the poor girl will ever find herself a husband."

Tempted to run a comb through her curls, Elizabeth stilled her hand. Sometimes, when she brushed the silky strands and counted out loud, she could curtail the whispers from her past, especially the memories of her mother.

Barbara Wyndham had died when Elizabeth was seven years old. A strong-willed woman, Barbara had embraced the notion that social equality should exist between men and women. She often told her little daughter the story of a simple peasant girl named Joan, who had fought valiantly for France.

Yet, even at the tender age of seven, Elizabeth saw that her mother didn't have any power. Everything she owned, including the White Hart, belonged to her husband, Lawrence Wyndham. Mama agonized over Papa's frequent gambling, but she had little say in the matter.

That would never happen to her, Elizabeth swore, as she penned her novels. Success was a viable method with which to assert one's independence, and B. B. Wyndham had proven herself very successful. However, if B. B. Wyndham couldn't finish *Castles of Doom,* all that success would have been for naught.

Shaking her head, Elizabeth crossed to the window overlooking Stratton Street. Coaches were lined up in both directions. The walk was crowded with women in luxurious capes, while men sported beaver hats and wide-brimmed hats and hats that scarcely spanned the crowns of their heads.

Grace was right, thought Elizabeth. Tonight was not the night for a lecture on the ills of the world. People were attending Mr. Beresford's "drum" because they expected to meet an authoress very much like the heroines in her books. Elizabeth knew that her heroines could best be described as vapid. All her leading ladies considered their chastity more important than their lives, and they fainted over a profanity. They spent much of their time in bed, recovering from some mysterious illness, and they could be counted upon to deliver, at the slightest provocation, a sermon on socially correct behavior. Her heroes were merely male versions of her socially correct females.

Elizabeth sighed. If boring characters were the price one must pay in order to remain the best-selling author of Minerva Press, so be it. She thought about her raven-haired knight. He might be many things, but he wasn't a gentleman.

A knock on the door interrupted her reverie.

"Enter." Turning away from the window, Elizabeth pasted on the public smile she employed at the White Hart.

Her hostess, Penelope Beresford, blew into the room like a ship in full sail. Penelope was followed by her tiny husband.

"Miss Wyndham, you look ravishing," Charles Beresford said.

While Charles reminded Elizabeth of a rabbit, his voice was deep, wonderfully mellifluous and soothing. She imagined God would sound similar.

"Everyone is talking about you," Charles continued, extracting a lace handkerchief and dabbing at his forehead. "They cannot wait to meet you. In the fortnight you've been here, I cannot tell you how many inquiries we've had concerning our lovely house guest. Isn't that true, Mrs. Beresford?"

"Absolutely, Mr. Beresford." Penelope spoke with a lisp, a common affectation, although the effect was marred by her voice, which, if raised one octave higher, could shatter porcelain ladies and rattle windows. "I believe you might even snare yourself a London husband, Miss Wyndham. What grand fortune that would be. Mercy! I would be quite overcome with the romance of it all."

Elizabeth bit back her first response. Even if she believed in marriage, at her advanced age she was far more likely to be attacked by an army of frogs than receive a serious proposal.

"I hope I won't disappoint you and your guests tonight," she said, retrieving her fan from the dressing table.

"Never!" Charles and Penelope cried in unison.

While the strains of a quadrille drifted up the stairs and through the open door, Elizabeth accepted Charles Beresford's arm.

If I cannot write about my knight's death, she thought with despair, *perhaps I can turn my talents to more contemporary novels. Or I can write articles for periodicals. Or poetry. Somehow, I must salvage my career.*

They walked along the hall toward the curved staircase that led to the ballroom. Elizabeth looked down upon the sea of people — ladies in their patterned silks, enhanced by the sparkle of jewels; gentlemen in hair both powdered and unpowdered, sporting tall wigs and wide wigs, satin breeches and richly colored coats.

None of the ladies and gentlemen are here for me. They attend primarily because the Beresfords host marvelous parties. B. B. Wyndham is an incidental attraction.

"We have a wonderful mix," Charles said, as they began their descent. "Everyone from politicians to fellow literary personalities. I spoke with Samuel Johnson only moments before we came upstairs."

"And so many gallants," Penelope gushed, the miniature glass garden in her hair fairly quivering with excitement. "They will be beside themselves when they discover that, despite your profession . . . er, talent . . . you are both lovely and unattached."

Charles began rattling off the names of the guests, most of whom were unfamiliar. Rather than appear an unsophisticated rustic, Elizabeth uttered oohs and aahs at what she assumed were the proper places.

I must not embarrass myself, she thought, her hand trembling on the banister. *For once I must act like a lady.*

Careful to avoid stepping on the hem of her gown, she placed one slipper-clad foot in front of the other.

She would not ask any personal questions. She would not look any man directly in the eye, nor challenge anyone who acted as if her brain had been construed from porridge. She would not debate any guest on why it was unacceptable for a woman to earn half as much as a man. For once she would behave like the heroines in her books.

Penelope's cheeks, held up by leather stretchers, reddened under her rice powder. "I just know this party is going to be a triumph for us all," she exclaimed.

"Indeed," Elizabeth murmured, trusting her reply was the reply of a heroine.

CHAPTER 3

As John Randolph Remington circulated through the crowd, he took note of the necklaces and bracelets and earbobs that adorned the women, the watches and knee-buckles and rings on the men. He also took note of the ballroom itself, in particular its entrances and exits. Earlier, he had spotted Lady Avery among the guests. While he had no real fear of being captured, the possibility added an interesting edge to the evening.

Despite his words to Zak, Rand hadn't been certain until the last moment that he would attend tonight's drum. By now he had read all of B. B. Wyndham's works, but none had shaken him like *Castles of Doom*. In her earlier novels the time periods were different, wrong. However, he was always able to recognize the man she referred to as Ralf Darkstarre in *Castles of Doom,* the man Rand thought he knew by his real name.

From her novels, he had concocted a

mental image of the author. Miss B. B. Wyndham would be small and fragile, with pale hair and eyes, and a quiet, modest demeanor. In his mind's eye, she was shaping up to look remarkably similar to the mournful blonde of his dream. And of course, like all proper females, she would be agreeable to her husband and tender to her children.

Except Elizabeth Wyndham wasn't married, Rand thought, as he dogged a servant bearing a tray of drinks. His inquiries had divulged that much information, along with her real name. Which meant that she was either so grotesquely ugly no man would wed her or she was as poor as Job's turkey. Or perhaps she was less conventional than her writings suggested.

Dancing couples passed with a swish of petticoats. As he wended his way toward the staircase where Elizabeth would make her entrance, he overheard snatches of conversation concerning the guest of honor.

"*The Critical* and *The Monthly* were most uncomplimentary. They said Miss Wyndham's imagination has become imbued with a disturbingly dark cast."

"I agree," stated a second dowager. "When that dreadful Darkstarre violated Lady Guinevere, I found it shocking. Guinevere seemed mesmerized rather than repelled, which is certainly not a proper reaction."

"But she's wasting away with remorse," countered a third dowager. "Which is only as it should be."

All music and conversation halted simultaneously. The Beresfords and their protégé had begun descending the staircase.

That cannot be Miss Wyndham, thought Rand. He had seen splendid women in his time, but none who possessed this creature's intense, scorching beauty. He followed her slow, graceful descent with fascination and disbelief. Who would have thought that someone who penned such anemic heroines could appear so lushly sensual? Elizabeth Wyndham didn't cause a man to ponder genteel flirtation. On the contrary, she conjured up vivid scenes of passionate, timeless lovemaking.

A gallant standing beside Rand said, "Brocade is not the height of fashion, yet Miss Wyndham is just as striking as I heard she was."

Elizabeth's low-cut gown blazed like a scarlet flame against the pale marble steps. Watching her, Rand realized how ridiculous he had been to equate this dramatic woman with her fictional characters, or even his dream memory.

However, her personality might not be as daunting as her looks. Before she was lost amidst a dozen whips, Rand glimpsed her downcast eyes and the modest tilt of her head. Experience had taught him that physically provocative women sometimes made less imaginative lovers than their plainer sisters. Most likely B. B. Wyndham was emotionally identical to her heroines, and her personality would prove as dull. In every novel save *Castles of Doom,* Elizabeth's ladies had suffered the most unspeakable violations at the hands of mad monks and lusty half-brothers and debauched kings. Yet the molested ladies still managed to remain as mentally unsullied as the Virgin Mary. Except for Guinevere. She had definitely enjoyed Darkstarre's attentions. Which meant what?

I'll never know, Rand thought, striving vainly for another glimpse of Elizabeth. A woman couldn't share his present life. Even if she could, he had an inexplicable feeling that *this* woman might single-handedly bring about his ruination.

Elizabeth felt as if she were a sheep surrounded by wolves, but her nervousness quickly subsided. As Charles Beresford performed countless introductions and she

40

noted the admiring stares and comments, her natural confidence returned. None of these smiling bucks had any idea she'd barely begun her final installment of *Castles,* or that Charles Beresford would soon be referring to her as the *former* pride of Minerva Press.

"Have you enjoyed your trip to London?" asked a gentleman at her elbow.

"Very much," she replied, casting him a coy look from behind her open fan.

"Have you been able to spend an afternoon at Bedlam?" asked a second. "I believe you would find it most entertaining. Perhaps I might escort you?"

Before Elizabeth could respond, a third said, "I'll wager Miss Wyndham would prefer Vauxhall Gardens, or perhaps a boating excursion along the Thames. Would you allow me the honor of your company on the morrow, Miss Wyndham?"

Elizabeth fluttered her fan and gave noncommittal answers. Even if she had been interested in any of these gallants, she hadn't journeyed to London in order to further her social life. While she had come partially in response to Charles Beresford's invitation and partially to withdraw money from her earnings so that she could pay her father's gambling debts, her main reason

41

had involved London's central library — or more precisely, what she hoped to find in its back rooms. Perhaps after she delved more deeply into the *Alcester Chronicles,* housed there, she would be able to overcome her writer's block and finish *Castles of Doom.*

". . . read all your books, Miss Wyndham. They show such charm and sensitivity."

Ordinarily, Elizabeth would have challenged the gentleman's choice of adjectives, but now she merely batted her eyelashes and murmured, "Thank you."

Another gallant chimed in. "I haven't read your novels, Miss Wyndham, but I intend to. I know I shall love them."

Elizabeth tossed her head and favored each of her would-be suitors with a dazzling smile, all the while thinking that London's beaus were really very little different from the Dales'. Put any farmer in satin breeches and ingeniously clocked silk stockings, paint his face and prettify his speech, and who could tell the difference?

Charles Beresford approached, accompanied by an imperious-looking matron and a young man.

"May I introduce Lady Avery and her nephew, Roger," Charles said. "I mentioned them to you before. They are the ones who so recently had that unfortunate incident with the highwaymen."

"The ruffians took my purse," Lady Avery said, "and all my jewelry, except for my wedding ring. And then the larger of the two, a veritable Hercules, had the effrontery to kiss my hand." She looked rather pleased.

"They also took Lady Avery's copy of *Castles of Doom*." Beresford sounded indignant.

"Perhaps they are fans of yours," Lady Avery said, her eyes crinkling with amusement. She led Elizabeth toward a hallway escritoire, then thrust the second volume of *Castles* into her hands. "When you autograph this, would you refer to the theft of your novel? I'm dining with the King and Queen tomorrow, and I believe they will be amused by the anecdote."

"It was actually all quite dreadful," Roger whined, as Elizabeth dutifully opened the book to its title page and began writing. "Though I suppose crime is common nowadays. Remember when the Prince of Wales, the Prime Minister, and the Lord Chancellor were robbed in broad daylight in the West End, and the Lord Mayor was held at pistol point at Turnham Green?"

Elizabeth didn't remember. Furthermore, she didn't care who robbed whom, so long as they left her alone. Signing her name with a flourish, she returned the book to Lady Avery.

"I trust the blackguards will soon be apprehended," muttered Beresford. "But as far as I'm concerned, hanging is too mild. I agree with that pamphlet we published a few years back, *Hanging Not Punishment Enough.* We should brand and torture lawbreakers, then force them into a life of servitude on a plantation."

"I personally found both highwaymen quite dashing," said Lady Avery. "At my age, the loss of a few trinkets seems a small price to pay for any adventure."

Fearing offense, Beresford quickly agreed. After mopping his brow with his ever-present handkerchief, he placed his hand on Elizabeth's arm and whispered, "Everyone is enchanted with you, my dear."

Elizabeth heard his words, but they didn't register. Beyond Lady Avery and her pompous nephew, Elizabeth had just spied the most extraordinarily attractive man. "Damme," she breathed.

"Did you say something?" Beresford asked.

Had Elizabeth been describing her reaction in one of her novels, she would have used words like "thunderstruck" and "heart palpitations," or perhaps her heroine would have fainted at the sight of the stranger's dark good looks. Elizabeth didn't swoon or blush or cry out, but she did feel light-headed. No. Light-headed was too sedate a description. Stunned was more apt. Yes. Stunned.

Far away, Beresford's voice dipped and soared, but Elizabeth could not hold onto it. She felt as though the stranger's gaze was probing the deepest recesses of her soul, and she shivered.

Beresford broke off mid-sentence. "Are you cold, my dear?"

Elizabeth shook her head. "I just thought I recognized someone I knew."

How peculiar, she mused. London — nay, all of England — was awash with handsome men, and she had glimpsed many a pleasing face. So why did she feel as if her stays were too tight and each breath a struggle? And why had she said that the stranger appeared familiar? But he *was* familiar. Perhaps he had once paid court to her?

Noodle-head! She would have remembered that lithe body, so straight and tall. Maybe she had seen him earlier in the day, or last Sunday at St. Paul's Cathedral. Maybe she had caught a glimpse of him from her window, or perhaps he had visited her father's inn.

But I would have remembered.

"Excuse me." Heedless of the surprised looks and raised eyebrows, Elizabeth wove her way through a blur of figures. The music, the rustle of skirts, the coughs and snuff-sneezes, the laughter and conversation all faded from her consciousness as she felt the room contract. However, once she was face to face with the stranger, she couldn't find anything to say.

This is absurd, she thought, striving to calm her racing pulse. In the Dales she had been proposed to more times than a month had days, and she discarded men as easily as she discarded the used nibs from her quill. Yet now she was virtually struck dumb.

"Who are you?" she finally blurted, and was immediately horrified by her *faux pas.* A lady must never initiate a conversation lest she be considered guilty of "too warm desires." A lady could only respond after a man had shown interest in *her.* And yet here she stood, Elizabeth Wyndham, heroine-for-a-night, behaving with all the subtlety of a streetwalker.

Rather than registering his disapproval, the stranger merely bowed and said, "My name is John Randolph. And you are the famed B. B. Wyndham."

"Yes." Elizabeth was struck by the raven color of his hair, which made his eyes appear even more blue. Her novelist's brain swiftly catalogued the strong line of his jaw, his full mouth, and his long, lean body. Most gentlemen used paint and strategically placed padding, but Mr. Randolph needed no such artifice to enhance his rugged good looks.

"What does the B. B. stand for?" he asked. "Bonny Bess?"

Elizabeth despised women who blushed, and yet she felt her cheeks flame. "Barbara Brownmiller," she replied. " 'Tis my mother's name. She was my inspiration and . . ." Elizabeth swallowed. "I have the oddest feeling we've met before, sir. Where might that have been?"

"I've recently been introduced to your books," he said, sidestepping her question. "I find them fascinating. Or perhaps I should say disturbing."

"I know we've met before," she insisted, although ordinarily she would have challenged the word *disturbing.* "Have you ever visited the Inn of the White Hart? Or the Theatre Royal in York?"

He shook his head. "I'm sure I would have remembered."

"Are you suggesting that I do not remember?"

"No. I meant it as a compliment, Miss Wyndham."

"Dance with me, John Randolph," she said, and was again astonished by her boldness. She prayed that no one had overheard. Hellfire! Her reputation would be forever ruined. She waited for a caustic reply, or even a polite repudiation, but he made no reference to her bad manners.

His eyes, she decided, were the color of the North Sea. She had used that phrase when she had penned her description of Ralf Darkstarre's eyes.

"What happened to your leg?" she asked, as they took their place among the line of couples.

"The War with the Colonies."

"You dance very well, despite your limp."

"I have wondered how we'd meet," he said.

Although he remained at a discreet distance, Elizabeth felt as if the earth had shifted beneath her feet, as if the very room had tilted. *Why?* Ordinarily, the warmth of a man's gaze wouldn't be unsettling. On the contrary, it would be invigorating. Or boring. What had Mr. Randolph just said about her writing? About *Castles of Doom?*

It was so difficult to concentrate.

"Why is it you've never married?" he asked.

His words brought her back to her senses, her *normal* senses. At first she was startled by his rudeness. Nay, she justified, he was simply inquisitive. Shocked by her advanced age, he had been unable to restrain his curiosity. Furthermore, his question was certainly no more rude than her question about his leg.

"I prefer a more independent path," she said. "I cannot accept the fact that everything we are, everything we can ever aspire to be, is contained within the duties of daughter, sister, wife and mother." Her explanation sounded shrill and false, even to her own ears, though he made no comment.

They danced past the orchestra, the statues from Italy in their wall niches, the portrait of Penelope Beresford above the mantelpiece. They passed the chaperones and young ladies seated in the chairs lining either side of the room, then the orchestra again.

"After reading your books, I had pictured you far differently," he said.

Elizabeth imagined his disappointment. Undoubtedly, he expected her to be like her heroines. True, they were somewhat vapid. But they were also sprightly and witty, amusing their male partners. They were sweet and compliant, so as not to arouse tempers. They were pure and self-controlled, successfully elevating morals — except when they were being ravished by monks and debauched kings. In other words, her heroines were the perfect complement to a man, something she could never be.

"How did you picture me?" she asked bluntly, abandoning any pretense at witty, sweet and compliant.

His gaze lingered on her bosom, and she was certain he disapproved of her décolletage. He probably expected her to wear a high-necked muslin frock patterned with dainty flowers.

"I think you are a very formidable force," he said.

A lady might be described in many ways but formidable could never be construed as a compliment. Elizabeth searched desperately for something clever to say, or better yet, something innocuous. "Where are you from?" she finally managed. "Your accent tells me you're not from these parts."

"I've lived in many parts of England. In my business I travel a good deal."

"And what business are you in?" Judging from his clothes, it was a profitable one.

But he merely shook his head. Elizabeth could smell food and burning candles and the faint sandalwood scent of John himself. She glimpsed their reflection in the wall mirror, the brightness of her scarlet gown and his deep blue jacket. Chandeliers shed their sparkle-bright tears while wooden cherubim seemed to swoop down from the rococo moldings. The music drifted to an end. Without asking, John ushered her outside, onto the terrace.

The boldness of Elizabeth Wyndham's gaze and her forthright manner perfectly suited her lush sensuality, Rand thought. As they paused at the railing, his inner voice warned him to lead her back to her drum, then return to the safety of the Rookery. On the other hand, he felt an overwhelming conviction that his first inclination had been correct. They *were* connected in some bizarre manner, for he had never been so powerfully attracted to a woman. In fact, during their dance, his mind had danced with images of lovemaking. He felt as if he already knew every enticing inch of her body.

He forced himself to keep his gaze on the starless sky. "You're from the Yorkshire

Dales, are you not?"

"You've done a bit of checking on me, sir. I'm flattered."

"I've never been to the Dales," Rand stated, thinking that the sultry air smelled strongly of coal ash, and more faintly of Elizabeth's perfume. Thank God he had introduced himself as John Randolph, an alias he frequently employed. The name Rand Remington was not unknown in London. After all, he had been a war hero, fussed over and feted by the very same aristocracy he now robbed.

He had instinctively withheld his name from the beautiful woman who stood by his side. Watching her approach him, watching her weave her way through the faceless dancers, admiring the luminosity of her black-hued eyes, the word *betrayal* had momentarily thrummed inside his head.

"You should visit the Dales, Mr. Randolph," she said. " 'Tis not unpleasant there, though you might find it quiet after London. I believe the most strenuous activity our justice of the peace has is signing the parish clerk's accounts."

"There is little crime, then?"

She laughed. "Indeed not. And if there were, Lord Stafford, our J.P., would be too impotent to deal with it."

The orchestra struck up a quadrille, and Rand silently congratulated himself on his self-control. Until he felt Elizabeth's hand close over his own. Slowly, reluctantly, he looked down into her eyes.

"I know why you seem familiar," she murmured. "I have long imagined someone like you in my novels."

"The hero, I trust," he said lightly. But he knew who she meant — Ralf Darkstarre. The knowledge was intoxicating and frightening, exactly the same mix of emotions he experienced while practicing his profession. Reaching out with his free hand, he stroked the contours of her face, lingering at a wispy curl in front of her ear. " 'Tis not only the darkness of our hair that is similar," he said, "but the darkness of our pasts."

John Randolph's words made no sense to Elizabeth, yet on some level they did. A voice whispered: *I have seen your face before. I have seen that look before.*

She felt as if her past had fallen away, as if there had never been a time when they hadn't known each other, so it wasn't only the chill of the evening shadows that caused her to shiver.

"We have met before," she whispered. "But why don't I remember?"

His finger caressed her earlobe, sending even more shivery sensations up and down her spine.

"Formidable is too mild a word for you, Bess. Dangerous is more apt." Cradling her chin, he turned her face, then touched his tongue to the ear he had caressed with his finger.

Elizabeth's heroines were always being "overcome." As she clutched John's shoulders, for the first time she understood the meaning of the word.

"Kiss me," she said, her tone not unlike the one she had used when she asked him to dance. But he merely continued exploring her ear. She felt like a marionette whose strings had been snipped. Only the tender strength of his palms against her chin kept her from sinking to the ground in a puddle of brocade. "Kiss me," she pleaded.

Rand traced Elizabeth's cheekbones. Then he stroked her brow. Finally, very gently, he caressed the fragile softness of her eyelids.

All at once, the crack of a pistol shattered the night.

From Stratton Street came shouts, the slap of running feet, and the clatter of horses' hooves.

A second shot sounded.

"Help!" somebody yelled.

Another screamed, "I think we hit him!"

Heedless of his bad leg, Rand raced down the terrace steps, followed by Elizabeth.

"What is it?" she cried.

"Sounds like a robbery." Rand feared he knew the identity of the robber. When he had left the Rookery, Zak had been well on his way to a roaring drunk. It would be just like him to put in an unscheduled appearance.

People were milling around the horses and carriages.

Tethered between a brown gelding and a black coach, Rand's stallion tossed his head.

A tall man wearing a beaver hat waved his pistol and shouted, "I hit him! I think I hit him!"

"What happened?" Rand asked a coachman standing by the front gate.

"A damnfool highwayman came out of nowhere an' thought to rob Lord Dunstable. M'lord pulled a pistol on 'im. Then the parish constable took off after the blackguard, bellowin' an' shootin'. I think they both hit 'im."

"Did you see what the blackguard looked like?"

"No. He stayed mostly to the shadows. But he would have made two of Lord Dunstable, I can tell you that."

A watchman had already gathered together a search party. "Follow me," he called, waving his torch in a smoky arc.

Rand tried to calculate where the parish boundaries were. He figured the demarcation would take place no more than three streets north, which meant that if Zak could reach the other side, neither the watchman nor the constable would have jurisdiction. Zak should be at least temporarily safe. But Rand must find him before the mob did.

"I'm joining the hunt," he told Elizabeth, who had remained by his side throughout.

"Where do you live? I want to see you again."

"That would not be wise for either of us." Rand traced her profile with his fingertips, lingering at her lips. Then he walked briskly across the street, untied his stallion's reins, and vaulted up into the saddle.

Belatedly, she called, "What do you mean? I must see you!" But he had already joined the crowd surging toward the juncture of Stratton Street.

"John!" Helplessly, Elizabeth watched the shadowy wave of men, on foot and on horseback, as they followed the bobbing eye of the watchman's torch. Then the torch and the men disappeared down a side street and she saw nothing at all.

CHAPTER 4

Hour after hour, Elizabeth listened to the watch call out the time. She heard the rumblings of the early morning delivery carts and saw the first traces of dawn, but still sleep eluded her. No matter how hard she tried, she couldn't shake the memory of John Randolph.

Despite his words to the contrary, she had hoped he would come calling. Three days had passed since the night of her drum, however, and John appeared to have vanished as completely as the mysterious highwaymen who had robbed Lady Avery. Moreover, when Elizabeth had questioned the Beresfords and others at the drum, not one person had known anything about John. Since London numbered nearly a million people, she had no idea where she could begin a search.

She accepted invitations to stroll in Vauxhall Gardens and visit Pall Mall's fashionable shops, but during each outing she had to restrain herself from racing back to the townhouse to determine whether John had appeared in her absence.

Had his interest in her merely been a ploy? Did he possess a perverse sense of humor? Perhaps from her books he had deduced her version of the ideal male and decided to act the part. No. If John had copied her heroes, he would have been perfumed and painted, his speech affected. Furthermore, why would he concoct such a scheme? He had never even met her.

Or had he?

The suspicion that they had met before still gnawed at Elizabeth, like a mouse gnawing at a piece of trap-cheese. Although she didn't care to ponder the possibility, perhaps John was akin to Walter Stafford, the Dales' Justice of the Peace. Lord Stafford had long pursued her, but his interest stemmed primarily from his conviction that she was a wild horse in need of being broken. "You are unappealingly masculine in your attitudes, my dear Elizabeth," was one of Stafford's most oft-echoed comments.

She knew that most men shared his sentiments, but the truth was that few women could afford to be so openly opinionated.

Even her Aunt Lilith, a strong personality, docilely allowed her husband's mistress to sup with them. Conventional wisdom, which Elizabeth suspected was merely a phrase concocted by men to keep women in their place, held that if a husband strayed, his wife was at fault. Had she been more loving and subservient, her spouse would never have been forced to find solace elsewhere.

Perhaps John had shown interest in Elizabeth Wyndham, Authoress and Spinster and Champion of Unpopular Causes, out of some evil-intentioned desire to prove his dominance. If true, she had responded correctly. Her body still throbbed every time she remembered their embrace. Her body had betrayed her . . . nay, her intellect had forsaken her, just as John had forsaken her with his abrupt and apparently permanent disappearance.

She heaved a deep sigh as she absently worried the folds of the counterpane resting beneath her chin.

I must not succumb to nerves or foolish desires, she thought. *I must concentrate on my forthcoming visit to the central library and forget all about John Randolph. I am financially independent. Why do I need a man? I cannot allow twelve years of hard work to suf-*

fer because my mind is filled with images of a handsome, dark-haired traitor.

Traitor? Where the bloody hell did that word come from?

"Traitor," she whispered. "Betrayer." Both words seemed an odd choice on the basis of a fleeting encounter, and they evoked an uneasiness in Elizabeth. The morning light streamed cheerily between the green moreen curtains, across the Turkish carpet, yet she felt as if the room was swathed in shadows.

The clock on the mantel struck eight. Summoning Grace, Elizabeth began her morning toilette. Generally by now she would have joined her host and hostess at the breakfast table. An early rising was an anomaly among the leisured class, which seldom stirred before noon. But Charles Beresford, who had inherited his publishing empire from his wife's father, continued his mercantile habits. When Penelope encouraged him to linger over his coffee and buttered toast, he'd say, "I've a great deal of work awaiting me, my dear," then reach for his greatcoat. Penelope would look distressed, but any mention of money — or more precisely, the disbursement of it — promptly improved her spirits. Penelope was currently infatuated with bronzes, and unless sidetracked, would spend the entire meal rhapsodizing over her latest Greco-Roman find. Her most recent "must have" was a statue of Fortuna. Elizabeth thought the yellowish-brown statue unsightly, if not unshapely, yet it carried a price tag that approximated her yearly earnings.

This morning Elizabeth had decided to avoid breakfast. While she figured she could prevaricate as well as anyone, she didn't want to inadvertently reveal her impending visit to the central library. Questions would surely follow, and Penelope, in her artless but brutally effective manner, would undoubtedly extract from Elizabeth the fact that she was hoping to solve her writer's block by means of an ancient manuscript.

With Grace's help, Elizabeth finished dressing. Then she sat in the window seat overlooking the street until Charles Beresford scurried off in the direction of Minerva Press. Successfully evading Penelope, Elizabeth ordered a carriage and set forth upon her mission.

"This is far nicer than the carriage we took from home," said Grace, rearranging her skirts. "The seat is a bit high, though. You'd think with all their money, the Beresfords would have insisted on softer cushions."

Elizabeth braced herself as the carriage

swayed 'round a corner, and tried to ignore her servant. Their journey south had taken six agonizingly long days. By the end of the first day, Elizabeth had contemplated in what ditch or lonely stretch of road she might deposit Grace. By day three, Elizabeth had wondered what ditch or road *she* might take refuge in.

Grace peered out the window. "So many buildings," she said, the expression on her angular face clearly registering her disapproval. "I've seen at least a dozen sprout up since we've been here. And all made of red brick. Why is that, I wonder?"

"I trust you've heard of the Great Fire, Grace."

"Mercy! When did that happen?"

"Last week," Elizabeth replied, even though the Great Fire had occurred more than a century past.

"Mercy!" Grace repeated. "The Beresfords' help are a snooty lot. They never tell me nothin'." She scrutinized the rows of spacious town homes where servants were scrubbing muck from the entrance steps. "No wonder everything's so filthy. I thought 'twas coal dust but it must be ashes." She clucked her tongue. "I remember last month when I was cleanin' the fireplace at the White Hart and yer mother —"

"Stepmother."

"— Mrs. Wyndham tells me to use wood ash to scour the andirons, but I like a mix with baking soda and some other ingredients, I forget which ones right now. I was cleanin' like I usually do —"

"Pardon me?" Elizabeth interrupted, already irritated beyond endurance. "I've never noticed your penchant for cleaning."

"I thought writers was supposed to notice everything. I wonder what kind of books ye write, Mistress."

Elizabeth's fingers tightened on her parasol. She felt the same urge toward violence that had overwhelmed her during the last leg of their journey from the Dales. If London had been but a few miles farther south, Grace never would have arrived intact.

In any case, at her advanced age she didn't need a chaperone. "Do be quiet, please," she said, as the carriage passed through a park where expensively garbed couples strolled beneath towering oaks. "You're giving me a headache."

"I've not seen one gent so handsome as Lord Stafford," Grace said, as she surveyed the scene. "I trust ye'll appreciate him more when ye return. I hear he's been seein' someone in Richmond who's a good ten years younger than ye, Mistress. Don't keep him waitin' too long, or ye'll lose him altogether."

"But he's not a real man," Elizabeth murmured, thinking of John.

"Whatever d'ye mean?"

"Real man are hard and muscular, with chiseled faces and callused hands. Real men wear rough woolens, and they have beards that would scratch my cheek, should I rub against them."

Delighted by Grace's shocked expression, Elizabeth continued. "Real men smell of leather and horses and sweat. They smell of sandalwood and the sea and faraway places, where no lace-cuffed gentleman would ever dare travel."

"Horses and sweat," Grace said with a disdainful sniff. "Mercy, Mistress, ye've just described Tim the Ostler."

John's hands are callused, Elizabeth thought, as she experienced an overwhelming sadness. Upon returning to the Dales, she would try unsuccessfully to conjure up John's face ten years . . . nay, ten weeks from now, and she would always wonder what she might have missed.

Damn the lawless footpad who had fumbled his attempt to rob Lord what's-his-name! Instead, he had stolen John and robbed her of John's kisses.

As Grace droned on and on, Elizabeth put aside thoughts of John and concentrated on her mission. What would she find at the central library? James Waterman, the curator, had agreed to translate portions of the *Alcester Chronicles.* Elizabeth believed she must be missing something pertinent about Simon de Montfort and the rebel uprising, something that the *Chronicles* would reveal. Mr. Waterman's reply to her written request had been so gracious, Elizabeth had momentarily forgotten that if she had been a man, she would have no need of the curator's assistance. If she had been a man, her childhood tutor, Lester Dubbs, never would have dared refuse to teach her Latin.

"Too much cultivation of the mind is selfish and unfeminine," Dubbs had been fond of saying. When Elizabeth pressed, claiming that no one need know, Dubbs had charged that she was trying to establish her mental equality with a man, an unacceptable ambition. "A woman doesn't need intellect to be successful in this world," he had said. She had begged, cursed and cajoled, but he would not be moved.

The carriage deposited Elizabeth in front of the library steps. "Remember what I told you about why we're here," she said to

Grace. "Mr. Waterman has been most kind in his compliments concerning my books and he wishes to discuss them with me."

If Grace knew the real reason for the visit, she would trumpet it to the world. *Hark! My high and mighty mistress can't write no more.*

Grace surveyed the library's imposing columnar front. "I wonder if bats are a problem," she said, her hands creeping up her mob cap. "I've never liked bats."

Once inside, they were greeted by the seemingly endless shelves of books. As they made their way toward the rear of the library, per Mr. Waterman's instructions, Elizabeth heard her maid emit disapproving grunts. Since she couldn't read, Grace considered books unnecessary, and she was surrounded by far too many of the bothersome things.

"Mercy!" she exclaimed. "I wonder who dusts them all."

"You never dust at home, so why would that concern you?"

Before Grace could spew a rebuttal, Elizabeth spied an elderly man who was carefully inspecting the binding of a book. After pointing her maid toward a seat, she approached the stoop-shouldered, white-haired curator.

"What a pleasure this is, Miss Wyndham," Waterman said, taking her hand in his. "I do so enjoy relaxing in the evening with your works."

"I'm surprised that a man of your learning would find my works interesting," she responded, charmed as much by the curator's courtly manner as his compliment.

"Hogwash, if you'll pardon the expression. Most other writers of Gothic novels seem determined to have our ancestors waving pistols and wearing wigs, which, in my humble opinion, are the biggest fashion nuisances ever created. And those silly writers make their characters live in ruined abbeys and crumbling castles, as if our forefathers actually built them that way."

Elizabeth had written more than her share of scenes that involved pistols, wigs, and dilapidated buildings, but she pretended to share Mr. Waterman's outrage. "While an author must keep contemporary taste in mind," she said, "we must also strive for verisimilitude."

"Exactly! Sometimes you paint a wonderfully accurate picture, Miss Wyndham. I am particularly enjoying *Castles of Doom.* I can imagine Lord Darkstarre striding through his Great Hall, followed by his yapping dogs and his mastiff. I can hear Ralf bellowing to his men, and I tell myself if Darkstarre did not exist, he certainly should have."

"That is high praise indeed," Elizabeth murmured, even though she privately wondered at the wisdom of having a madman as the most unforgettable character in one's work.

"Listen to me ramble," Mr. Waterman said with a self-deprecating laugh. "I assure you, I am not generally so voluble."

He beckoned her to follow him. As they walked down the poorly lit hallway, Elizabeth thought: *In a few minutes I will know.* But what would she know? The hall seemed to contract, and she felt as if the shadows were smothering her, as if someone pressed a gray feather pillow against her nose and mouth. From a great distance, she heard an eerie howl. It sounded like the laughter of a demented soul.

Elizabeth felt faint. Not enough air! Not enough light! Struggling to breathe, she raised her hand and pressed her palm against her mouth. At the same time, she pinched her nose with her thumb and first finger. Then, realizing what she had done, she dropped her hand and placed it over her racing heart.

She continued forward, taking deep breaths, trying to keep her panic at bay. Why did she experience such an overwhelming terror? She had never feared the unknown before. Was she afraid that her raven-haired knight — a man conjured up out of her imagination — had actually lived and breathed? No. Her trepidation had to do with his *death.*

But Ralf Darkstarre didn't exist, had never existed!

Elizabeth told herself that reason was stronger than fear. She told herself that the hallway sustained a draft, an annoying influx of air that caused the flesh beneath her sleeves to goosebump. Her petticoats swayed and swirled, as if caught in the throes of a nautical cat's-paw, but she told herself that the swirl was caused by the draft, or perhaps her swift movements, certainly not by her trembling limbs.

". . . excited about showing you the *Alcester Chronicles.* They were written by monks from Alcester Abbey, not far from Evesham." The curator turned halfway 'round to face her. "By the way, it appears that you're not the only one interested in the *Chronicles,* Miss Wyndham."

"I . . . I beg your pardon?" she managed.

"A few days ago, or was it a week — my memory has such a way of slipping — a gentleman also asked to be shown the manuscript. He seemed a pleasant young man, well-garbed and courteous. He told me his name, but it escapes me." Waterman's faded blue eyes disappeared behind a web of smile wrinkles. "I fear I can remember names centuries old more easily than the name of someone I met five minutes ago."

Halting in front of a door, the curator reached for his ring of keys and bent over the lock. "He limped."

"Who limped?"

"The gentleman. Not a severe impairment. He might have returned from a grueling ride."

John Randolph, Elizabeth thought. "Was this visitor in his early thirties, a shade over six feet, with dark hair and blue eyes?"

"Could be." Mr. Waterman removed the key from the lock and returned the ring to its rightful place. "It's so hard to say."

"Was his name, by any chance, John Randolph?" Elizabeth pressed. "Did he say where he lived? Anything concerning his occupation? Anything at all that you can remember?"

Even as she tried to jog the curator's memory, she knew the odds against John strolling into London's central library, looking for the *Alcester Chronicles.* Such a coincidence defied all reason. And yet, by his own admission, he had read her books. Maybe he had been particularly interested in *Castles of Doom,* and wanted to learn more about the ending. But how would he have heard of such an obscure chronicle? And if he had stumbled across its existence, why not just reach for a dozen translated histories? Why would anyone save an historian or a desperate Gothic novelist show any interest in the ancient manuscript?

It must be somebody else, Elizabeth decided. In a crowd of people, at least one individual would possess a limp. A person could fall from his horse, be born with a bad leg — a dozen things might cause such a condition. Why, even the gallant who had escorted her through Vauxhall Gardens had affected a rather sprightly hobble.

"My treasure house," Waterman said, stepping aside to allow Elizabeth entrance. "I would not trade one of these manuscripts for all the gold in the kingdom."

Glancing around, Elizabeth felt a smile crease the corners of her mouth. She saw that a skylight bathed the tiny room in a pleasant natural light. The furnishings consisted solely of a huge cluttered desk and a chair. Glass bookcases, which stretched from the floor to the ceiling on three sides, displayed dozens of bulky manuscripts.

"Just think," Waterman said, gesturing toward the cases with his elegant hands. "Some of these works are hundreds of years old."

"Yes," breathed Elizabeth.

She imagined a monk, his tonsured head gleaming softly in the light from a large window. Seated in a high-backed chair, his legs rested on a footstool beneath his desk. His right hand, encased in a fingerless glove, toyed with a quill. Raising the quill, he dipped its tip in a nearby inkhorn and began writing on the lined parchment. He paused to flex his fingers. Lowering the quill, he gazed out the window. He looked mortally sad. Something terrible had happened, a great tragedy that he must record . . .

Elizabeth blinked and the monk faded. Sometimes, during her writing, she conjured up vivid scenes so realistic she could almost believe she had actually witnessed them. When Mr. Waterman said she aimed for historical accuracy, he could not know that much of her so-called research was her imagination.

"Do sit down, Miss Wyndham." The curator pulled out the lone chair. From behind one of the glass doors he retrieved a manuscript. Then he cleared a place atop his desk.

Elizabeth noted that the book's binding was adorned with a plate of carved ivory, while its clasp was of worked silver.

Waterman maneuvered his spectacles atop the bridge of his nose. "St. Bernard used to say, 'Every word you write is a blow which smites the devil.' A very Catholic concept, but I find it charming, don't you?"

"Charming," she echoed.

He opened the *Chronicles.* A shaft of sunlight fell upon the book, illuminating each page as he carefully turned it. Elizabeth saw an occasional huge initial denoting the beginning of a chapter, plus numerous illustrations too small to identify. *Such startling colors,* she thought, experiencing a mixture of anticipation and disquiet. *I never dreamed they would be so intense.*

"Would you like me to begin with the Battle of Evesham, or earlier?" Waterman asked.

"Earlier, please. There's so much I don't know."

The curator ran his finger down the column of Gothic script, uttering a word here and there. "Yes. This seems a likely place, Miss Wyndham."

He began with Simon de Montfort's lineage. The Montforts were from France, where Simon's father had been one of those who had crushed the Cathari heresy. Which meant that Simon's heritage was a dark one, for thousands had died rather than recant their beliefs.

A legacy bathed in blood, Elizabeth thought, suppressing a shudder. When Mr. Waterman continued, she squeezed her eyes shut. His voice was gentle, even soothing, as he recounted Simon's marriage to Henry the Third's sister, Eleanor, and the events that gradually tore apart the king and his brother-in-law. Mr. Waterman detailed Simon and Henry's struggle for power — the profligate ruler and his unyielding subject fighting over the power of the barons.

Concentrate, Elizabeth! Soon you will know. Know what?

The curator's voice lulled her into a peculiar relaxed state, which hovered between sleeping and waking. Images swam before her. Images of cavernous rooms and narrow stone hallways. Images of armed riders racing toward forests so dense they looked like black walls. Images of bearded men clustered together, hatching conspiracies.

"We're nearing the civil war," said Waterman, and Elizabeth could tell by the sound of his voice that he had looked up from the

Chronicles. "Of course, this accounting favors the barons' point of view. However, this is the part that should interest you most, Miss Wyndham. Am I correct?"

"Yes." Her feeling of well-being faded, along with her sensation of floating upon a river of timelessness.

Waterman resumed reading. His tone was louder, more forceful. "For that short time, de Montfort virtually wrested the crown from King Henry and ruled England. His enemies termed de Montfort's rule the blackest time in history."

"Black," Elizabeth whispered. Somewhere, Simon de Montfort was connected with something black. Yes. That was important. That was the key. Opening her eyes, she leaned toward the curator. "Was the color black related to Simon de Montfort? Was it used as an epithet, something like 'the Black Montfort' or 'Simon the Black'?"

"No. Why do you ask?"

A memory stirred in her mind, a memory from long ago. "Did the monks refer to his black deeds or his black heart?"

The curator shook his head, but she persisted. "What about his followers? Somehow I associate the color with him."

"Not that I can recall." Waterman removed his spectacles and polished them with his handkerchief. "But perhaps it could be so, Miss Wyndham. I have read much, and my memory grows as feeble as my body."

Staring at the pages, Elizabeth felt her uneasiness turn once more to an overwhelming, inexplicable fear. She gripped the arms of her chair and forced herself to remain seated, even though every instinct urged her to flee.

"This year saw a great battle between King Henry and many of the barons of the realm," Waterman read. He went on to detail the army that His Majesty was assembling and Simon's response. "The news concerning the King's actions reached the wiser party, including the much to-be-revered Lord Simon and his most trusted barons, men such as Gilbert of Clare and Ranulf Navarre, also called Ranulf the Black."

"Stop!" Elizabeth cried. An icy gust of wind seemed to blow across her. "Ranulf Navarre. Ranulf the Black. There it is."

The curator smiled. "You are well-informed, Miss Wyndham. His is not a name well-known outside scholarly circles. I have read countless histories, but only a few lines about Navarre. The *Chronicles* deal with him more extensively than any other source."

"Tell me about . . . this man."

I must have read about him before, she thought. *But where? Especially if he is only an incidental footnote.*

Most likely she had heard a similar name and confused the two. But how could the name Ranulf Navarre cause confusion? And why would the mere utterance of a dead knight's name cause her to feel something akin to panic?

"Tell me about this man," she repeated. "Please."

"Ranulf Navarre was Simon's most trusted advisor, Miss Wyndham, but the *Chronicles* mention very little about any man's personality. The king's chroniclers merely refer to him as evil."

"Yes," she said faintly. "Is there a physical description of Ranulf Navarre?"

Ranulf Navarre. Ralf Darkstarre. The two names echoed off the corridors of her mind. *Ranulf Navarre. Ralf Darkstarre.*

The curator peered at her from above his spectacles, and for the first time Elizabeth sensed disapproval. An historian would never concern himself with the physical description of a footnote. Only a silly woman would favor such a description.

"The monks did not devote their efforts to a man's appearance," Waterman said, his

77

voice brusque. Then, relenting, he added, "The monks might occasionally describe a king, Miss Wyndham. However, they did not detail the few men who stood on the perimeters of history."

He returned to his reading, but Elizabeth no longer listened, for she now knew that she could never finish her novel.

Navarre-Darkstarre, Navarre-Darkstarre, singsonged her mind.

"They assembled at the vale of Evesham and —"

"Thank you so much, Mr. Waterman." Elizabeth bolted to her feet. "You've been too kind. I've found out everything I needed to know."

The curator looked startled. "Well, I hope I have been of some help." After returning his spectacles to his pocket, he extended the *Chronicles* toward her. "Would you care to hold the manuscript, Miss Wyndham? I feel you are a kindred spirit, that you revere history as greatly as you do the printed word. I have found that the mere feel of parchment beneath my fingers is quite moving, and I believe that you would feel the same way. Am I correct?"

"Yes. No. Yes." Elizabeth stared down at the manuscript, at the brilliant red and gold initial writhing like a serpent down the right margin, and she knew that no power on earth could make her touch that book.

"Go ahead," Waterman urged. "Touch your history, Miss Wyndham."

"What do you mean, *my* history?"

"It is all our history, is it not? Don't fret. The parchment is extremely durable. You cannot hurt it."

"I must go," Elizabeth whispered, and before the curator could protest, she turned and fled from the room.

CHAPTER 5

Elizabeth braced her feet against the opposite side of the coach. The road was abominable, and they hadn't even begun the last steep climb toward the White Hart. Her gloved fingers tightened around a leather-bound copy of *Castles of Doom.* Inside the hollowed-out book was two hundred pounds, one-fourth the sum she needed to pay off her father's gambling debts. Charles Beresford had promised to transfer the remainder by post.

"I cannot allow you to travel with eight hundred pounds on your person," he had said, his voice decisive.

Penelope had agreed. "Remember Lady Avery's dreadful happenstance," she had warned, thrusting a small bronze of Calliope, the Greek muse of poets, into Elizabeth's hands. An appropriate good-bye gift.

Charles Beresford's "gift" had been even more agreeable, for he had handed over her financial balance sheet.

Contemplating the fiscal rendering, Elizabeth felt a sense of accomplishment and satisfaction. *I don't need a man for anything,* she told herself. *A plague on men in general, and John Randolph in particular.*

After she devised a suitably inaccurate ending for *Castles,* she would write a book about John. She would concoct some dangerous profession for him, perhaps soldier of fortune. Or pirate. Did pirates exist in the Middle Ages?

No matter. Whatever the vocation, John would be jilted by the woman he adored, then die of some dreadful, lingering disease, perhaps leprosy.

Elizabeth's more immediate concern, however, was with her homecoming. She had hired an expensive coach at Harrogate, and she wore a fashionable muslin purchased in London. "There goes Bess, the landlord's daughter," everybody would say. "Doesn't she look the stupendously successful authoress?" All right. Maybe they wouldn't say *stupendously successful.* Maybe they'd say she was sitting pretty. Or well-heeled.

At the thought, she slumped down and pressed her heels harder, allowing her legs, rather than her rump, to absorb the jolts.

"I swear, when we reach home, no one will ever talk me into leavin' again," Grace said, her voice somewhat muffled by her handkerchief. "I cannot tell ye how much I hate travelin'."

Elizabeth removed her gloves and flexed her fingers, trying to alleviate their stiffness. It had rained much of the day and she looked forward to nestling beneath a mound of quilts in the privacy of her own bedroom. Still, after five days spent listening to Grace's coughs and groans and complaints, she felt duty bound to contradict everything her maid said.

"Travel is a wonderful experience, Grace."

"Not when ye're carryin' all that money." Leaning across the seat, she tapped *Castles of Doom* with her index finger. "What'll ye do if we're robbed?"

"Who's going to rob us out here? Ghosts?" Elizabeth pulled back the curtain and stared through the window. Patches of fog criss-crossed the highway, catching on bare branches, rock walls, and the stubble of surrounding fields.

"I like ghosts better than highwaymen, Mistress."

Elizabeth bit her lip, deflecting an acrimonious retort. During the first part of their journey, they had shared the coach with a hangman who had spent the trip from London to Coventry regaling them with tales of the highwaymen he had executed.

"Remember when Mr. Cooke told us 'bout that one highwayman what cut the finger off a lady who wouldn't part with her ring? Ah-ow-oo!" Grace's screech echoed throughout the coach's tight interior. "Then there was another what slit open the stomach of a passenger who'd swallowed her jewels."

"That was merely Mr. Cooke's way of flirting with you, Grace. Highwaymen are more likely to be patricians down on their luck. Don't you remember what the papers said about the Gentle Giant and his Quiet Companion?"

"Ye know I can't read."

"They said that highwaymen are the elite of the underworld."

Grace sneezed into her handkerchief. The coach plunged forward. Elizabeth tried to gauge their whereabouts from various landmarks. Earlier, they had passed through the town of Ripon, which meant they must be somewhere near the ruins of Fountains Abbey.

With a sigh, she resumed her former position, and — during a particularly loathsome jounce — nearly smashed her head against the top of the coach.

"Well, I can tell ye this much," said Grace, her cheeks flushing a dull pink. "The only reason the Dales've not been overrun by cutthroats is 'cause of Lord Stafford, God bless 'im."

"It has nothing to do with Lord Stafford, Grace. What self-respecting highwayman would waste his time in a place that has more sheep than people?"

"Ye'll not give Lord Stafford credit for nothin', Mistress. What'll ye do if a highwayman swoops down on us this very moment and takes every shillin'?"

"I still have over two thousand pounds on account at Minerva Press." Dropping *Castles of Doom* into her lap, nudging the statue aside with her hips, Elizabeth rummaged through her traveling bag until she found her statement, which she waved before Grace's eyes. "Look at this. I've saved more money than most people make in a lifetime."

Even as she pointed to the bottom line, she thought: *Why am I justifying myself to my maid, who cannot read the bottom line and would not be convinced if she could?*

She jammed the paper back into her bag. "I know this may seem strange, but I'm proud of my independence. Even if I were nicer to Lord Stafford, and he really meant his marriage proposals, once we were wed I would have no say over any of my funds. He could burn every pound if it pleased him, and the law would be on his side. I shall never risk losing what I have worked so hard to achieve."

Which sounded fine enough, thought Elizabeth, except that, despite her brave words, despite her considerable fortune, after she finished paying off her father's debts, she would be considerably less independent. Especially if she couldn't finish *Castles of Doom.*

Suppose her writing career was indeed over? Then she'd simply devise some new way to earn a respectable living. She might return to teaching; years back she had taught reading and spelling at a dame-school. How about portrait painting? She had a bit of talent with the oils.

Grace unballed her handkerchief and searched for a dry spot. "Ye're a peculiar woman, Mistress, if ever I've known one."

"You're right, Grace." Elizabeth's gaze returned to the window and the darkness, as if seeking something beyond the fog, beyond the abbey ruins. This was one of those moments when she knew she had made a monumental mistake by not marrying and having children and conforming to society's dictates.

Where did it all go wrong? she wondered. *How did I ever get so out of step with the rest of the world?*

Once she had thought herself in love with a local sheepherder. She had terminated that relationship when she realized that she and her shepherd had little in common beyond the physical.

Her stepmother, Dorothea, had never unearthed the affair, not that Elizabeth gave a tinker's damn what her stepmother believed or disbelieved. Dorothea, however, had set her sights on Lord Stafford, and Elizabeth's lack of virginity might be considered an impediment.

Lord Stafford reminded Elizabeth of her father, except Walter Stafford accrued possessions while Lawrence Wyndham accrued debts. Elizabeth knew, beyond the shadow of a doubt, that if Walter meant his marriage proposals, and if she accepted, she would be nothing more than a Lord Stafford possession. She also suspected that her frequent refusals merely fueled Walter's desire to possess her.

" 'Tis dreadful dark outside," Grace said. "Blacker than a night should be. I wish the coachman'd stop and light the lanterns. I hope the fog don't get worse. I hate fog. I could tell ye tales of men ridin' out upon the Dales, ne'er to be found again."

"Please don't." Pressing her shoulders against the coach cushion, Elizabeth attempted a stretch.

Grace searched inside her traveling bag for yet another handkerchief, knocking over Elizabeth's parasol in the process. "If a highwayman had a mind to mischief, this would be the night he'd pick. I wish the White Hart was closer. I wish it wasn't so lonely 'round here."

"How many times do I have to tell you? There are no highwaymen, and that's the end of it." Hoping to avoid any further complaints, Elizabeth peered through her window again.

The bobble-wheeled coach had begun the final leg of the route. Large portions of the highway, snaking its way through the increasingly bleak Yorkshire countryside, remained hidden by the restive fog. A quarter moon struggled against a bank of clouds, then vanished, leaving only a feeble glow, like the halo 'round the head of a saint.

Only we don't believe in saints anymore, Elizabeth thought, settling back against her seat. *At least not the papist kind.*

Ralf Darkstarre and Lady Guinevere

would have believed in saints. Simon de Montfort and Ranulf Navarre would have believed in saints.

Elizabeth shivered. Ranulf the Black. What manner of man had he been? And from where did she know him?

The coach eased to a stop, and the long stretch of silence soothed her ragged nerves. "The coachman has dismounted from his perch," she said, pulling back the curtain. "He's lighting the lamps, helped by the guard. So you can rest assured —"

"They're takin' an unseemly long time. And they'd best not be enjoyin' a nip along with their business. Drunken drivers are a menace. They'll be unable to handle the horses, and the beasts'll be spooked by the weather, run away, and we'll crash over the side of the hill somewhere, and we'll all be killed. 'Tis what ye deserve for thinkin' to travel, Mistress."

"Do be quiet, Grace." The voices of the coachman and guard had grown louder, as if they were quarreling. Lowering the window, Elizabeth poked her head out. "What's going on here?"

The fog glided in front of the horses like a ghost upon a stairway. The coachman's and guard's arms were raised. Elizabeth saw an enormous man on horseback pointing a pistol at them.

She sank back onto her seat. "Dammit to hell!"

Grace covered her ears with her hands. "Mistress! Not even a stablehand uses such words."

"What do you expect me to say? We're being robbed."

"Robbed? Mercy! I told ye highwaymen might butcher us."

"Hush." Cautiously, Elizabeth peeked through the window again. As if summoned by Grace's words, the highwayman approached. He was unusually tall and quite bulky. Obviously, this giant of a brigand had not taken to crime because he was in danger of starving.

"Stand and deliver!" he boomed. His voice was distorted, most likely from a pebble in his mouth.

"Lord in heaven," Grace wailed. "What'll we do?"

"Shush up and let me think," Elizabeth hissed. Too bad she had packed her ladies' pistol in her trunk, tied topside. She would have to settle upon something other than murder to rid herself of the highwayman. But rid herself she would. She had no intention of relinquishing so much as a shilling.

"Stand and deliver, I said!"

"Get out, Grace," Elizabeth whispered, thrusting her book beneath the straw. "Tell him I'm ill. Tell him I've fainted. Tell him I need his help."

" 'Tis a lie, Mistress. He'll know I'm lyin' and shoot me."

"Just do it, damn you."

While Grace scurried from the coach, Elizabeth removed her plumed hat. Then she pulled free her hair pins and shook her head. She hoped this highwayman, like so many others, had a weakness for women. A feeble distraction at best, but it might grant her enough time to formulate a proper plan.

She heard Grace's words tumble, one over the other.

In response, the highwayman hollered, "Get your arse out here, ye poxy bugger, before I drag ye out."

Perhaps this highwayman hasn't read his own press, Elizabeth thought. She saw the muzzle of a pistol, thrust through the coach window.

"I'm sorry to be a bother, sir," she said, "but I'm so frightened. If you could only help me —"

"Out *now,* before I blast ye from here t' York!"

This highwayman was definitely not one of the chivalrous types. "Hold on a minute, you bloody bastard," she muttered.

Retrieving her parasol, she placed Penelope's bronze within easy reach of her right hand. Then, flinging open the door, she studied her enemy. He was positioned only a few feet away, his horse facing her. A skittish animal, the horse snorted and stomped, especially when the coach door slammed against the coach's frame. Leaning forward, Elizabeth raised her parasol and snapped it open, directly into the horse's eyes. It whinnied, shied, and swung its haunches. The highwayman swayed in his saddle. Elizabeth grabbed the muse statue and cracked the highwayman over the head.

He toppled to the ground.

She jumped from the coach and ran toward his prone body. Exhilarated by the ease with which she had foiled the robbery attempt, she poked the man vigorously with her parasol. He appeared to be unconscious. Such a huge fellow, yet she had bested him with minimal effort.

The brute groaned and stirred.

"I wonder if I should hit him again," Elizabeth said to nobody in particular.

"I wouldn't if I were you."

She spun around. A second highwayman sat astride a black stallion. This one was hatless, and his hair, black as the cloak he wore, curled untidily around his head. A mask hid the lower half of his face, and his pistol was pointed at her breast.

"Damme," she breathed. Then, louder, she said, "I don't suppose you'd believe me if I told you that I didn't mean to hit your friend."

"I don't suppose I would, dear-r-r lady."

His voice possessed a Scottish burr, and there appeared to be something vaguely familiar about him. Was it the way his hair curled upon his neck? Or was it something about his demeanor? He was tall, not as tall as the other man, but tall enough. His eyes . . . *dark blue,* she thought, *or perhaps black.*

"You're a dangerous woman," he said, "which means you ha' something to hide."

"No, I'm poor." Tossing her parasol back inside the coach, she cradled the statue across her bodice. "I was angry at your companion because he frightened my maid and disturbed my journey. I swear I have nothing."

"Your coach looks first-rate, m'lady."

"The coach was an extravagance I could ill afford."

He gestured with his pistol toward his prostrate companion. "You strike me as a most resourceful woman. I'll wager you would not be above a bit of trickery to ha' your way. I canna' see your face, so I canna' read your expression. Please step before the lights so that I may ha' a better look at you."

After a moment's hesitation, Elizabeth obeyed. While he scrutinized her face, she felt increasingly uncomfortable. Despite her words to Grace, highwaymen were not always patricians down on their luck. Furthermore, they had been known to force their unwanted attentions on their victims.

"Your gown is expensive," he finally said, lowering his pistol, "but your jewelry is of the most indifferent quality."

The highwayman seemed to be weakening, thought Elizabeth. However, the brute with the head wound was now stirring, and she feared his volatile reaction. If she wanted to escape with her money, she must act decisively. Perhaps the dark-haired highwayman might be susceptible to a little feminine charm.

"I swear I'm just an impoverished spinster," she said, shifting her cloak to expose more of her bosom. "The most expensive thing I own is this bronze, a gift." She displayed it, slightly raised. "I have nothing else."

Pocketing his pistol, he laughed. "Since 'tis impossible for me to believe that some-

93

one as lovely as you could utter a falsehood, I must accept your word. I see no point in further distressing you, so we shall just agree that a mistake has been made and you can be on your way."

The wounded highwayman jerked his bloody head up, then struggled to his knees. "Are ye mad? That strumpetin' whore tried t' kill me. She's hidin' somethin', a bit full o' jewelry, or lord knows what. And if I've ever seen anyone actin' peery, 'tis that one." He nodded toward Grace, who was bouncing from leg to leg and twisting her handkerchief in her hands. "You! Tell me! What's your mistress hidin'?"

"Nothing," Elizabeth cried.

"Nothing," Grace parroted, her voice weak. Like a human pendulum, her face moved back and forth between the coach and the highwayman.

"Go get it," the wounded brute barked. "I'll not shoot ye in the back. *Move,* lass!"

"No!" As Elizabeth stepped forward, Grace screeched and scrambled inside the coach.

"Stay where ye're at, ye double-poxed, long-arsed, salivated bitch in grain!" The injured highwayman groped for his pistol. "Don't come anywhere within strikin' distance."

"But —"

"Don't argue," he growled, waving his weapon none too steadily in her direction.

"Cousin, take care," said the dark-haired highwayman. "Your pistol might go off by mistake." Dismounting, he stepped in front of Elizabeth.

Grace descended from the coach. Eyes feral, she stumbled — and dropped Elizabeth's book. Apparently deciding the wounded giant's pistol was less frightening than her mistress's wrathful expression, she scurried over to the coachman and guard, whose hands were still raised.

Despairingly, Elizabeth watched the giant retrieve the sheaf of bills from her book.

"Lord a'mighty," he said. "Grunting cheat! Not bad for a bloody poor spinster."

"If you steal that, you'll be robbing me of my independence and all my hopes for the future." Elizabeth's eyes brimmed over with tears, which were only partially forced.

"Why not allow her to keep it?" the dark-haired highwayman said.

His partner shook his head, as if to clear it. "Has that crack on me head affected me ears, or have ye gone daft? Me sawbone's bills alone will run me hundreds o' pounds."

"Your reputation would be assured by such a chivalrous act," Elizabeth pleaded, turning toward her ally. "You would both become immediate legends, like the Gentleman Giant and his Quiet Companion."

The wounded highwayman snorted while the second affixed a rope to the guard and coachman's wrists, binding them together. Grace thrust out her hands, but the dark-haired highwayman shook his head.

Elizabeth rushed on. "I'm a sister of the quill, an authoress. Perhaps I could even compose a tale about you, forever immortalizing you in print, like *Tom Jones.* Wouldn't that mean more than mere money?"

"I wouldn't mind being immortalized," the dark-haired highwayman said. "It seems a fair trade, cousin."

"What in God's name has come over ye, ye bloody flat? Ye think to return a bloody fortune so that this toad's harlot can fill some bloody reader with fancy lies about ye? I say we keep every damned shillin'!"

"I have brilliant powers of observation," said Elizabeth, losing her temper. "I shall report everything I've seen to the local justice of the peace. He'll track you down and you'll hang from the nearest gallows."

The injured highwayman leveled his pistol at her heart. "Then maybe I should save meself a lot o' trouble by poppin' ye right now."

Still cowering near the guards, Grace wailed. "They'll slit our throats and open our stomachs and fill them with stones, then throw our bodies into the stream. Oh, we'll die, Mistress, and 'tis all yer fault."

"Enough," said the second highwayman. "If you must take the money, take it, but there's no sense in threatening anyone." As he returned to his horse, Elizabeth saw that he walked with a slight limp.

"Damn my soul," she whispered, dropping the statue.

Why hadn't she figured it out immediately? His broad shoulders, stalwart chest, lean hips and muscular thighs. His hair, the shape of his eyes. *John Randolph was a highwayman!*

She turned her attention to the wounded highwayman, now wobbling toward his mount. She knew exactly who this pair was: the Gentleman Giant and his Quiet Companion. Most likely they had planned to rob the Beresfords, then something had gone amiss. Whereupon John, remembering what she had said about the Dales' bumbling justice of the peace, had retreated north.

The Gentleman Giant leaned across his horse until his balance steadied. Easing himself up into the saddle, he groaned. "If I'm not dead now," he mumbled, "I should

97

live forever."

John had also remounted. Elizabeth figured he knew who she was and thought to spare her. Which seemed commendable enough, except they still planned to leave with her two hundred pounds.

"Sir," she said, taking a step toward John.

"Yes, m'lady?"

Placing her hand on his thigh, above his glossy brown boots, she gazed up into his eyes. "I have long imagined someone like you in my novels."

He stared down at her for a long moment. Then, moving his mask away from his mouth, he cradled her chin between his palms, lowered his head, and kissed her hard upon the lips.

The Giant's raucous cheers and Grace's renewed wails overlapped his words.

"I'll return your money, Bess," he said softly, "and that's a promise."

"When?" she asked, ignoring the sensations that coursed through her body. She felt as if she had just swallowed a bolt of hot lightning.

"In my own time."

CHAPTER 6

Why should I believe him? Why should I trust him?

John trusted *her,* thought Elizabeth. She knew his name and had seen him all too clearly during Beresford's drum. He could have shot her to protect his identity.

But she had a feeling John wouldn't kill a woman, no matter what the circumstances, so that justification didn't hold water.

How about this? If she gave Lord Stafford a physical description and the inept lawman somehow managed to capture the Gentleman Giant and his Quiet Companion, she'd never recover her two hundred pounds.

She must believe John's promise. She really had no other choice. Besides, betrayal was repellent.

All these thoughts ran through Elizabeth's mind as the coach turned into the yard of the White Hart. Distractedly, she gathered her things together.

"Remember, Grace. Do not say one word about the unfortunate incident."

"You mean the robbery, Mistress?"

"I mean the unfortunate incident."

"But we must tell Lord Stafford. No respectable woman will be safe so long as those two monsters are free."

"I'd hardly call them monsters. They did us no physical harm. I'll take care of the matter myself, in my own way. Do you understand?"

As the coachman blew his horn, Elizabeth peered through the window. She saw that the area was crowded with incoming and outgoing carriages, stable hands, guards and passengers. *I hope no one is awaiting me,* she thought. On the other hand, she had sent word with an earlier coach, so no doubt she would receive a hearty welcome.

The coach rumbled to a halt beside the grooming shed, adjacent to the stables. A cheer went up and a small crowd immediately surrounded Elizabeth's window. She saw her father, dark as a Gypsy, a big grin on his face. She saw Dorothea, looking as deceptively fragile as the crystal drops that hung from a chandelier. And Walter Stafford, half a head taller than those around him.

Most women would call Stafford handsome. He did not possess the dark ruggedness of a Ralf Darkstarre or a John Randolph, yet he could easily pose for one of Elizabeth's book heroes. A cauliflower wig cascaded down his narrow shoulders, enhanced by his padded coat. The rest of his body lacked the muscularity of a Ralf or John, but his visage was noteworthy. Mahogany brows shaded pale blue eyes whose intense expression often unsettled her. His nose was long and straight, his lips too thin, bowed on top. But this small discrepancy was disguised by a mustache and a well-trimmed goatee. When all the facets of Lord Stafford's face came together, he looked like an imperial pirate.

"Remember what I told you," Elizabeth warned Grace, as the coachman pulled down the steps. "Not one word."

She opened the coach door to cheering and clapping, but before she could descend, Grace pushed her aside and tripped down the stairs. "We was robbed by two horrible highwaymen!" she yelled.

The welcome party uttered a collective gasp.

Strong arms lifted Elizabeth from the coach, and she gazed into her father's shocked face. "Did they hurt you?" he asked. "Insult you in any way? Lay a hand on you?"

"No, of course not. It wasn't —"

"I've never been so afraid in my life," Grace cried. "They said they'd kill us, and do all manner of unspeakable things."

Another collective gasp.

Grace began sobbing. She glanced around, as if seeking solace, then collapsed against Lord Stafford's chest.

Ignoring Grace, Stafford looked at Elizabeth, his eyes narrowed to slits. "What exactly happened? Where were you when you were robbed? How much money did they take? What jewelry?"

She attempted a smile. "It was nothing, really. Just a misunderstand—"

"They took *all* of Mistress Elizabeth's money."

"No!" Dorothea's hand flew to her mouth. "Not your entire fortune."

"Of course not," Elizabeth snapped, irritated by what she considered her stepmother's inappropriate concern.

None too gently, Stafford pushed Grace away. "How much, Elizabeth?"

Grace shook herself like a dog who had just emerged from a lake. "It was more than two hundred pounds, m'lord."

"It was less than twenty."

"But Mistress —"

"I know how much I lost!"

Elizabeth felt her father's arms tighten around her. "I'm just glad you weren't hurt," he said. "And since you have much more on account, 'tis no calamity."

"I thought you told us you were going to return with the first installment of our loan." Beneath her powder, Dorothea's face was as white as curdled milk. "Which is it, Elizabeth, twenty pounds or two hundred?"

"I assure you, everything is fine. My funds are still intact." Handing Papa her statue and parasol, she retrieved her bank statement from her traveling bag. "It's all here on account," she said, waving the paper in front of a dozen startled faces. "The robbery was a minor matter, I tell you. The highwaymen were courteous and apologetic, a couple of patricians down on their luck."

"Patricians, my arse." Stafford jerked the statement from her hand. "This looks fraudulent to me, my dear. I suspect you've not only been robbed, but you've been duped by your publisher, which is hardly a surprising turn of events. Women have no place in the business world."

Elizabeth snatched the paper back. "Enough! I know what I'm worth, and I know what I was robbed of, and I refuse to discuss this further."

"My dear Elizabeth," Stafford said, his voice and manner solicitous, the attitude of a rational man attempting to soothe an hysterical woman. "You've so often told me that your scribbling would afford you a decent living. I fear, however, that you have no head for figures, and I suspect that you've been deluded by a disreputable businessman. Which means, my dear, that you've risked spinsterhood for naught."

Elizabeth pictured the Beresfords' palatial town house, her shelf of published books, the sums she had periodically withdrawn from her account, and she felt like whacking Stafford over the skull with her parasol. "If *your* name headed this document," she said scornfully, "you would have no doubt as to its authenticity. You seek to discredit me and Minerva Press simply because it angers you that a woman can earn a comfortable livelihood through her own efforts."

"My beautiful Elizabeth, how I do admire your spirit. Unfortunately, locked up with your books, you know nothing about the real world. Twenty pounds is hardly a comfortable livelihood." He held up a hand to still her heated protests. "Nevertheless, you have been robbed, no matter how paltry the sum. Since today is Sunday, the Sunday Trading Act relieves the authorities of any responsibility. I mean, of course, for the reimbursement of your money."

"Yes. And since it was such a paltry sum, I don't even plan to pursue it."

"What? Do you have a fever? Are you overcome with fear?" Stafford stretched to his full height and looked down his long narrow nose, as he always did when trying to intimidate her. "Of course you'll pursue it. You must. Those blackguards will not stop with one coach. Now, give me a description of them, anything you can remember. I shall attempt to jog your memory with pointed questions. What were their clothes like? Their accents? What kind of horses were they riding?"

"It was dark. I couldn't see well. Their horses looked like horses. They wore masks." She smiled. "The men wore masks, not the horses."

"One was hugely tall with a big belly," Grace offered. "And the other one wore a black cloth over his face, and his hair was dark, I think."

"What else?"

"They both had pistols, and the dark-haired one pointed his at Mistress Elizabeth."

"Yes?" Stafford prompted impatiently. "What else?"

Grace considered. "I was so scared, m'lord."

With her maid's powers of observation, Elizabeth figured the highwaymen were in no immediate danger. Stafford then questioned the coachmen and guard, who recalled little more than the pistols and masks.

"I am sorry this happened," said Lawrence, still holding Elizabeth's parasol and bronze. With his free hand, he patted her head. "It was fortunate you did not carry a large sum on your person." He glanced toward Dorothea, then focused on Elizabeth again. "That's my Bess. 'Tis a blessing you inherited your brains from your mother, not your old papa."

"We must pursue this in all haste," Stafford told Lawrence, who was one of the local constables. "If those brigands think to terrorize the Dales and thwart me, their reign will be short, their end brutal."

"Aye. So it will, m'lord."

The men gathered together in an excited cluster. The ladies, save for Dorothea, comforted Grace.

Brown eyes bright, Dorothea faced Elizabeth and spoke in a low, angry voice. "You'd better hope Lord Stafford is wrong and you are still a wealthy woman. If there's no two thousand pounds on account, in a few months' time you'll lose your entire inheritance, and your father and I will be homeless. How will you feel about that?"

"Before Papa wed you, he seldom gambled," Elizabeth replied. "Perhaps his marital unhappiness has forced him into reckless habits."

"Your father always gambled. If you think otherwise, your illusions have become reality." Dorothea lifted her chin, and with an air of dignity remarkable in so petite a woman, she walked back toward the inn.

Clutching her traveling bag, Elizabeth followed. "Welcome home," she muttered.

But everything wasn't pure disaster. Far from it. John Randolph was in the Dales and they would meet again. He had said so. She would make certain of it. He had promised to return her money, and somehow she knew, deep down inside, that John was a man who honored his vows. The only danger lay in Lord Stafford finding him before she did. But Stafford couldn't find his way home. How could he be expected to find a couple of highwaymen intent on hiding from him?

After she met up with John, she would retrieve her two hundred pounds and talk him into giving up his life of crime.

Then what? Perhaps she'd write a novel

about him, something like *Confessions of a Former Highwayman.*

Reforming John would be the first order of the day, Elizabeth calculated.

She couldn't let herself fall in love with a man who might end up swinging from a hangman's noose.

CHAPTER 7

And Lady Guinevere murmured to her beloved, with tears trembling at the corners of her shining eyes, "Dearest husband. Now we shall ne'er be parted again."

Elizabeth put down her quill and rubbed her temples. With that paragraph, *Castles of Doom* was completed. It had taken her eight weeks, during which she had been plagued with nightmares and distracted by her search for John. Yet, ultimately, she had triumphed. Rather than relate the rebels' true fate, she had consigned Simon de Montfort and Ralf Darkstarre to exile in France. Tomorrow she would post the manuscript, and soon she would be reading flattering reviews, or scathing ones, depending upon its reception.

She wondered what James Waterman would think. Perhaps the library curator would simply shrug his stooped shoulders and condemn her to his list of "silly writers." On the other hand, Simon de Montfort was probably laughing at her from the bowels of the earth, sharing his mirth with Ranulf the Black and Lucifer.

The candle flame atop the girandole sputtered, as if from a sudden draft. Elizabeth stretched, then massaged her stiff neck. Outside, mist painted the diamond panes of her casement window. It was a night reminiscent of the night when she'd last seen John.

Since then, the Gentleman Giant and his Quiet Companion had plagued the Dales. They had proven remarkably resourceful — and active. In addition to the usual mélange of thefts, they had robbed post boys carrying mail from York, and they had even prigged a coach while it was changing horses in Middleham, virtually under Lord Stafford's aristocratic nose.

Despite his abominable language and disgraceful behavior toward Elizabeth, the Gentleman Giant treated others graciously. Lawrence Wyndham told of interviewing a lady who had refused to part with her favorite ring. The gallant Giant had said that a kiss on the lovely hand wearing it would constitute fair trade.

John, however, remained a nebulous figure. Nebulous to Elizabeth, as well. He had obviously lied about seeing her again, although he couldn't simply present himself at the White Hart and ask for Miss Wyndham. She had questioned everyone who might have conceivably come in contact with John, from Woodale to Horsehouse, clear to Middleham. But she had invariably been met by blank looks, or sly winks, or a curt shake of the head. Nobody seemed to know anything at all about the slender, dark-haired highwayman.

Small wonder John and his companion have achieved such success, she thought with an unladylike snort. *They must be bribing half the Dales.*

A coachman's horn blasted, announcing the arrival of yet another carriage. Elizabeth drew her shawl closer around her neck and shoulders, hiding the white fichu that adorned her blue woolen dress. The very stones of the wall seemed to radiate cold, and she fancied she could decipher faces clinging to the window panes — spectral faces bleeding into drops of rain.

Suddenly, inexplicably, she thought of the watchers who had attended her mother's funeral. They had waited for Barbara to move, but Barbara had remained motionless. They had watched to see if Barbara would bleed, but she hadn't bled.

Elizabeth heaved a deep sigh. Even after twenty-one years, she still thought of the watchers when her mood was melancholy or the night's shadows lay especially heavy, like cobwebs inside a long-abandoned room.

"Stop this," she admonished, but her normally comfortable bedroom had been transformed into an alien, sinister place. The fog swirled against her ground floor window. Quickly, Elizabeth stood, causing the girandole's flames to dance. The melting wax from one of the candles coiled round its shaft and spilled beyond its holder, in the manner of a winding sheet.

A bad omen.

"Ridiculous," she whispered. Good Lord, she should be celebrating. Her career was intact, her literary reputation saved, and soon she would regain her inheritance. Except for her failure to find John, life couldn't be better. Well, it could. Charles Beresford could send her the money he owed her, Walter Stafford could leave the Dales, and Dorothea could — no!

It was better not to contemplate a fitting fate for her stepmother. Elizabeth had already consigned Dorothea to the rack in *The Conqueror's Conquest.* For her next endeavor, she thought she might place Dorothea inside an iron maiden. And snakes would add a nice touch. Dorothea was terrified of snakes.

As soon as Elizabeth entered the common room, she was enveloped by a feeling of warmth and good cheer. An inviting fire burned in the huge stone fireplace. The air was redolent with tobacco, pork pies, wet wool, smoke and hickory. Servants bearing pewter trays loaded with food and homemade beer scurried to and from tables, accompanied by clacking plates, conversation, and a sprightly tune, compliments of Dorothea and her pianoforte.

Elizabeth crossed to her father, who was shaking awake one of the regulars, asleep at the bar. "I'm all finished, Papa," she said. "We shall post the manuscript tomorrow and instruct Mr. Beresford to send the whole amount you need by return post. He should have sent the money after my London visit, but in his last letter he said he was waiting for the completion of *Castles.* Now 'tis finished, and we still have six more weeks before your note is due."

Lawrence had become increasingly morose as the mortgage deadline neared. Face brightening, he said, "I promise I shall never look at another card or bet on another cock fight for the rest of my life, Bess. I've learned my lesson."

Dorothea launched into a new melody. Passengers from the latest coach settled at their respective tables. A sprinkling of lords and ladies, some wearing far more jewelry than was safe considering recent circumstances, supped on the roast capon, lamb, and pork pies. A young couple, the woman with a baby in her arms, lounged on a bench near the door. The baby had huge brown eyes that seemed to register awe at everything it witnessed, from its mother's finger to the swinging pendulum of a nearby grandfather clock. Elizabeth quickly passed the family on her way to the parlor. Cozy domestic scenes — and babies, especially babies — were better ignored. Sometimes, when she considered how she had forfeited children along with marriage, she felt a deep, aching sorrow. She told herself that the mothering instinct was just another basic animal urge, like the need to protect one's territory. After all, she lived in an age of reason, where everything could be explained away by science, including inappropriate yearnings.

The parlor was deserted save for a handful of locals playing cards or billiards. Since John's arrival, Elizabeth figured business had decreased by half.

"Be ye ready t' finish our draughts game, Miss Elizabeth?" called out Daniel, one of the regulars.

She slid across the bench opposite him. "I've not bested you in so long, I don't know why you bother." Daniel had recently lost his wife of forty years, and he spent much of his time at the inn. Although Elizabeth made it a point of honor never to acquiesce to a man in anything, she generally let Daniel triumph.

While he agonized over every move, her mind swirled as relentlessly as the fog. Where was John tonight? she wondered, drumming her fingers on the tabletop. Was he gazing into the darkness, remembering their all too brief encounters?

Hardly, she thought, expelling her breath on a derisive sigh. *A man of broken promises is what ye be.*

Suddenly, Elizabeth had the strangest feeling she'd uttered those exact words before, and she couldn't control the small gasp that escaped her lips.

"Don't be so impatient," Daniel admonished. "You young folks nowadays are always in such a hurry."

"I wasn't. I'm not in a hurry, truly." How could she explain that her gasp had been evoked by fear, not impatience?

While Daniel tentatively fingered the board, Elizabeth vowed to ignore her recent unease. Instead, she contemplated her next move — with John.

Once she had retrieved her two hundred pounds, she would forget him, for the truth was plain enough. He didn't care one whit about her. If he did, he would have been as irresistibly drawn to her as Ralf Darkstarre had been drawn to Guinevere. Besides, while John was attractive, he was a disreputable sort of handsome. Chapbooks wrote that highwaymen were romantic and dangerous and bound for the gallows, where women would weep and men would cheer. Which seemed an apt summation of John and his impending fate.

I won't shed a tear, she vowed. *You are neither a proper hero nor a proper villain, John Randolph. My lovers would never be so cavalier in their treatment of the heroine. They would not dare, or I would kill them off in the first chapter.*

"I've bested ye again," Daniel cackled. "A second game, Miss Elizabeth?"

She shook her head. "I believe I shall go for a ride."

"In this weather?" Daniel gestured with his pipe toward the window, where mist clung to the glass like a frightened child.

116

" 'Tisn't fit for man nor beastie."

"Then it should suit me just fine."

Vapor rimmed the wooden sign above the inn's front door. The painted white hart seemed to leap from the surrounding darkness, as if seeking the warmth and laughter of the interior. Elizabeth raised her face to the drizzle, perversely enjoying its cool caress against her cheeks and brow. Heading toward the stables, her petticoats swished upon the cobblestones like whispered voices, and once again she thought of the watchers.

What is wrong with me tonight?

As she passed the shoeing shed and smithy, she heard a man say, "Pay close attention, you dolt," and she stiffened like a fox who had just heard the first bay of hounds.

"You must check every cloak-bag," Walter Stafford continued. "If you find one empty, sound the alarm. Highwaymen carry bags for show rather than to burden their horses."

"Damme," Elizabeth breathed. She had thought Stafford would be well on his way home by now. Yet here he was, making a nuisance of himself with poor Tim the Ostler.

"Aye, m'lord," said Tim. "Ye've told me all this before."

"Notify Master Wyndham immediately if any guest seems unduly concerned over the owners of the horses," Stafford persevered. "Or if they question you about the owners' occupations, their destinations, or when they plan to resume their journ— why, Elizabeth, what are you doing out here?"

"Obviously, I'm taking a stroll."

Stafford held her knuckles to his lips, and the ruby ring on his finger caught the stable light. "You are looking especially enchanting this evening, my dear." He rearranged her shawl, which had slipped from one shoulder. Then he *tsked* his tongue against the roof of his mouth. "Whatever could you have been thinking of to have left your hat and gloves inside?"

"I was contemplating a brief stroll, my lord, *alone.*"

Walter Stafford hesitated, unsure whether to use the frontal assault he usually reserved for his social inferiors, or to feint. With Elizabeth Wyndham, one never knew what might work, if anything would. The woman was a conundrum, which was precisely the reason why he had been unable to forget her.

"Dear Elizabeth, this meeting is extremely fortuitous," he said, bowing his head so that his nose was leveled at her thick dark lashes.

"I see so little of you these days with your writing and other, er, pastimes. Really, all that close work must be hard on your eyes, not to mention your personal life." Stroking the froth of lace at his throat, he laughed mirthlessly.

Angry, Elizabeth refused to look at him. Instead, she stared at the ruby on his ring, which glistened like a drop of fresh-pricked blood.

"My personal life is as I wish it to be," she finally retorted, lifting her chin.

Walter scowled, for a woman should never be so openly contradictory. Elizabeth Wyndham had neither tact nor good manners, but she did have damnably fine breasts. There wasn't a finer pair in all the Dales. "Speaking of your personal life," he said, keeping his voice steady, attempting a sangfroid he didn't feel, "I assume you're still planning to do me the very great honor of acting the devoted companion during next week's fête. I have been keeping company with a wealthy widow who yearns for my escort, but you agreed so many months ago and your mother —"

"Stepmother!"

"— said that you have been eagerly anticipating our engagement."

"If you have found yourself a wealthy

119

widow, my lord, I'll not hold you to your promise."

"Dear Elizabeth," he began, clasping his hands in front of him, purposefully flashing the ruby ring that dwarfed his index finger. "Dear, dear Elizabeth, I would not consider reneging on my promise. It's just that sometimes you seem more concerned with making a statement than acting the woman, and many men might find that a bit off-putting."

She arched an eyebrow. "And you, my lord?"

Stafford hesitated once again, his eyes raking her body. Damnably fine. "No, I don't find you off-putting," he said, and even to his own ears, his voice sounded rough, throaty. Aware that such naked desire would only further alienate her, he shifted his attention back to Tim. "I've been helping your ostler sharpen his powers of observation, my dear. Even someone as dimwitted as Tim might inadvertently supply information which will rid this area of the scourge that has descended upon us."

"Yes, we all know how lawless the Dales are. Even the sheep have criminal records. Really, my lord, from your attitude one would think that you were a member of London's Bow Street Runners, rather than someone who spends his time issuing ale-house licenses."

Stafford's smile was peculiar. "I have not always lived in the Dales," he said. "And you comprehend very little about me, though I remain eager to rectify that deficiency. Despite your doubts, my dear Elizabeth, I am confident that those two scoundrels are very nearly within our grasp. I've studied them and their minds, and I know them better than they know themselves. I must confess, I'm more concerned with the quiet one than his flamboyant partner."

Her heart slammed against her bodice. "And why is that, sir?"

"The loud one has obviously assimilated the same propaganda as most of the populace, who believe what they read about in chapbooks and what they see in *The Beggar's Opera*. But I sense the quiet one is conducting his own private war with society. He is the one who must be caught. And he will be. For when it all comes down to it, despite their superficial differences, highwaymen are stupid and lazy. They live only to drink and whore and gamble. They rely solely on a pistol to intimidate their victims, a mask to disguise their features, and a fast horse for escape. Beyond that, they have no imagination."

Which sounds remarkably like you, thought Elizabeth.

"I don't believe these men are stupid or lazy," she countered. "They certainly work hard at their trade. And I need not remind you that they made short work of the watchmen you posted. The Gentleman Giant and his Quiet Companion tied the watchmen up, took their places, then proceeded to rob every person who passed by. That, my lord, takes imagination."

Stafford threw back his head and laughed, as if Elizabeth had just related *the* most amusing anecdote. "I love wit in the fairer sex, my dear, which is one of the reasons why I remain so smitten with you. Watchmen are old and decrepit. Anybody could thwart them, even a woman. Not that some of you aren't extremely capable," he amended, "although *your* independence afforded you ill when you were faced with danger."

Before she could reply, a stable boy arrived with Stafford's horse.

Stafford removed his heavily scrolled gold pocket watch, its fob-seal encrusted with diamonds. "Oh my. I've enjoyed our chat, but I must be on my way. However, the prospect of spending an entire day in your lovely company will warm my heart on the cold ride home."

He swung up onto his horse. "I was distressed after reading *Castles of Doom*," he said, leaning sideways. "I've read all your books, you know. Some were acceptable, but *Castles of Doom* was most definitely not."

"And why is that, my lord?"

"You may possess the face of an angel, but your mind seems to work in an inappropriately masculine manner. Lady Guinevere was not always as chaste as she should be. She seldom knew her place, and on more than one occasion she was downright contumacious."

"Contumacious? Did it ever occur to you that Guinevere was stubbornly disobedient because circumstances forced her —"

"She was rebellious!"

"If I am so *contumacious,* I should think you'd quit asking me to marry you."

"I've always enjoyed a challenge." Stafford reined his horse around. "And I warn you. I'm just as dogged in the pursuit of love as I am in my quest for justice."

Still angry, Elizabeth watched him melt into the fog-shrouded highway.

Tim sidled up to her and thrust his hands through his pale, uncombed hair. "That one likes to talk, don't he?"

"Pay him no mind. Lord Stafford likes to annoy people."

"Aye." Tim smiled his cherubic smile. "The quiet highwayman don't keep his spoils, Mistress. He gives it over t' them in need."

"That's called a bribe, Tim. Hush money."

"Nay, Mistress. He gives over his boodle t' them wot's hungry an' sick. He give Old Fife a cow."

"A cow," Elizabeth repeated, dazed. She had pictured John in many guises, but never altruistic.

"Aye, Mistress. Old Fife's daughter died i' the straw, birthin' a baby, an' there weren't no wet nurse hereabouts, nor coins fer one wot bided far off. That baby fared poorly, no more 'n this side o' the grave, 'til the quiet highwayman brung Old Fife a cow."

"Did the baby live, Tim?"

"Aye."

"Thank God."

"Nay, Mistress. Thank the highwayman."

Elizabeth watched her ostler walk toward the harness room. With a sigh, she veered toward the stalls. Lantern lights dropped soft golden circles upon row after row of browns and blacks and roans and horses the color of tonight's fog. The scent of ammonia, leather, and hay from an overhead loft enshrouded her while she made her way to Rhiannon, her mare. Elizabeth heard a stable boy's whistle, the cursing of a groom who had dropped something, and the stirring of the horses.

Rhiannon greeted her with a soft nicker. Elizabeth wrapped her arms around the mare's neck and rested her cheek against the smooth chestnut coat. Something about Rhiannon's warmth and the darkness in the high-backed stall caused Elizabeth to feel as alone as the moor owls who skimmed the gills.

"I'm trapped," she whispered to her mare. "I am twenty-eight years old, a spinster without prospects. My life is half over and what do I have to show for it? Lord Stafford was right. I am too masculine. I don't fit in anywhere. I may rail against a woman's lot, and name a hundred things I find unjust, yet I have no idea what would make me happy."

She thought of Old Fife's baby and the brown-eyed baby. She thought of the couples leaning against each other while they conversed or shared a slice of lamb or smiled together over some shared memory.

I don't want that, she thought, leading Rhiannon from her stall. *But what do I want?*

Deciding a saddle was unnecessary, Elizabeth mounted her mare from a block, then plunged into the fog. She often rode out on fitful evenings, when the weather was as unpredictable as her moods. She especially enjoyed racing across the countryside, with the thunder growling and the rain slashing her face. She loved the charged air and the power of a storm, which empowered her as well. This was a quieter night, designed to soothe rather than excite the soul, but her soul was in need of soothing. She felt protected by the fog, which nestled deep in the valleys, settled thick upon the bracken, and obliterated the treeless landscape. Elizabeth felt as if she could wrap the fog around her like a cloak, perhaps even hide from the world.

What lay beyond the ravines and caves? York, of course, and London, and beyond that France and Spain, India and America. But what else? Her Aunt Lilith told stories of a magic world filled with spells and bindings and enchanted happenings. Elizabeth desperately wanted the world to be like that tonight. If it was, she could make a wish and bring her books to life, or she could change her destiny with the utterance of a spell, or she could —

A pistol cracked.

Elizabeth reined in Rhiannon and looked

around. It was impossible to determine direction or distance. She heard a shout, seemingly cut off in mid-cry. Then she heard hoofbeats, cutting across the fields, racing toward her. She saw the swirl of a black cloak, the blur of a dark horse, and she felt the earth shake beneath her as the horse and rider thundered past.

Could that have been John plying his trade? But he and his partner always worked together.

"John!" Elizabeth called.

Her only answer was silence.

CHAPTER 8

Elizabeth awakened from a fitful sleep. The wind rattled her shutters. She rolled over on her side. The shutters rattled again, as if someone shook them. She sat up.

The night had carried fog, but no wind.

Crossing to the window, she raised the sash, swung open the shutters, and leaned out. Her long, unbound hair tumbled over the window's ledge.

John sat astride his black stallion, bathed by the moonlight. "I thought you'd never awaken," he said. "I nearly broke my whip beating on your shutters."

"How did you know which room was mine?"

"I know everything about you, my bonny Bess."

He looked so pleased with himself, she could not help but return his impish grin. "I've looked everywhere for you," she confessed, propping her elbows on the window's ledge. "Nobody would tell me anything."

"That's why highwaymen always have limited funds. Bribery is expensive."

"I've heard you do more than bribe. I've heard you help those in need."

" 'Tis merely a drop in the bucket." John removed his hat, shook the moisture from its brim, then rested it on his saddle horn. "Despite your low opinion of your justice of the peace, he's made life difficult for my partner and me, and I have a feeling that things are about to get much worse. 'Tis time we moved along."

"But Walter Stafford is a cork-head. He cannot find his snuffbox, let alone a criminal."

"You underestimate him, Bess. I think you're soon going to learn that there is more to Stafford than he generally presents to the world."

She felt her skin prickle. "What have you done now? Have you been up to more mischief?"

Ignoring her questions, he retrieved a coin purse from beneath his cloak, then tossed it to her. "I am honoring my promise, Bess. Since you work so hard for your money, I didn't think it fair to keep it forever."

Elizabeth estimated the purse's weight.

"This is far too heavy for pound notes."

John shrugged. "In my business, I have to improvise."

She studied him, his dark hair sweeping untidily across his forehead, his eyes sparkling with excitement. *Who are you? An ordinary man who's fallen into lawlessness, an altruistic outlaw, or someone "at war with society"?*

According to chapbooks, highwaymen were brought into the trade because of gambling debts or a disinheritance or some other acceptably genteel reason. Why had John become one?

"Do you think to repay me with your ill-gotten funds, John Randolph? Was it you I heard earlier tonight? Were you out in the fog, waylaying coach passengers?"

"What were *you* doing out in the fog?"

"Celebrating," she fibbed, even though she had a feeling he might understand her restlessness. "I've just finished the last installment of *Castles of Doom*."

"How does it end?"

"You must purchase a copy to find out."

"I'm serious, Bess. How does it end?"

"Happily ever after."

"Ralf Darkstarre . . . does he die?"

"No," she replied uncomfortably, remembering the *Alcester Chronicles*. She also recalled the curator's comment about a man who limped. "John, do you read Latin?"

"Darkstarre doesn't suffer a bloody death?" he pressed, ignoring her query.

"I just told you. He does not. Conventional wisdom says that Gothic romances must end on a happy note."

"But Darkstarre was the villain."

"Not to Lady Guinevere. I mean, he was a villain, of course he was, a thoroughly reprehensible rebel . . ." Cheeks aflame, she swallowed the rest of her explanation, and instead gazed down at the purse she held so tightly against her palm, secured by her clenched fingers. "If I accept this, will the law consider me an accessory?"

John laughed. "You don't give a hang what the law says. I suspect you're every bit as rebellious as I am."

Elizabeth was flattered by his characterization, but her rebellions were largely in her imagination. "I don't consider an occasional comment about a woman's sorry lot the same as holding a man at gunpoint," she said. "Why don't you retire, John? Find yourself a more respectable way to thumb your nose at society and —"

"Never," he interrupted, his expression so fierce she recoiled, momentarily afraid of him. "Besides," he said, his manner again smooth and unruffled, "if I were a respectable merchant or craftsman, I would not have robbed Lady Avery. And most likely I would not have happened across *Castles of Doom.*"

"I should have guessed. You picked up my volume along with your booty, and when you had some free time between robbing people, you read it." She saw John's knee-high black boots glimmer in the moonlight. His stallion pawed the cobblestones. "And you were so impressed, you simply had to meet me," she added sarcastically.

"I can't decide whether I'm pleased we met, or terrified."

"Terrified? Whatever do you mean?" She dropped the purse on the floor and pressed her hands against her heart.

Standing in his stirrups, he entwined his fingers through her unbound hair, drawing her to him, brushing her lips with his own. Elizabeth's breath caught in her throat. "John," she whispered. She nearly added: *I do love thee,* but that was absurd. He had stolen from her. He was a rogue, a good-for-naught, a scoundrel. Still, it seemed right to tell him she loved him.

Rather than speak, she kissed him, softly at first, then harder, more urgently. As her mouth opened under the onslaught of his tongue, she felt her limbs grow weak. As if they had kissed like this a thousand times before, as if they had lain together and he had stroked every inch of her body, as if she had already felt his hands caress her breasts and thighs, as if she already knew what it was like to feel him inside her, to own him as her beloved. And all the while her mind whispered: *I do love thee.* And all the while she knew it was true, that she did love him, that she had always loved him.

"Enough," he said, pulling away. Elizabeth stumbled backwards, bent over double, her hands beating at the air for balance. Then, standing upright, she extended her arms in a gesture of supplication.

Rand had seen that identical gesture before!

Of course he had. Many of his ladies had offered up just such a gesture, begging him to return to their beds. But none had stood above a window's casement, ebony hair shrouding a white nightshift. He contemplated climbing through Bess's window, but suddenly she was gone. Feeling hollow and cold at the loss of her warmth, he watched the room flicker and glow. She had lit a candle.

Darkness was much more tempting than light, even though he would love to see her body enshrined by candlelight, her womanly curves visible, nay, *defined* by the taper's illumination. But he couldn't treat Elizabeth Wyndham like one of his London bunters. She would require a covenant of promises, a commitment he was unwilling to give. At the very least, she would insist he forfeit his life of crime.

After his niece's fiery death, he had pressed his lips upon a Bible and sworn revenge. Revenge against whom? The upper classes, of course. Would Bess consider his present activities fair trade? Rand doubted it. Sometimes he wondered if his actions stemmed from another motive. Perhaps he wanted to atone for sins committed in his past by playing the sainted Robin Hood. What sins? Could the death of the American rebels be considered an offense against God? Rand thought not. In battle, one killed or was killed — a simple concept. Anyway, Rand had a feeling his transgressions had been committed five hundred years ago, a ridiculous concept.

Bess stirred a host of emotions in him that were better left buried. He didn't want to think about the past or how they might be connected. Yet even as he told himself that a man only lived once and any other notion bordered on madness, somehow it didn't seem mad. On the contrary, it seemed eminently logical.

Elizabeth poked her head out through the open window. "You really are a scoundrel," she said.

"I try to be." He raised his whip in a mock salute. "Get some sleep, Bess. Dream of your highwayman. Dream of Rand."

"Rand?"

"My given name is John Randolph Remington," he confessed, wondering if his slip of the tongue had been intentional. Was he challenging her trustworthiness? "My friends call me Rand, not John." He grinned recklessly. "I would have you call me Rand, Bess, especially in your dreams. And now, goodnight."

"Wait!" she called. "When will I see you again?"

But John . . . *Rand's* horse was already racing across the cobblestones. Only after the stallion's hoofbeats had died away did Elizabeth retrieve the discarded coin purse and walk over to her writing table. Darting a quick glance toward *Castles of Doom,* she focused on the purse. From inside, she retrieved a gold watch, a ruby ring, and more guineas than she could easily count.

As if she held a scorpion's tail, Elizabeth quickly dropped the purse onto the tabletop.

The guineas and jewelry followed. Mesmerized, she stared at the watch with its diamond-encrusted fob-seal.

"Now you've done it, John Randolph Remington!" She didn't know whether to laugh or curse. Picking up the ring, raising it to the candle's flame, she slowly twisted it around, allowing the ruby to catch the light. "Impressive," she said dryly.

But the blood-red ring had looked even more impressive when it had graced the finger of Walter Stafford.

CHAPTER 9

As Rhiannon loped across the countryside, Elizabeth reveled in the fragrance of the moorland grass, the sight of the valleys falling away on either side, and the feel of the wind caressing her curls.

Pinned to her petticoat was the blasted coin purse.

She had decided to hide it in the peel tower, but this morning was her first opportunity to do so. With all the recent hysteria, should she merely stroll through the inn yard alone, some do-gooder would insist on finding her a male escort.

In the teeth of Dorothea's protestations, Elizabeth had persuaded her father to ride ahead, saying they would rendezvous nearby at West Scrafton. Today was Walter Stafford's Midsummer's Eve party, which, despite the robbery, was taking place as scheduled. That exacted a bit of courage on Walter's part, for Rand had humiliated him beyond reason. When a raving Stafford had arrived at the inn, he had been naked as an egg. Rand had stolen the lawman's clothes along with his horse.

Feeling guilty over her part in the crime, no matter how incidental, Elizabeth had vowed that she would be nicer to Walter. Aware that he would wholeheartedly approve, she wore a stylish riding dress, purchased at a second-hand shop in York. Dorothea had altered the outfit, making it *au courant,* using as a model a fashion baby mailed from Paris. What Elizabeth might have regarded as an act of kindness had been dispelled by Dorothea's remark that a woman could never snare a wealthy husband garbed in a dress that dated back to the Year of the Flood.

A blue cloth skirt over billowing petticoats hid Elizabeth's breeches and boots. A blue cloth coat, very low-cut, nipped her waist, then flared out at the back. Beneath the long-sleeved, velvet-cuffed coat was a cream silk waistcoat. Much to Grace's relief, Elizabeth had added a white lawn fichu, draped loosely around her neck, then fastened at her bosom with a brooch. The fichu hid the rising mounds of her breasts, or accentuated them, depending on one's point of view.

Perhaps she covered her bosom to avoid Walter's penetrating gaze. Nevertheless, she would behave like a proper escort. A demure demeanor, ladylike rather than masculine, compliant rather than rebellious, should diminish Walter's fury, and he might not be so determined to shoot Rand on sight.

Walter Stafford wasn't the only one upset by the robbery. The entire Dales were scandalized, at least those who had something worth stealing. Since the Gentleman Giant and his Quiet Companion always worked in tandem, the populace feared the arrival of yet a third highwayman. Carriages rode with armed escorts, the papers cried for the culprits' immediate capture, and the roads crawled with posses. Elizabeth was certain Rand had long left the area, which was undoubtedly best, even though she wondered how she would ever see him again.

Fearful the coin purse would be discovered, she had concluded that the safest place for it was pinned inside the waistband of her petticoat. She didn't dare leave the stolen goods in her room, and she couldn't pawn the jewelry. Following the example of John Fielding, the famous head of the Bow Street Runners, Walter had availed himself of the local papers, publishing descriptions of each stolen article. His ring and watch now topped the list. Every day Elizabeth worried that she would be found out and accused of the robbery. Hadn't she taken her ride soon after Lord Stafford's departure? Suspects had been found guilty on as little evidence and women were not exempt from the hangman's noose. Until events calmed down, she would simply bury the purse and go about her business.

Damn John Randolph Remington! He had returned her money, albeit in guineas and jewelry, but now she couldn't spend it.

Elizabeth raised her face to the sun. In keeping with her newfound desire to be agreeable until safely divested of the coin purse, she had allowed her stepmother to slather an ointment on her face. The ointment smelled of vinegar and apples and it was supposed to subjugate the sun's rays. According to Dorothea, Elizabeth's unfashionable complexion was one of the main reasons she had not yet snared a husband.

Someday she would like to live in a place so hot it would blacken her skin. During her research on *Richard of the Lion's Heart,* she had become intrigued with the Holy Land and its climate, so very different from the north of England with its cold weather and relentless winds. The Holy Land was . . .

well, holy, while dark things formed in the north — ghosts and demons and evil spirits.

She dismounted at the peel tower. It had been erected in the fourteenth century during the time of the bad king, Edward II, when Robert the Bruce had ravaged the borderlands at will.

Reaching beneath her skirt, she unpinned the purse, then entered the tower. Its roof and three of its four walls had long since crumbled. Periodically, farmers carried off stones to erect fences and cottages. Tough grasses had replaced the hard-packed earth upon which frightened Northerners had huddled against marauding Scots.

She sometimes spent hours at the tower, writing or gazing up at the clouds and dreaming. Once she had fallen asleep, but that had been a mistake. The Dales were steeped in history. First Anglo-Saxons, then Danes, then the Normans had swept across the area in violent tidal waves. Folktales and the ancient mounds of the dead bore witness to bloody confrontations. Perhaps that was why she had dreamed of shadowy knights on horseback, engaged in some sort of battle. Perhaps that was why she had awakened screaming.

Today her throat felt dry as she picked her way across the rubble to the western wall, but nothing disturbed the silence save for the whisper of displaced pebbles, the bubbling trill of a curlew, and the distant bleats of sheep. Selecting a landmark, Elizabeth buried the purse.

How did my life come to this? she wondered, replacing the rocks. How did she ever become so enamored with a highwayman? Why would she want somebody so absolutely wrong for her?

She knew why. A country squire could never compare with a highwayman and the romantic, outrageous legends that sprang up about his deeds. Despite gossip to the contrary, Elizabeth knew that, deep down, she possessed a romantic nature. Didn't she breathe life into men who had never existed? Men like Ralf Darkstarre, the perfect lover?

Unfortunately, the only lover a highwayman could embrace was Death. Elizabeth pictured Rand shot down while fleeing from the law. She pictured him sprawled in the moonlight, his linen shirt black with blood.

A lump as big as an acorn filled her throat and her eyes blurred with tears. Sometimes a vivid imagination was a hindrance. "But most likely you're in Scotland now," she whispered, dissolving the lump.

Rising, she brushed off her skirt. Someday, somehow, they would meet again, and when they did, she would persuade Rand to give up his life of crime.

"Yes, we shall meet again," she said. Directly overhead, a buzzard, wings outstretched, rode the wind across the sky. "And next time I'll not let you get away."

CHAPTER 10

Rand left the highway to travel his own route. During his two months in the Dales, he had come to know the area well, a necessity in his profession. Sometimes he and Zak stayed with friendly locals, but more often than not, they hid out in the remains of lead mines, or in such ruins as Fountains Abbey. Rand had grown to love the Dales' bleak beauty. He enjoyed walking along the river beds and stone fences which networked the moors like the wrinkles on an aging face. Under different circumstances he might have entertained plans for settling in the area.

But it was time to go. Past time. He detoured around Horsehouse, a cluster of stone houses where packhorses were fed and rested. Hadn't he and Zak robbed a goldsmith right outside the town? Or was it a minister? Or could it have been a post boy? There had been so many, Rand had trouble remembering.

However, he had no trouble remembering a flower-like face, dark eyes bright with an unfathomable expression that made his need to escape even more vital. Once he would have courted Bess and —

Zak and I court danger if we stay here much longer.

Unfortunately, Zak had become enamored with a tavern maid in Coverham, and he balked at leaving. Ever since the theft of Walter Stafford's clothes and valuables, Rand had decided it would be safer to separate, and Zak had spent the entire time with his Annie.

No wonder Zak gets caught. Whatever part of his anatomy he uses for thinking, it isn't his brain.

Rand shook his mane of unruly hair. Zak had promised they would leave for Scotland today, and Rand meant to hold him to his promise.

Zak had agreed they'd meet at Roova Crag. Since the crag was visible for miles around, Rand figured Zak couldn't possibly get lost, or stumble into one of Stafford's patrols.

His bonehead cousin hadn't even bothered to acquaint himself with the area!

" 'Tis no mystery why highwaymen are so

easily caught," Rand told his stallion. "Some of us are just plain stupid."

He had long ago decided that Elizabeth was wrong about Stafford's intellect. The lawman was both perceptive and persistent. And Stafford possessed sufficient London connections to piece together the fact that Rand and Zak were the Gentleman Giant and his Quiet Companion. Early on, Rand had realized that it wasn't only the Dales' sparse population that accounted for its low crime rate. The last three highwaymen who had dared intrude upon Stafford's jurisdiction were still hanging in chains atop Roova Crag. Those particular robbers had made the mistake of holding up a local judge, one of Stafford's friends. Angered by the judge's refusal to part with his valuables, the trio had divested the judge's coachman and footman of their clothes, tied them up, and thrown them into a pond. Then the high-waymen had shot the horses, demolished the coach, and hanged the judge. Unfortunately for them, they had tried to sell their stolen goods to one of Stafford's many spies.

Rand didn't regret his own robbery, or even the impulsive theft of Stafford's clothes. In the army he had encountered dozens of officers like Stafford, men who had been pampered all their lives, who had inherited or purchased their ranks in order to increase their fortunes at the expense of their troops. If he could even momentarily discomfit the Walter Staffords of the world, Rand considered the possibility of death worth the risk.

Or at least he had until he encountered Elizabeth Wyndham. He recalled the scene beneath her bedroom window, the touch of her silken hair, the taste of her lips, her breath warm in his hair. Her flowery, female scent had rendered him indecisive. He hadn't responded with pretty words or insincere promises, but for the first time since the American War he longed for a normal existence. A damn shame it could not be. His Bess was fraught with danger. She didn't evoke images of a hangman's noose. Nay, his perception of her was that of a conspirator. Why, he couldn't say. He only knew that, should he continue to spend time in her presence, he was doomed.

Wasn't he doomed anyway? Wouldn't his feelings for Bess erase the past, dispel the ghosts and — damn! Only a young, foolish lad would conclude that "love conquers all."

"Love is a babble," a man sang at the top of his lungs. "No man is able to say 'tis this or 'tis that, 'tis full of passions, of sundry fashions, 'tis like I cannot tell what."

No mistaking that singer, Rand thought, as Prancer picked his way up the rocky path. Zak had beaten him to the summit.

A pistol cracked. Rand instinctively ducked, even though he could tell that the shot was aimed in the opposite direction. Raising his head, he saw Zak, garbed in a satin waistcoat, black velvet breeches and white silk stockings. The bloody fool was reloading his flintlock.

Beyond Zak, the skeletons of the hapless highwaymen, clothed in tatters, appeared silhouetted against the sky. Their iron cages creaked in the wind, and their limbs swayed, keeping time to a melody only they could hear.

"Cousin!" Rand called.

Zak spun around and grinned. Then he turned back to the gibbet, aimed and fired. One of the skeletons increased the tempo of its dance. Zak aimed a second pistol and pulled the trigger. The pan flashed, but didn't fire.

"Damn!" Zak shook his pistol at the gibbet. "Ye toad's harlot! What's wrong with ye this time?"

"You didn't hit the cage, nor the corpse." As Prancer carefully made his way around various mounds and tussocks, Rand added,

"Maybe your priming is wet or your flint's dulled."

"Or maybe this pistol's a piece of shit." Zak poured powder from his large main flask into the first gun's muzzle, then jammed the patched ball down with a ramrod.

"What the hell are those?" Rand gestured toward a string of horses tethered nearby.

Zak's swarthy features brightened. "Ain't they a fine bunch? I thought t' take them t' Middleham. They're havin' a horse fair there today. Annie told me."

Rand frowned. "We're highwaymen, not copers. Besides, Stafford lives in Middleham. You've pulled some gormless stunts in your time, cousin, but peddling stolen mounts in Stafford's town would number among the most idiotic."

Zak jammed one of the pistols behind his belt. " 'Tis no more gormless than makin' the bloody pimp walk butt-naked in the fog. Anyway, I bought them beasts fair and square. I've got me a bill of sale right here." He waved a piece of paper in front of Rand.

Rand knocked it away. "That's about as worthless as your word. You bloody fool! Do you want to end up like *them?*" He jerked his head toward the swaying skeletons.

149

Zak grinned. "Ye're a sour one today."

Dismounting, Rand slowly circled the grazing horses. If Zak had bought them and planned to make a profit, they couldn't be quality animals. Rand knew well enough how to fix horses. A lean horse could be temporarily fattened with a glut of unwholesome food. One suffering from a broken wind might be "cured" by keeping it short of food and water, or giving it grease dumplings. A rambunctious horse might be beaten just before it was displayed, making it appear quiet and manageable. A listless horse might be confined to a dark stall. Once freed, it would bound out of the barn and, startled by the daylight, toss its head and prance about like a colt.

Zak shoved his beaver hat off his forehead, where it perched precariously atop his wig. "What'd I tell ye? Won't they fetch me a fine amount o' rum cole?"

Rand grunted, then ran his hand down a bay gelding's foreleg. "This one's lame."

"What d'ya mean?" Zak puffed out his chest.

"I know how you fix a bad leg, cousin."

Copers had a thousand tricks, thought Rand. They might soak the leg in water, or they might hammer a tiny stone between the shoe and the hoof's most sensitive part after first removing a sliver of flesh. Thus the good leg would be lamed, and to an inexperienced eye the horse would appear normal.

Zak assumed a sorrowful expression. "I can't believe ye would accuse me of bein' a bite. Them animals are sound."

"Sound? Look at that chestnut mare. You've stained its legs to hide its blemished knees."

Zak placed his hand over his heart. "I swear on me brother's grave, 'tis not so."

"Both your brothers are alive and kicking, which is more than I can say for these sorry mounts."

"Ye've wounded me, cousin."

"I don't know what you're going to do with this *fine bunch,* Zak, but you're not selling them. We're bound for Scotland."

Zak's expression sobered. "Annie says she's with child, and I promised t' scrounge up enough ridge t' see her and the baby through for a year. I can't just go off and leave her t' fend for herself."

"What about the fifty guineas from our last robbery?"

Zak shrugged his massive shoulders. "A man has expenses." He thrust out his right leg to display a shoe with silver buckles. "These stampers cost a fortune, and Annie was in need of some new lurries."

"Are you daft? Annie must be all of two months pregnant. She doesn't need a new wardrobe, and if she does you can send her money from Scotland."

"*Ye* waste yer boodle on cows an' such!"

" 'Twas not a waste. Old Fife's baby was knocking at death's door."

Zak snorted. "I s'pose all the other buggers was knockin', too."

"Look, cousin, I told you from the very beginning that I'd only keep enough to survive, that I'd give the larger portion of my share to those in need."

"Annie *was* in need. I promised her, Rand, and I'll not disappoint her. Ye know what it's like t' be soft on a lass. Ye're soft on that Wyndham woman, though only Our Lord himself knows why. I'd sooner handle a rabid dog than that one."

Judging from Zak's stubborn expression, Rand knew the argument was lost. Nevertheless he said, "I'll have no part of your blasted horse fair." He crossed to the edge of the crag where the valley spread fifteen hundred feet below. The village of West Scrafton huddled in the distance, and alongside it, riders on the king's highway. "I have a bad feeling about this, Zak. I had that dream again last night. If you go through with your wild scheme, something's bound to happen."

Zak came up behind him. "Ye must visit me sawbones, lad. Them black moods ain't healthful."

"Something always happens after that dream."

"I'll be careful, 'tis a promise. I know what I'm doin'."

It was against Zak's nature to be careful, Rand thought. And whenever Zak said he knew what he was doing, it was a sure sign he didn't know a blessed thing.

"I'm not askin' ye t' go with me," Zak continued. " 'Twould be more chancy with the two of us skulkin' about. Meet me at the crossroads north of Middleham at midnight. Then I'll be off t' Scotland meek as ye please."

Anytime Zak planned something on his own, trouble followed. Rand knew that all the common sense in the world wouldn't sway his cousin, so he would have to attend the fair in order to keep a close watch. But he must not bruise Zak's pride. That would only make the brash bull-shooter more reckless.

" 'Tis agreed, midnight," Rand said, forcing a nonchalance he didn't feel into his voice. "Don't be late," he added, leaping atop Prancer.

Zak grinned and raised his pistol in mock salute. "Ye'll see, cousin. 'Twill go as smooth as a bunter's bottom."

Heading down the path, Rand heard Zak's cheerful bellow.

"Love is a wonder, that's here and yonder, as common to one as to mo'e. A monstrous cheater, every man's debtor, hang him, and so let him go."

"Hang him," Rand echoed. Then he shivered, for he feared the song's words were an omen.

CHAPTER 11

"I can't tell you how excited I am to be meeting an authoress," said Lady Marston, slipping her arm through Elizabeth's. "*Castles of Doom* is so vivid. I just finished the second installment and I love Ranulf Navarre. He's deliciously evil, isn't he?"

Elizabeth gaped at her admirer. *Ranulf Navarre? Why would Lady Marston mention the name of Simon de Montfort's baron?*

"I . . ." She swallowed. "I beg your pardon?"

"I said, I find Ralf Darkstarre deliciously evil, don't you?"

"Yes, evil." Elizabeth quickly regained her composure. Her mind was playing tricks on her. Perhaps the peel tower had stirred her imagination.

As Lady Marston continued, Elizabeth smiled at the circle of beaming faces. Almost all of the ladies were far older than she, domestically settled, and desirous to hear about the peculiar but assuredly interesting life of a writer. Elizabeth rather enjoyed being the center of attention. Several ladies hailed from London and were summering in the Dales. They seemed eager for any diversion from the slow country pace, and Elizabeth was more than happy to oblige them.

"Why is it that you've never married?" asked Lady Marston. "I have a nephew in Coventry who would be perfect for you."

Elizabeth gave one of her standard responses. "As another author, Lady Chudleigh, once wrote, 'Wife and servant are the same, But only differ in the name.' I prefer my single state."

Dorothea's nostrils flared and she fanned herself vigorously. The other ladies laughed.

"I think you should write your next book about highwaymen," said Mrs. Wright, the wife of a country squire. "Dear me, did they have highwaymen in the Middle Ages?"

"If they did not, they should have," Elizabeth replied diplomatically.

"Remember when Claude Duvall terrorized the highway?" Mrs. Wright patted her generous bosom as if stilling her heart. "Of course you wouldn't, Miss Wyndham, since that was before your time, though unfortunately not before mine."

"I've read about him." *Indeed, who hadn't?* "They say he was arrogant, insolently charming, and equipped with such an overpowering sensuality that maids, widows, wives, rich, poor, and vulgar women all enjoyed his bed. He sounds intriguing, doesn't he?"

"Ahem," Dorothea interjected, obviously disturbed by the improper turn of the conversation. "He wasn't before my time, Elizabeth, and, if memory serves, Claude Duvall was even better known as a liar, a cheat and a card sharp."

As always, Elizabeth felt duty-bound to contradict her stepmother. But before she could utter one word, Walter Stafford appeared at her side. "I must apprehend our guest of honor," he said, sounding like the lawman he was. Lacing his hand in the small of Elizabeth's back, he guided her toward the music room.

"Have I told you how radiant you look today?" he asked, ushering her inside.

"Thank you, my lord."

Walter waved his perfumed handkerchief at several guests, two-fingered the handkerchief back inside his cuff, then sat Elizabeth upon one of the settees and joined her there. "I have visited London and Bath and many of the kingdom's most fashionable resorts," he said, "yet I have never seen a lovelier woman." He touched her hat, which tilted rakishly over her forehead. "I do believe you're missing one of your ostrich plumes, my dear, and I noticed earlier that your shoes were a bit scuffed, which is no wonder. White kid might not have been the wisest choice. But other than your shoes and hat, you are perfection."

Just before entering Walter's house, Elizabeth had exchanged her boots for a pair of slippers. She had also tidied her hair and donned a hat. Now, ignoring his remarks, she pretended an interest in the entertainment — an indifferent interpretation of Handel. Soon her attention wandered. She studied the carpet, patterned with flowers, baskets and fruit. She studied the walls, paneled with damask silks in pale hues. She tried to calculate the cost of Walter's remodeling. Her host pressed his thigh against hers. She shifted away.

Without warning, she heard the music alter its cadence, though no one else seemed aware of this obvious discrepancy.

Elizabeth's breath came in hot gasps and every instinct urged her to flee. The melody sounded familiar, yet she had no earthly idea where she had heard it before. Clear-toned and mellifluous, it evoked images of celebration. And death.

Body ramrod stiff, eyes staring straight ahead, she willed her limbs to remain motionless. Then, after the obscure melody had faded, along with the last solemn notes of Handel, she experienced relief. And an almost overwhelming sadness.

Walter clapped politely. Rising from the settee, he signaled for silence. "Miss Wyndham recently had one of her poems published in *The Spectator,*" he announced. "You will do us the honor of reading it, Elizabeth, won't you?"

While she complied, Walter watched her hungrily. Two words came to mind — ripe and voluptuous. Several curls had escaped from her formerly neat club, yet even the undisciplined hair enhanced her aura of sensuality. Despite her physical attributes, he wondered whether he didn't desire Elizabeth primarily because she presented a challenge. He knew he was attractive. He also knew that he was the wealthiest man in the Dales and could have his pick of the ladies, even though men outnumbered women. In the cities the mix was reversed, and desperate fathers sometimes bribed bachelors to propose.

You wouldn't be so arrogant if we lived in London, Walter thought, yet perversely Elizabeth's haughtiness merely added to her charms. Rapidly *diminishing* charms. Time would inevitably take its toll. A man of his age, forty, was at the height of his desirability, while any woman past twenty could best be described as a shriveling bouquet. Soon Elizabeth would sprout crow's feet, a drooping jaw line, a thickened waist and a sagging bosom. Soon no man would have her.

Anticipating her impending decay did not make him feel any better. He indulged in sex with other women, of course, but he fantasized that it was Elizabeth he dominated. Now that he doctored yet another inflammation of his genitals, he was forced to limit his sexual encounters. Perhaps his celibacy partially accounted for his inability to shake Elizabeth from his thoughts.

A scowl creased his brow, negating that last notion. While it was common knowledge that physical desire and romantic love were violent mental disturbances of short duration, he had been intrigued by Elizabeth for five years, ever since his arrival in the Dales. He feared he was obsessed by her.

He felt a hand on his shoulder and turned, hoping his expression, rather than words, would reveal his annoyance. The butler whispered, "Reverend Farnsworth is here, my lord. He said he must see you. He further states that he has been victimized by a heinous crime."

Fully expecting that the highwaymen had struck again, Stafford hurried outside. Reverend Farnsworth, wearing around his neck the white Geneva bands of his Presbyterian ministry, was leading a horse up and down the drive. Walter had never seen the reverend appear so agitated, except during his recent sermon against the "Frogs." Those foreigners were destroying England's existing social structure, Farnsworth had thundered.

"I believe I've been sold a doctored horse, Lord Stafford," Farnsworth huffed. In his black coat and hose, he looked like an enormous beetle. " 'Twas earlier in the day, near Coverham. The gent had a string of fine-looking mounts, and I purchased one at a very good price. But I was told that this gelding here is seven years old and from his lumbering gait I suspect he's far older."

"There's only one way to find out." Walter pulled apart the roan's lips and displayed its teeth. "As you know, I am an expert on horseflesh. See those black marks on the crowns of your gelding's incisors? They generally disappear by age nine, so seven could be feasible. Aha!" He ran his finger along the teeth. "Real infundibulate have a ring of pearly enamel, which these lack."

"What does that mean, m'lord?"

"Bishoping. Those marks were burned by a hot iron."

Reverend Farnsworth's eyes widened. "The gent said this gelding was the property of a nobleman who had gone abroad. That is the reason he offered up such a good price."

"What an ancient line. And he probably showed you a second horse that he swore was ordered to be sold by the executors of a deceased minister. No doubt he had tales for each animal, and all equally false. I'm afraid you've been duped."

"No!" Farnsworth could scarce believe that anyone would cheat a man of the cloth. "What is this world coming to? If you want my opinion —"

"Tell me about the coper," Stafford interrupted, impatient to return to Elizabeth.

"He was large, well dressed, and he could talk the ears off a person. I've not seen him around these parts before, m'lord, but he wasn't a Frog. He was an Englishman."

Wonderful description, Walter thought sarcastically. If Farnsworth were any more specific, half the Dales would be under suspicion. "The chap most likely thinks to

162

sell his horses in Middleham, Reverend. I have various patrols on the road, and you might give them a description. I am quite certain my men will scour the fair looking for a large, talkative gent."

"Yes, well, I trust you will further investigate the matter, m'lord. Come to think of it, he might have been a Frog with a false accent." Shaking his head, clutching the roan's reins, Farnsworth turned to leave.

Walter slipped back inside the music room, but Elizabeth had finished her piece. Dorothea Wyndham sat at the pianoforte, accompanying Lady Marston, who was warbling an unidentifiable tune.

Pretending to sip lemonade baptized with brandy, Elizabeth scanned Lord Stafford's face. She feared he had been called away because of Rand, but Walter soon dispelled her fears with a brief recounting of Farnsworth's plight.

After Lady Marston had lurched through her finale, they all enjoyed a leisurely dinner. Then Walter offered his guests a choice of cards in the drawing room or bowls on the green. For the Wyndhams, he suggested a tour of his latest renovations.

Lawrence exclaimed over Walter's expanded stables and racehorses, while Dorothea waxed poetic over his new dairy, which had been constructed with marble walls. The milk, cream and butter were stored in porcelain vessels, cooled by splashing fountains.

"Isn't this lovely, Elizabeth?" Dorothea's hands fluttered over the Stafford seal, engraved on one of the butter churns. "I've never seen such a magnificent dairy."

Elizabeth thought the room resembled an enormous mausoleum.

Dorothea was even more impressed by Walter's garden, renovated in a Gothic style, complete with grottoes and artificial ruins. "This makes me feel so pleasantly melancholy," she said, clapping her hands in delight over a crumbling tower and a broken archway. "Doesn't it you, Elizabeth?"

"It must have cost a fortune," offered Lawrence.

"I have a fortune to spend." Walter turned to Elizabeth. "I confess that after reading *Castles of Doom*, I sympathized with poor King Henry. He lavished so much money on the arts and architecture and was vilified for his pains."

"But in Henry's case, the money belonged to his subjects," she countered.

"If one believes in the divine right of kings, Henry was totally justified."

"That is an outmoded notion, or at least thinking people find it so." Every time Walter opened his mouth, Elizabeth felt that her scheme to play the demure companion was in jeopardy. Temper simmering like a pot of boiling water, she walked away. Almost immediately, she spied a hermit's cell. The small religious house might dispel her hostility. Peering inside, she stifled a scream.

A monk knelt in the shadows, his head bent forward, his hands steepled in prayer. Elizabeth shivered violently. A whisper of the mournful, melodious chant she had heard inside the music room floated through her memory.

She blinked several times, thinking the monk was just another one of her visions. It couldn't be a real monk, for Catholics had no power in England. Furthermore, any man with position and money was Protestant, and would never harbor a Roman clergyman, no matter how perfectly the clergyman enhanced the decor.

"Very lifelike, isn't it?" Walter stood at her elbow. "Of course, 'tis merely a stuffed figure. I thought he might add a pleasing touch of gloom."

"Why is it that we hate papists, yet we strive so hard to reproduce their traditions and mimic everything about them?"

Walter laughed. "My dear Elizabeth, one can enjoy the look of an era without believing in its deceptions."

"Didn't you mention earlier that we might visit a bull baiting in Middleham, my lord?" Dorothea asked, obviously fearful that Elizabeth would start another argument.

"Aye," Lawrence said. "I'm always eager for a bit of wagering. I mean, I would be if I still gambled. I'll just enjoy watching, eh Bess?"

"Yes, Papa. I'm anxious to attend, as well."

But more precisely, she was anxious to get away from the kneeling monk in his gloomy cell.

CHAPTER 12

A large crowd clustered around the center of a field where a black bull had been tied. A fifteen-foot rope, secured by an iron ring affixed to a stake, circled the bull's horns. Several men stood on the sidelines, along with their bulldogs. The men restrained the dogs by holding onto their ears. The dogs whined or yapped at the bull. Common folk and powdered lords debated the strength of the bull and the skill of the dogs.

Rand kept to the outskirts, positioning himself so that he had a clear view of the horse traders beyond. Though he seldom lost sight of Zak, he didn't dare move too close. Standing together, they might trigger some observant victim's memory.

This is madness, Rand thought, as he watched his cousin collar a rotund farmer. How could Zak bring defective horses to a town renowned for its breeding of blood stock?

In fact, the entire area was dotted with huge stables. Many had been constructed from the stones of Middleham Castle, sprawled above the town. For some reason, the castle's jagged silhouette further reinforced Rand's uneasiness. Yet nothing sinister had occurred, it was nearly sundown, and Zak had been successfully cheating people for hours.

Rand studied the faces of those awaiting the bull baiting. No one paid any attention to him. He was dressed in a coarse woolen tunic, tight-fitting breeches, and home-knit hose. His hair fell free, without even a queue to hold it in place. Rand thought he looked plainer than all but the poorest yeoman farmer, and was well pleased with his disguise.

He noticed a tall man in a double cauliflower wig who moved majestically through the crowd. *We've placed the hangman's noose around our own necks,* he thought, recognizing Walter Stafford. The lawman tilted his head toward his companion, a woman clothed in a blue riding outfit. Despite the ostrich-plumed hat that shadowed her eyes, Rand could never mistake Elizabeth Wyndham's sun-kissed complexion, nor her slender waist and rounded hips. He felt a rush of anger. Elizabeth possessed the power to destroy him, if she chose. Rand had heard rumors, but he had summarily dismissed them all. She so obviously loathed Stafford that any gossip about her being his mistress or his fiancée was ludicrous.

What if her scorn had been pretense? Had she fingered Rand as the highwayman, eagerly relating a detailed description to Lord Walter Stafford, the most dangerous man in the Dales?

Impossible! She could not have responded so ardently to Rand's embraces if she wore a mask of duplicity — or would she?

Lady Guinevere had acted in a similar manner when confronted by Ralf Dark-starre, unable to resist his effortless seduction. In fact, that was the very same scene which had scandalized the dowagers at Beresford's drum.

At that moment, the signal was given and a gray dog was released to run at the bull. "Scrag him, Cornwallis!" screamed the dog's handler, his voice rising above the excited murmur of the spectators. Rand positioned himself at the back of the crowd where he would have a clear view of Elizabeth, Stafford, and Zak.

In the ring, Cornwallis darted toward his adversary. The nameless bull turned a horn.

Trying to get beneath the bull's belly in order to seize his muzzle or dewlap, Cornwallis circled behind the bull's tail, barking all the while. From the sidelines, the dog's companions echoed the sound.

Elizabeth, who was far nearer the action than she wished to be, covered her ears. She hated the violence inherent in such events and regretted her earlier eagerness to attend.

The bull pawed the earth. Its breath emerged in angry snorts. Cornwallis edged closer, slinking on his belly. The bull charged, sliding his horns beneath the dog. Cornwallis flew into the air. The crowd gasped. Handlers ran to break the force of the dog's fall. Dazed, Cornwallis shook his head and staggered to his feet.

The crowd cheered, though Elizabeth was sickened by the entire business. Was she the only one who found such sport cruel? She felt alien to those around her, alien to their values and perceptions and the world they inhabited.

I don't belong here. But where do I belong?

The dog darted in, catching the bull's dewlap. The bull roared and twisted and kicked, breaking free. He charged forward until he reached the end of his tether. His head snapped back, and he slammed to the ground.

Elizabeth's hands balled into fists. *How brutal we all are,* she thought, looking away from the bull, now bellowing in rage and pain. But what could one expect from a society that considered public hangings entertainment? Reluctantly, she focused on the ring again.

The bull rocked his head from side to side. Blood dripped from his mutilated dewlap.

Today we watch a bull bleed. Soon it will be Rand.

But Rand and his companion were long gone.

The crowd screamed further encouragement at the dog, who had once again attached himself to the bull's throat. The bull tossed his head upward. The dewlap tore. Cornwallis tumbled to the earth, then scrambled back to the safety of his handler.

"Well done!" Walter's shout joined the crowd's applause.

Elizabeth raised her eyes to the evening sky, gradually melding into twilight. The town of Middleham clung to a hillside. In the distance, she could see the remains of Middleham Castle. Once the castle had housed kings and queens, knights and ladies. Now townspeople exercised their horses across the surrounding plain while wild birds nested among its ruins. But tonight was a special time when special things happened. Would the ghosts of the dead meet for one last banquet?

She shivered, filled with the same apprehension she had experienced when she spied the praying monk. On tiptoe, she spoke against Walter's ear. "I am going for a stroll, my lord, and shall meet you later."

"I shall count the minutes, my dear," Walter said, but his gaze remained riveted on the ring, where a second dog had just been loosed on the bull.

As Elizabeth made her escape, she saw a full moon — lush and golden — inch above the moors. The air was warm and smelled strongly of wood smoke. Nightingales called from the darkness of the copses while insects whispered.

Midsummer's Eve was believed to be a time when restless spirits walked the earth. On the hillsides, bonfires had been lit to hold them at bay, and young men made a game of leaping across the edges of the flames. She strolled among the revelers, stopping every once in a while to scrutinize the foot races and wrestling matches. She watched the husbands who smoked their pipes and passed around bottles of gin. She watched the wives who gossiped and, at the same time, watched their children. She envied the lovers who drifted toward the privacy of hedges.

A fiddler began to play. Couples joined hands and circled the bonfires. The tempo of the music increased. Spectators stomped their feet and clapped their hands. The dancers whirled, faster and faster, keeping time to the screech of the fiddle. The bow ran up and down the strings — wailing, beckoning, threatening, promising.

As the firelight shimmered off sweaty faces, muscular arms, bare chests and flat stomachs, Elizabeth ached for her own man. Not any man. One man.

Where are you, Rand? she silently pleaded, watching sparks explode heavenward where they soon disappeared into liquid blackness.

" 'Tis a night made for love," a man whispered.

Elizabeth turned in surprise. "Rand! Are you real, or am I imagining you?" She traced the muscled ridges of his chest, then quickly dropped her hands, as if she had just encountered the bonfire's flames. "You certainly appear solid enough, but what are you doing here? Why haven't you left the Dales?"

"My partner saw fit to stay a while longer.

I'll be meeting him later, at midnight. Then we shall leave straightaway for Scotland."

Elizabeth nodded. "Midnight. The hour when the veil is lifted between this world and the other. Be careful. You might meet a parade of ghosts on your way to Scotland."

"You speak nonsense, Bess."

"Yes. We are rational people and such things do not happen." She looked around, afraid someone might be eyeing Rand with suspicion, but they were in a secluded spot, surrounded by prickly hedges. Rand must have seen her earlier and followed.

"I've not been noticed," he said, indicating his garments.

I would notice you, she thought. *So would any other right-minded lass.*

Despite his clothes, his bearing was every bit as proud as an aristocrat. His stance was straight and tall. Had his solid chest been clad in armor, it would have stopped a dozen arrows. The moonlight flashed over his hair, causing it to shine like polished onyx. Long, thick strands fell below his broad shoulders.

The butt of a pistol had been thrust into the belt of his breeches, so she smoothed his shirt over it. "I had to bury your blasted coin purse, Rand. The jewelry was useless to me. Lord Stafford lists all stolen goods in

174

the paper, which means every pawnbroker has a description."

"Is that why you're angry with me?"

"I'm not angry."

"Yes, you are. Otherwise you would not have been Stafford's companion at the bull baiting. I thought you hated him."

"I don't hate him. He's slimy, insignificant, and I pity him. Nevertheless, I agreed to this engagement months ago."

"That strikes me as a feeble excuse. What did you and Stafford talk about, Bess? Did you mention me? Did you tell him who I am? Have you betrayed me?"

The accusation cut between them. *Betrayal.* For long moments, Elizabeth found it impossible to speak, let alone formulate a response. "I would sooner die than conspire against you," she finally said.

She saw him turn away and run his fingers through his hair. His fingers were long and blunted on the tips. He had strong, callused hands, hardly the hands of a gentleman. Those hands and fingers would feel rough against her skin.

"Take me with you," she blurted.

Even as she spoke, she knew the impossibility of her demand. She must sort out her father's financial difficulties. The eight hundred pounds from Charles Beresford would arrive any day. Then she and the barristers and the note holders must begin the laborious process of settling the Wyndham accounts. If she left, her father would lose everything. There was also the matter of the final installment of *Castles of Doom.* Soon it would be published with all the attendant obligations.

Yet none of that mattered, not when Rand stood beside her, so close his sleeve brushed her bodice.

"I must admit that I can think of far less agreeable companions," he said. "But I cannot take you with me."

"Why not?"

"For one thing, your reputation would be destroyed."

"I don't give a fig for my reputation!" The warmth of the night pressed upon her. The writhe of the fiddle coursed through her veins, like blood, like the pounding of her heart. "I insist that we run off together. Now! Tonight!"

"Bess, please listen. If we ran off together, eventually you would realize that your happiness lies in being wed to a country squire, surrounded by country children, growing stout and middle-aged in your comfortable country house."

"No, Rand, I've never wanted that."

"Occasionally, on a summer evening like this one, you might wonder what happened to me, but it will be an idle thought, soon gone." He traced the outlines of her lips with a gentle finger. " 'Tis the way it should be, Bess."

Her throat ached from holding back forbidden words, from wanting Rand and all the pleasures implicit in the night. "No, you're wrong," she whispered. "I would never stop wondering."

"Never is a long time."

"I refuse to spend my life concocting exciting lives for other people. I refuse to end my life drowsing over an almanac, my spectacles slipping from my nose, my gouty leg propped atop a stool. I don't want to remember a Midsummer's Eve long ago, when you and I chatted so politely about what can and cannot be." The moon hung like a paper lantern beyond their heads, beyond the leaping flames of the bonfires. "I crave different memories."

" 'Tis better thus." Rand cupped her chin. "To think back upon me, as I will you. I shall be the man who never aged, the man who remained a mystery, so you can make me anyone you wish me to be. 'Tis better to imagine than to know."

Rand was mistaken, thought Elizabeth.

Sometimes her imaginings proved far worse than reality could ever be.

"If we really knew each other," he continued, "you would accuse me of being cruel or indifferent, and I would nag you for not properly darning my hose. We would uncover all sorts of annoying truths and our love would slip into routine."

"That's not the real reason, Rand. You think to protect yourself by weaving a web of words. You fear me for other reasons, don't you? I've sensed it from the very first."

" 'Tis not fear, Bess." He slipped his arm about her waist. " 'Tis all so complicated, what I think sometimes."

The fiddle music ended abruptly, as if it had been severed by a sword. Elizabeth heard Rand's breathing, and her own. The shadows wrapped them together like a cloak. She looked up into his eyes.

We have stood like this before, she thought, *when the night was known by another name, when the night was called St. John's Eve.*

Suddenly, she began to weep.

"Ah, Bess, my bonny Bess." Rand's voice was tender. "Are those angry tears?"

"Yes. No." Gasping for breath, she slipped from his arms to the ground below, landing on her knees.

Rand knelt in front of her, then pressed

178

her face against the coarse wool of his shirt. "All right, my dearest love," he crooned. " 'Twill be all right. I'm here, Bess, and we have a few more hours."

"I don't want you for 'a few more hours.' "

"Hush." With his finger, he tilted her chin. "I cannot make love to a weeping woman, even if the moon causes her wet eyes to shine like all the stars in the heavens."

"You *have* read my books," she said with a sniff.

He laughed low in his throat. "I need no book to do this." He removed her fichu, fumbling at her brooch, then thrust his warm hand inside her bodice.

She gasped as he caressed one full, aching globe.

"Nor this." With his free hand, he unbuttoned her coat, then her waistcoat. "Nor this." Drawing her breast from her shift, he lowered his head and began to tease her nipple with his tongue.

The fiddle started up again, and Elizabeth felt the blood course hotly through her veins. Gently pushing Rand's face away, she settled prone upon the ground.

He removed her slippers and tossed them aside. Raising her skirt and petticoats up toward her waist, he jerked back in surprise. "Bess! You're wearing breeches!"

"I rode to the peel tower."

"My London ladies never wear breeches beneath their skirts."

"I don't want to hear about your other women, Rand. I shall be your first woman, just as you shall be my first man."

"Am I not your first man?"

She felt a blush stain her cheekbones. "I was sixteen."

"Ah, sixteen. I don't think I was ever sixteen."

"Of course you were. You must have been."

"My logical Bess." Without further ado, he removed her breeches, tossed his pistol toward her slippers, took off his own clothes, then straddled her hips.

His movements were so swift, she had no time to study the magnificence of his lower body. But it didn't really matter because his lips were nuzzling her bosom again. She wove her hands through his hair and pressed his face closer, until his mouth was filled with her breast. She ached to fill her mouth with something, too. Releasing his hair, she grasped one of his hands and sucked his first finger.

To her surprise, his finger inside her mouth consumed her with such a craving that she felt her own warm moisture accrue, and she found herself digging her heels into the hard-packed earth. Urgently, she lifted her buttocks.

"Whoa, Bess. Let me move up a bit. There. Now we fit."

They did fit! Elizabeth vaguely wondered how that was possible, especially since the passive organ inside her was growing thicker by the moment.

She panted and Rand's finger slid from her mouth. He snaked his arm between their bodies. With that same wet finger, he rubbed her intimately, tenderly. Behind her closed eyelids, she saw bonfire flames and sparks exploding heavenward, until they disappeared into liquid blackness. Nay, not blackness. Color. All the colors of the rainbow.

The fiddle began a new refrain, a simple tune, but Elizabeth heard a different melody. It sounded like a lyrical thread woven through a tapestry, and it was the very same melody she had heard inside Lord Stafford's music room.

Panic clawed at her heart. She knew Rand would take what he wanted of her, then leave her all alone. His voice would mock like a bow across a fiddle. His laughter would ring in her ears long after he had ridden away; laughter that conveyed a bitter triumph. It had always been thus.

Rand seemed to sense her fear. Slowly, he moved his hands over her body, caressing her as he would a terrified child. At the same time, he disengaged himself from her.

She calmed at his deft strokes. "I cannot do this," she whispered, both relieved and frustrated by his withdrawal.

" 'Tis all right, little one," he soothed. "Put your clothes back on and I shall hold you in my arms."

"But I want to know you!"

"You know me, Bess."

"Aye. Perhaps I should have said I want you."

"I want you, too, but not against your will."

" 'Tis my will that wants you," she whispered, her whole body feverish with his touch. Despite his obvious control, she felt his erection rise, hot and hard against her belly.

Staring up into his face, she saw nothing more than tender concern. Why was she hesitating? She had loved this man from the moment they met, perhaps even longer. Trusting her panic would disappear, she guided him into the deepest recesses of her body. "I have no doubts," she said, "none at all."

Rand heard the conviction in her voice. He felt a rush of gratitude, then a rush of renewed desire. Murmuring endearments, cradling her backside, he moved within her until she whimpered with pleasure. And yet he still sensed a fearful reluctance.

Sweat beaded his brow. Sliding free, he rubbed the head of his erection against the cleft between her thighs.

At first Elizabeth lay motionless. Then, unable to endure the gratifying agony, she pushed his hand aside and impaled herself on his hardness. "I have no doubts," she repeated, her legs lifting around him.

"Nor do I," Rand whispered, as he felt her nails rake his back. He heard her sob his name. The anxiety had given way to eagerness.

Joyfully, he thrust again and again, deeper each time.

Elizabeth pressed herself more firmly into his straining groin, yet somehow he managed to insert his fingers and search out the tiny nub at the center of her desire. She caught her breath, but released it when her quivers coiled into one huge burst of uncontrollable ecstasy. She heard Rand moan, and she felt a new wetness, and she was vainly triumphant at her power to cause that wetness.

"Bess, my Bess," he cried, pumping his hot offering into her body, bringing her to an apex of delirium that was even more explosive than the one before.

She thought she couldn't possibly endure a third tempestuous convulsion, but his kiss, as long and deep as his thrusts, provoked yet another satisfying spasm of completion.

Afterwards, fully clothed, she lay in his arms and listened to the fiddle.

Then she stared into his eyes, as blue as the North Sea. "Now you will have to take me with you," she murmured.

He shook his head. " 'Tis impossible."

"But I have just given you my heart."

"You have given me far more, Bess. You have given me memories, and dreams that won't jerk me out of a restless sleep. However, you must return to Lord Stafford. I am certain he is desperately search—"

"No! I must stay by your side. Earlier, I wondered where I belonged. I don't have to wonder any more. I belong with you."

Rand kicked at a clump of brush. "Do you believe what you read in the chapbooks, Miss Wyndham? Do you think the life of a highwayman is so damnably romantic? Think again. There is hunger and sleeplessness. Lurking behind every corner is the shadow of the hangman's noose. If you want to ponder romance, Bess, visit Roova Crag."

"But you don't have to be a highwayman, Rand. You can —"

"Coper!" somebody shouted. "Help! I've been robbed!"

Other shouts joined the first. The voices came from the horse fair.

Elizabeth saw Rand's face freeze into a mask of utter helplessness. "What is it?" she cried.

"My partner. I never should have left him. I love you, Bess. I always have and I always will."

Rand turned and ran toward the noise. He saw Zak leap up onto a horse, kick at one man, and beat away at a second with the butt of his pistol.

"Bloody pimps!" Zak shouted.

Several more men surrounded him. Zak's horse reared and flailed at the would-be captors, scattering them. Rand spotted Walter Stafford, standing off to the side, watching.

Stafford raised his arm and leveled his pistol.

"No!" Rand bounded forward and jostled Stafford's arm. The pistol discharged harmlessly at the moon.

Stafford cursed and reached for Rand. But several men descended on Stafford, peppering him with questions about what had happened and what should be done. Amid all that chaos, Rand managed to shake off Stafford's frantic grip.

Zak thundered past, heading toward the highway.

'Tis all over, Rand thought, running for his own mount. Zak had gone too far. Most likely Stafford had already linked Zak with the Gentleman Giant. Rand knew that the roads would be crawling with posses. He and Zak couldn't possibly meet as planned.

Damn Zak! Most of the traders had packed up and gone home, but Zak had one horse left, the chestnut mare with the blemished knees. Rand had followed Elizabeth, figuring nobody would buy the bloody mare, thus nobody would discover the cheat. But he hadn't considered that a customer might return to finger Zak.

Unfortunately, Rand knew exactly how his cousin would react to tonight's events. Exhilarated by his brush with danger, Zak would be out prowling for more. That was the way it always was with Zak. The closer he came to getting caught, the more chances he took. Which was the reason why the law always snared him in the end.

I have to find him before Stafford does, Rand thought, spurring his horse.

Standing in the glow from a bonfire, Elizabeth refastened the brooch at her neckline. She filled her eyes, mind, and heart with the last sight she would ever have of Rand Remington. Then she fled headlong down the hill, toward the bull baiting.

Chapter 13

"I'll escort you home in my post chaise," Stafford said. "Early tomorrow, my footman will deliver your mare. For your own safety, my dearest Elizabeth, I must absolutely insist."

Her first inclination was to refuse. Absolutely refuse. She wanted to ride Rhiannon. That way she might encounter one of Stafford's unskilled patrols, and they would tell her that the highwaymen had slipped through their fingers once again.

'Tis better to know than to imagine, she thought, twisting Rand's words.

On the other hand, if Walter was with her he couldn't orchestrate a manhunt. While she still held his expertise in contempt, she wasn't sure how clever Rand's companion was. Walter might even come up with an uncharacteristically brilliant revelation, and he would undoubtedly share it, if only to impress her. He had already made one passably shrewd deduction — that Middleham's coper was the Gentleman Giant.

As they bumped along the rutted highway, Elizabeth watched the moon spin its light upon the moors. She and Walter sat facing Papa and Dorothea. Stafford's post chaise was elegantly gilded and scrolled but Elizabeth considered the interior far too cramped, and its front third was open to the cold night wind. Nevertheless, the wind soothed her flaming cheeks, yesterday's rain kept down much of the road dust, the stars looked uncommonly close, and the night-song of a thrush trilled melodically.

The time she and Rand had spent together now seemed blurred and distant, like figures seen through the mist. From the very beginning, everything about Rand had been bittersweet and remote, not to mention unconventional. She likened herself and Rand to actors whose most important parts were being played offstage. She wondered why he aroused in her such strong emotions, and why his conversations almost always sounded enigmatic.

She thought back to their first encounter and her certainty that they had met before. But where? When? And why did she have a sneaking suspicion that he knew something about their relationship that she didn't? Why did he often seem ambivalent, as if he were alternately drawn to her and repulsed by her?

Squeezing her eyes shut, she pressed her head against the cushions. An inner voice whispered: *Long ago, Bess. Don't you remember? Don't you know?*

If they had met before and loved before, didn't that justify tonight's passions? Not that she needed justifications. She and Rand belonged to each other. They always had, and they always would. "I love you, Bess. I always have, and I always will." Comforting words, unless "always" was of brief duration.

She knew Rand had ridden away in desperation, rather than triumph. There had been no mocking laughter. And yet the breathless panic she had experienced was very familiar. Could the haunting melody she'd heard earlier, so beautiful, so sad, so *threatening,* have something to do with her panic? Or her nightmares?

Noodle-head! Her blasted nightmares had no sound, unless one counted her violent, albeit silent, screams.

". . . wonder what happened to the other highwayman," Walter was saying. "Why did they split up? They have always worked as a twosome."

190

"The interpretation is as plain as the nose on one's face," said Elizabeth, opening her eyes. "The other highwayman is dead, or he has left the Dales."

Walter patted her hand. "My ethereal, beautiful, but obviously misinformed Elizabeth. You are certainly not the best judge of their modus operandi. May I remind you that you were robbed at gunpoint, not fleeced by a coper?"

"You were robbed as well, and in a most humiliating —"

"Precisely. My point exactly. The Quiet Companion changed his method of procedure when he robbed me. I wonder what that means?"

"I have no idea, and I sincerely doubt you do either."

"Elizabeth," Dorothea warned, "remember your manners!" She turned her face toward her husband, as if seeking concurrence, but Lawrence was asleep.

Walter inserted a pinch of snuff up his nose. "It's quite all right, Mrs. Wyndham. I'm sure Elizabeth regrets her tart tongue. Now, back to the missing highwayman. For one thing, it is quite safe to say that he wasn't dead a fortnight ago. The Giant has switched from highway robbery to doctoring horses . . ." Stafford paused to sneeze.

"I simply cannot comprehend your reasoning, sir." Elizabeth yawned, feigning disinterest.

"The answer is obvious, my lovely but sometimes sophistic Elizabeth. The pair quarreled. Which means once we catch the Gentleman Giant, who I have always considered to be the less intelligent of the pair, he will lead us to his partner."

"Unless his partner is dead or has left the Dales," she repeated stubbornly.

Dorothea gave her an angry glare. Elizabeth turned away, effectively ending her part in the conversation.

Walter's sneeze had roused Lawrence. While the others continued talking, Elizabeth attempted to pierce the secrets of the night. Her ears strained for the sounds of gunfire, her eyes for any movement. She tried to imagine what was happening beyond the feeble glow of the carriage lanterns. Something must be, for the darkness suddenly seemed to possess an ominous waiting quality. Had Rand caught up with his cousin? Had they eluded the patrols? Were they racing for Scotland? Or were they engaged in a battle this very moment?

She could hear nothing save for the squeaking of the post chaise and the voices of her companions. She could see nothing save for clumps of trees, stone walls, and abandoned buildings, crouching just beyond the light.

But it wasn't midnight yet, Elizabeth thought with a shudder. When the witching hour finally flourished, the trees, walls and buildings would be populated by ghosts.

"I'm so pleased you're here to protect us," Dorothea said to Walter. Her lips turned up in the closed smile that always reminded Elizabeth of a sly cat. "I feel so much safer in your company."

"Before the evening is out, my men will have snared at least one, possibly both of the thieving scoundrels, never fear."

Dorothea cast a wide-eyed look into the darkness, as if she momentarily expected it to disgorge a host of demons. "I know that with you . . . and Mr. Wyndham, of course . . . I am safer here than I could possibly be anywhere else. Still, I do feel a bit exposed."

Elizabeth stifled a snort, amused by her stepmother's sudden vulnerability. The only thing Dorothea truly feared was poverty.

Walter reached for another pinch of snuff, then hesitated, as if he wanted to share a secret. Folding his hands on his lap, he said, "When I apprehend the Gentleman Giant and his Quiet Companion, it will be nearly as big a coup as my most famous capture."

"And who was that?" burbled Dorothea.

"I can say, in all modesty, that I was entirely responsible for the incarceration of Jacob Halsey, the Quaker Highwayman."

"Goodness! Did you hear that, Elizabeth? Isn't Lord Stafford full of surprises?"

Elizabeth dismissed Walter's assertion as hyperbole. Jacob Halsey had plied his trade to the south, around Bedford, a far more populated area. Walter might arguably be an adequate justice of the peace in a community with more sheep than people, but he couldn't ply his trade elsewhere.

"Lord Stafford has told me some right funny tales about Halsey," Lawrence said. "Tell them the one about old Jake and his fight with the beadle, m'lord."

Walter chuckled. "It seems Halsey and this beadle had a fierce altercation. After Jake knocked the unfortunate man to the ground, he said, 'I see thou canst exercise thy long staff pretty well, but I'll prevent thee from using thy short one tonight.' Then Halsey nailed the poor fellow to a tree by his foreskin." Walter laughed heartily, slapping his padded thigh.

Dorothea, who maintained she could not stand profanity in word or deed, laughed even more heartily. "You do tell a story so well, my lord. Doesn't he, Elizabeth?"

"What time is it, please?"

Reaching into his embroidered waistcoat, Walter removed a silver pocket watch and held it beneath the lantern's glow. "Nearly midnight," he replied. "Look, Elizabeth, my new watch has a most erotic scene, set in an arched aperture. It depicts a lady and a gentleman, with the gentleman's . . . er, activity . . . in constant motion. I find it quite amusing."

"Goodness," Dorothea said, peering at the watch. "If the gentleman is doing what I think he is doing, m'lord, your new timepiece is rather risqué. And amusing, to be sure," she quickly added.

"I shall have you home in another half hour," Walter told Elizabeth, noticeably disgruntled at her lack of interest.

Midnight! She had never been out so late on Midsummer's Eve, and she wished it were true that supernatural things happened. The north was famous for its abundance of ghosts. Her Aunt Lilith swore that once, on the road to York, she had seen the ghost of a bishop. In front of the bishop had been a coffin, covered by a black velvet shawl fringed with white silk. The coffin had swayed through the air, unsupported by human hands.

"Do you believe in ghosts?" Elizabeth asked no one in particular.

Dorothea frowned, Lawrence shrugged, and Walter laughed.

"I'm not surprised you would ask such a question," he said, absently caressing the lace at his throat. "While you are uncommonly bright for a woman, your sex is never logical."

Elizabeth heard Rand say "My logical Bess." He had said it just before he removed her breeches, just before he —

"Ghosts cannot exist, my dear," Walter continued, his voice somewhat shaky. "They go against the laws of nature."

Startled, Elizabeth peered at him more closely. Despite his declaration, he looked decidedly unnerved. He was even clutching at his chest. If she was describing him in one of her books, she might say he looked *apoplectic.*

She remembered the words he had spoken last week, outside the stables. "You comprehend very little about me." He was correct. She really didn't know much about him. Still, it was interesting to speculate that the mere mention of ghosts would set him all aquiver. It made him less pompous, more empathetic, more . . . human.

With a sigh, Elizabeth returned to the

scenery. Lights from an occasional farm-house softened patches of darkness, as did the lamps from other coaches, far in the distance, shining like cat's-eyes.

The horses finally reached the foot of the dale, where they began their last arduous climb to the White Hart. Exhausted, Elizabeth started to nod off, until she heard the sound of pounding hooves, like a roll of thunder. Gunfire cracked.

"No," she breathed. "Please, God, it cannot be."

Misunderstanding, Walter said, "Don't worry, my dear. I'll protect you." He whipped a rifle out from under the seat.

Dazed, Elizabeth watched Walter and her father draw pistols from their belts. Then both men stood and leaned out of the chaise.

"What is it?" Dorothea asked.

"Get down on the floor," Walter ordered. "Someone is coming up fast."

Dorothea settled on the carriage floor-boards, as if she were arranging herself atop a delicate armchair.

"I'm safe right here," Elizabeth said. Fearful that the rider might be Rand, she wanted to stay where she had the best view.

"Now is not the time to be adventure-some." Walter pushed her down beside Dorothea. "Maintain a steady pace," he called to his driver.

Elizabeth popped her head up.

Walter shoved her back down. "Do not disobey me! I'm about to snare a highwayman and I'll not be distracted by some troublesome female."

"I hope the highwayman blasts you to hell and back again," she whispered.

Dorothea kicked her in the shins.

Frightened by the gunfire, the horses picked up speed. The carriage swayed and jerked, slamming Elizabeth against the seat. The air reverberated with rifle fire and hoofbeats.

Dorothea just sat there, clasping her hands tighter, her bouncing rump the only indication that something was amiss. "Hole-hole-hold still," she warned, her voice rattling from the jolts rather than alarm. "Don't you dare moo-moo-move."

Ignoring her stepmother, Elizabeth peered over the rim of the chaise. Figures raced past, of no more substance than shadows in the night.

Lord Stafford's patrol!

Who were they chasing? Rand or his cousin? It couldn't be Rand. He had said he wanted to leave the moors. Why would he detour? Maybe he sought an escape, any escape, from the men who had converged upon him from all directions. Elizabeth prayed it wasn't Rand, told herself it couldn't possibly be Rand, and truly feared it was Rand.

Let him live! Please, God, let him live!

"I hope they leave him alive long enough to tell us where my . . . your money is," Dorothea said. She had wadded her shawl, skirts and petticoats beneath her backside, so that her clothes, rather than she, would absorb the bumps. "I begrudge that man even a handful of shillings. And if he cannot come up with my . . . your entire twenty pounds, he'll have to answer personally to me."

The highwayman edged alongside the coach. Elizabeth tried to ascertain his shape and size but he was just a blur, hurling through the darkness.

The coach lurched and Lawrence sprawled on top of his wife.

Walter braced himself and aimed his pistol.

Thinking to deflect the barrel, Elizabeth staggered upright. The carriage lurched once again, hurling her to the floor, but somehow she managed to rise to her knees. Walter fired. Simultaneously, the highwayman pointed his pistol in Walter's face. The barrel flashed, illuminating the darkness.

Walter collapsed on the seat.

"Don't let his face be blown off!" Dorothea screamed.

Blinded by the explosion, Elizabeth groped for Walter. "Are you all right? Did you shoot him?"

"The bastard's gun misfired." Rearing up in his seat, Walter aimed his rifle. "I'm fine, but *he* won't be."

Blinking furiously, Elizabeth saw the highwayman veer away.

Walter fired.

Horse and rider abruptly parted.

"He's down!" Walter exulted. The carriage lurched to a halt. He and Lawrence leapt from the chaise.

The air appeared to breed riders everywhere, all racing toward the fallen highwayman.

Elizabeth slumped against the seat, gulping in the acrid odor of sulfur. Her heart slammed against her bodice. She heard the excited babble of voices, the labored breathing of the carriage horses, the jangle of their harnesses. What if Rand had been the highwayman? What if she had watched Walter kill him?

Dorothea eased up from the floorboards. "Is it over? Has anyone been hurt? I pray the blackguard's still alive so that he can lead us to our . . . your money."

'Tis Rand, Elizabeth thought. *They killed his partner and he came after Walter for revenge.*

But how could Rand know that Walter was escorting them home?

Her chest felt so constricted she could scarcely breathe. The downed highwayman must be Rand. Earlier, she had experienced a premonition, just like her Aunt Lilith was always talking about.

Elizabeth saw Walter stride toward her. "Do you know the man's identity?" she asked. "You . . . you didn't kill him, did you?"

"I merely grazed him, my dear. He'll be coming 'round any moment. Then we'll be able to question him." Walter grasped her hand. "Come with me. Perhaps you'll be able to identify the thieving bastard. After all, you were as close to him as we are to each other right now."

Closer, she thought. *Much, much closer.*

"I'm afraid to look," she cried. "I mean, I'm much too overcome. My heart couldn't stand any more excitement."

"I'll have a look at him," said Dorothea, gathering up her rumpled skirts and bounding from the opposite side of the carriage. "That man has a few things to answer for."

201

"My dear fragile Elizabeth." Walter lifted her down. "Never fear. You'll be safe with me."

Yes, she thought. Perhaps she should know. It couldn't be Rand. And if it was, she could save him. "No, he's not the one," she would say. "You must be mistaken."

But any reprieve would be short-lived. Walter ruled the Dales. This wasn't London. A trial, if there was a trial, would be brief, orchestrated by Lord Stafford. He would surely hang Rand, with or without her identification.

She stumbled upon the ruts in the road. Ahead, torches pinpointed the location. Darkened figures, like silhouettes upon a wall, circled the fallen man. From a far distance, the peal of church bells chimed the hour. Midnight.

Smoke rose like wraiths from the flickering lights. The torches lit up the dark as they snaked down an invisible hill, bringing her . . . bringing her . . . what?

Her surroundings seemed to recede into a vague netherworld, and she trembled. She remembered the praying monk inside Walter's garden cell, and she realized that clergymen carried the torches down the hill — a long line of cowl-clad monks.

How could she possibly know this? A feeling of dread, unlike anything she had ever experienced before, immobilized her. She swayed against Walter.

"Are you all right?" he asked. "There, there," he soothed, his arm encompassing her waist.

She felt disoriented, uncertain of time and place. She also feared she might faint.

"There, there," Walter repeated.

Elizabeth heard him, but his words didn't register. Her mind was numb with horror. She couldn't look at the fallen man. She knew exactly what she would see. What she had plotted to see. What she would see forever more in her nightmares.

Walter drew her forward. The circle of men parted, giving way. The torches wavered, then steadied.

Elizabeth gazed down at the body. She screamed. And screamed. And screamed.

Gradually emerging from her fog of shock and terror, Elizabeth heard Walter and her parents conversing in the hallway beyond her bedroom.

"I don't know what happened to her, the poor thing," said Papa. "This is so unlike Bess."

"Perhaps," Walter said, "she was overcome by his monstrous size, or his cursing."

203

Dorothea laughed. "Elizabeth has never been squeamish, Lord Stafford. I've heard her swear like a stable hand, so I cannot understand why the sight of the highwayman would distress her so. Even if she recognized him as the man who robbed her, she hardly seemed all that upset following the initial robbery. Why would she suddenly turn into such a . . . well, female?"

"She was behaving like a female even before she looked down upon his features, Mrs. Wyndham. I suspect Elizabeth craved my protection, which is how it should be. The weaker sex must be defended to the last man."

"Quite right, m'lord. While we were cowering together on the carriage floor, Elizabeth whispered in my ear. She said that you were her salvation. Those were her very words."

Elizabeth wanted to shove those very words back down her stepmother's throat, but she was afraid to open her eyes. She might see something horrible in what she had always assumed to be her safe, comfortable bedroom.

I am going mad, she thought. *They shall lock me away, and I shall be alone with my imagination and that awful thing.*

She finally raised her lashes when she

heard the door creak open.

Her father entered with a sleeping potion.

"No, Papa, I don't want to sleep. I might dream about it."

"What? Please, Bess, tell me what has distressed you."

She slumped back onto her pillows. How could she explain? How could she tell her father about something that hadn't even been there? Perhaps the torch lights had unnerved her. Perhaps her imagination, primed by thoughts of Midsummer's Eve, had deceived her. And yet, even now, she knew that she had seen a body sprawled upon the ground. It had been clothed in a scarlet cloak, or maybe a surcoat — she could not be certain. Nor could she tell whether the scarlet color emanated from the man's clothing or the man's blood.

Elizabeth was only certain of three things. The man's black hair and black beard, and the fact that his head had been severed from his body.

CHAPTER 14

August–November 1787

With a heavy sigh, Elizabeth examined the words she had just penned:

You have been mine before,
How long ago I may not know,
But just when at that swallow's soar
Your neck turned so,
Some veil did fall — I knew it all of yore.

As she replaced her quill and paper inside her writing box, she wished some veil truly would fall. She often felt overwhelmed by loneliness, as if Rand had died rather than disappeared. While she realized full well that these feelings were out of proportion to reality, logic could not mend the gaping hole in her life.

My logical Bess.

At first her memories of Rand had consumed her. The lush, golden moon. The scent of wood smoke. The crackle of the bonfires. The carnal screech of the fiddle. Now her memories comforted her, even though she sometimes believed that Rand had been conjured up from a dream.

More recently, she had been plagued with dreams of another kind, so wrenching that she had begun to dread the night. Upon awakening, she couldn't remember their content, only the emotions they evoked. She was fairly certain her dreams weren't about the headless man, for she had attributed that apparition to Midsummer's Eve and her Aunt Lilith's influential tales. So why did she experience such abject fear? Why did she perceive a ghastly horror so intense she felt hollow inside?

Nay, not hollow. Drained.

With a sigh, Elizabeth locked her writing box. Then she stood and brushed the dirt from the back of her skirt. She yearned to stay, but the peel tower was two miles from the inn and she had promised to serve Lord Stafford pork chops from a slaughtered ground squirrel.

Pig, not ground squirrel.

According to the locals, a woolbird was a sheep and a ground squirrel was a pig and a three-legged mare was nothing more than a gallows.

God's teeth! She was so tired of the Dales, so tired of the "exotic" names applied to animals and instruments of death.

Furthermore, she didn't want to serve Walter anything, especially herself. After formally proposing marriage, he had talked at length about traveling to London for their honeymoon.

She desperately needed to visit London, but not with Walter Stafford.

She desperately needed to pay Charles Beresford a visit!

Since the Gentleman Giant's execution, her writing had been practically nonexistent.

Zak Turnbull, not the Gentleman Giant, Elizabeth amended. Zak Turnbull had refused to reveal the identity or the whereabouts of his companion, yet he had shouted his own name just before the noose tightened around his thick neck.

On the day of the hanging, Elizabeth had developed a blinding headache, so painful she had "forfeited the festive event." Father and Dorothea had been properly sympathetic, but Walter had kept silent, his mahogany brows cresting. Afterwards, Elizabeth had sought out Tim, her ostler. According to Tim, the condemned man had shouted: "Don't forget me name, Stafford. 'Tis Zak Turnbull, an' I'll haunt ye 'til yer

208

own bloody death."

Now Turnbull swung from his cage atop Roova Crag.

Rand had apparently left the Dales. Nobody had sighted him, not even at the hanging, much to Walter's disappointment and chagrin. Certain the Quiet Companion would attend, Walter had posted a dozen armed sentries.

Elizabeth's thoughts returned to London. Beresford had not posted her eight hundred pounds and the mortgage deadline rapidly approached. Surrounded by the accouterments of wealth, her publisher might not have believed that his successful authoress was penniless. She had sent him another letter, her third.

Walter had repeated his suspicions that her account rendering looked fraudulent, but he was wrong. He had to be wrong.

If she traveled to London, she might not feel so trapped by memories and melancholia. After retrieving her money, she might even recover from this cursed inertia.

Elizabeth walked away from the peel tower, away from the coin purse still rotting beneath the dirt. The sky was an explosion of purple, lilac, red, amber and orange, while the cottony streaks of clouds had deepened to black. She turned her face upwards, hoping to catch the colors on her cheeks and feel them upon her closed eyelids. Behind her, the jagged wall cast its cooling shadow. She sensed the tower's loneliness and its isolation, which matched her own. Opening her eyes, she spied a man striding across the valley. He walked with a limp.

"Rand!" she called.

He paused and looked in her direction before hurrying on.

Hiking her skirts, Elizabeth chased him until he vanished into the gathering darkness. She had not seen his features clearly, but she was almost certain the man had been Rand Remington.

Shortly thereafter, the robberies resumed.

A coach marked the Midnight Flyer rattled into the inn's yard. Vaguely, Elizabeth noted that all was hustle and bustle. Tim and several other grooms led horses to and from the rows of parked carriages. Coachmen blew their horns. Guards unloaded trunks and passengers. Servants lit the yard lamps.

Elizabeth waited impatiently for Walter, who was questioning the coachman of the Flyer, robbed on its last run. Walter was duly distressed over the presence of yet another highwayman, but Elizabeth didn't believe he had connected the latest crime surge with the Quiet Companion.

"I hope Lord Stafford catches the fiend before our ball," said Dorothea, fluttering her hands. "Or perhaps the inconsiderate brute will suspend his activities for that one special occasion."

Elizabeth disguised her grimace within a discreet cough. The Harvest Ball was the White Hart's annual subscription ball, held the first week in October, and Rand, or whover, had successfully eluded Walter's patrols for weeks. Dorothea had porridge for brains if she thought Rand, or whoever, was philanthropic enough to take a breather.

"We'll capture him, wife," Lawrence soothed. "Unlike the Gentleman Giant and his Quiet Companion, this one is careless and attacks far too often. Last week it was three robberies in one night. Sometimes he just tosses his ill-gotten gains along the side of the road, and we suspect he hands over all coins and banknotes to the locals, especially those in need. Obviously, this clod-plate is too stupid to realize that the point in robbing somebody is to enrich oneself."

Elizabeth said nothing. If Rand was the highwayman, as she believed, he was probably making his presence known in order to bait Lord Stafford. Several times she had ridden out alone, hoping to find Rand, but she had found only rain showers, cold upon her face.

After Walter had finished, he and the Wyndhams rode toward Wyndham Manor. Walter was negotiating with Papa to pay the mortgage on Wyndham Hall and renovate the dilapidated manor house. Should Elizabeth wed Walter, the family's entire debt would be wiped out.

It might be nice to have Wyndham Manor brought back to life, Elizabeth mused. When Father had accrued his gambling debts, the manor had been put under the care of trustees. She had been born there, and her mother was buried there, but the Wyndhams had vacated it long before her novels had begun to show a profit.

She had a sudden thought. Suppose she agreed to wed Walter? Only she would insist that a clause be inserted into the agreement. If she paid Lord Stafford back within ninety days, the engagement would be null and void.

Why would Walter agree? He would. She knew he would, especially since he had firmly stated that Beresford was a cheat. Walter's pride would disallow any chance that he might be mistaken. Besides, he oft boasted that he enjoyed a challenge.

She would visit London directly after the Harvest Ball and reclaim her eight hundred pounds. No, her entire fortune. Then she would return to the Dales under armed escort, repay Walter, and that would be the end of it.

Belatedly dismounting, Elizabeth saw that Walter, Papa and Dorothea had lit lanterns. The eerie glow illuminated the outside of the tree-shrouded house.

"I'll be along presently," she said, still thinking about her scheme. It was not unlike the move on a chessboard but she had never lost at chess. Her father had taught her the rudiments of the game, whereupon she had beaten him soundly the very first time they played.

"Don't wander a great distance, dearest," Walter warned. "Remember. This is not far from the very spot where you were robbed."

"I'm not likely to forget, my lord, and I can take care of myself."

"I recall the last time you wandered off." Lawrence's brow furrowed. "We found you screaming among the Fountains Abbey ruins. I thought we'd never calm you down."

"I was ten years old at the time," Elizabeth said, unable to keep the irritation from her voice.

"Some patterns of behavior never change, daughter. I've seen it in great generals who —"

"I assure you, Papa. I won't wander off."

Still irritated, she watched Walter and her parents disappear inside the manor house. Their lights drifted through the windows from room to room, reminding her of the fox fire she'd seen over bogs and brakes and water meadows. Such lights were known as "corpse candles." Since the flames appeared at the level of a raised human hand, a ghost was said to walk invisible, using the candles to light its way. The sight of corpse candles was said to presage death. A servant had seen such a light just before Barbara Wyndham's violent fall.

Abruptly, Elizabeth turned away from the flickering lanterns. "Where are you?" she whispered. "Why do you hide from me?" She tried to penetrate the darkness, to somehow mingle her thoughts with Rand's. Perhaps she might will him to come to her.

Walter appeared, instead. "Do join us, dearest," he said, taking her by the arm. "This involves you, too."

The interior, never spacious, seemed even smaller. Due to its tiny rooms, Wyndham Manor reminded Elizabeth of a labyrinth rather than a residence, and as soon as she

214

walked through the doorway she felt suffocated.

"Do you enjoy being back in your childhood home?" Walter asked, a smile stretching his thin lips.

Somehow, Elizabeth managed a nod.

While Walter and the others assessed the years of damage, she climbed a staircase, then pushed open the door to a bedroom. She had been born in this room, which smelled of cold and mildew. Although she knew her mother had died here, she could remember very little about Barbara beyond the funeral and the watchers seated in the shadows, and she had to admit that Barbara herself might have been conjured up out of shadows. There was a portrait of Barbara inside the White Hart's parlor. A quilt she had sewn adorned Elizabeth's bed. And there were flashes of memories. A gentle hand caressing. A melodic voice reading bedtime stories. A perfumed handkerchief.

Elizabeth spat on her own handkerchief. She then rubbed vigorously at the dirt-encrusted window pane until she had clarified a small portion of glass. Her mother's grave was out there. Rand was out there, as well, and tonight she must find him. Motionless, she allowed the room's darkness and the night's darkness to wash over her.

She must tap into Rand's mind, into some sort of consciousness that linked them together. She sensed the time for their reunion was at hand. She had sensed it all evening, which was why she had waited so impatiently for Walter.

Squeezing her eyes shut, Elizabeth concentrated. Finally one word came to her. *Abbey.*

Built in the twelfth century, Fountains Abbey had been inhabited by Cistercian monks. It was located in the Skell Valley, which consisted of dense woods, uncertain terrain, and numerous springs. The abbey had fallen into decay, but Elizabeth thought its ruins looked impressive.

She walked across the tangled grass toward the cluster of buildings. Stone outlines from the chancel's trefoil arches and lancet windows created a chiaroscuro against the distant swell of the valley. An inky stain of ivy spread out across the abbey walls and overlaid the ragged rooftops. A lone church tower thrust above the other buildings like a fist brandished at the sky. The stars and moon were obscured by clouds, and the atmosphere was oppressively thick.

Entering a long vaulted cellar, she halted, letting her eyes adjust to the darkness. At

216

one time, part of the cellar had been used as the Cistercians' frater and she could visualize the white-habited monks drifting toward their dining tables. Only the renewed rustling of her gown and the distant murmuring of the River Skell disturbed the cellar's silence. Fountains Abbey possessed a tranquility which she attributed to the hallowed ground, or the souls of the dead monks.

As she neared the edge of the cellar, she heard her own footsteps, fluttering like birds caught in a net. She halted again. Her nape prickled. "Rand?"

"Turn around."

She obeyed, and saw him step out from behind one of the columns. "I knew you were here," she said, running toward him. "I felt you calling to me."

Rand pocketed his pistol. "Sorry, Bess, but I wasn't thinking of you, nor anything else. I was asleep." He enfolded her in a quick embrace before pulling away. "You tried hard enough to find me, haunting the roads until I considered robbing you again, merely to discourage your persistence. Why can't you let me be?"

"If you truly wanted to be left alone, you would not have returned to the Dales."

"I've a score to settle with Stafford."

What about me? Did you think to come back because of me? Even once?

Immediately, she realized that her silent queries were silly and senseless. What did she expect him to say? *Yes, I thought about you when I ran for my life. I thought about you when they were choking the life from my cousin. You were in my thoughts, Bess, night and day.* If Rand had answered thus, she would have regarded him as an insincere gallant.

By mutual, unspoken consent, they left the cellar and walked among the ruins. A small portion of moonlight filtered through the clouds, enough so that Elizabeth could drink in the sight of Rand. She rested her arm upon his. They might have been a lord and his lady strolling through their gardens.

"What are you doing here?" Rand asked, breaking the spell.

"I slipped away. Lord Stafford and my parents are nearby, at our old manor."

"Still keeping comfort with that bastard, are you? I should think you could find yourself a better suitor."

"I have," she said, gazing up into his face. "I'm happy to see you again, my love, but don't you know you're courting death?"

"Perhaps I mean to court it, Bess. Perhaps the knowledge that life can be yanked away at any moment is what makes life so exciting."

"Really! Do you miss your cousin so much you'd follow him?"

"I miss him so much I'd avenge him. Moreover, my attitude has less to do with Zak than . . . events."

"What do you mean?" When he didn't respond, she said, "Tell me why you're not some respectable farmer or solicitor. Tell me why you chose to become a highwayman."

"I don't remember."

"Yes, you do."

"All the remembering in the world cannot alter anything. If I told you my life story, I would still remain what I am. You think to change me but you can't."

"I don't want to change you. I want to understand you."

He considered for a long moment, then shrugged. "I was a soldier, Bess, a respectable soldier. I fought at the Battle of Guilford Court House. Some call it the turning point of the war, but I only know that we marched and marched. The weather was miserable, snow and rain. Cornwallis had chased the Colonials out of the Carolinas. But once we entered Virginia, we were outnumbered by their reinforcements. We had to retreat to the south. Earlier, Cornwallis had destroyed many of our supplies so that we could march faster. He had also laid waste to the countryside. Thus, we were forced to retrace our path over scorched earth which yielded precious little in the way of food."

Elizabeth imagined the blackened fields, the starving men, the bone-weariness, the despair.

"When we finally met the Colonials," Rand continued, "we were outnumbered two to one. I'll never forget the countryside where we made our stand. The golden hills and dark woods, and the courthouse off to one side. I still can't bear the sight of rolling hills and forests. That's why I shy away from the south. I mislike the very thought of Dorset or the Cotswolds or the Vale of Evesham, especially Evesham. So similar. They almost seem interchangeable . . ." He faltered, his eyes bleak.

Elizabeth was familiar with the Battle of Guilford Court House. For days . . . nay, weeks, her father had talked of nothing else. Ultimately, Cornwallis had ordered his gunners to fire grapeshot, which had proven disastrous to both sides.

"A black cloud appeared, racing toward us, as if driven by demons. It finally stopped to hover above the enemy."

The timbre of Rand's voice had changed. Elizabeth attributed the sudden huskiness to emotion, and she longed to reach out, hold him, mitigate his painful memories.

"The cloud frightened us, for it came out of nowhere. It was an evil omen. We knew it. Lightning flicked like serpents' tongues, and thunder growled, but only drops of rain emerged."

"Lightning?" The whole scene sounded familiar. Perhaps she had read about the storm in the press.

"We saw the cloud and we were terrified, for we had already sensed our cause was lost. We believed God had sent the blackness to hide our forthcoming tragedy. It was so dark we could barely see the abbey, though occasionally we could hear the prayers of the monks."

Elizabeth blinked, surprised. She hadn't known America possessed abbeys. America was so young. Its abbeys would be fresh and beautiful. America's abbeys would not reveal the inevitable decay wrought by King Henry and the dissolution.

"We marched up the slopes of Green Hill, right into the heart of the enemy. We were so outnumbered. It was futile, of course, but I didn't care. I still loved battle. What made it particularly difficult was that in many cases we were not fighting strangers, but brothers and friends."

Elizabeth knew that to be true. During the American War, loyalties had often been hopelessly tangled. General Cornwallis himself had opposed many of the acts leading up to the Revolution, and countless officers had refused to serve against the Colonials. On the other hand, fully half of all Americans had remained loyal to England.

"We crashed into the enemy line." Rand's voice was a harsh whisper. "All around me, soldiers were falling. I heard the shouts and screams but I pressed on. A thousand deaths made no difference. I loved the very thought of war. The smell of the horses, the noise, the fear, the blood. I had fought so many battles, this seemed but one more. We had always been victorious before. Our cause was just. Why would we not prevail again?"

Elizabeth had a hard time imagining Rand as the war lover he portrayed himself to be. Obviously, the Battle of Guilford Court House had been his turning point. It had changed him, as war must always change men.

"The wings closed in on either side, crushing us. Then I knew. We would all die, there on Green Hill."

Not all, thought Elizabeth, but the losses had been tremendous. One fourth of the General's command had been killed or wounded.

"Is that when you hurt your leg?" she asked. "When General Cornwallis fired into the line?"

"No. My horse fell on me."

Elizabeth winced. She imagined the snap of breaking bone, the pain and fear he must have experienced. "How dreadful," she said softly.

"A broken leg was the least of my problems." He ran his fingers through his thick, dark hair. "That was the end, at least for me. Both sides were right. Both sides believed in what they were fighting for. Both sides were wrong. And nothing mattered anymore. I felt detached from the entire business. It all seemed so irrelevant. Something happened to me that day on Green Hill."

"And now society's rules seem just as irrelevant." She wanted to say something more profound, something comforting, something that would put the past in perspective and reroute Rand's life, but she couldn't find the proper words. Instead, she reached out and caressed his smooth-shaven cheek.

He jerked back, as if emerging from a trance. "You must return to your parents, Bess. There is danger here."

"Danger from whom? Do you consider me dangerous?"

Yes, Rand thought. How could he explain? She wanted to make love, and he knew he would be ineffective, if not brutal. The memories he had just revealed had left him with a bitter taste in his mouth. He could smell blood. He could hear the screams of the wounded. He could see the shapeless forms of the sightless dead.

He watched Elizabeth tilt her head. The moon spilled its light across her face. Her eyes glistened with unshed tears, but her lovely mouth appeared resolute.

"I want you, Rand," she said. "I want you now, tonight, evermore."

"No, Bess."

"Aye." She unbuttoned her coat, then her waistcoat. Her slippers, skirt and under-clothing were soon shed, until her lithesome body was shrouded by nothing more than moonbeams. Her hands, sure and steady, began divesting Rand of his shirt.

"No," he repeated, batting her hands away. Then, almost trance-like, he removed the pins from her neat club and stroked the shiny masses of her hair.

"Do not build a wall," she pleaded. "Do not keep me out. I want to love you."

"I don't know what love is," he replied bitterly.

"Of course you do. Did you not mean it when you said you loved me?"

"I meant it, Bess, I swear. 'Tis because I love you that I don't want to do this. I would only hurt you, betray you, and soon you would grow to hate me."

"Never! Even if I hated you, I would love you. Please lay beside me and help me prove how much we love each other."

This was all wrong, he thought. He should be wooing her. He had always wooed his ladies. Bess, however, was unique. She didn't play the coquette and she didn't play the whore. She didn't even seem to realize that her honesty would precipitate his defeat. If he said no again, she'd simply drag him down onto the grass and feather him with kisses until he was helpless.

She raised her arms, inviting him, cajoling him. The motion revealed the delicate bounce of her breasts. Moonlight made her nipples extrinsic, the color of dusk, the color of shade. She was so fragile, so vulnerable, so overpowering. He could smell his own lust and he could feel his body trembling and he could no more master his hunger for her than he could master his dreams of the past.

Elizabeth glimpsed Rand's face as he bent to kiss her. His features were all shadow and moonlight. She felt his mouth come down upon hers in a violent assault, stealing her breath. Her head whirled. She felt powerless, overwhelmed by her own desire and the hard, unyielding press of his body. After a short space or long minutes, she couldn't determine which, he drew back. Head still spinning, she gazed into his face.

Rand's face, but not his face. The darkness of hair, but darker somehow. The same features, but not the same. Coarser. Bolder.

Unable to accept this obvious illusion, she reached up to stroke his face again. This time her fingers encountered a beard. She yanked her hand away. Behind her, she heard the chanting of the White Monks and the rustle of their ghostly habits. "Who are you?" she whispered, her heart rising and beating against the pulse in her throat.

The moonlight teased his face, revealing, hiding. Strong white teeth flashed against his beard as he said, "Do you not know me, Janey?"

She felt as if her legs were being sucked

into quicksand. She tried to force herself to turn and flee, but her body seemed without strength. "What did you call me?"

Clouds crept across the moon, encasing the ruins in darkness once again. When Rand spoke, his voice was as it should be. "Do you insist on propriety, Bess. After all that has passed between us, would you have me call you Miss Wyndham?"

"No. Of course not. I only meant . . ." She struggled to see his face, fearing she would encounter that someone else, that dark, brutal, exciting someone else, who was as desirable as he was repellent.

Something moved within, an ancient memory. Her mind almost grasped it before it floated away, like the souls of the dead monks.

"I thought . . ." She shivered, as if a chill wind had sprung up, even though the air remained oppressively stagnant. "I was mistaken. I have been imagining things."

He laughed. " 'Tis your vocation to imagine things, Bess."

"True," she replied. But in a sudden burst of insight she knew. Her raven-haired knight. Somehow she had blended the two together in her mind. Either that or there was another more frightening explanation, one she didn't dare consider, one that might drive her mad.

She sighed. Rand had spoken of turning points, but their relationship had passed its own turning point a long time ago. She experienced anticipation, fear, and a strange sense of fatalism, as though she had embarked on a journey into an uncharted land and she couldn't steer or change the direction, no matter how hard she tried. *Why would you want to change the direction? This is where you belong,* a voice inside her whispered.

Rand seemed unaware of the fact that they had been momentarily suspended in an illusory realm. Beginning where he left off, he cradled her chin in his strong, callused hands.

She felt his lips claim hers. His lips were moist and warm, soft and firm, yet they moved with a hungry fervor. She inhaled the scent of horse, leather and sandalwood, but this time the monks were silent. The earth spun and her head whirled, but this time it was her reaction to Rand's kiss. And this time, when the moon reappeared, it smiled.

Elizabeth noted that the moon's smile was sideways, crooked, just before Rand lowered her to the ground and slid his palms beneath her breasts, rendering all contemplation impossible.

If she had been more aware, more coherent, she might have thought the moon was mocking them.

Afterwards, she lay in the crook of his arm and listened to the rhythmic cadence of their heartbeats.

"Will I see you again?" she asked.

"Yes."

"When?"

"In my own time."

CHAPTER 15

The Harvest Ball was always held on the night of a full moon so that participants would be guided by its light. Guests from as far south as York had purchased tickets, all the surrounding inns and assembly rooms were packed to the rafters, and woe to the boarder who desired private accommodations.

With that last thought, Elizabeth smoothed her lavender silk gown, a gift from her Aunt Lilith who had arrived this morning. Lilith had toted a vast array of baggage, but no husband. He was consumed with business affairs, Lilith had stated resolutely. Elizabeth surmised that her uncle's affairs were, at best, the consumption of gin, at worst, an *affaire d'amour.* Damn all men!

After plaiting her thick braid with a blue love knot, Elizabeth leaned out the open bedroom window. A pumpkin-colored moon illuminated the carriages stretched along the highway. She swallowed a yawn, her fifth or sixth; she had lost count. "Dorothea says this will be the best ball ever," she told Lilith, who shared her room. "I hope she's right."

Lilith fastened her own sapphire bracelet around Elizabeth's slender wrist. "Why shouldn't she be right? The weather is fine, the crowd grows by the minute, and you have an attentive suitor in Lord Stafford. What more could anyone ask for?"

"I . . . nobody has sighted the highwayman," Elizabeth stammered, then realized she hadn't answered her aunt's last query. Or perhaps she had.

"There are patrols everywhere. He would never attack tonight." Lilith studied her niece. "Would he, Elizabeth?"

She pretended not to hear by closing the window, retrieving her hand mirror, and carefully inspecting her face. Rand had said "In my own time," but a full week had passed without even one glimpse of him. Her body ached for his touch, and she felt bewildered, nay, *betrayed* by his indifference.

Far more disturbing than Rand's absence, however, was the memory of her raven-haired knight. She had seen him at Fountains Abbey. It hadn't been a trick of the fickle moonlight or her vivid imagination. It was the same face that teased her when she wrote her novels, the face that haunted her dreams. Which meant what? She didn't dare contemplate what it might mean. A part of her was even relieved that Rand had made no effort to visit. As much as she loved him, she also feared him. No. She didn't fear Rand, only the secrets he held and the unsettling things that happened whenever they were together.

Impulsively, Elizabeth gave her aunt a hug. Then she gathered up her skirts and exited the room.

Walter waited near the front door. A lively tune, dominated by a racing fiddle, intruded from the courtyard.

"Good evening, my lord." Wishing he were Rand, Elizabeth curtsied, keeping her back and shoulders straight so that her gown's fitted bodice concealed more than it revealed.

Nevertheless, Walter's gaze lingered on her breasts. "You dazzle me, dearest," he said. "In truth, you are by far the most beautiful woman here tonight. No. In all of the north. In all of England. I cannot wait to get you to London." Grasping her by the upper arms, he kissed her on the lips.

Startled by his boldness, she shoved him away.

He gave her a naughty-boy grin. "I couldn't resist," he said. "You look so perfect, and your eyes shine brighter than your sapphires."

She smelled the wine on his breath. "If my eyes shine, they shine because I am angry. I do not appreciate your rude behavior." Elizabeth realized she was overreacting, but his lips had provoked such revulsion, she felt like cleansing her mouth. "If you don't want to quarrel, I suggest you control yourself."

"I'm sorry, dearest. It's just that I have come to a decision which shall change my entire life, and I am exuberant at the very thought of it. And, in truth, you looked as if you wanted to be kissed."

"Really, Lord Stafford!"

"No, no, I was mistaken. On my oath, I will comport myself like a gentleman."

He led her out into the courtyard, adorned with enormous baskets of flowers. Dorothea thought the blooms lent fragrance and color to the evening, and she was probably right, but Elizabeth found the smell cloying, almost nauseating. Paper lanterns and decorations wound around the light posts, the tables of food, and the platform upon which the band played. Father was flinging about the mayor of Middleham's plump wife, while Dorothea stood on the sidelines, smiling her cat-smile.

Elizabeth bit back a greeting. Her father was no longer her beloved papa. Despite his words to the contrary, he had wagered on the bull baiting and lost several pounds. Walter had promptly settled the debt, and Lawrence now praised Lord Stafford's virtues like a well-trained parrot.

"Let us find a quiet spot in the garden where we can talk," Walter said. "I have decided we should be married immediately and we must discuss our plans."

Speechless, totally aghast, she allowed him to pull her toward the privacy of a secluded hedge area. "But I haven't agreed to wed you," she said when she finally found her voice.

"Stop playing coy, Elizabeth. You should be flattered that I am such an ardent suitor. I've met hundreds of women, most richer, many younger, and all with less independent dispositions, but it is you I want. I can't explain what it is about you, perhaps it is merely the fact that you're so reluctant . . ." He paused, shaking his head. "In any case, I've already approached your parents with a formal offer and they're delighted."

"Of course they're delighted. They pant like thirsty dogs. Our marriage would relieve them of all financial burdens. Does that not make you think twice?"

"I have thought twice, more than twice, and I've concluded that your hand in marriage is well worth the paltry sum I've loaned your father. I would pay triple the amount just to bed you, my pet, but bedding you is not enough. Not anymore."

Elizabeth suppressed the urge to slap him. Lord Stafford would definitely appear in her next novel as a villain whom her heroine would torture in an exquisitely diabolical manner.

"Let us leave our relationship as it has been," she said, striving to maintain her composure. "We enjoy each other's company, at least most of the time. I don't want more, and I don't believe you do either."

"That's not true." Walter groped for her hand. "I'm forty years old, and I've worked my entire life for this moment. Now that I'm comfortable and have achieved a certain position, I want to savor the fruits of my labors."

What fruits? What labors? she wondered. Aside from his job as justice of the peace, Walter had probably never labored. Why should he? The Stafford family was arguably one of the oldest and wealthiest in all of England.

Her gaze sought the moon, rising above the moors. A black cloud drifted across its golden-orange face. A sudden gust of wind tossed the lanterns and, at the same time, changed the direction of her thoughts. During this past week, she had dwelled endlessly on two things. If Rand really cared for her, he would have pursued her. And perhaps Rand himself was too dangerous to be pursued.

The man at Fountains Abbey had both attracted and frightened her. A shiver passed through her that had nothing to do with a second gust of wind. Had Rand really called her Janey? Who was Janey? And who was Rand Remington? A soldier disillusioned by war? Or a specter from the past who would ultimately betray her?

You betrayed him, an inner voice whispered.

Making a sudden decision, she said, "I shall travel to London with you, my lord, but only to retrieve my money from Charles Beresford. You see, I have never wanted to marry any man."

"But I want to marry *you,* Elizabeth. What a fine couple we would make. We could spend our winter season in London and savor the company of London society. You might even continue your scribbling, in between children of course."

"Sir, you are very persuasive," she murmured, biting back a sharp retort, "but I don't love you."

"I don't love you, either. Since when has love been a necessity for marriage? However, I do desire you. Beauty is always a door opener, Elizabeth, and will go a long way toward making up for your common origins and your lack of wealth."

"I'm pleased to hear that," she said, thinking she would chain her Walter-like villain to a dungeon wall, where rats would nibble at his bare toes and spiders would crawl across his body. "I'll contemplate what you have so generously offered, my lord. I cannot promise more."

"Don't keep me waiting, Elizabeth. Once I make up my mind, nothing can dissuade me. I've already decided that we should be wed next week, in London."

"You're insane," she hissed, turning away.

He caught her braid and reeled her back, like a fisherman reeling a fish on a line. Then, almost fussily, he tidied her hair. "You know I'll win in the end, my pet, so why fight me?" He reached into his pocket. "I have something for you."

Elizabeth felt Walter wrap her fingers around a narrow box. She fumbled at the clasp. A primitive golden rope of a necklace nestled inside the box.

He held it up so that it was detailed by the moonlight.

"I first viewed this in London last year, inside a toy shop of all places," he said. "I was haunted by its beauty, but I could think of no woman it really suited. Once you and I became more intimately acquainted, I kept picturing how perfect you would look wearing it, so I sent a servant back to London expressly to purchase it for you."

Mesmerized, Elizabeth stared at the necklace. Forgetting her anger, forgetting even the small ache Walter had produced by his yank on her braid, she tried to steady her wobbly limbs.

"It does suit me," she finally said. "I've never seen anything like it."

But she had, although where and when she couldn't say. Tentatively, she accepted the necklace from Walter. But as soon as it touched her palm, she gasped. She wanted nothing more than to hurl it away, for it felt ice cold. *'Tis just a necklace,* she thought, as the metal warmed to her body heat.

"You do like it, then?"

Elizabeth nodded. " 'Tis a wondrous piece

of jewelry, my lord."

He removed it from her hand and placed it around her neck. The coil initially felt heavy and foreign against her breastbone, but after a few moments it felt as if it belonged.

"It's very old, isn't it?" she murmured, vaguely aware that she should return the gift straightaway. But her arms felt weighted, graceless. In fact, her whole body might have belonged to someone else.

"The proprietor swears it dates from the thirteenth century and was involved in some sort of baronial wars, but his story is most likely fabricated." Walter smiled. "Whatever its origin, it was made for you."

Elizabeth curled her fingers around the necklace. Just above the moors, the pale moon hovered. Around her, the tables and footpaths were hung with shadows. During the Middle Ages people believed the shadow was a man's soul. "I'll wear it everywhere," she said.

"I prefer you wear it 'round your neck," said Walter.

He laughed at his own jest, and Elizabeth wondered why every time she touched the heavy golden rope she felt like crying.

Elizabeth and Walter joined other couples

inside the common room.

For the past several months, in anticipation of the Harvest Ball, dancing masters had been teaching single women the latest fashionable steps. Subscription balls were wonderful places to impress eligible gentlemen, and eligible ladies circled the dance floor like buzzards circling a carcass. The orchestra, which had traveled all the way from Richmond, played a variety of music, most prominently minuets and lively galliards. Heat from a hundred bodies, as well as candles, caused perspiration to bead Elizabeth's forehead. The orchestra, far too large for the room, assaulted her ears.

Walter bowed to her. When he took her hand their eyes met, but she couldn't read his expression. Then his gaze moved down to her breasts. Nay, her necklace.

As the dance glided to its conclusion, she became aware of a commotion outside. Subscription balls often bred altercations, so at first she paid little heed to the excited voices.

Abruptly, the orchestra stopped playing. Wig askew, a portly man rushed toward the center of the dance floor, followed by his equally plump wife. Both appeared disheveled, though judging from their dress they were well-to-do. Elizabeth saw that the woman's neck, ears and fingers lacked jewels.

"Shit," Walter muttered, then offered a hasty apology.

"We've been robbed!" shouted the portly gentleman. "And not a mile down the road!"

"A monster wearing a vizard stopped our carriage at gunpoint," his wife cried. "I recognized him since we were robbed once before, near York. It was the Quiet Companion." After imparting this dramatic addition, she swooned.

Several people rushed to her aid, while more clustered around the gentleman, firing questions. Walter strode outside, bellowing something about how the fiend would soon be cold meat. Dorothea stood beside her sister, Lilith. Wringing her hands, Dorothea looked alternately horrified and enraged.

Elizabeth stood alone on the dance floor. She cursed Rand and at the same time prayed that tonight he had not overplayed his hand.

A strong wind had sprung up. Elizabeth lay in bed, next to her aunt. She listened to the shutters rattle and watched the moonlight shimmer through the wooden cracks. The ball had ended hours ago. Walter and her father had organized a patrol, and the rest

241

of the guests had departed in frightened groups. Like sheep headed for the slaughter — or the *shearing* — she thought with dour amusement.

She had to concede the boldness of Rand's act. He must have been aware of the wrath he would incur, yet he had willingly risked the danger. She could imagine him galloping along the dark ribbon of road, his cape flying. Who would be the recipient of his largess this time? Penniless locals or slumdwelling Londoners? No wonder Rand was so in love with death, she thought with a sigh. Both shared the same profession. Just like a highwayman, death lurked in the shadows, leaping out unexpectedly to rob one of that which was most precious. Not gold watches and silver-threaded purses, but life itself.

The wind continued rapping at the shutters. Mindful of her sleeping aunt, Elizabeth eased up in bed and cocked her head. The rhythmic *tap-tap-tap* repeated, and she was almost certain she heard someone whistle. Rand? It couldn't possibly be Rand. He was reckless, impetuous, but he wasn't stupid. Gliding from the bed, she raised the window and pushed the shutters open.

Bathed in a pool of shadows, Rand waited. "Are you mad?" she whispered. "What are you doing here?"

"I told you I'd come for you in my own time."

"But 'tis far too dangerous. The roads are swarming with patrols. You must be gone before Lord Stafford catches you."

Rising in his stirrups, Rand caught a strand of her hair and brought it to his lips. "Ride with me, Bess," he urged. "Out under the moon."

She hesitated. Although her recent animosity had disappeared at the sight of Rand, a tryst was much too rash, fraught with known — and perhaps unknown — hazards. She turned her face toward Lilith, who appeared to be sleeping peacefully.

"You can't risk it, love." The wind tore her words away. In a few days, she might be on the road to London. In a few days, he might be caught and on the road to the gallows.

"Hurry, Bess, we haven't much time," he pressed, while his mount pawed the ground impatiently.

The sight of the stallion's restlessness made up Elizabeth's mind for her. The slap of her bare feet followed her out the front door. She raced toward Rand, who swooped her up behind him, then swiveled in his saddle. Beneath the luminescent moon, his eyes danced. "Are you ready, my bonny Bess?"

"Where are you taking me?"

Laughing, Rand dug his heels into his stallion.

As they raced across the moors, the moon sped after them. Ragged strips of clouds played hide and seek with the stars. The wind tore through Elizabeth's shift, lashed Rand's hair against her eyes, and iced her fingers. The horse seemed to skim the rugged terrain, an extension of the wind and night. Burying her face against Rand's back, Elizabeth closed her eyes and allowed herself to be swept along. She blanked her mind to the possibility that Walter would uncover them, that even now Lilith was alerting Dorothea. If this moment was madness, and it most assuredly was, she would deal with the consequences later.

Rand reined in his stallion. The jagged walls of the peel tower loomed before them. Clouds closed over the moon like a fist, plunging them into darkness. Rand dismounted and she felt his hands pulling her down to him. She burrowed against him, suddenly afraid, but he gently pried her face loose from the linen of his shirt. His kiss was filled with tenderness — and something else. Exaltation? No. His slow exploration of her lips conveyed a yearning for the years they had not spent together, a surrender to the years, or months, or even weeks they might yet spend together. It was the sweetest, most profound kiss she had ever experienced.

When the moon broke free, Rand led her into the depths of the peel tower, and she responded to the pressure of his knee between her thighs by sinking to the ground. His hands cradled her back as he followed her descent, his knee still in place.

He kissed her palm and sucked her fingers. If the suck of his fingers had once fueled her desire, the suck of hers caused a throb that was almost unbearable. Sensing her need, he guided her wet fingers beneath her shift and placed them on the very core of her womanhood. His hand applied pressure to her fingers as he stroked back and forth. With a moan, she wrenched her hand free, pushed his face toward her breasts, and silently implored him to taste her nipples. He tightened the white cotton of her shift. Then he filled his mouth, shift and all, with her breast, until she cried out, wanting more, needing more.

She felt chagrin at the sound, but Rand said, "Cry, scream, howl, my love. We are alone and the moon does not care if you express your pleasure. Neither do I."

He rose to his feet, and she experienced a vulnerability that had nothing to do with her state of undress; a forlorn isolation that made her breath catch in her throat. Before she could express her grief, she felt the weight of his body settle upon hers. He was nude, gloriously nude, and this time more than a knee wedged itself between her thighs.

She felt his mouth claim hers, hot and demanding, so that when she screamed and howled, he swallowed her cries and they became a part of him. Her body raged with need. Thrashing wildly beneath him, she sobbed his name over and over.

He halted her frantic writhing with his hands, tender yet firm, and an uncontrollable shudder rippled through her frame at his pervasive penetration. For the first time in her life she craved complete male dominance, and her lusty cries of pleasure, along with her violent quivers, gave credence to her restive desire. At long last, when she had nothing left but whimpers, Rand grasped her buttocks, and his thrusts were rough, without gentleness of any kind, just as she wanted them to be.

Past and present melded together. Elizabeth saw the face from Fountains Abbey; the face of the man who haunted her. His hair curled long, blacker than black. His beard was as dark as the night. His mouth was sensual and cruel, his nose straight, aristocratic. His eyes were more than compelling. Mesmerizing.

A part of herself slipped free. She was Bess, but she joined with someone else. In the depths of her mind, she knew his name. She could almost call it out. The man she loved and hated. The man she had betrayed.

Just as she hovered on the truth, Rand exploded inside her. Then he slumped on top of her. She felt his heart gradually slow against her chest, felt the sweat from both their bodies, felt the cold biting earth assault her buttocks. Beneath her shift, Rand's hands cradled her back.

" 'Tis over then?" she murmured.

"Nay, sweet Bess, 'tis just beginning."

Before she could question the ambiguity of his statement, he led her from the tower and covered her with his cloak. Then he swung up onto his stallion and settled her behind him.

"What if they are waiting for us?" she asked, as Rand's horse once again galloped across the rugged terrain.

"They won't be."

"How do you know?"

"I just do. My fate is not to be shot down in some damnfool courtyard, where a white hart passively guards the front door. I prefer to run like a hart. If I am shot down, it must be on the highway, or in the forest."

She wanted to ask what *her* fate was, but she bit her lower lip, maintaining a silence that was permeated with fear.

He sensed the fear, if not the reason. "They won't be waiting," he assured her.

He was correct. The courtyard was deserted. While passing the stables, Elizabeth fancied she glimpsed Tim's pale face, but she dismissed it as a trick of the dawn's light.

Riding toward the inn's entrance, Rand felt Elizabeth's warm breath in his ear. During their weeks of separation, he had reached an incessant conclusion. She held the key that would unlock the secrets of his past, a past that had occurred five hundred years ago. He had meant what he said about running with the hart, but he now knew that Bess must run by his side. He had known it from the moment they met. He had fought it, but the battle had been lost before it had truly begun.

He helped her slide from his horse, then leaned sideways to kiss her. "I'll be back for you tonight," he said. "Together, we shall leave for the south. I'll deal with Stafford another time."

As Elizabeth handed Rand his cloak, she heard her heart pound. " 'Twould be madness," she countered, aware that her inner joy belied her words.

"I won't go anywhere without you." Rand tilted her chin. "You and me, Bess. After tonight we're linked together once again."

"What do you mean?"

"We both have things to uncover, things that will inevitably be revealed to us if we stay together. You've felt it from the very start. So have I," he said, his voice a harsh whisper.

Elizabeth caught his hand and brought it to her lips. "I don't understand why this is happening."

"Neither do I. But I do know that I love you. Come with me, wherever that might lead. I won't let the past hurt you, I promise."

For the first time he sounded unsure, but she merely said, "Life without you holds no promise, Rand. I shall follow you to the ends of the earth."

"Cornwall should be far enough."

She released his hand, but clung to his boot and stirrup. "I don't want you to leave me. I have a premonition —"

"Hush. *I'm* the one with premonitions."

"Why can't we leave now, Rand? Why?"

"You are clothed in nothing more than an insubstantial nightshift. I may be a rogue, Bess, but I would never steal a half naked woman."

"Give me but a few minutes to change my clothes," she pleaded, ignoring his tease.

"No. 'Tis almost dawn, and daylight's far too dangerous, even if I were on my own."

"We can hide in Fountains Abbey."

"Would they not search for you there? Everywhere?"

"Yes. Of course they would. My father found me at Fountains Abbey when I was ten. I had ridden there on my pony. I was skirling, screaming, frightened out of my wits. I cannot remember why, though I'm fairly certain it had something to do with my nightmares."

"I wish I had been there to hold you, comfort you."

"So do I, but I think we were not meant to meet until now. And please don't call me logical. 'Tis just a feeling."

"A feeling we must explore together. I'll be back tonight, Bess." His lips brushed hers. "I love you."

She watched him ride away, then opened

the inn's front door. Furtively entering, she groped her way toward her bedroom. Her feet felt like blocks of ice and her hands were numb. Perhaps the sudden chill was caused by Rand's departure, or perhaps her elusive childhood memory, but she couldn't stop shivering.

The door to her chamber remained open, just as she'd left it. She stepped inside, only to see Lilith and Dorothea seated on the bed, waiting for her.

CHAPTER 16

Elizabeth felt completely detached from the two women, as if they were fictitious characters resurrected from one of her early novels. Her emotions remained firmly centered on her encounter with Rand. He was her reality. *I'll be back tonight, Bess. I love you.*

"So . . ." A multitude of sentiments, ranging from contempt to fury, was conveyed by Dorothea's one word. She stood, her motion tremulous rather than fluid. "Close the door, you slut!"

As if she were sleepwalking, Elizabeth obeyed. Lilith remained on the bed, twisting folds into her nightshift. Her aunt had betrayed her, Elizabeth thought, but what other choice did she have?

"Do you realize what you've done?" Dorothea's delicate features contorted with anger.

Elizabeth didn't care about anything save

riding south with Rand. A part of her warned that she should try to brazen her way out of this predicament, but her mind remained as numb as her extremities. "I have done nothing wrong," she finally managed.

Dorothea made a disgusted sound. "You have run off on some midnight tryst, which could ruin everything. Lord Stafford will pay off our mortgages and complete the renovations on Wyndham Manor." She advanced toward Elizabeth. "But you must sign the marriage contract first."

Elizabeth's bare feet were beginning to ache. She wondered how her feet could feel numb and ache at the same time.

"Who is he?" Dorothea asked.

Elizabeth shook her head.

Dorothea slapped her.

"Sister, please!" Lilith half rose from the bed. "There is no need —"

"I asked her a question which she had best answer."

Elizabeth pressed her hand against her cheek. Dorothea had never struck her before. The fact that her stepmother was upset enough to lose control jolted Elizabeth from her inertia. "He is no one you'd know," she said.

Dorothea inclined her head toward her

sister. "When you rode off, Lilith had a clear view of him from the window. She said he looked like a man she saw at Zak Turnbull's execution, the surgeon who cut him down. I'll find out sooner or later, so why not make it easy on both of us? Tell me now."

"No. Never. I'm sorry to spoil your plans, but I will not marry Walter Stafford."

"Where did you meet your lover? How long have you been sneaking off to rut with him? Do you realize what you've done? If word of your promiscuity leaks out . . ." Dorothea wrung her hands.

"I don't care about any man except . . . him."

"How quaint. You're starting to believe your own novels. Real women don't forsake their futures for love, Elizabeth. If they do, they invariably regret it. Once you consider what I've said, you'll realize I'm right and we shall leave for London as if nothing has happened." In a tone several degrees colder than Elizabeth's hands and feet, Dorothea added, "Because nothing *has.* Do you understand?"

"Yes. But if you force me, I shall tell Lord Stafford the truth. I'll tell him that I'm in love with another man, that I've lain with somebody else."

"Frankly, I don't believe that would deter him. Anyone can see that he's bedeviled by you."

Terror stabbed through Elizabeth. She had long suspected that Walter's dogged pursuit of her was fueled by her constant refusals and obvious disdain. If she had only played the flutter-fanned coquette, the empty-headed damsel, if she had only portrayed one of her book heroines, his interest might have dried up years ago. Walter wasn't bedeviled. He was possessed.

"You'll do as I say, you pig-widgeon," Dorothea continued. "I'll not sacrifice my future for your whims, nor your romantic fancies. I'll not allow you to indulge yourself as you please, and neither will your father. We leave for London on the morrow."

Elizabeth felt all the color drain from her face. A pig-widgeon was a simpleton. Dorothea could not have uttered a more demeaning epithet. Elizabeth had striven her whole life to avoid such an appellation, and she had succeeded brilliantly. "You bitch!" she cried. "I won't bed Walter, I won't marry him, and I won't travel to London with him. And should I tell him the truth, he'd spurn me forever."

"What truth is that?"

Goaded beyond endurance, beyond caution, Elizabeth blurted, "My lover is a highwayman. *The* highwayman!"

Lilith gasped. Dorothea stiffened.

I've bested you now, Elizabeth thought triumphantly. *You and Father will disown me, but I'll be rid of Walter Stafford forever. More importantly, I'll be free to leave with Rand.*

Silence charged the room. From the kitchen came the first sounds of the servants. Dorothea bent her head and tapped her teeth with her forefinger, a signal that she was calculating events and molding them into her favor.

Uneasy, Elizabeth edged backward until her buttocks pressed against the door. Her father, always the military expert, would have said she had made a tactical blunder.

Dorothea finally smiled her cat-smile. "Leave it to you to conjoin with a thief and a murderer —"

"He has murdered no one!"

"— though I do thank you for the information. Ultimately, it will make my task so much easier." She motioned toward the corner washstand. "Make yourself presentable. We're to meet with Lord Stafford after breakfast."

"I will not marry him," Elizabeth insisted. "I shall tell him so, and you cannot stop me."

"I can stop you." Dorothea opened the door. "I suggest it would be mutually beneficial for all concerned if you refrain from mentioning anything about a lover. Such an admission will lead to questions regarding his identity. Lord Stafford may not be many things, but he is a dedicated justice of the peace. If he knew you had rutted with the highwayman, he would only intensify his efforts at bringing the scoundrel to justice. Such an admission, far from solving your problems, would seal your lover's death warrant. Make no mistake about that!"

"Lord Stafford's a bumbler. We have nothing to fear from him."

"I believe Zak Turnbull challenged Lord Stafford's competence. True?"

"Yes," Elizabeth replied, albeit reluctantly. A fist knotted in her stomach.

"Would it not be easier to go to London with Stafford?" Dorothea's cat-smile never wavered. "Your compliance would remove his presence from the Dales and your highwayman could slink away to freedom. Unless you do as I say, your lover is headed straight for the gallows."

The fist grew and widened, drawing Elizabeth's breath from her lungs.

Dorothea's smile widened as well. "Wash

257

your face and bathe your lover's scent from your body. Lilith, don't let her out of your sight!"

Eyes downcast, Elizabeth entered the parlor and groped for a chair. Clasping its upholstered sides, she sank down onto its padded cushion and stared at the red, blue, and green rug. With one foot, she inched the tasseled edges apart.

When she finally raised her lashes, she saw Walter and her parents grouped at the opposite end of the mahogany-paneled room, near the tiled fireplace. A sheaf of papers rested upon a writing desk, while a silver service perched atop a table draped with white linen. The pleasant aroma of coffee permeated the room.

"Did you sleep well, Bess?"

Her father's tone accused her of heinous offenses against God and nature. Dorothea had told him about the highwayman.

"I asked you a question, Bess."

"I slept very well, Father," she fibbed.

"Well, I didn't. I spent the night freezing my arse off, chasing some bastard across the moors. Some bastard who —"

"Hush, dear." Dorothea cast him a warning look. "We can discuss that later. For now, we have other matters to address." She removed a silver cup from the tray and nodded sharply at Elizabeth. "Coffee, daughter?"

I'm not your daughter! "Yes, please."

Elizabeth gazed over her stepmother's head, toward a painting of Lake Windermere. The passivity of the painting only increased her anxiety. Accepting the coffee cup, she curved her hands around its warmth. Even after a hot, almost scalding wash, her extremities still felt chilled.

"The papers have been drawn up," Dorothea said.

Elizabeth squeezed the silver cup until her fingers burned. "And what exactly is in those papers?"

"It is a standard agreement." Walter's gaze shifted back and forth between Elizabeth and her parents. His nose twitched as if he could smell the tension, thick as pea soup. Or perhaps he had simply shoved a few pinches of snuff up his nostrils.

Dorothea casually rearranged the spoons on the tray, but her gaze remained fixed on Elizabeth, willing her to obey. Father also glared at her. Walter extended a quill pen.

Rising from the chair, Elizabeth placed her cup on the hearth, then accepted the quill. Her movements were slow and deliberate, along with her thoughts. It made no

259

difference what she signed because she had no intention of going through with the marriage. Rand had said he would come for her tonight. *He* had employed logic this time, but she understood his motive. He had left her at cock's crow, and daylight was one of their enemies. Tonight, cloaked by darkness, familiar with the terrain, they would avoid the patrols. On the morrow, when Stafford arrived, she would be gone. She could sign her name in blood for all it mattered.

"What are you waiting for?" Lawrence's voice had gained several decibels. "Sign the damn papers!"

"Do you not think I should read them first?" Elizabeth asked sweetly.

"No wonder women aren't allowed to be soldiers. They can't follow orders."

She tried to meet his gaze defiantly, but knew that her expression revealed a yearning for the past, for the papa who had cuddled and protected her. "You plan to accompany us when we travel to London, do you not?"

He shook his head. "I'll remain here. Lord Stafford has endowed me with certain responsibilities and I must prove myself worthy of his trust."

Rand, thought Elizabeth. Father didn't want the highwayman captured. Father wanted him dead. That way he would never reveal her "promiscuity."

She settled her face into a serene expression, but her mind raced.

Father was a gambler. He would always gamble. Settling her father's debts would merely lead to more erratic wagers, more devastating losses. Elizabeth felt an habitual twinge of remorse. However, she no longer wanted, nor needed, her inheritance.

Rand was her legacy now.

Storm clouds had gathered, hiding the stars. Elizabeth wished they would hide the moon. Wending her way toward the stables, she prayed for rain. The steady patter of raindrops might disguise the sound of hooves while a deluge would surely cover any footprints or horse tracks.

The whole day had been interminable. Seconds felt like minutes, minutes felt like hours, and the hands on the clock seemed to inch backwards. Elizabeth had packed her traveling bag, asking Lilith's opinion on this gown and that one, thanking her profusely when she insisted Elizabeth keep the sapphire bracelet from last night.

Meals — without Walter's presence, thank goodness — were welcome respites, although Elizabeth couldn't swallow one morsel. Instead, she chatted about her forthcoming marriage. "I'll continue my writing, what Lord Stafford calls my scribbling, in between children."

Smiling sweetly at her stepmother, Elizabeth continued, "After I confront Mr. Beresford and demand my money, I'll ask him if a torture device surrounded by snakes is too profuse. A multitude of snakes. A chamber floor carpeted with snakes. I can hear them hissing. I can see them slithering inside the iron maiden through its . . . eyes? Nose? Mouth? What do *you* think, Dorothea? God's teeth, you're so pale. Do you feel faint?"

"My sister can't abide snakes," Lilith had reprimanded, but Elizabeth could see that her eyes crinkled with amusement. "Lawrence, help your wife to her room and give her an opiate. Elizabeth, let us retire as well. I am exhausted by last night's events."

Exhaustion was an understatement, Elizabeth now thought, placing her feet carefully on the path that led to the stables. Before they had finished even one game of backgammon, Lilith had fallen asleep, her snores punctuating the clock's rhythmic ticks.

It gave Elizabeth the perfect opportunity to saddle and bridle Rhiannon. Better yet, she would nonchalantly ask one of the stable hands to help her. Then she would pretend distress, explain that she had forgotten something in her room or that she was momentarily indisposed. When Rand rapped on her shutters, Rhiannon would already be saddled and —

"Dammit to hell! I can't help it if the bloody horses get upset, Tim. We're talking about catching a criminal here."

Elizabeth jerked away from the open stable door.

"But with so many men crawling about, Master Wyndham, 'twill make the beasts all worked up."

" 'Tis just for tonight, Tim. As soon as the highwayman sets foot at the inn, it'll be as good as slipping a noose 'round his neck."

Outmaneuvered again, Elizabeth thought, hurrying back across the courtyard. Why oh why had she mentioned Rand? She should have sewed her mouth shut. Dorothea had surmised that the highwayman would return tonight. She had discussed it with Father and he was laying a trap. Lord Stafford had not been informed, of course. He might ask too many questions. For example, he might ask Dorothea where and when she had obtained the pertinent information.

I must warn Rand. But how?

Startled by a flurry of activity, Elizabeth

halted. Her mind was still dazed by the scene she had witnessed inside the stable, but she could see that servants carried Lilith's trunk toward a waiting coach.

Lilith followed. Spying Elizabeth, she said, "I think it best I leave tonight. I trusted your compliance, but as soon as I shut my eyes you fled from the room, free as a bird."

"Please, Aunt Lilith, don't leave. Your abrupt departure would alert Father and . . ." Elizabeth swallowed the rest of her plea when she realized that her father had already been alerted.

"Everything has turned into such a bloody horror." Lilith dabbed at her eyes with her handkerchief. "I'm sorry I told Dorothea about your liaison. At the time I thought it best, but frankly I'm no longer sure."

"Then you must help me. John means to come for me tonight, and Father is laying a trap."

"What are you talking about?"

"The highwayman. His name is John. Tonight, when John arrives, he'll be captured, probably killed on the spot. You must head for York, then double back and wait for John at the crossroads. Call him by name and tell him *Bonny Bess* insisted you intercede. Dorothea said you saw him from the window and at Turnbull's execution, so you know what he looks like. Please, Aunt Lilith, you must warn John to stay away, that the inn will be swarming with lawmen."

"You don't realize what you're asking of me, Elizabeth. Your John is a thief, a murderer."

"He has murdered no one."

"He's a criminal!"

"Tell John that Lord Stafford and Dorothea are taking me to London on the morrow. Tell him I have no choice. If I refuse, I shall undoubtedly be forced to travel against my will. Tell him I'll give Lord Stafford the slip and meet him as soon as I can. Tell him to wait for me at the peel tower."

Lilith balled her handkerchief between her palms. "I must not get involved in this."

"If you don't warn him, he'll think I betrayed him . . ." She almost said *again.* "If you don't warn him, they'll kill him. And without him, I might as well be dead."

"I dreamed about the Harvest Ball, Elizabeth. When I awoke, I was weeping. It was a premonition. If you ride off with your highwayman, something terrible will happen. And if I help, I'll be setting in motion tragic events."

"Would you rather be a party to John's murder?"

"I would rather be left out of this completely!"

"It seems such a little thing, to warn John. Furthermore, if you had not betrayed us, your intervention would not be necessary. Please, Aunt Lilith, please. I'm begging you."

"All right. I'll think about it. But I cannot promise."

Elizabeth waited by her window. She watched the moon rise higher and higher. She watched the shadows of her father's men as they raced across the inn yard, or crouched behind the wagons and carriages.

The moon climbed to its zenith. No hoofbeats disturbed the silence. No rider appeared along the highway. The moon edged westward.

"Thank you, Aunt Lilith," Elizabeth whispered.

Near sunrise, she crawled into bed. By cock's crow, she had formulated a workable plan.

CHAPTER 17

Elizabeth clasped her hands around the pouch she had hidden inside her muff and settled her boot-clad feet against the warmed bricks on the floor. Walter's coach was making good time, nearly ten miles an hour, but its rocking motion threatened to put her to sleep. So did last night's vigil. With an effort, she straightened her back against the rolled damask cushion. *I must stay awake. I must go over my plan once again and make certain I've left no stone uncovered.*

Stones still covered a coin purse, filled with a ring, watch and guineas. It was one of the reasons she wanted to meet Rand at the peel tower. She could hear his laughter when she handed him the purse, her dowry, stolen from her fiancé. She might have a vivid imagination, Elizabeth mused, but she could never devise such a subtle plot twist for one of her own novels. Admittedly, she still felt an occasional pang of guilt at her unintentional participation, but then she'd recall Walter's comment about paying triple to bed her. He had been mortified at the theft of his clothes, not the loss of a "paltry" two hundred pounds.

Ever since the coach had rumbled out of the White Hart, Walter and Dorothea had kept up a constant chatter. Elizabeth joined in often enough to appear accommodating, so that Walter would truly believe she meant to marry him. Her hand tightened around the hidden pouch. Once they stopped for the night, she would administer belladonna to both his and Dorothea's drinks. Elizabeth would wait until they were both unconscious, then flee.

During the writing of *Betrayed by a King,* she had researched poisons. In *Betrayed,* wicked Queen Eleanor of Aquitaine had murdered the beautiful, sweet, but undeniably naive Blanche by dumping belladonna into her mead.

I shall just administer a tiny amount, Elizabeth thought. *Enough to give Walter and Dorothea a good night's sleep.*

Although her forthcoming escape was uppermost in her mind, Elizabeth raised the window shade and gazed out at the scenery. Early evening had arrived, but much of the

268

horizon's grayness could be attributed to the numerous coal, brick, and ironworks spewing forth pollution. This part of York was a study in contrasts. Stately mansions, owned by industrialists and great lords, nestled amid parks of surpassing beauty. The seemingly natural parks possessed perfectly placed trees, sham ruins, and placidly grazing sheep or deer, which were kept in their respective pastures by sunken ditches. Only the numerous industrial villages, clustered around mine shafts, marred the idyllic picture.

"I've been inside many of the residences around here," Walter said. "Dearest, please pay me some heed."

"Yes, my lord." With a sigh, Elizabeth turned away from the window and settled her muff more securely in her lap, as if she held a temperamental Pomeranian rather than a tubular covering for her hands.

"You've been entertained inside England's grandest houses, haven't you, my lord?" Dorothea was giving full vent to her euphoria over obtaining Walter as a son-in-law. "And you've probably even lived in them."

Walter smiled ruefully. "To be perfectly honest, I enjoyed entrance to many of these residences as an ordinary —" he coughed as if embarrassed "— working man."

"You have not always been a gentleman of leisure?"

"Now that Elizabeth and I are to be wed, I fear it's time to confess something, Mrs. Wyndham. While I am indeed a member of the Stafford lineage, I'm a fourth cousin from an impoverished family in Birmingham."

Dorothea looked as if a physician had just informed her that she had only scant moments to live. "But what about all your money and property?"

"I earned every shilling and inherited not so much as one acre of land. I am a magnate, Mrs. Wyndham, with a magnate's rank, power and influence."

"Do tell!" At the mention of rank, power and influence, Dorothea had regained her former enthusiasm. "Lord Stafford has secrets he's been keeping from us, Elizabeth."

"Secrets," she echoed politely.

"I left Birmingham for London as a very young man. I was employed by the Bow Street Runners, and in all modesty, I must admit that I established some prominence. Sometimes we Runners solved crimes outside London. That is when I first gained entrance to mansions such as we've passed."

Attention caught, Elizabeth leaned toward

him. "You were a member of the Bow Street Runners?" The Runners was a well known organization of detectives. They had provided the first effective alternative to London's ancient — and inefficient — system of watchmen and parish constables.

"Yes, dearest." Walter preened. "I was rather good at it, I might add, and made a bit of a reputation. Wealthy people often employed me to provide protection against pickpockets. Eventually, I obtained more than a cursory knowledge of London's underworld. It was an interesting job, but not one in which an honest man could become rich. I gave it up in order to pursue a far more profitable though less prestigious occupation."

"And what was that?" Elizabeth asked, fearing the answer. Even without further disclosures, Walter's revelations were unsettling.

"Some called us thief-takers, others bounty hunters, but whatever the name, we tracked down criminals for monetary compensation."

"You're a bounty hunter?" Elizabeth tried for a calm, casual demeanor. "Why did you not mention that fact before?"

"Because I'm retired. And while bounty hunting can be a very lucrative profession, it doesn't enjoy an elevated status. Not that I was ashamed of it, but I wanted to begin an entirely new life as a gentleman. It was the primary reason I moved to the Dales, so far away from all reminders of my past."

"Fascinating," Dorothea exclaimed. "And that's how you came to know London so well."

"I *knew* London. For the past five years I've seldom visited. But it hasn't changed so much that I'll be unable to squire you about and entertain you."

A bounty hunter, Elizabeth thought, squirming in her seat. Walter knew all about crime, which probably meant he already suspected her of planning to poison him.

Walter patted Elizabeth's muff. "You seem a bit pensive, my dear. Are you not excited about our journey and our marriage?"

"Of course." *A Bow Street Runner. A bounty hunter.* She actually felt her eyes widen at the impact of his revelation.

"I own a small but lovely residence on Great George's Street," he continued, "which is one of *the* addresses in London. I purchased it out of the profits I've made as a business partner in a local gambling establishment."

"Goodness," Dorothea cooed. "You have your hand in so many things. Won't he make a fascinating husband, Elizabeth?"

"Fascinating," she echoed dutifully.

"I can't wait to show you all that London has to offer, dearest."

Walter had assumed a fatuous expression, Elizabeth noted, not unlike the coxcombical whips she'd met at Beresford's drum. It was remarkable how Walter slipped in and out of his various roles. No doubt he was a great actor. He had certainly fooled her.

"We shall boat down the Thames," he said with enthusiasm, "and visit the theatres in Drury Lane. And we must stroll the pleasure gardens, especially Vauxhall and Ranelagh, so that we may take tea there and be seen. I want to be seen with you, Elizabeth. Your beauty is your primary asset, which will surely enhance my reputation."

"Don't forget shopping," Dorothea gushed. "You promised you'd take us to Pall Mall and St. Paul's Churchyard and the Strand. Didn't you purchase Elizabeth's necklace in the Strand?"

"Indeed. I paid seventy-five pounds for it, which is undoubtedly more than it's worth. But my extravagance was well rewarded when I saw the expression on Elizabeth's face. She said she would wear it everywhere, didn't you dearest?"

"Yes. Everywhere."

"I said I preferred it 'round her neck." Walter chuckled, then removed a pinch of snuff from his powder blue snuffbox, covered with frolicking nymphs and satyrs.

Dorothea laughed, while Elizabeth clutched her golden coil of a necklace. *I'm in a carriage with a man who made his living tracking down criminals. What have I let slip? What does he know about me that I don't know he knows?*

"And you did promise you would purchase a wedding gown for Elizabeth and at least one new gown for me," Dorothea pressed.

"Of course. But may I remind you that I've already spent a great deal paying off your mortgage, Mrs. Wyndham? You must comprehend that, while I am a man of means, my funds are not unlimited." He passed Dorothea his snuffbox, then addressed Elizabeth. "Once we arrive in London, is there anything you specifically wish to see, dearest?"

"The Tower of London sounds interesting." Elizabeth felt as if she had just been consigned to it. She peered through the window again, avoiding Walter's incisive gaze. In the distance, a couple strolled across a stone bridge that dissected an artificial lake. The lady's golden parasol bobbed like an autumn leaf caught in a current. Lights, the color of buttercups, sprang from the interior of a mansion perched atop a hill. Walter had gained entrance to those homes as a bounty hunter.

"If you want to visit unusual sights," Walter said, "may I suggest Bedlam? It provides hours of entertainment. The woman who tried to assassinate His Majesty is incarcerated there. Margaret somebody-or-other. She's a barber's daughter who believes the Crown is rightfully hers, and if she does not become regent, England will be washed in blood."

Elizabeth shivered. *Washed in blood!*

"Speaking of the king," Dorothea said. "Is there any truth to the rumor that His Majesty has suffered some sort of fit?"

"Unfortunately, yes. While no one has officially mentioned the king's illness, a very good friend of one of His Majesty's body servants sent me a drawn out missive and told me all about it. King George apparently suffers from the Flying Gout, which flew from his legs to his head."

Dorothea clapped her hands. "Do tell. Oh, won't it be fun to be related to somebody who knows something about everything? Elizabeth, pay attention!"

"Something about everything," she murmured, turning her face toward Walter.

Reaching inside his coat, he withdrew a brandy flask from the pocket in which he also carried a pistol. After taking a long pull from the flask, he proceeded to detail King George's obsession with a certain Lady Pembroke. According to Walter, the king sometimes believed Lady Pembroke was his wife and he would order his true queen to get away from him.

"You're remarkably well-informed, my lord," Elizabeth said softly. "What else do you know that you haven't told me?"

A shout obliterated Walter's reply. The coach lurched to a halt. Walter opened the door and leaned out. "Shit," he swore. "Dammit t' hell! We're being robbed."

Elizabeth saw Rand, framed in the doorway. He wore his polished boots, doeskin breeches, white shirt and black cloak. Seated atop his black stallion, his arm was steady as he pointed the muzzle of his pistol at Walter's chest.

"Hide your necklace," Dorothea muttered, stuffing a pair of emerald earbobs and a bracelet down her bodice.

"Outside! Now!" Rand gestured toward the coachman, who sagged against the horses. "You're at my mercy, Stafford, so I suggest you stand and deliver."

Rand had made no effort to disguise

himself. But even while Elizabeth decried his foolishness, she admired his courage. She descended from the carriage, followed by Dorothea, who whispered, "If this scoundrel is who I think he is, should we emerge from this alive I'll strangle you myself. Whatever you do, don't admit to knowing him."

"I shall keep his identity a secret," Elizabeth whispered back, tossing her pouch-filled muff toward a clump of dense, prickly brush. "And that's a promise."

"John Turpin!" Walter exclaimed. "Have you given up dissecting corpses?"

Elizabeth blinked. *Who the bloody hell is John Turpin?*

Rand grinned. "I prefer robbing bastards like you, m'lord."

"I suspected you were Zak Turnbull's accomplice all along." Walter smoothed his coat and adjusted his sleeves, as if readying himself for a social engagement. "I don't know how you gave me the slip after Turnbull's execution, but it is of little consequence. Men such as you never learn and never change their way of life. That's why you're as good as dead."

"Perhaps. But you have something I want, Stafford, and I've come to take it."

Maintaining his attitude of unconcern,

277

Walter brushed an imaginary spot from the front of his coat. "And what might that be, pray tell?"

Rand gestured toward Elizabeth with his pistol.

Walter's eyes widened. "Miss Wyndham?"

"Me?" Elizabeth wrung her hands and fluttered her lashes. "Oh dear, what are you going to do with me?" This was far more exciting than lacing drinks with belladonna.

"I believe you know full well what I plan to do with you. I haven't followed this carriage just to exercise my horse."

Straightening to his full height, Walter eyed Rand as he would a recalcitrant servant. "You may take our worldly goods, Turpin, but you are not to lay a hand on Miss Wyndham. It will go hard on you if you despoil her in any way."

"Hard on me?" Rand laughed. "You can only stretch a man's neck so far, Stafford. I have nothing to lose and everything to gain. *Everything,*" he repeated, his gaze probing Elizabeth's face until his eyes met hers.

Only she understood the true meaning of his words. Clasping her hands in front of her bodice as if she could still the rapid beat of her heart, she heard Dorothea groan.

"Miss Wyndham is betrothed to me!" Walter shouted.

"That is precisely why I want her. Besides, you're not going to live past the next few minutes. Say your prayers, Stafford, and say them quickly."

"Murder!" Dorothea screamed. "Somebody help us!"

Rand removed his attention just long enough for Walter to whip out his hidden pistol. "I have earned myself another reward," he exulted, "and rid England of another vermin." Extending his pistol arm toward Rand, he ordered him to throw his weapon to the ground.

"Shoot him!" urged Dorothea. "That bloody bastard is worth the same dead or alive!"

Elizabeth gaped at her stepmother, but she understood Dorothea's desperation. It was the same desperation that had caused Father to lay last night's trap. What fools they were to think that Rand would betray her. She hadn't betrayed him, had she? *Had she?*

Walter cocked the trigger on his pistol. Almost negligently, Rand kicked his booted foot against Walter's arm. The pistol flew free and skittered across the ground, its discharge swallowed by meadows and copses and spreading sky.

"You'll have to do better than that," said

Rand. "If you think to challenge me, make it worth my time."

He turned to Elizabeth, who shook from head to toe. The death of a lover might be a staple in her novels, but in real life the possibility was decidedly unnerving.

"Pick up Lord Stafford's pistol, Miss Wyndham. Then take all jewelry and purses, please. And that snuffbox. It looks as if it might be worth a few guineas."

"You can't mean to do his bidding," Walter huffed.

"I'm in no position to argue, my lord. Dorothea, I believe you have some earbobs and a bracelet stuffed down your bodice."

"After they hang you, they'll disembowel you and shave off all that pretty black hair. Then they'll dip your body in tar before they chain you in irons." Dorothea's words were directed at Rand, but her gaze remained fixed on Elizabeth.

"Do be quiet, Dorothea," Elizabeth warned. "You'll provoke the highwayman and that could prove dangerous, if not imprudent."

Elizabeth retrieved her stepmother's valuables, then ran her hands rapidly over Walter's clothing and through his pockets. He spread his arms, inviting her frisk. At the same time, his eyes shot daggers. Did he disbelieve her ploy of helplessness?

"Very good, Miss Wyndham," said Rand. "Please place the items in my saddlebag."

After she had complied, he lifted her arm, caressed her wrist with his thumb, and kissed her palm.

"You scoundrel," she said, feigning anger. "As you know, my fiancé is a justice of the peace and he was once a bounty hunter. If you steal me away, he will hunt us down."

"No doubt," Rand murmured, wrapping her hand around a rope. "Take this and return to your companions, Miss Wyndham. Now, tie the foul-mouthed lady to the coachman."

"I'll have your hide for this, Turpin!" Walter shouted. "I'll make certain you're whipped senseless before we hang you."

"Empty threats." Rand's expression hardened as he directed his attention, and his pistol, once again at Walter. "I have a vengeful memory, and a long one. A life for a life, Stafford. Yours for Zak Turnbull's."

"What are you doing?" Elizabeth rushed back and clung to his stirrup. "You can't really mean to kill him."

Leaning over in his saddle, Rand whispered, "You're supposed to be afraid of me, remember? You're not supposed to tell me what I can or cannot do."

She positioned her back to the others. "I don't care. You cannot murder a person in cold blood, even if he deserves it. I told Dorothea and my Aunt Lilith that you had murdered no one."

"A bald-faced lie, my love. I was once a soldier."

"Rand, please!"

"Keep your voice down, Bess. You'll ruin everything."

"Tell Walter you've listened to my heartfelt pleas and have decided to spare him because you can't stand to see a woman in distress."

"A *beautiful* woman in distress."

"I'm warning you, Rand Remington, I won't be a party to Walter's killing. *That* would ruin everything."

Rand studied her for a long moment. Then he straightened in his saddle and addressed Walter. "You're lucky your fiancé is so persuasive, Stafford. Next time we meet, 'twill be a different story. Tie his lordship to the lady and the coachman, Miss Wyndham. You may remove Stafford's wig. It might prove useful. In America, savages scalp their victims, but this is England, more's the pity."

"I'll see you hanged, you bloody bastard," Walter railed.

"Gag him, Miss Wyndham. Rend a piece

of petticoat from the lady."

"I'm sorry, my lord," Elizabeth said, summoning what she hoped was a convincing sob. "But at least I saved your life."

His eyes blazed. By obeying Rand, the law would consider Elizabeth Wyndham a criminal, at the very least an accessory. A child could be hanged for stealing a handkerchief. What would they do to her?

Rand looped a rope over the driver's seat, backed his horse until the rope tightened, then pulled the coach over on its side. Its upended wheels spun round and round, whispering in the dark.

Twilight had vanished, giving way to the night's black cloak, a highwayman's cloak. Rand extended his hand to Elizabeth. "Mount my horse, please."

Biting her lip to keep from singing her joy, still feigning a fearful demeanor, she let Rand settle her atop his stallion, directly in front of him.

They had traveled only a short distance when he said, "Did you doubt for a moment that I'd come after you?"

"There was no need. I had everything under control."

"We make a fine pair, I'll grant you." He kissed her nape before digging his heels into his stallion's flank.

The horse bolted from the meadow, onto the deserted highway.

The rays from the rising sun illuminated the forest, which rested like a dark fleece upon the rolling hills. Turning off the road, Rand guided his stallion into the forest's chill depths. Elizabeth followed on the gray mare Rand had purchased from some nameless individual at some nameless inn along the way. Their entire journey had been a bewildering succession of side roads and open fields, possessing a distinct air of unreality.

They plunged farther into the woods. The trees grew more impenetrable, as if daybreak had given way to night. Bracken *whooshed* against their horses' legs. Finally, Rand dismounted. He held out his arms and Elizabeth slid from her mare. Then she remained wrapped in his embrace, not thinking, just enjoying the caress of his hands, the beat of his heart, the warmth of his body. If they had not been reunited, surely she would have died for want of him.

"What next?" she said. "What is your plan?"

Rand kissed the tip of her nose. "I hate plans, Bess. They destroy life's excitement."

"Who the bloody hell is John Turpin?"

284

"A reprehensible rogue who resembles me. I've oft used the alias."

"How much time do we have before Walter is on our trail?"

Rand shrugged. "Not long, I trust. Nor do I want to stay too well hidden. I meant it when I said I had a score to settle. I'll let Stafford follow us until I decide to catch him."

Elizabeth sighed, resigned to the inevitable. Next time she would not be allowed to stay Rand's hand. "Did you know Walter was once a bounty hunter?"

"Yes. And a member of the Bow Street Runners."

She leaned back to better study Rand's face. "How did you know?"

"After Zak's execution, I visited London. I have family there. Besides, even in a city of a million people, 'tis not difficult to ferret out information."

"I wish you'd forget about revenge. Ultimately, Zak's utter disregard for the law led to his capture."

"Are you defending Walter Stafford?"

"No. Of course not."

"You weren't really going to London with him. You wouldn't have betrayed me, would you Bess?"

"Never!" *You betrayed him long ago.* She

buried her face against his chest. *Don't you remember? Don't you know?* She tried to drown out the mocking whisper with words. "Even if Walter had not hanged your cousin, you'd still feel obligated to leave a deliberate trail. The possibility of danger excites you, doesn't it?"

"Perhaps." He grinned. "But the possibility of danger excites you, as well."

"The possibility of death does not," she replied somewhat primly, noting that the grin on his lips lingered, unchanged. Delicious fear shivered through her. Was he right? Did she court danger? All her recent actions said she did.

Her gaze skimmed his face. A face that had never left her thoughts since their very first meeting. A face that had dominated her thoughts since her very first book.

That perception triggered a rush of excitement in her blood that had nothing to do with the possibility of danger.

Or perhaps it did.

Rand reached out and gently grasped her shoulders. "I love you, Bess. I always have, and I always will."

He drew her close and lowered his mouth to her breasts, and she half feared, half anticipated the return of her raven-haired knight.

The knight didn't appear, but she sensed him waiting in the shadows, just beyond her sight. The man she hated and loved and feared. The man who seemed to have spanned five hundred years, only to torment her once again.

Elizabeth rested her head upon her bent knees. The small of her back pressed against the grooved bark of a giant oak.

Through half-closed eyes, she watched Rand arrange for them a bed of bracken. They must sleep during the day, he had said, and ride through the night, until they had traveled a bit farther. If Elizabeth craned her head, she could see a gray patch of morning sky, but the forest remained wrapped in secret shadows. They were safe here. For the moment, they were safe.

Rand straightened and faced her. "Listen to me, Bess. If things somehow go amiss and we're ever captured, you're to say you had no choice but to obey me. Under no circumstances will you try to rescue me or champion me. You'll denounce me to everyone. Is that clear?"

"No one need ever find us, Rand. If you give up your revenge scheme, we can remain invisible for as long as we wish."

His mouth twisted. "The wind is invisible,

Bess. Ghosts are invisible. Since we are neither, we must consider the possibility of capture."

Stroking a patch of lichen, she could almost believe they were ghosts, or memories lost in a forest. "We won't be caught unless we want to be," she insisted.

Rand returned to the task at hand. While working, he hummed to himself. Elizabeth listened to his song, interspersed by the *sip-sip-sip* of a wood warbler. Her fatigued mind began to drift, riding with the music's rise and fall. Then her eyes snapped open and she jerked upright. "What is the name of that song, Rand?"

"I have no idea." He placed his cloak atop the bed of bracken. " 'Tis just something that came into my head."

"You've never heard it before?"

He shrugged. "I haven't much thought about it."

Elizabeth felt as if a dozen centipedes crept down her back. She had heard that very same melancholy melody at Lord Stafford's fête. Trying to shut out the memory, she said, "You never did tell me, Rand. Where, exactly, are we headed?"

"We can travel to Cornwall, 'tis where I'm from. Or to Dover, and beyond to the Continent." He eyed her speculatively. "Or we might go to Evesham."

"What's in Evesham?"

"Answers, perhaps. At least some of them."

"Answers to what?"

"To how we're connected. To our past."

"You already know far more than I do." She clutched her knees against her breasts. "Why won't you tell me? Perhaps we can figure it out together."

"What did you see the night they captured Zak?"

"What makes you think I saw anything out of the ordinary?"

"I was nearby. I heard your screams."

She stiffened. "It was a trick of my mind. I don't want to think about it."

"I need to know, Bess."

"And I need to know what's at Evesham, and how you could sing a song supposedly foreign to both of us. Why did you call me Janey? Did I really lie with you that night at Fountains Abbey? Or was it somebody else?"

"What the bloody hell are you talking about?"

"Fountains Abbey. You called me Janey, and you looked . . . sounded . . ." Her heart fluttered like a captured bird. Rand didn't remember. Nay. Rand didn't *know*. Had she imagined the roughness of his countenance? His beard? Had that been a trick of her mind, too? "You looked and sounded like someone from my . . . from the past," she stammered.

Rand gazed at Bess's face, pale and flower-like beneath the masses of her dark, tangled hair. Someone from her past?

He desperately wanted to explain, but how could he explain something he himself didn't fully comprehend? Furthermore, he suspected that any explanation might cause her to suffer the black moods he experienced. That would be disastrous. He needed her strength, her stubbornness, her determination.

His lips curved as he recalled her frequent rides across the moors, after his return from London. How many times had he been tempted to intercept her? He had told himself over and over that such an action would place her in grave danger. Then she had sought him out at Fountains Abbey, drawn to him, as he was drawn to her, by some invisible bond linking them together. Once again he had tried to dissuade her, claiming he had been asleep, not thinking of her — a bald-faced lie. He had thought about nothing else *but* her.

If his quest to discover the secrets of the

past proved futile, he would leave England and start a new life. However, she would stay by his side; two shadows melding into one. He couldn't let her go, even though he recognized the reality of his capture and death. They might have days, weeks, perhaps months to enjoy each other, but he now knew that a life without Bess was no life at all. In any case, she wouldn't accept his dismissal. She never had, not since the beginning.

"Why did you call me Janey?" Bess repeated.

"I don't know." Rand nodded toward the bracken. "Come, my bonny sweetheart," he urged. "I'll not cry out another woman's name, and that's a promise."

CHAPTER 18

The next afternoon, Elizabeth and Rand skirted Nottingham. The spires of its cathedrals thrust above the autumn-tinted trees, while factory and chimney smoke blended into a glowering sky. An earlier rain had muddied the highway, deepening ruts and making travel difficult. Elizabeth ached for a long rest, yet she knew the soaked ground would be even more uncomfortable than her saddle.

On a lonely stretch of road they came upon an overturned coach. Trunks and boxes were strewn about. The coach, scarlet in color, possessed a coat of arms with the representation of a castle on its gilded doors. A liveried coachman and a guard both bent between the wheels, peering at the undercarriage.

A beautiful blonde woman lifted her silk skirts and picked her way through the mire. "Can you help us? I am the Duchess of

Newcastle. As you can see, my husband and I have run into a bit of poor luck." After glancing toward Elizabeth, who had stolen clothing from various hedges and was dressed as a man, the lady gave a little *moue* of disgust, then focused on Rand.

"What happened?" he asked.

"Our carriage has a broken axle." The blonde lady was Elizabeth's own age, and had been blessed with slanted green eyes, a lush figure, small white teeth, and a dimple which she now displayed for Rand's benefit. "You look like a capable gentleman, sir. You'll help us, won't you?"

Rand turned in his saddle and winked at Elizabeth. "Watch this!"

"Don't you dare!"

Elizabeth drummed her fingertips against her brown velvet breeches as she watched Rand guide his horse closer. The blonde lady sidled toward him, dimpling and oozing sensuality. From the front of the carriage, her husband appeared. The duke was short and stooped and ancient. Pouches of skin surrounded his protuberant eyes, while a receding chin melted into the flabby folds that hid his neck.

"We're run into a problem, sir." From the jeweled buckles on his shoes to his laced shirt and green velvet coat, the duke was spattered with muck, and yet Elizabeth thought his manner still carried an unmistakable air of authority.

"It would appear that way." Rand's hand rested on his doeskin breeches, not far from his pistol.

"Damme," Elizabeth breathed. She was now certain that Rand was going to rob the duke and duchess. *That* would erase the lady's dimples.

"Our axle has snapped clean in two," the duke said. "I had thought to send my guard, but if you rode back to Nottingham it would be much quicker. I'm bound for London and had planned to make Coventry by nightfall. I haven't a lot of time."

"I haven't much time, either," Rand said.

"But my business is important."

"Really, Charles!" The blonde lady smiled at Rand. "If you would address this gentleman a bit more tactfully, I'm sure he would help. He looks . . . agreeable."

Ignoring his wife, Charles pulled out his timepiece. "We're already hours behind schedule."

"That's a fine watch," Rand said.

Here it comes, Elizabeth thought, pulling down her wide-brimmed hat to conceal her face. She rested her right hand on the butt of Lord Stafford's pistol, which she now carried in the belt of her shabby breeches.

Rand grinned. "I'm a connoisseur of watches," he said, "and I've a mind to add yours to my collection."

The duke blinked.

Rand pulled out his pistol. "Hand it over."

"Dear me," said the blonde lady. "We're being robbed. I should have known. You're far too handsome to be respectable."

Rand raised his voice and addressed the servants. "On the ground! Spread your arms and legs!"

While the men scurried to obey, Charles said, "You cannot do this. There are four people here who can identify you. It would be the height of foolishness for you to proceed —"

"Give me your coat and your purse. And just to make this equitable, m'lady, why don't you hand over that diamond ring?"

She removed it from her finger. "The last time we were robbed, the highwayman apologized. He swore he was from a good family and had been brought to crime by his weakness for gambling. Will you not even offer an insincere apology?"

Rand shook his head. "I never apologize."

Handing him her ring, she thrust her breasts forward. "Would you like my necklace as well, Sir Highwayman?"

"No. It shines far brighter 'round your beautiful neck."

Elizabeth fumed.

The blonde lady dimpled.

"While I realize you've seduced every man from here to Cornwall, Katherine," Charles told his wife, "I ask that this once you *pretend* to be well-bred."

Katherine's green eyes slanted even more, if possible. She held her tongue, but Elizabeth could see that it took a vast amount of self-control.

After ordering the duke to prostrate himself beside his servants, Rand beckoned to the duchess. When she reached his side, he encircled her with his arms and kissed her hard upon the lips.

Raising his head above the mud, Charles flushed angrily.

Elizabeth gasped.

Rand reached into his pocket, removed Walter's snuffbox, then wrapped Katherine's hands around it. "So you'll not forget me."

"How could I forget you?"

Rand kicked his stallion and raced away.

Elizabeth followed. Once safely out of sight, she turned on him in fury. "Why did you kiss that creature? And right in front of me! Damn you to hell, Rand Remington! You embarrassed me and enraged the lady's husband."

"That's precisely why I kissed her. The duke will remember me. And the snuffbox has Stafford's name inside. I'll wager Newcastle will waste no time tracking Stafford down. The duke might even put a handsome reward on my head."

"You didn't have to *kiss* her!"

"Nothing infuriates the nobility more than to think the lower classes might be forgetting their place. They fear we shall rise up against them, like Simon de Montfort did."

Elizabeth felt as if a knife had pricked her. "What do you know about Simon de Montfort?"

"I met him in *Castles of Doom* and was merely using him as an example, like Oliver Cromwell or some other rabble-rouser." Rand stared into her eyes. "Never doubt that I love you, Bess, or that I would ever want any woman but you. What I did, I did for a reason."

"But I felt so awful when you kissed her."

"I apologize." Lifting Elizabeth from her saddle, Rand settled her across his lap.

"You never apologize," she reminded him.

"I never have until now." He gently thumbed away her tears. "I would have embraced the devil himself to infuriate the duke, but I wish now I had employed some other method. I love you, little one, and I'm truly sorry I caused you distress."

"*She* often felt distressed, I think."

"Who?"

Elizabeth opened her mouth to speak, before shaking her head. The other woman in her life wasn't the Duchess of Newcastle. The other woman in her life appeared to be a lady dead five hundred years. A lady she could not even say for sure had ever existed.

The town of Alcester, in Warwickshire, was located at the juncture of the Alne and Arrow Rivers. From her vantage point inside the King George's Inn's tiny room, Elizabeth fancied she could hear a whisper of current somewhere in the darkness. She gazed out the narrow window. Timber-framed buildings reflected the light from the rising moon. Unable to sleep, she listened to Alcester fold itself inward, like the petals of a flower. She could almost swear she heard her fellow travelers settle atop their lumpy, lice-ridden beds.

King George's could learn from the White Hart, she thought. *Father's bedrooms have quilts and looking glasses and chamber pots. These rooms have filth.*

Not that she was homesick. She really didn't have a home. She and Rand had been on the run for seven days. During that time, they had zigzagged, backtracked, and traveled in such a circuitous fashion she generally had no idea where they were, although Rand sprinkled clues at every stop. In Coventry, he had pawned all the items they'd stolen, which meant that while Elizabeth might be totally confused, Walter would eventually unravel their route.

Staring into the night, listening to the murmur of the water, Elizabeth tried to overcome the fear gnawing at her stomach. It wasn't fear of Walter or the law, but something more . . . primitive. She sensed similar emotions in Rand, or at least a withdrawal. Since their arrival at Alcester, he'd scarcely spoken.

She heard a groan and swiftly made an about-face. Rand stirred, then jerked upright, as if snapped by a rope. "Nightmares?" she asked softly.

Leaving the bed, he walked toward her. "I've never liked this part of England." He placed his hands upon her shoulders. "I always sleep troubled here."

Elizabeth stroked his fingers. "I feel the same. But I can't think why since I've never been here before."

"We are near the Vale of Evesham," he murmured, as if that explained everything.

"You once said you misliked the south because it reminded you of the war."

"Yes . . . the war."

"Perhaps we should have traveled a different route."

"There are answers in Evesham, Bess, if we're up to facing them." Rand's hands tightened on her shoulders.

Tell me what you know right now! Elizabeth didn't voice her command. The closer they came to Evesham, the less certain she felt. Did she really want to explore anything? Did she really want answers?

"Get back into bed, my love," she said. "You're shivering."

"So are you. Come with me."

"Soon."

Soon blended into minutes, then an hour, and she remained by the window. The quarter moon now rested directly above Alcester. Wisps of clouds crept across clusters of stars. From the street below, the sound of a flute or shepherd's pipe wafted upward.

Elizabeth's breath caught in her throat. The tune was the same one she had heard at Walter's fête, the same tune Rand had hummed.

Fumbling with the latch, she swung open the window. Music drifted in upon the sudden breeze, slow and mournful, piercing to the soul. She squeezed her eyes shut and allowed the strain to curl around her, tugging at her. It teased her with its memory of something more, something she could not identify.

She opened her eyes and glanced toward Rand. He tossed and turned, his teeth clenched. Elizabeth wanted to crawl inside his dream and help him fight his demons. Since that was impossible, she hastily donned her breeches and shirt.

Exiting the inn, she followed the thread of the music. The streets were deserted. She halted, one bare foot suspended. Now the music seemed to be coming from everywhere and nowhere.

A jumble of images sprang into her mind. She was waiting in a dark exactly like this one. It was so dark in the stone passageway, and cold, for it had always been cold, even on the hottest summer days. She was waiting for someone — someone unpleasant. They shared a secret that would destroy her life. And save it. While she waited, she heard the music, emanating from the banquet hall below.

Without warning, the music ceased. Elizabeth lowered her foot and looked around. Why was she standing alone on a deserted street? Why did she feel so cold? And why did the word *betrayal* pound inside her head like a kettledrum?

"I'm in Alcester," she said, clenching her fists. " 'Tis Tuesday, the fifteenth of October, and I'm cold because my feet are bare." She didn't try to explain away the word *betrayal*, since she feared the little voice, possibly Janey's voice, would whisper: *Don't you know, Bess? Don't you remember?*

Stepping on pebbles and floorboards as if they were rosebuds and fur pelts, Elizabeth returned to her room. She slipped into bed beside Rand, then tried to ignore the fear writhing inside her like a snake, twisting and turning on itself.

The next morning she and Rand ate breakfast in the common room. They had purchased wigs and clothing at a second-hand shop, and were dressed as a merchant and his wife. Elizabeth thought they blended well with the handful of other couples who shared the low-ceilinged room.

As she poked at the pancakes on her chipped plate, she said, "This food's worse than the blasted bedrooms."

Rand merely watched two men enter the inn. One was indistinguishable from a thousand other working-class men, while the other was tall and emaciated.

"He looks like a fugitive from a bone pile," she blurted.

"He's poor, Bess. Poverty and hunger go hand in hand."

"That's why you try to help the poor."

"Please, sweetheart. Don't imbue me with altruistic motives."

"But they *are* altruistic, Rand. Old Fife's baby would have died had you not bought a cow with your ill-gotten gains. My ostler told me," she added.

"The tales of my kindheartedness are vastly embroidered."

"Nonsense. You could have *stolen* the cow. And you purchased my mare, rather than stealing her." When he didn't respond, she sipped her coffee, which tasted like mud. Then she speared a piece of bacon. Fat bubbled on both sides, and she decided to forgo meat with her meal.

Rand abruptly stood. "We must hurry if we're to make the port of Dover as we planned," he said loudly.

"Dover? I thought we —"

"Hurry! We have well over a hundred miles yet!"

"Why are you shouting?"

Rand leaned over and whispered, "Would you please quit asking questions and do as you're told?"

Once outside, he walked quickly toward the stables. "I'll wager those two men are bounty hunters, Bess, which means Stafford has already plastered handbills and reward posters from here to Plymouth."

"Are you certain? They looked like ordinary men to me. Maybe a bit scruffier than usual, but —"

"Who do you think goes after those rewards? I know I'm right. I've developed a sixth sense about this sort of thing."

"In your business, you have to," she muttered, reaching the stable entrance.

They retrieved their horses with a minimum of fuss.

Beyond the inn, Rand dismounted in front of a sprawling four-storied building bearing the sign JOHNSON'S ANCIENT AND MODERN PRINT WAREHOUSE. Their horses mingled with a half dozen others, plus several carriages.

"Go inside and wait for me, Bess, while I rid us of those bounty hunters. I want *Stafford* after me, not anybody else."

She watched Rand race back toward the stables. Then she tethered Prancer and the mare she had christened Greylag, named for the common grey wild goose. Finally, she entered the warehouse.

The main room contained a clerestory

which bathed the hundreds of prints in natural light. Elizabeth pretended to study the prints. Rand must be wrong, she thought. It was too soon for bounty hunters. The ordinary reward of forty pounds for a highwayman would not entice them so quickly. Perhaps the Duke of Newcastle had offered an additional sum, but wasn't that too soon as well?

On the other hand, Walter had ties with the Bow Street Runners. Rand said the Runners kept in touch with magistrates all over England, and the magistrates often spread handbills at inns and stables. The Runners also published the *Quarterly Pursuit* and the *Weekly or Extraordinary Pursuit,* detailing criminals who had escaped from their original districts. According to Rand, the success rate of those two papers was fairly high. With Walter masterminding the chase, Rand could be right.

By the time he returned, she had leafed through eight how-to books on plant drawing, and couldn't remember the contents of any. As he escorted her out the door, she whispered, "What is going on?"

"Nothing now." Rand helped her mount Greylag. "But I wasn't wrong. According to the stable hand, those damnfool thief catchers are bound for Dover in hot pursuit of their reward."

"How did they find out about us?"

"A handbill, I would imagine."

Elizabeth's fingers crept up to clutch at her golden necklace, hidden beneath her prim white collar. "Are we still bound for Evesham? Perhaps we should forget about the past or snaring Walter and get as far away from here as possible. I don't care about revenge. I want to escape. Please, my love."

Rand compressed his lips and said nothing.

He was playing the Quiet Companion again.

The Vale of Evesham was a fertile spot, nestled in a long loop of the River Avon. Orchards were scattered among the recently harvested fields, and the surrounding area was dotted with abbey ruins. Green Hill dominated the sky's vista. Elizabeth had never seen Green Hill before, nor did she know its history, and yet the very sight of it filled her with foreboding. Rand apparently felt the same, for he remained uncommunicative.

Despite their mutual unease, they headed toward Green Hill as relentlessly as spawning salmon struggling upstream. If they passed travelers or farmers in their carts, or mail coaches, or boats gliding upon the River Avon, Elizabeth couldn't say. All she saw was Rand's broad back and his stallion's haunches.

Above Green Hill, a flock of birds strained across the morning sky. Elizabeth recalled an old wives' tale which told that such birds, from their vantage point above the earth, could easily observe strangers and changes of any sort. Thus, they were considered heralds of death.

Rand finally reached the base of the hill. Elizabeth nudged Greylag alongside Prancer. The remains of an abbey, leveled save for a bell tower, sprawled in one corner. "It seems peculiar that the Battle of Guilford Court House took place on a hill of the very same name," she murmured, "and with an abbey as well."

Rand gave her an enigmatic look, but did not reply.

They dismounted at the remains of Evesham Abbey. A cloud passed over the autumn sun, plunging the hill into shadow, hiding the brightness of the grass. Elizabeth shivered, then watched Rand gaze up at the cloud. His face expressed such intense concentration she knew he must be remembering something.

Her heart began a dreadful pounding, not unlike a funeral knell. "This is a place of blood, isn't it?"

"May God have mercy on our souls," he said. "For our bodies are theirs."

Fear prickled Elizabeth's nape. "What is this place? You know, don't you?"

The cloud edged beyond the sun. Its rays again warmed her.

"Wait for me here," said Rand.

"Where are you going?" Even to her own ears, her voice sounded strident with fear.

"I'll be back by dark."

"I want to go with you."

"Whatever is revealed to me will be revealed to you. We're linked, Bess. You know that. You've known it from the start."

"I don't want to be alone." She placed her hand on his arm, as if that could stay him. "There are memories here."

"There are memories everywhere." He lifted her hand and kissed her palm, before turning away and striding up the hill.

Elizabeth watched his mantle swirl around his boots — a black mantle which should have been red. She watched the sun glint across the blackness of his hair, which should have been even blacker. She saw his shaven chin, which should have possessed a beard, and she felt as if a hand squeezed her throat.

"Don't go!" she screamed. "I'm sorry! Don't leave me!"

She ran after him, but he was far ahead of her, and by the time she reached Green Hill's summit, he had vanished.

Leaning over her, he smiled.

His beard was raven-colored, as was his hair, thick and curling below his ears, covering the coif which rested upon his nape. A black hawk was emblazoned across the front of his wine-colored surcoat. His long sword was belted low on his left hip. He grinned at her as he bent to kiss her good-bye. She hated him. Hated him and clung to him, sobbing into his hawk.

"Don't go! I'm sorry! Don't leave me!" She loved him, even if she had betrayed him, betrayed them all.

She didn't stand on the parapet and watch him ride away, though she usually did. She would watch him die, instead.

From the coolness of the abbey, where the monks chanted the Hours of the Dead, she viewed the battle. The royal forces outnumbered the rebels so completely, it would be murder rather than battle, but he would not have chosen any other way to die. She had given him that much, at least.

The fighting was savage and disjointed. Above the chants of the monks, she heard the cries of men and horses, the ringing of swords. She spotted his lord's banner near the crest of the hill — the red vertical lines angled across the gold. She knew he would be there, where the fighting was fiercest. Fighting not so much for his lord's cause, but because he loved war more than life. He loved war more than food or drink or beautiful women or sunsets; more than swift horses, land, and friendship. Certainly more than her.

The sky blackened and a wind sprang up, howling through the abbey. She began to cry. She wanted to call him back and tell him that she hadn't meant to betray him, but she could not reclaim the days. Instead, she must reap what she had sown, in all its bitter harvest.

Around him knights dropped as suddenly as if felled by the lightning that cracked across the sky. One hundred sixty knights on the rebels' side, but only a handful remained. He was one, of course, fighting as if he were a new knight and it was his first battle. But he was a man of forty-five, and it was his last.

Knights surrounded him. Knights that belonged to the king. Twenty knights for every rebel. The sky grew darker and darker until she could see only two things clearly — the flash of lightning and the flash of swords. His horse reared above the other mounted knights. She glimpsed a blur of red just before his surcoat disappeared and his horse toppled over and the knights closed in on him.

"Ranulf!" she screamed.

Elizabeth awakened.

The night's chill bumped her perspiration-streaked body and cooled her cheeks, awash with tears. The abbey ruins surrounded her. She saw Rand, leaning against the bell tower, his arms folded across his chest, his gaze directed toward the darkness that was Green Hill.

"Ranulf," she whispered. The name had always been there. Even before her visit to the central library, the name had been a shadowed outline in her mind.

She crossed the ruins, trembling from the remnants of her dream. Disentangling Rand's arms, she pressed her face against his shoulder. She didn't look to see whether the man who stroked her back was Rand or Ranulf. In this blighted place, soaked with the tragedy of the past, it might be either.

Finally, she raised her gaze to his face. "You mixed up the two battles, didn't you? It wasn't only the Battle of Guilford Court House you told me about at Fountains Abbey, but an ancient one."

"The Battle of Evesham. Simon de Montfort had overthrown Henry and ruled England for eight months. He died up there, at the crest of Green Hill. His body was hacked to pieces. His head was cut off, his legs and arms . . . everything mutilated. It was a reminder of what happens to traitors."

Elizabeth shuddered. She could imagine such a sight. Or had she personally witnessed it? "You also died, didn't you?"

"I think so. Sometimes I know I did. As a boy, I used to relive the battle in my dreams. I was riddled with wounds, but 'twas my horse that fell on me, breaking my leg. Then it was an easy matter to finish me off." Releasing her, he moved away from the tower. "Here, I can believe the truth of those dreams."

"Dreams," she echoed, swallowing a sob.

He turned, facing her. "I would suffer what Zak called black moods, but I hadn't dreamed of Evesham in years, not until the night preceding Lady Avery's robbery, shortly before I met you. After Beresford's drum, I researched the *Alcester Chronicles*." He gave her a lopsided grin. "I resisted temptation, Bess, which required an almost inhuman effort."

"Temptation?"

"You were in London, my love, so close I

could almost reach out and touch you. Then, when I inadvertently robbed your coach, I knew for certain. You were the one. I didn't want to reopen those memories, and yet I couldn't let them be. I kept picking at them, like a child picking at a scab."

"But what have I got to do with your memories? I know we're connected, Rand, but how?"

He shrugged. "You tell me."

She gazed beyond him, toward the blackness of Green Hill and the dark sky, unmarred by stars. The Battle of Evesham had taken place earlier in the year, when summer had been at its fullest, when the earth had smelled of flowers and hay and sleepy rivers and soft rains. "You called me Janey. Is that who we were? A knight named Ranulf and his lady Jane?"

"Ranulf Navarre. That was his name. Perhaps you are right, Bess, I don't know. Sometimes it seems that way."

"But the rebirth of a soul isn't scriptural."

"Do you have a better explanation?"

"England is an ancient country and so much has happened here. Perhaps we're trapped in some sort of whirlpool, filled with memories."

"Perhaps."

"If we really are those people, Ranulf and

Jane, I assume we're supposed to learn from the past." *You betrayed him,* her little voice whispered. *Does he know that?* "Are we supposed to atone for our past sins in this life?"

"I have no idea, but I'm sure we'll find out." He extended his arms, and she nestled against his warmth. "If you want all the answers, I think I know where we can find them. Ranulf Navarre is buried at Southwark Cathedral, in London."

"London? But we can't! 'Tis far too dangerous."

Terror stabbed through her. Should they uncover the truth, Rand would learn that she had betrayed him. She didn't even know the manner of betrayal and she couldn't face such painful revelations. She had lived through them once, centuries ago. Why suffer the past all over again?

"Why have we been brought back?" Rand asked, his voice soft. "If we live several lives, why are we the only ones who remember our past? There must be a reason. We can't walk away from it or we shall be doomed to repeat it."

"Do you really think so?"

"I think we should go to London."

Elizabeth's mind raced. For weeks she had sworn she'd confront Charles Beresford. Hadn't her carriage ride to London been

314

undertaken with that thought in mind? True, she had sacrificed her independence, her most precious commodity, in order to keep Dorothea from revealing Rand's identity. But she had decided that, after drugging Walter and her blasted stepmother, she would find Beresford and demand her money.

Having already conceded that her father's addiction to gambling was no longer her problem, she would use her fortune for an escape, perhaps even passage to America. She and Rand would be free. Freedom required money. She had money. It was so simple when broached in those terms.

She wove her fingers through Rand's hair. She had oft stroked Ranulf's curls, so thick and black. After the battle, Green Hill was black, its curtain of darkness pierced by a line of torches, held aloft by the monks who brought Ranulf back to her. *But Ranulf had gone to his death ignorant of her betrayal.*

Elizabeth's logic deserted her. "Leave it rest in peace," she cried. "Please, Rand!"

He tilted her chin and stared into her eyes. "What do you know that you are not telling me?"

She shook her head vehemently. "Make love to me," she implored.

"No, Bess, not here, not now."

"Don't you understand? We can only defeat death by proving that we are alive. Making love will prove —"

"No! You want an illusion, Bess."

"Love isn't an illusion. Love is an emotion."

"My emotions are drained!" he shouted. "I have neither the will, nor the strength. Love is *not* the answer, Bess."

"Then what is?"

"London."

"I don't believe you." She touched his cheek, then drew her finger slowly down his jaw and across his lips.

Her motion was a deliberate tease. Heat radiated through Rand's loins as he captured her finger between his teeth and ran his tongue back and forth.

"I don't believe you," Bess repeated, freeing her finger and using both hands to draw him down, onto the grass. The bell tower loomed above them.

Rand felt her firm legs beneath his breeches. He smelled her warm female scent. Taut and helpless, he was unable to turn away from her mesmerizing gaze, and yet he saw nothing but love in her eyes. She was right. This wasn't an illusion.

He kissed her breasts, all the while caressing the soft whorls between her legs. Then he unfastened the flap of his breeches, spread his hands against the ground, and buried himself deep within her. With a soft moan, she rode his erection, as she had once ridden across the moors, her body demanding his thrusts.

Instead, he reached his hand up and crushed a strand of her hair between his fingers, rubbing the dark silk, striving to slow his breathing and bring it under control. *Her* breath was still ragged, but he felt her belly relax against his. He began again, his hands caressing. This time she responded like a cat, curving sinuously into his strokes. He heard throaty purrs of pleasure.

Rand remained inside her, hot and hard, until her purrs became happy whimpers. Then and only then did he thrust, until her body quivered and his body quivered and the ancient bell tower rang with the music of their ecstasy.

Afterwards, watching him sleep, Elizabeth understood that neither tears nor pleas nor threats would deter Rand's obsessive need to probe the otherworldliness that was Ranulf Navarre.

Their next destination would be London.

CHAPTER 19

Elizabeth stared into the dark, her senses alert. Her ears strained for the sound which had jolted her out of a deep sleep. Her eyes sought any unusual movement, but everything seemed in order.

Around ten o'clock they had rented a room in an inn on the outskirts of Oxford. Elizabeth had no idea what time it was now, nor how long she'd slept. She only knew that something had changed. Beneath her shift, her skin felt itchy.

Sending out invisible tentacles, she probed the darkness. Then, gradually, she began to relax, deliberately easing the tenseness from her muscles. Rand lay beside her, his eyes shut, his breathing regular.

Perhaps I was dreaming, perhaps I'm still dreaming.

Something scraped just beyond the door, which was locked from the inside. Easing herself up, she ran her fingers through the scrim of sleep-tousled hair that shaded her eyes. Door locks could easily be picked.

She inched her right leg sideways until it touched Rand's breeches. His hand squeezed hers. "If anything happens, escape out the window," he whispered.

Maneuvering toward the edge of the bed, he leaned over and retrieved his pistol.

Elizabeth had no wish to jump from a second-story window, but now was not the time to argue. Rolling from the bed, crouched on the floor, she groped for her own pistol.

Metal scraped against metal. There was a loud click.

Chest bare, feet bare, Rand strode across the tiny room and stood behind the door.

Elizabeth raised her head and shoulders above the straw mattress. Moonlight streamed through the narrow window and pooled upon their clothes, folded across the bottom of the bed. The shadows fashioned by the rumpled blankets gave the appearance of bodies.

Perhaps 'tis a servant checking all the doors, she thought hopefully. *Or somebody who mistook our room for his. Such things do happen.*

The door creaked open. Elizabeth's heart drummed so loudly, she was certain Rand could hear it. Not only Rand, but the intruder. He would track her by the booming of her heart.

Rand raised his pistol and pressed his body against the wall.

A hand appeared, then a head. Despite the moonlight, it was too dark to distinguish any features.

Elizabeth watched the rest of the man slip into the room. He was so thin, he might have been a skeleton. He was tall and faceless and totally unexpected. Elizabeth imagined Death would appear like that. Except Death wouldn't point a gun at the bed. Death wouldn't have to. He'd merely beckon and — damn! The bounty hunter! The one who looked like a fugitive from a bone pile. Rand hadn't fooled him, after all.

Crouching down lower, she felt her legs tremble, as did her hand when she cocked her pistol. She crawled around the foot of the bed and once again peered toward the door.

She saw Rand step behind the skeleton man. At that very moment, a second man entered the room. His gun barrel gleamed, and Elizabeth could see that it was pointed at Rand's back. Rearing up, she fired. A roar rattled the window and a flash illuminated her hand.

"No, Bess!" Rand yelled.

She thought she saw a dumbfounded look on the skeleton man's face, and she suddenly realized that her pistol's bright flash had clarified a portion of her own face.

Rand's shout had given away his position. The skeleton man spun around. Rand slammed him across the skull and he collapsed on the floor next to his partner.

"Let's get out of here." Thrusting his pistol into the waistband of his breeches, scooping up their boots, Rand headed for the window and fumbled with the latch.

"Hurry!" she cried, her fingers curling around the handle of the traveling bag that contained their disguises.

Rand flung open the window and leaned out. "Part of the common room juts directly below, so we need only ease ourselves onto its roof."

Elizabeth was shaking so badly she could scarcely stand. Repeatedly, she looked over her shoulder at the two motionless shapes on the floor. "Do you think I killed him?"

"I don't know." Untangling her stiff, clawed fingers from her pistol, Rand stowed it inside one of his boots. "Perhaps you just nicked him."

Footsteps sounded in the corridor, voices from the adjoining room. Swallowing her fear, Elizabeth allowed Rand to shove her through the window's narrow opening. He followed, whereupon they hurried along the roof line then dropped to the ground. She felt her knees and ankles protest but no bones snapped, thank God. Passing the kit to Rand, she thrust her feet into the boots he tossed her, then ran toward the stables.

Was the skeleton man chasing them? Elizabeth twisted her head and glanced over her shoulder. She saw lights spring from various windows. It seemed an eternity before they reached the horse sheds.

Rand retrieved her pistol and handed it over. "Try to look fierce," he whispered.

Gritting her teeth, Elizabeth aimed her gun toward the stable boy while Rand tugged on his boots. Then he saddled their mounts. Luckily, the stable boy was frightened out of his wits, for her gun wasn't primed.

Had it been primed, she could not have pulled the trigger.

"I didn't kill anyone," she muttered under her breath. "I just nicked him." But even if she had killed him, what choice did she have? He would have shot Rand. He would have shot her. Damn Walter Stafford and his blasted reward!

As she swung up on Greylag and they clattered out of the inn yard, Rand said, "You shouldn't have fired at the bounty hunter, Bess. I could have handled the situation." His voice chastised, and she was appalled, for she might very well have saved his life.

They raced through Oxford's sleepy streets and beyond. Moonlight glinted upon the River Thames, which wound along farms and pastureland. The river seemed to chase Prancer and Greylag, but — fortunately — it was the only thing that did.

Cold air stung Elizabeth's cheeks and sliced through her linen shift. Her mind raced in concert with her mare's pounding hooves. The flash of her pistol had illuminated her face and Rand had called her Bess. *I'll hang from the gallows alongside Rand,* she thought, swallowing a sob.

Would that be so bad? She didn't want to live if he died. Janey had betrayed Ranulf because she feared death, but Elizabeth had a feeling that life without Ranulf had been a living death.

She would not make the same mistake.

They rode until dawn, as if demons pursued them. The horses were ready to drop, so they halted, hiding within the depths of a dense forest. Exhausted, Elizabeth was much too fretful to sleep. Suppose she wasn't hanged? Suppose she was merely imprisoned? That would be far worse than a swift strangulation. Hadn't she oft written about dark, dank cellars filled with all sorts of vermin?

Walter Stafford would be the worst vermin of all.

Why didn't Rand hold her, soothe her, at the very least say something comforting?

"I would have taken care of the matter," he finally stated, his voice stern, though tempered by fatigue. "There was no need to shoot the bloody fool."

"He was going to kill you." While Rand tethered the horses, Elizabeth stretched out beneath a tree. The cold and damp from the earth invaded her back. She sat up.

Rand loomed above her. "We'll be safe in London, Bess. I know my way about. After we do what we planned —"

"*You* planned!"

"— we'll swing south to Dover. From there we'll head across the Channel."

"Why don't we go straight to Dover or the nearest port? I don't want to hang, Rand."

"Nor do I. But we must visit Southwark Cathedral."

"And Charles Beresford," she added, somewhat reluctantly. "We need escape money." She thought he might protest, deeming a woman's help unacceptable, but he nodded. "I'm so frightened, Rand. Please sit beside me. Please hold me."

He complied, and she pressed against him.

I should be shot, Rand thought, hugging her closer. *Bess acted heroically, and I scolded her. I treated her like Zak, when she's braver and smarter than both of us put together.*

"By shooting that bounty hunter, you saved your lawman's life," he said, trying to explain his callousness. "Now I must make certain Stafford does not catch up with us. 'Tis a pity that flap-dragon'd son of a bitch won't die, after all."

Four major roads radiated outward from London. At points along the way, turnpikes had been set up. Turnpike keepers collected tolls, but they also watched for criminals. As travelers streamed past the booths, keepers distributed handbills which detailed crimes and suspected perpetrators.

Dressed as male servants, Elizabeth and Rand approached London along the Oxford Road. As they neared Shotover Hill, a popular place for highwaymen, Elizabeth saw two iron-caged men hanging from a gibbet. Since their flesh remained largely intact, the men were recent arrivals. Carrion crows perched upon the bars, feeding. Other crows circled overhead. Elizabeth couldn't keep her eyes off the birds, drifting above the corpses or creeping across the cages.

Swallowing bitter bile, she began to tremble. *That's how Rand and I are going to end up.*

Beneath her breeches, her legs goose-fleshed. Beneath her shirt, her necklace felt like a choker.

Nearing the turnpike, Rand maneuvered Prancer closer to Greylag. "By now the handbills will have been printed and distributed," he said. "The innkeeper will have described us and everyone will be on the lookout."

"I'm aware of that," she snapped. "Which is why it would have been much safer to arrive after dark."

"The roads are usually patrolled at night and the keepers maintain a sharper eye. Trust me, Bess. 'Tis safer to enter during the daylight hours."

Trust me. Elizabeth thought Ranulf might have said the very same thing to Janey. Ever since Green Hill and Evesham Abbey, she had found it difficult to distinguish the difference between herself and Janey, Rand

and Ranulf. Rand had even begun to grow a beard, which increased his likeness to Ranulf. Sometimes Elizabeth felt as if she'd cast aside her own identity. Who was she? Ranulf's Lady Jane or Rand's Bonny Bess?

After passing through the turnpike, she relaxed. Rand was correct. They were just two among thousands traveling toward London. The very press of people would protect them.

The dread she had experienced at Shotover Hill receded. Maybe last night's intruders had been robbers rather than bounty hunters. In that case, nobody would investigate.

Long before Elizabeth reached London, she smelled it. A brisk northwesterly wind carried coal smoke and various other disagreeable odors. The day was bleak and cloudy. St. Paul's Cathedral, the Tower, and Westminster Abbey had disappeared, covered by a leaden mantle that obscured the entire city.

"London isn't always so dirty," she murmured, remembering her first visit.

"What you see is coal smoke from glasshouses, earthenware factories, blacksmith shops and dyers' yards, not to mention thousands of fireplaces. Believe me, Bess, 'twill get worse before it gets better."

"But the Beresfords —"

"Reside where it's cleaner. Prentices scrub the fronts of the houses. Many houses possess high steps so that ladies can enter their carriages without ever touching the muck below."

"What's wrong with that?"

"Nothing. Except the lords and ladies blind themselves to the human urine and stagnant water that befoul the streets. They don't see the butchers who toss offal from their shops, nor the raw sewage spouting from broken sewer lines beneath the pavement. They don't see their grand coaches splash filth upon pedestrians, unless of course they are careless enough to leave their windows open, whereupon they themselves get splashed."

In sporadic fits and starts, Rand guided them toward the city outskirts. Elizabeth peered through the drizzle of coal dust which seemed to emanate from the clouds. The road was a maze of hackney coaches, sedan chairs, carts, wagons and riders. The hooves and iron-rimmed wheels shook the ground in a constant rumbling, like the start of an earthquake. Sedan chairs for hire clustered around Charing Cross. The statuary upon the cross was covered by a pall of coal dust, just like everything else. The dress of the pedestrians who clung to the footpaths provided the only spots of brightness.

Rand leaned closer. "Just think what you missed, Bess, living all those years on the moors."

An hour passed before they entered Temple Bar, the only remaining gateway into the City. The smell from garden privies and basement cesspits was so noxious, Elizabeth gagged. Rand bought her a nosegay from a vendor, which she promptly thrust against her nose.

This is so very different from my first visit, she thought, *when the sun shone and I saw the best parts of the city.*

By the time they reached the Strand, the cloudy mist had become something akin to seepage. Umbrellas bloomed. The noise increased. Beggars cried for alms. Ballad singers stood on every street corner. Hawkers of ballads yelled and waved their sheets. Collectors for the penny post rang their bells. Scavengers with carts and bells pushed among the shoppers, as did vendors of fruit, pies, fish, and quack medicine.

Elizabeth had developed a terrific headache. Deciding her nosegay smelled of coal dust, she tossed it away.

"Don't despair, Bess. We've neared our destination." Rand turned down one of the countless side alleys that spiked Fleet Street. "There's a decent inn here. It will do for one night."

On the corner, a knife sharpener ground knives upon a wheel. A milkmaid yodeled her wares. "If I have to listen to that all night, I'll never sleep," Elizabeth groused.

"Would you prefer the Beresfords?" Rand snapped, then ran his hand wearily across his brow. "I'm sorry, Bess, that was uncalled for. But at least now you understand why I try to ease some of the suffering, though 'tis truly a drop in the bucket."

With a sigh, Elizabeth dismounted in front of a small inn. Several floral arrangements graced the bay windows overlooking the court, and she felt mollified by the brightness. From the shadows at the edge of the yard, a thin wail emerged.

Tentatively, she approached the shadows and bent over. The noise came from inside a bundle of rags. "Dear God, 'tis a baby!"

"Don't touch it!" Rand slid from Prancer.

Elizabeth straightened. "But we can't just leave it here. We can't just let it die."

"London is filled with abandoned babies, Bess. Children are often maimed for begging purposes, or simply deserted. 'Tis not pleasant, but nothing can be done."

She stared down at the tiny, pinched face.

"It seems so unfair, especially when I've been so long barren."

"Barren? What are you talking about?"

A fist knotted inside her stomach. "I don't know why I said that. I didn't mean to. What should we do with the baby?"

"We can't take it with us."

"But you saved Old Fife's baby."

"That was the Dales. London has her own ways," he said, attempting to explain the unexplainable. "Should you try and rescue all the children, you would find yourself the mother of fifty thousand."

"I don't want to rescue thousands. I want to save one. How much money do we have left from the sale of the duchess's diamond ring?"

"Thirty guineas. Why?"

"Hand over ten . . . no, twenty guineas."

Puzzled, he drew the coins from his purse and pressed them against her palm.

She scooped up the weightless bundle, then backtracked toward the milkmaid. "Here," she said. "I'll give you ten guineas if you take this little one home with you."

The milkmaid shook her head. "I have three at home already."

"Fifteen guineas."

"Your master don't care," the milkmaid said. "Why should you?"

Momentarily, Elizabeth had forgotten that she was garbed as a man. Deepening her voice, she said, "Twenty guineas and that's my last offer."

"For twenty guineas I'd take the devil's own spawn. 'Tis a bargain."

"My master has spies all over London, so if you leave the baby on another street I'll find out. Then I shall find *you* and run a sword through your gullet. Do you understand?"

The milkmaid snatched up the guineas. "That I do, sir."

Elizabeth returned to Rand, who led her to their room. Once inside, she tossed her mantle upon the bed and sank down beside it. She felt as if she had just run a foot race. Would the milkmaid grow to love the child? Or would she discard it when the guineas were spent? Elizabeth thought she heard a thousand baby wails, blending with the rain that drummed upon the tile roof. Rand was right. She couldn't save them all.

"London is a brutal place," she said mournfully. "I don't like it here. I remember the dancing and the theatre and the pleasant strolls. I remember London as magical."

"Poor Bess. Tomorrow, just before we meet up with my cousins, I shall take you boating. That should revive your spirits."

"Are you insane? We must visit Southwark Cathedral and Charles Beresford. I should think you'd be anxious —"

"No, love. First an outing, then Southwark."

His mouth tightened and she knew from experience he could not be swayed. "All right, I'll boat with you. I'll even ply the oars. Does that make you happy?"

"Yes. But 'tis *your* smile I crave." Tossing her hat aside, he removed the pins from her tightly coiled hair. Then he combed the silken strands between his spread fingers.

"Could you have left the baby all alone?" she asked, resting her head in his lap. "I mean, had I not been along?"

"No, Bess. I would have delivered it to a foundling home. Yours was the better solution, I think."

Elizabeth heaved a deep sigh. If circumstances had been different, she would have kept the abandoned baby. After all, she had petitioned God with a thousand masses, a million prayers, begging him to cure her barrenness.

A shudder coursed through her. The Protestant Elizabeth would never petition God with masses. But the Lady Jane would. Once again, Elizabeth realized that she had melded five hundred years into the present.

Rising from the bed, she crossed to the window. Black beads of water slipped down the glass and blurred Rand's reflection as he crept up behind her.

"I wonder what we shall find at Southwark," he said, slipping his arms around her waist. "Will the sight of Ranulf Navarre's tomb provide us with what we need to know?"

Elizabeth removed her neckband and fingered the golden coil of rope upon her neck, thick as a hangman's noose. She had betrayed Ranulf, that much *she* knew. Rand didn't. If he found out, would it destroy their love?

Lady Jane's betrayal had occurred five hundred years ago, and yet Rand was obsessed with the past. Once they left England, would the ghosts that haunted them remain in Evesham? "If you truly loved me, Rand, we would pay Charles Beresford a hasty call, then flee London."

"I truly love you and we shall visit Southwark on the morrow. Don't fret, Bess. If we cross paths with your bloody lawman, I'll protect you."

What about Ranulf Navarre? Will you protect me from him? Who shall protect you, my love? Not Lady Jane. She betrayed you, though you know it not.

A log popped in the fire. Elizabeth felt Rand remove her shirt, then her breast binding. Bunching her hair with his hand, he rained kisses down upon her neck and shoulders.

Outside the window, London's black rain fell. But at least it would not fall on the face of one nameless baby.

Elizabeth sighed. *I cannot save them all. I wish I could. Just as I wish I could save Rand from himself.*

Chapter 20

"Oars! Oars!" the boatmen called out, as Elizabeth descended the stairs below the Tower of London. Garbed in natty uniforms, swarming over the docks, the watermen tried to solicit rides along the Thames. All wore embossed plates on their doublets, displaying the arms of their various protectors. Rand motioned to a young man who wore the arms of the Lord Mayor. Other boatmen castigated their rival by shouting good-natured obscenities.

Rand's choice possessed a lanky build which had very nearly outgrown the gawkiness of adolescence. "My name is Davey, sir," he said, his ears red. Davey's voice insisted on changing octaves, and Elizabeth kept her laughter at bay by biting down hard upon her lip. "I charge sixpence for two," the lad continued. "Double that if you would pass London Bridge."

"What say you, lass?" Rand winked. "Dare

we risk the tide? Some consider it dangerous."

"Yes, I know." She adjusted her green silk hood so that more of her face was visible. "Why not take the risk? I seem to enjoy dangerous things."

After Davey had helped them into his brightly painted red boat, Rand said, "I trust you can swim, Bess."

"I never learned." She squeezed his hand. "I shall let you save me."

"I never learned, either. I guess that means we sink or swim together."

"Hasn't it always been thus, my love?"

Davey removed the tent overhead and Elizabeth glanced around. The turrets of White Tower, belonging to the Tower of London, thrust above the bank on the opposite side of the river. City roofs peeked above the Tower walls. Thousands of red and green boats glutted the shoreline.

Rand looked toward the Tower. "That's where I first found out about Ranulf Navarre."

Before Elizabeth could question him, he changed the topic. "Thirty thousand watermen work the Thames, Bess. It was even worse during the war. Watermen can't be pressed into naval service so everyone wanted to navigate the blasted river. I swear

I saw the Prince of Wales himself haunting the docks."

They glided into the main flow of traffic. The Thames was so densely populated, Elizabeth couldn't see the water, though she certainly smelled it. Davey said that trout, lampreys, porpoises and salmon were caught from its depths, but Elizabeth could scarce credit the lad's veracity. The stench alone would kill any living thing.

Lowering her hood, she settled against Rand's arm and tried to ignore the enormous vessels on both sides of their small craft. Davey was now singing, "Row the boat, Norman, row to thy leman."

Her stomach felt hollow. Davey was so young. Surely someone so young couldn't be wise in the ways of the river. "I trust you were teasing when you said you couldn't swim," she murmured, turning her face toward Rand.

He merely grinned.

She gazed upwards. Just like her hopes and dreams for a bright future, the sun shone intermittently. Following their boat ride and a midday meal, she and Rand would visit Southwark Cathedral. Then they would pay Beresford a call. Tonight, God willing, they'd be bound for Dover.

Until recently, London Bridge had been

the lone bridge across the Thames, and Elizabeth knew from her first visit that the rise and fall of the tides flowing through its narrow archways produced wicked rapids. Six months ago she had firmly refused any offer of a boat ride. Why had she accepted today? Because Rand admired courage?

As they neared the bridge, she fancied she heard screams. "Rand!" she cried. "People are drowning!"

"No, Bess. 'Tis the various songs of the watermen."

The roar of the river heightened while the boat increased its speed. Truly frightened, Elizabeth buried her head beneath Rand's somber wool coat. Waistcoat buttons dimpled her cheek and brow. A spray of water drenched her cloak and her gown's hem flounces. The boat lurched and jumped. A wave slammed against her body. The boat shuddered.

This is the end, she thought, clinging to Rand. They would drown. Her unidentified body would be washed up on the shore and be buried in a pauper's grave. She heard the mocking echo of Rand's words: *Just think what you missed, Bess, living all those years on the moors.*

" 'Tis over, my love." With an exultant laugh, Rand lifted the front of his coat. "You can come out now."

"I honestly thought we might drown."

He shook his head. "We live a charmed life. Our fate is not to breathe water until we breathe our last."

"Of course. Your fate is to run with the hart," she said, remembering his statement outside her father's inn. She wanted to ask him what *her* destiny might be, hart or hearth, but she bit back the question. Perhaps he wouldn't have the answer. Perhaps she didn't want to know.

Finally, mercifully, they disembarked at Westminster Bridge, then strolled across one of the bridge's two pedestrian paths. Rand had made plans to join his London cousins, Billy and Thomas Turnbull, Zak's younger brothers. Elizabeth tried to summon enthusiasm, but she still felt shaken by the boat ride. And even though she was surrounded by so many people, she experienced a sudden vulnerability. Walter might be ensconced in one of the scrolled and gilded carriages forever rattling along the roadway.

Midway across the bridge, she and Rand met Billy and Tom. During the subsequent conversation, Elizabeth kept thinking Billy looked familiar. Since he was short, stocky, and possessed a thatch of wheat-colored hair, he didn't resemble Rand, so she couldn't attribute her notion to a family resemblance.

"I've a good eye for faces," she said, staring at Billy, "and I'm certain I've seen yours before."

"Billy's a pugilist." Rand grinned. "He's hoping to make the Championships next year. He's been the subject of several newspaper articles and written up in the *Gentleman's Magazine.* Perhaps that's where you saw him, Bess."

"You don't look at all like your cousin, Mr. Turnbull," she pressed.

"I'm the spittin' image of me father, Miss Wyndham, more's the pity."

"Pity?"

"Me dad was a thievin' bastard."

"If Billy scores at the Championships, his future will be assured," Tom said, unperturbed by his brother's epithet. "Billy will make a fortune . . . handkerchiefs, mugs, statuettes, all with his gruesome face painted on 'em." Tom nudged his brother good-naturedly, then grinned at Elizabeth. "On the other hand, I plan to make my fortune in a less hurtful manner. I'm employed as a croupier at one of London's finest gambling establishments, Shepherd's. Perhaps you've heard of it."

"I believe my publisher mentioned Shepherd's. He visits often, with his wife." Elizabeth studied Tom from beneath her lowered lashes. He might be a good five years younger, a shade prettier, his build less powerful, his clothes more foppish, but at first glance his resemblance to Rand was startling.

"I expect my job to be a stepping stone to wealth," Tom said, stroking his beard. "I'm tired of poverty. I'm tired of living in some flat over the buttock bawds at Covent Garden. Nightly I see the richest lords and ladies drop thousands of pounds in one sitting. Why them and not me, I ask myself."

"And wot's yer answer?" Billy teased.

"No reason, I tell myself. I've refined my tongue, and Mr. Shepherd gives croupiers a percentage of the take. Someday I'll have enough to buy my own establishment."

"I applaud your honest ambition, Mr. Turnbull." Despite Tom's resemblance to Rand, despite his friendly personality, Elizabeth mistrusted him, though she couldn't say why. Due to recent tribulations, her instincts had become more sharply honed, or maybe it was because Tom shared Walter's unctuously sincere manner.

They lounged at the side of the bridge, above the glittering Thames. Gaily dressed couples strolled past, the women sheltered beneath frilly parasols. Admiring one such parasol, Elizabeth felt her nape prickle — something was amiss in Rand's disposition. Turning slowly, she saw that his hand pressed hard against the stone railing. His gaze was riveted on a large vessel moored nearby. Gray from lack of paint, the vessel sported a splintered mast, a total absence of rigging, and a hull blanketed with barnacles.

Rand gestured toward the abandoned ship. "Whenever I cross this bridge, I cannot help but think of Zak. He was imprisoned in that hulk. When I left for the American War, he went there for robbery."

Elizabeth wrapped her cloak more tightly around her, as if the green silk might somehow provide some warmth against the chill of Rand's disclosure. "There are people in that wreck?" she asked, appalled.

"London might seem a fine place t' you, Miss Wyndham," Billy said, "but for the rest of us . . ." He shrugged. " 'Tis a truth that England don't believe in prisons. She would rather rid herself o' scofflaws by shippin' 'em off t' the American colonies or Australia, places far away. When the American War came along and transport was scarcer than hen's teeth, the law mewed up convicts in old ships. 'Twas less costly than buildin' new prisons."

Elizabeth's hands tightened on the balustrade. A sudden wind off the Thames tugged at her sodden cloak and whipped her hair across her cheeks.

"To save space, prisoners are packed together on three decks," Rand said. "The newest arrivals are put on the lowest and those few who survive on top. The air is foul, of course, and I needn't tell you about the food. At night the hatches are screwed down and the men left to kill each other in the darkness, or plot revenge against those who put them there."

He sounded so caustic and bitter, Elizabeth wanted to take him in her arms and comfort him. God's teeth! No wonder Rand was so contemptuous of authority.

Overhead, seagulls circled and screeched. The shoreline was cluttered with beached pleasure craft, tumble-down shacks, fishermen casting their nets, and washerwomen pounding clothes against the rocks. Billy and Rand's attention remained on the prison hulk, while Tom ogled passing ladies.

"Soon after I returned from the war, Zak was released," Rand continued. "Our grandmother, who had taken it upon herself to raise all the Turnbull boys, managed to nurse Zak's body back to health, but his soul was scarred. Zak and I were a pair. He hated everyone and I hated everything."

Elizabeth could understand Rand's impotent rage toward a system that was so uncaring, so unjust, but she asked her question anyway. "Knowing that you could end up in such a place," she said, nodding toward the ship, "how could you have stolen so much as a shilling?"

"Because they'll never catch me."

"I would imagine that's what Zak said."

"I'm not Zak."

" 'Tis true we Turnbulls are the black sheep o' the family," Billy said, "which on the whole is fairly respectable. Our downfall began with our mother, Franny."

Tom removed his attention from the passing parade long enough to say, "Do not bother Miss Wyndham with the sordid tale of our past, Billy. The day is far too lovely, and so is she."

"I don't mind," Elizabeth said. While Tom might be far younger than Walter Stafford, he had effectively learned to ape the bored, arrogant manner of the upper classes.

Billy launched into his tale of Frances Remington's march to perdition. Although Franny had died during his infancy, Billy knew all about his mother's infatuation with, and marriage to, a handsome ne'er-do-well, who persuaded her to share in his illegal activities.

"Includin' prostitution," Billy said. "At least till she was twenty-three and past a good age. Then Father involved Mum and Zak in petty thievery. When Mum was twenty-nine and Zak fourteen, they was caught and sentenced t' die."

"Our mother was beautiful, so they tell us," Tom said. "With long dark hair, much the color of yours, Miss Wyndham. Our grandmother, who repeated the story more times than I care to count, said Mother remained gay and lighthearted, even up to the time they pulled the bucket out from under her."

Billy's powerful hands balled into fists. "For part of Zak's 'instruction,' the authorities forced him to watch Mum kick the bucket. Zak was supposed t' be hanged, but he cried. The crowd yelled at him for his cowardice and the hangman had to chase him 'round the scaffold."

No wonder Zak had developed such a careless bravado, thought Elizabeth. He wanted to wipe out the scorn he had endured when he was only fourteen.

"My family had ridden up from Cornwall for the execution," said Rand, "so we witnessed the entire event. I was a mere lad, but I remember it well."

Rand could scarcely be heard above the scraping of the iron carriage wheels or the music of the street musicians playing below. Elizabeth had learned that when he was agitated, Rand's voice became deceptively low-pitched.

"Zak scurried about that scaffold for what seemed like hours," he continued, his voice bitter. "When Zak was finally caught, the hangman threw him to the ground and strangled him with a silken cord. Near death, Zak was pulled to his feet, splashed with a bucket of water, then tied to the tail of the very same horse that had pulled Franny's cart."

"How dreadful!" Elizabeth knew she could never reproduce the scene for one of her novels. Unfortunately, the majority of her readers would be delighted rather than sympathetic.

As if to confirm her last thought, Tom said, "Grandmother told us the crowd didn't care. They were overjoyed."

"After Mum's death and Zak's release, our grandmother stayed in London t' help raise us," said Billy. "Our father, God rot his twisted soul, died some years later."

"He was hanged?"

"No, Miss Wyndham. He was knifed by a

Bow Street Runner. They say that when the blade pierced me dad's gut, gin flowed from his belly and soaked the street."

Elizabeth's hand closed over Billy's fist. She had meant her gesture to express compassion, but the words she summoned surprised her. "I know I've seen you before, Mr. Turnbull. Have you ever visited the Dales?"

Billy shook his head. "Jacob . . . me dad did. He said the moors was bleak and lonely. He said the sheep was prettier than the wimmen. Now that I've met you, Miss Wyndham, I can see that Jacob lied through his teeth."

"Did you not attend your brother's execution, Mr. Turnbull?" Elizabeth asked, sidestepping the compliment. "I, myself, could not watch."

" 'Twas too quick, Miss Wyndham. Rand told us all about it . . ." Billy paused, his eyes slits. "We owe Lord Stafford a grudge."

"Not me," said Tom. "I plan to remain law-abiding, though I could be corrupted for a good price." He appraised Elizabeth, giving credence to a sexual innuendo. "My cousin has all the luck with the ladies, Miss Wyndham."

She didn't know whether to thank Tom or smash his skull with a parasol. Since she didn't possess a parasol, she murmured the socially acceptable, "Indeed."

After bidding the brothers good-bye, Rand and Elizabeth continued their stroll across the bridge. Mind reverberating with frightful images of "scofflaws" living aboard an abandoned ship, Elizabeth clutched his arm. She wanted to rush back to their little room and lock herself in until she and Rand could flee London. Walter was wrong. Highwaymen didn't get caught because they were lazy. They got caught because they never knew when to quit. Rather than tempting fate, they taunted it.

"We must leave London," she said. "I don't care about some tomb in Southwark Cathedral, or a past that died five hundred years ago. We must visit Beresford, then flee England. The only thing left for us is to take up residence in some foreign country where we shall live long enough to grow old and respectable."

"Where is your courage, Bess? I love you for your sense of adventure, and I can't imagine either of us growing old and respectable. I think I'll buy you something to lighten your mood." With a dismissive wave, he disappeared inside one of the shops.

Tempted to follow, cursing him for leaving her without his protection, Elizabeth drifted toward a board of posted notices. Her eyes probed advertisements for the current theatre attractions, the latest fairs, the menagerie and armory at the Tower of London. There were handbills seeking the return of stolen articles. One headline announced:

**FIVE HUNDRED GUINEAS REWARD
FOR THE ARREST OF A HIGHWAYMAN
USING THE NAME JOHN TURPIN**

Damn! Walter knew Rand by that name! She snatched the sheet from the board. No portrait, but Rand's description followed, as well as a list of his crimes, including "the kidnapping of a gentlewoman, Miss Elizabeth Wyndham." Any interested parties were to contact the Bow Street Runners, or Lord Stafford at One George Street.

Wildly glancing about, she imagined she saw accusatory eyes everywhere. Then she saw Rand striding toward her, a grin on his face.

"I had something printed up and . . ." At her stricken expression, he stopped midsentence. "What is it?"

"Handbills! 'Tis for certain they're all over London. We must get out of here right now, head for Dover. Damn! The horses. First we must return to the Strand, I mean the inn —"

"Calm down, Bess."

"I won't calm down. Don't tell me to calm down. You may place little value on your life, Rand, but I don't want to die. Five hundred guineas means we'll both end up swinging from a hangman's noose. I love you, just like Franny loved her Jacob, but when I kick the bucket out from under *my* feet, I won't be lighthearted."

"Hush! We'll leave directly after Southwark Cathedral."

"I don't give a hang about your blasted cathedral! Hang. That's funny, Rand. Hang!" She began to laugh, a high, shrill wail.

"Unless you want to draw attention to us, you'd better control yourself," he said. "Please."

"I feel ill," Elizabeth mumbled, swallowing her laughter. She swayed and would have fallen had Rand not reached out and caught her.

"Lord, you're burning up. Lean on me, sweetheart, there's a good lass." He hailed a post chaise and helped her inside.

"I'm sorry, Rand. I despise illness of any kind, but —"

"You caught a chill from the river, that's all."

That wasn't all. Her eyes hurt, even her teeth hurt, and her limbs felt as if a giant hand was kneading bread dough. "Walter knows we're here," she murmured feverishly, waving the handbill.

Rand removed the paper from her fingers. "We've known all along that Stafford might be in London, Bess. But this doesn't mean he knows *we're* here."

"He's probably given handbills to every pawnbroker, stable hand, informer, and innkeeper, including ours. By the time we reach our lodging, 'twill be swarming with lawmen."

"I've never been much good at reading in the dark." Rand reached for the window shade, hesitated, then held the paper up to his nose. "Now I know where Stafford lives, which is more than he knows about us."

"George Street. He told me so. He also told me that highwaymen always get caught."

"John Turpin doesn't exist, love," Rand soothed. "And as far as the physical description goes, dozens of people, including my cousin Tom, match it. Five hundred guineas is a princely sum. I'll wager I enraged the Duke of Newcastle beyond endurance."

"If you had not kissed his wife, the duke would have dismissed the robbery. What are a few baubles to a duke? You wager with our lives. You wager with our love."

"Hurry, driver!" Rand shouted. "Bess, we shall be home soon."

"We do not have a home," she whispered, just before her head lolled against his shoulder.

Rand handed Elizabeth a venison pie, cheese, and an apple he had purchased from various street vendors. "You can't stay cooped up here forever, Bess."

"I've been ill."

"You were ill for one afternoon and one night. Then your mysterious malady disappeared almost as quickly as it appeared."

"Are you saying that my illness was a sham?"

"No. I think it was brought on by the handbill and your fear of Stafford."

Tears pricked her eyes. "You're probably right, but I felt unwell, and that's the truth."

"Of course it is." Gently grasping her by the shoulders, he pulled her from the bed, guided her toward the table, and forced her to sit. "You must eat something."

"I cannot." She crumpled a piece of cheese between her thumb and finger.

"When you're gone, I'm certain you'll never return. I imagine you picked up by one of Walter's spies, then hauled off to Newgate or the Fleet. I imagine us hanged."

"Would you rather starve to death?"

"Don't tease."

"That wasn't a tease. Look, I know London well enough to slip past anyone as easily as a mouse in a hole. Believe it or not, nobody pays me the slightest heed."

She saw that despite his words he seemed upset. "What's amiss now?" she cried, dreading his answer.

"I made some inquiries concerning Charles Beresford. He's gone, Bess."

"Gone? Where?"

"He set sail for America. Creditors were circling his home like buzzards, only there was no corpse to feed upon."

"You visited his home?" The thought of Rand's daring, and his foolishness, mitigated her anger at Beresford. "But you could have been captured. The handbills must be all over London . . . even Stratton Street."

With a shrug, he stoked the fire, then poured them each a glass of claret.

Clutching the goblet's stem, Elizabeth tried to control her shivers. Rand had sought out Beresford on her behalf, but she never would have given him permission had she known his intent.

Permission, hah! Rand thrived on danger and excitement. Her words would not have dissuaded him. Wasn't that one of the reasons she loved him? Because she couldn't bend him to her will? But she couldn't bend Walter, either, and she didn't love him.

She wondered why she didn't feel more rage toward Charles and Penelope, even though she now realized that they had always lived beyond their means. Her drum was probably an expense they could ill afford. Unless they had used *her* money to finance it, she thought with a mental huff.

True, she had suspected Charles's duplicity, but deep down inside she hadn't really believed it. God's nightgown! Had he at least published the last volume of *Castles of Doom*?

Elizabeth pictured the Gainsborough painting and Penelope's costly bronzes, just before it hit her. B. B. Wyndham, Daughter of the Quill, was as poor as a church mouse. And yet, to her surprise, she realized that Elizabeth Wyndham was far more concerned with Rand's recklessness. Gone were the days when she could wave an account rendering in front of noses and feel satisfied. Gone, just like Charles and Penelope Beresford, damn their souls!

Rand retrieved his wool coat from the wardrobe and wrapped it around her shoulders. Immediately, she felt a bulky packet press against her breast. "Your coat, the inside pocket," she gasped. "More handbills?"

"Handbills? Lord, I forgot." He pulled a newspaper from the pocket, then smoothed the paper and placed it upon the table.

Elizabeth looked down. The headline on the front page read:

RAND REMINGTON
DECLARES HIS LOVE
FOR BONNY BESS,
THIS MONDAY, 22 OCTOBER, 1787.

"I had it printed especially for you," Rand said, his fingertips brushing back the dark, silken hair that shaded her eyes. "I thought it would please you as a memento when we're old and respectable."

"Old and respectable," she echoed. "That *was* a tease and one I don't appreciate, though I do thank you for the headline." She groped for the apple, bit into its ruddy skin, then spit. "This tastes of coal smoke. Everything here smells and tastes peculiar."

"I promise we'll leave London tomorrow, Bess."

"Why not now?"

"We must visit Southwark."

This time anger did rage through her. "When we're caught, I shall denounce you! I shall say horrid things about you, and you'll deserve them all!"

"That's exactly as it should be. I'd expect you to do no less. Nobody will blame you if you play the innocent."

Instantly deflated, she cried, "I wasn't serious!"

"*I* was."

She heaved a deep sigh. "Have you seen any more of those wretched posters? London's covered with them, isn't it?"

"The only thing London is covered with is soot. Believe me, if I thought we were in any real danger, I'd leave immediately."

"No, you wouldn't. You'd woo danger, just like you wooed me."

"I didn't have to woo you, Bess. You chased me across the moors until I had no choice but to succumb."

"If Walter should find us, we're both as good as dead."

"Only I, Bess. The posters made no mention of the bounty hunter, which means one of two things. The man didn't die, or Stafford would rather ignore the law than see you hanged. Either way, you're safe." He refilled her goblet. "Drink, love. I've never seen anyone who can remain as sober as you, even after a full bottle's worth. If I were so inclined, I'd place you inside a tavern, challenge the most boastful cock-a-whoop, then wager."

"Don't you dare." She offered him a thin smile. "Over the years, I've developed a good head for wine."

"A good head is one thing. You're a bottomless pit. Drink up, Bess."

Outside, London's church bells tolled the hour. Glancing toward the window, Elizabeth could see nothing but a patch of black sky, though it was impossible to say whether the blackness occurred from the lateness of the hour or the polluted clouds.

She drained the wine from her goblet, then shifted her back against the slats of her chair. "I wish I could change the past, Rand. I wish I could make all the ghosts go away."

"On the contrary, my love. You have a way of resurrecting even more." He walked over to the fireplace and leaned against the mantel.

The flickering flames cast his hair in red, played across his rough features, and silhouetted the line of his chest through his shirt.

Grabbing a poker, he stabbed at a log.

Elizabeth knew his resurrection remark referred to Evesham and Southwark. What would they encounter inside the cathedral? The answer to their quest? Or even more ghosts?

Rand poked at the log until it disintegrated into a hundred glowing coals. Elizabeth wished she could pulverize her trepidation so easily.

What the bloody hell would they find at Southwark?

CHAPTER 21

Southwark Cathedral's square tower, sided with four steep pinnacles, disappeared into a porridge-thick fog. Near the cathedral gate a priest read a burial service, his words directed toward a coffin being lowered into a poor hole, halfway across the cemetery. The huge pit contained several tiers of caskets, but wouldn't be closed until it was completely filled, which made the resultant odor unbearable. Pinching her nose, Elizabeth rushed past, heading toward the sanctuary of the cathedral nave. But the stench from the poor hole lingered like a bad dream.

The nave was draped in shadows. Surrounded by the chilled stones, Elizabeth shivered. From her research on *Castles of Doom,* she knew the original church had been rebuilt in the early thirteenth century. Although she had never written one word about its interior, it appeared vaguely familiar. A charwoman dusted the great stone screen behind the high altar in the choir, a screen Elizabeth *knew* had been added to the original structure. A curate showed a portly gentleman the tomb of the medieval poet, John Gower, while a handful of worshippers knelt in the chantries. Otherwise, the cathedral was empty.

Reluctant to move forward, she hung back in the shadows. Some of the cathedral's effigies were painted, some arranged in lifelike poses, others in attitudes of death. Hoping to postpone the ultimate shock of recognition, Elizabeth studied the various stone faces. When Rand bent forward to read the name from yet another brass plate, she said, "That isn't them."

He straightened. "Who is them? I thought we were looking for Ranulf."

"Of course we are." But she knew that wherever they found Ranulf, they would also find Janey.

Upon approaching the north transept, Elizabeth's heart raced.

"Maybe Navarre isn't at Southwark after all," Rand said, entering the transept behind her. "The historian who told me was ancient. Perhaps he was confused."

"No. I think not." A vision flashed through her mind — the image of a fair-haired woman atop a bay mare, followed by a two-wheeled cart drawn by black horses. In the cart rested the coffin bearing the woman's husband.

We shall find Ranulf and Janey tucked inside a chantry, she thought, as the tap-tap of her boots echoed off the vaulting. Beneath her shirt and breeches, her flesh felt cold, clammy, yet perspiration beaded her brow, soaked her breast binding, and dampened the masses of hair hidden by her hat. Rather than the gown she had worn during her boat ride, she had chosen a man's garb. That way, should Walter lurk anywhere nearby, she might escape detection.

Circling the transept, peering into every dark corner, Elizabeth's dread intensified. "They're not here," she cried. "They should be here."

The curate passed by, alone now. Elizabeth ran toward him. "Father, where are they?"

"Who?"

"Ranulf and Janey. They should be over there, in that corner, in this transept."

The curate shook his head. As if appealing for help, he glanced toward Rand. "I'm sorry. I have no idea what the young man is talking about."

"Ranulf Navarre," Rand clarified. "One of

362

the leaders of Simon de Montfort's rebellion."

"Ah! Ranulf the Black and Jane of Winchester. Due to their great age, they've been moved to a more prominent place, closer to the central altar."

Elizabeth raced forward until she saw them. Then she knelt on the icy paving stones in front of the tomb chests. Time had ravaged them both. Their faces were chipped and worn, nearly unrecognizable. Once they had been flawless. Once she had traced the outline of Ranulf's smooth, cold profile.

Now she ran her fingers across Ranulf's broken nose and cheekbones, caressing the pocked and damaged granite. With an almost inhuman effort, she suppressed the wave of emotion that threatened to overwhelm her, most especially the desire to weep. If she began to weep, she'd never stop. She had already shed too many tears for Ranulf, cried herself to sleep more nights than there were seasons of the moon.

Rand's hand rested on the crown of her hat. "Ranulf Navarre, 1220–1265," he read from the brass plate. "Jane of Winchester, 1235–1270. So that's how it ends."

"They chopped you to bits, just like Simon. I saw it happen, from Evesham Abbey. I don't know why they didn't put your head on a pike, as they did the rest of the leaders. Instead, the monks brought your head back to me."

Rand closed his eyes, as if visualizing her words. But he couldn't know what she'd seen. He had been dead by then. He couldn't know what she'd done, or how she had felt when the flickering line of torches made their way down Green Hill — the torches that lit the way for the monks who had carried Ranulf's mutilated body back to her.

"I brought you here," Elizabeth continued, her voice a harsh whisper. "Since you were a traitor, they wouldn't take you elsewhere, not at Evesham, nor Winchester, nor Gloucester. For five years I sought a suitable place where I could put you at rest."

The curate approached. "Were the Navarres your ancestors?"

Rather than answering, Rand said, "What can you tell us about them?"

"They make an interesting tale. Of course, much of what we know has been passed down, so I can't speak for its veracity. Ranulf the Black's wife asked to be buried next to him, yet we're fairly certain that she was the one who betrayed him. Some say Jane of Winchester was responsible for the ruin of Simon de Montfort and the rebels' defeat at Evesham."

Scarcely breathing, Elizabeth rose and faced the curate. Her fingers touched her necklace, hidden beneath her shirt.

"How did Lady Jane betray him, Father?" Rand asked.

"After the traitors took over, they held the king's eldest son, Prince Edward, in their custody. One day, while out racing, the prince simply rode away on a horse that had not been winded. It had all been arranged beforehand. Royalist troops met Prince Edward, then escorted him to Wigmore Castle. The prince, of course, went on to destroy Simon de Montfort at Evesham."

"But how was Jane involved?"

"Prince Edward's escape plan was carefully set forth in advance. Lady Jane was thought to have masterminded the escape."

Elizabeth's hand squeezed her necklace. She knew. Oh, God, she knew. She had sent the prince this very necklace as a sign of her faith, as well as her identity. The necklace was her talisman. Ranulf had presented it to her on their wedding day, and she had always worn it.

Ignoring the curate and Elizabeth's male garb, Rand said, "Is that true, Bess? Did you betray me?"

His voice sounded devoid of any emotion,

but his face was in shadow. "Yes," she said.

She had met Prince Edward in a cold passageway near a banquet hall. They had formulated their plans there, to the sound of a haunting melody. The same music that had played at her wedding.

Trying to outdistance the sudden flood of memories, Elizabeth walked blindly away. She wanted to scream, cry, beat her fists against Southwark's walls. She had hated Ranulf. He had placed everything and everyone above her, even other women. Worst of all, he had left her alone countless times. Alone in that wild border land with only the undisciplined servants to keep her company. Servants who whispered behind their hands while she ached inside and mourned for her husband's return.

"You are barren," Ranulf had mocked. "I will pack you off to a nunnery and marry someone young and fertile."

He had never carried out his threat. There had been a bond linking them — a bond of mutual need and weakness.

Coming up behind Elizabeth, Rand said, "It does not matter, Bess. Ranulf and Lady Jane are two bodies long crumbled to dust. We need not accept any connection to us."

"But we *were* connected. I can see her now. She was me, and yet she looked nothing like me. A tiny little thing, with hair so pale and fine, so colorless."

As an atonement for her conspirator's role, she had found Ranulf sanctuary at Southwark. Afterwards, she hadn't really died, just faded away, like the colors in her hair. She had been relieved to lay beside him, encased in stone, where he could never leave her.

"If 'tis so, what does it mean?" Rand asked. "Must we replay our former lives? Will I die a bloody death? Will you betray me all over again?"

"I would never betray you! I love you more than life itself!"

"Then what does it mean?"

She could only shake her head.

"We shall leave London on the morrow," Rand said, after they returned to the inn. "We've done what we came here to do, and I've not lived thirty-four years so that Walter Stafford can have the pleasure of watching me hang."

Thirty-four. Not a very great age for a man. Janey had died at thirty-five. "Why can't we leave right now?" she asked.

"We need money," he stated, his manner cool and distant. "Your fortune no longer exists."

"I'll sell my necklace," she said. Immediately upon exiting Southwark Cathedral, she had removed the symbol of her betrayal. "When the shops open, I'll sell the damn thing. Then we can rid ourselves of England forever."

Rand nodded sharply. Turning his back, he gazed out the window.

She sank onto the bed. It was dark and shadowy in their little room; dark and shadowy like Southwark Cathedral, like the passageway where she had met Prince Edward. Everything was collapsing around her and Elizabeth had no idea what to do. She sensed Rand's unspoken condemnation. Shedding her boots, she tore her breeches and shirt from her body, aware that they still retained the smell from Southwark's poor pit, or at least she thought they did.

"Here, Bess, let me help you."

She hadn't heard Rand's approach. Now she felt him unravel her breast binding. "I'm sorry," she whispered.

"There's no need to apologize." He tossed his own garments aside, then settled on the bed beside her. "In truth, I've been acting the fool."

His voice sounded sincere, but there was an underlying edge of bitterness. "By all that's holy," she said, "I love you."

"And I, you."

At long last, she relinquished the hold on her grief. Her limbs shook, tears coursed down her cheeks, and she glanced wildly about, as if she might pluck a handkerchief from the air.

Rolling onto his back, Rand settled her quivering form atop his, then pressed her face against his shoulder. She wanted to explain, but how could she explain something that was just a memory, that no one could even prove had happened. "We're fairly certain she betrayed him," the curate had said. *Fairly certain.*

"I am not Ranulf, Bess. I won't leave you."

She felt his hands glide down her back. She loved his hands, callused from so many years of hard riding, yet capable of infinite tenderness. Although he applied a light pressure, running his fingertips over the indentation of her waist and the flaunt of her buttocks, her skin burned. It had always been thus. She had always loved his hands.

Rising to her knees, she stared down at his face and saw her desire mirrored in his eyes. Suddenly she was wild to have him, but he gently grasped her upper arms and pushed her away. "You don't want me," she whispered. "There are too many memories between us, shared and unshared."

"I'm tired, that's all."

The clock in their little room ticked away the minutes. Rand lay motionless, his eyes shut, but Elizabeth didn't believe he slept. Several times she reached out for him, but she always drew back. He was clearly not in the mood to be touched. Leaving him, she walked over to the window.

From the shadows of their bed, Rand watched Elizabeth. Her head drooped. Yesterday he would have gone to her, comforted her, but now he watched, knowing that he was the cause of her sorrow.

What the bloody hell was wrong with him? *Bess* hadn't conspired against him, and yet Rand had a feeling she would ultimately betray him. He couldn't explain how he knew this, it defied all logic, but the feeling was there, buried deep, and it wouldn't go away. Finally, he drifted off to sleep.

Near dawn, he felt her violent thrashing and pulled her into his arms. "Wake up, Bess! You're having a bad dream."

"I dreamt I was killing you. I'm killing you, Rand, just as I killed Ranulf."

"That's not true. You didn't kill Ranulf, and I was only half alive until we met." *That's what I should have said before,* he thought.

370

Despite her core of strength, Bess was so vulnerable. Rand was reminded of a willow he had once seen. Whipped by the force of a violent windstorm, the willow's branches had merely brushed the ground. His Bess was like that willow, standing straight and tall after the storm had passed.

Rand had once believed he could bend without breaking, but now he wasn't so sure. He felt defenseless. He had no sword sharp enough to parry the thrusts of the past, and his pistol would be useless against ghosts.

Bess, however, was no ghost, and right now she needed him as much as he needed her. Very gently, he pushed her onto her back and spread her legs. She was hot with her own moisture.

Rand was on fire, as well. Yet he schooled himself to move slowly. If he could not express his emotions in words, he would prove it with his lips. His mouth branded hers, possessive, hungry. Their kiss was the present . . . and the future.

A groan tore from his throat as she reached out, clasped him firmly in her grip, and rubbed the head of his erection against the cleft between her thighs. He smelled her warm female scent. Taut and helpless, he was unable to turn away from her steady gaze, and yet he saw nothing but love in her eyes. Not the slightest hint of betrayal.

Only love.

She still held him as he slid inside her, and the feel of his erection slipping through her fingers was almost more than he could bear.

With a soft whimper she dug her heels into the mattress, arched her back, and rode him, as she had once ridden across the moors. His mouth possessed hers, his tongue seeking entry. He felt her tongue respond, teasing, gliding. A shiver rippled through her. Then another. Inching his hands beneath her buttocks, he thrust once, twice, three times.

Still reeling from her ecstatic quivers, Elizabeth managed to wrap her legs around Rand's hips and take him even deeper. She heard her own throaty mews of pleasure as the perfect harmony of their flesh conjoined in a mutual burst of satisfaction. She felt the proof of his passion, yet he remained silent, and his silence was louder than his usual moans of capitulation, louder than any endearments he might have uttered.

Afterwards he held her tightly, almost desperately, while she nestled her body against his and feigned sleep.

CHAPTER 22

The sign "Dealer in Foreign Spirituous Liquors" was found in front of almost every shop in the Strand, whether grocer's, milliner's, haberdasher's, or furrier's. While each shop specialized in specific items, most carried a variety of goods.

Elizabeth entered a pewterer's shop. The hour was early, the establishment newly opened. Once she sold her necklace, she would buy a couple of greatcoats so that she and Rand could pretend to be merchants. He, along with his cousins, had gone to purchase supplies and a pack mule. Later they would meet back at the inn.

Although she wore a brown woolen gown and a black shawl, as did dozens of other women, Elizabeth felt exposed, vulnerable. When the shopmaster approached, she gingerly removed her necklace from her purse and placed it on top of the counter. The very touch of the golden rope was now loathsome to her.

"How much will you give me for this?"

The master turned the necklace over in his hand. "Fifteen pounds."

"But I paid seventy-five."

He held the necklace up to the window's light. " 'Tis not worth seventy-five. Its workmanship is crude, the style is not popular, and I'd have trouble selling it."

Snatching the necklace from his outstretched hand, she returned it to her purse. "Thank you for your time."

When she reached the door, he said, "Twenty pounds."

She turned around. "Not enough."

"Twenty-five. That's a goodly amount for a woman, even in London."

Elizabeth walked out.

She repeated the scene several times. All the offers were insultingly low. *They believe I'm stupid,* she thought, entering an ironmonger's establishment, cluttered with kettles, pots and watches. *If I were a man, they'd offer me double.*

The ironmonger offered her ten pounds.

Next, Elizabeth tried Harold Harvey's Toy Shop and Miscellanies. In addition to toys, the shop sold jewelry, trinkets, bucklers, clothing, umbrellas and snuffboxes.

Mr. Harvey himself serviced her. He was

short, pear-shaped, and wore his own hair, which was thick and gray and fell over his ears. "Ah!" he exclaimed, after she handed him the necklace.

" 'Tis lovely, isn't it?"

"Aye," Harvey agreed. "I've always liked this particular piece of jewelry. I sold it myself, you know."

"You did?" Elizabeth's heart plummeted as she recalled Walter's comment about finding the necklace inside a toy shop. Glancing over her shoulder, she fully expected a watchman to emerge from the corner, shaking his clapper to summon assistance.

"A very unusual necklace," Harvey said. "I wouldn't be likely to forget it."

Though Elizabeth wanted to flee, she hesitated. Mr. Harvey's revelation might mean nothing at all. Would Walter have been astute enough to visit the toy shop on the off chance that she might, out of all the shops in London, enter this particular establishment? Why would he even dream that she'd sell her necklace? She had read lists in the *Public Advertiser* and other papers, detailing the items Rand had stolen, and the necklace had never been mentioned. As far as Mr. Harvey was concerned, what difference did his previous ownership make?

Walter had not personally bought the necklace. He had sent a servant. Harold Harvey had met Lord Stafford once, and their casual chat was probably no more unusual than a dozen other brief conversations.

The threat was negligible. "I must sell my necklace," she said, summoning a deep sigh. "My mother has taken ill and I am in need of funds."

"I'll give you twenty pounds."

"My mother's servant paid seventy-five."

Harvey studied her. Elizabeth sensed he was eager to complete the purchase.

"It graced my window for a very long time," he finally said.

"I must have at least fifty pounds. Even at that price you'll make a fair profit."

"All right. But I don't have fifty pounds on hand. Come back in an hour."

"I can't do that, Mr. Harvey." She retrieved the necklace. "I need the funds immediately."

His gaze wavered between her and the necklace. "I'll send a prentice for the money. A half hour. No longer, I swear."

Elizabeth considered. Too risky. She shook her head.

"One moment, please. I just remembered that I have money in my lockbox upstairs." Harvey scooped the necklace out of her hand. "I'll be back directly. While you're waiting, peruse my goods. Perhaps you'll see something of interest."

Before she could refuse, he disappeared into the back room. Elizabeth glanced around the shop. Beneath shelves that contained cloth dolls and wooden animals was a rack of clothing. She picked through the meager selection, contemplating a worn but heavy greatcoat that looked to be her size.

The shop bell rang. An elderly woman entered, picked up a silver sand box for drying ink, peered inside, set it down, and began rummaging through a box of lace. All the while, she hummed a monotonous tune that set Elizabeth's nerves on edge.

Finishing with the lace, the woman held some whalebone stays against her generous stomach.

Damn! The shopmaster was taking much too long. Elizabeth considered walking out, but she didn't want to leave her necklace. "Mr. Harvey!" she called.

He appeared, his face shiny with perspiration. "I'm having a bit of trouble," he said. "I seem to have misplaced the key to my lockbox."

"I don't want to wait any longer. My mother —"

"Now I remember where I put the key." Harvey removed a handkerchief from his pocket and wiped his brow, streaking his face powder. "Please, I crave your patience. This time I'll only be a moment."

"I don't care. I've changed my mind. Please return my necklace so that I might go elsewhere."

"All right, if you insist." He licked his lips and wiped his palms on his vest. "But I really would pay you top price."

"Mr. Harvey, I want my necklace. Now!"

At that moment the elderly woman waddled toward the counter, waving the whalebone stays.

"If you'll just wait while I take care of this lady," Harvey implored, "I'll give you some lace for your mother. It might cheer her up."

"Please hurry, Mr. Harvey."

He dawdled over the woman's transaction so long Elizabeth thought she would scream with frustration. She watched him fumble with the wrapping paper and string, and she decided she couldn't linger any longer. Mr. Harvey was either an incredible bumbler, or he was deliberately stalling.

"I'll return in an hour," she fibbed.

"Wait," he protested. "I'm nearly finished."

Elizabeth made an about-face.

The shop bell rang, an ominous sound.

She heard Harvey expel his breath on a long sigh of relief.

Walter Stafford entered the establishment.

Elizabeth stood there as if paralyzed, but her mind raced. She should have known. She *had* known. The moment Mr. Harvey disappeared into the back room, he must have sent a prentice for Walter. This toy shop was, without doubt, one of the first places Walter had contacted.

Why do I always underestimate him?

Walter was holding out his arms. "Elizabeth, dearest!"

She forced herself to run toward him, even embrace him, as if she were indeed his fiancée and had been captured against her will. "I'm so glad you've found me," she said to Walter's diamond buttons. "I've been so terrified."

He patted her back and made appropriate soothing sounds. Elizabeth raised her face. Behind Walter stood a Goliath of a man dressed in the Stafford livery.

Two of them! Oh, God, what am I going to do?

Rand had said to denounce him. Although the very thought was odious, she'd try. After all, her own survival was at stake. She would stall, as Mr. Harvey had successfully stalled,

379

so that she might devise a plan of escape.

"It was horrible, my lord. I prayed every night that you'd rescue me."

"I have men searching from Scotland to Plymouth, Elizabeth. Did that blackguard harm you? Rape you? Where is he? I swear I'll kill him."

"Kill him," she echoed weakly.

"I've been frantic, dearest. How did you ever get away from John Turpin long enough to sell your necklace?"

"He . . . drank sometimes. He took opium, too. He even inhaled ether." Rand had described such drug dens, a common part of London's underground, and it sounded sufficiently debauched to possess the ring of truth. "He threatened dire consequences if I escaped, but this morning, while he slept, I slipped away and wandered the streets until I happened upon the Strand. I was so frightened, nearly out of my mind. Then I remembered what you said about the toy shop. I didn't know you had contacted Mr. Harvey. I told him I needed money for my sick mother. That way if John searched the Strand for me . . ." She stared beseechingly into Walter's face. "He let me keep the necklace . . ." *Why?* she thought frantically. *Why would he do that?* She remembered Zak's hanging, the first one, where the hangman had strangled Zak with a silken cord. "John oft twisted the necklace round my throat if I would not do his bidding, until I was nearly dead from strangulation. Then he would laugh."

Forgive me, my love.

"John was bigger, stronger," she cried. "I tried to escape countless times, but he always found me. Once he lashed me to my horse. He didn't beat me, but I was beaten in spirit, unable to shout for help, or even beg assistance from strangers. I feared every man. I think I might have shunned the very men you sent in pursuit, the ones who read your handbills . . ." She swallowed the rest of her words, aware that she was revealing far too much information.

"There, there, you're safe now. We'll go directly home, to my residence. The carriage waits outside. I'll have a servant retrieve your necklace."

If he gets me in his coach, I'm doomed! As Walter led her from the shop, she saw a constable's wagon parked directly behind Walter's carriage. Armed guards bristled from the wagon's rooftop, while a half dozen mounted men surrounded it.

"Now that you're safe, you must tell us where John Turpin is," Walter said. "I assume he's near here."

Elizabeth swayed against him. "I feel faint, my lord." Collapsing on the shop stoop, she put her head between her knees.

While Walter sent his servant Grosley for vinaigrette, Elizabeth desperately tried to devise some way to give approximately fifteen men the slip.

Kneeling beside her, Walter said, "My brave darling, you're going to be fine." He accepted the vinaigrette from Grosley and waved the bottle in front of her nose.

Elizabeth coughed and jerked her head aside. The smell was powerful enough to revive a platoon of swooning elephants.

Walter helped her rise. "Sit in the carriage, dearest. Soon you'll feel better."

She shook her head. "I prefer to walk. The cold air might revive me."

"Grosley and I will walk with you. But first you must tell me what you know about Turpin's whereabouts. You must remember something, Elizabeth."

" 'Tis difficult. I've been so confused. We never went out, except at night. During the day he never left me alone. Oh, I can't talk about it. The memories are too painful."

"I understand completely. But you must have some idea. Does he bide near the toy shop? The Thames? St. Paul's? Use your powers of observation. As a writer, you must have them. Think, Elizabeth. Where did Turpin keep you?"

She pretended to ponder his question while she pondered escape. How the bloody hell could she obtain more favorable odds? First, she would have to get rid of the law-men.

"I do remember something about our lodgings, my lord. From my window I could see Covent Garden. We were in a tiny side street, near a flash house," she added, making up details as she went along. "I cannot recall the name of the inn, but it had a bay window in front with two broken panes. That's all I remember, except for an abandoned baby near the gate."

Walter conversed with the lawmen, who immediately departed for Covent Garden. Now she would only have to rid herself of Walter and Grosley. With one man on either side, she walked along the footpath. Walter also maintained his arm around her waist, ostensibly for support.

"Would you buy me a pastry from a vendor, my lord? I find that your protection has rejuvenated my appetite."

Walter snapped his fingers and Grosley scurried toward a vendor.

Her serene expression never faltered, never betrayed the trepidation that grew with every step they took. "Wine," she said. "There's an inn. A glass of wine might —"

"I have an even better idea. Why don't we all eat dinner?"

She managed to choke down a venison pie and a glass of claret, hoping fate would intervene. Rand would be expecting her return, and by now he'd realize something was amiss. Walter's carriage, parked outside the inn, had the Stafford coat of arms painted on its doors. To further stall, she ordered a roast leg of lamb, peacock steaks, and rice pudding.

"Didn't that monster ever feed you?" Walter asked.

"Of course he did, but I couldn't eat. I feared he might —" *get caught,* she almost said, just before she clamped her mouth shut.

"You feared his attentions. I understand. Turpin twisted the necklace?"

"Yes."

"Strange. You have no marks on your throat."

"I did, at first. After John broke my spirit, he merely threatened."

"I can't imagine anyone breaking your spirit, Elizabeth."

"I told him I preferred death, but he wouldn't let me die."

"*He* shall die, and that's a promise. You look so pale, my dear. Does Turpin's pending death distress you?"

"No. The memory of my ordeal has made me unwell." Rising, she clutched her belly. "Perhaps another glass of wine might settle my stomach."

"Help yourself."

Walter glared at her while she drank, and she realized that her stall game was at an end. Completely subdued, she allowed him to guide her to his carriage and heard him tell Grosley that he was dismissed. Once they were seated, Walter said, "I want to get you home. I am indescribably eager to witness your reunion with your mother."

"Stepmother," she replied. Then his words pierced the fog inside her head. "Dorothea's here? In London?"

"Of course. Concerned with your safety, where else would she be? Rest your head upon my shoulder, dearest."

"Thank you, but I'm feeling much better." Actually, she felt much worse. Walter had said home, most likely his residence on George Street. It might as well be India. Once they left this part of London, she would be totally lost.

What was he doing now?

He had retrieved a bottle of red wine from

the carriage floor, uncorked its top, and extended it toward her. He wanted her drunk so that she might inadvertently reveal more information. *Pompous ass!* She had consumed many a bottle with Rand and he had admired her clearheadedness. Defiantly, she took several swigs from the bottle.

She heard Walter urge her to drink more. After she had complied, he said, "Something has bothered me from the beginning, Elizabeth. Perhaps you can help me with my uncertainty."

In the dimness of the carriage, she couldn't interpret his expression, but the affected tone had disappeared from his voice. She knew what that meant. Walter Stafford, lawman, had emerged. Warily, she waited for him to continue.

"One thing in particular doesn't make sense. Why would Turpin kidnap you? Am I not correct when I say that you barely knew each other?"

"Yes, you are correct."

"So you knew each other *slightly,* but not intimately."

"Yes. No. You are deliberately confusing me and I really do feel unwell."

"You've dribbled wine down your chin." He whipped out a handkerchief and wiped her face. Dropping the handkerchief, he snaked his arm around her back and rested his hand just below her breast. "Why did Turpin steal you away, Elizabeth?"

Walter put something in the wine. She felt her head lurch downward until her chin rested upon her chest. *He had this planned all along.*

With his free hand, Stafford snatched the bottle and tossed it out the window. "You've had enough, my dear, more than enough. I don't believe I've ever told you how much a drunken woman disgusts me, though it is sometimes necessary."

"Nes-necessary?"

"In order to insure compliance."

"Are you threat . . . threatening me?"

"Why should I threaten you when you're already at my mercy?" Cupping her chin, he forced her head upright and stared into her eyes. "Answer me, Elizabeth. Why did Turpin kidnap you?"

"Revenge," she slurred. "John often said he would make you pay for his partner's death. What better way than to pirate your fiancée and despoil her?"

"Of course. How simple. Simple and diabolical. Yes, that sounds plausible. And yet I sense something more. Why didn't he let you go once he had raped you?"

"He . . . enjoyed me."

"Yes. Who wouldn't? Tell me, Elizabeth, was John Turpin the man who robbed you on your return from London?"

Although her head whirled, she weighed her response carefully. Walter was trying to trap her, had already trapped her, but she couldn't comprehend the reasoning behind his questions. She only knew that she had consistently underestimated him.

"It might have been John," she replied. Even to her own ears, her voice sounded as if it came from inside a deep, dark hole. "I cannot say for certain who robbed me. The highwayman hid his face with a viz . . . vizard. Please, my lord, I fear I am truly ill . . . and so . . . so tired."

"A few more questions and you may sleep, *dearest.* Why did you scream when you saw Zak Turnbull? Open your eyes and pay attention, Elizabeth. Midsummer's Eve. Remember? My guess is that you thought Turnbull was the other highwayman."

"Did not," she mumbled, her mouth filled with pebbles, her stomach lurching.

"Then why did you scream?"

Despite Walter's fingers clamping her face, Elizabeth slumped forward. She felt him release her chin and tug at her hair, until her throat was so taut she couldn't swallow. Her limbs felt like logs. She didn't have the strength to push him away. *Rand,* she pleaded silently. *Rand, help me.*

The coach's interior swam before her eyes, and she felt herself slipping further and further down into the abyss. When the carriage wheels encountered a nasty bump, she merely flopped like a rag doll, even though Walter was forced to loosen his grip so that he might balance himself on the seat.

Just before the relief of total oblivion fell upon her, just before she plummeted toward the carriage floor, she heard him say, "Shit! This time I've overplayed my hand."

CHAPTER 23

With an effort Elizabeth opened her eyes and tried to focus, or at least clear the cobwebs from her brain. Her hands dangled from the arms of a chair, her legs were at an awkward angle, and her feet rested upon an embroidered foot stool. The tall-case clock read three, or was it fifteen minutes past twelve? No, the noon hour had progressed long ago, so it must be three.

"Poor darling." Dorothea materialized, seemingly out of nowhere, and wrapped Elizabeth in a perfumed embrace. "You're safe now. You must rest until you get your strength back. No. Don't say one word. Lord Stafford has told me everything." Dorothea nodded toward Walter, who stood by the window.

Everything? Elizabeth grimaced. *Not bloody likely!*

Dorothea minced over to the fireplace, her short steps prim, affected, and Elizabeth was struck by her stepmother's grandeur. Dorothea was beautifully made up, her coiffure flattering, her gown's décolletage daring. From a distance she looked youthful. In a voice as cold as the diamonds around her throat, she said, "Did you get him, m'lord?"

"My men are searching Covent Garden. If I don't receive a favorable report soon, I'll join the search." He strode across the room until he reached Elizabeth's chair. "Your daughter has recounted a most harrowing tale, Dorothea, including rape and near-strangulation. Yet she managed to escape, which, in my opinion, was very courageous."

Elizabeth bit down hard on her bottom lip to prevent an acrimonious reply. She mustn't defy him. Not yet. Not until she had fully recovered from the drugged wine.

Trying to control her shaking limbs, she glanced around the small but elegant drawing room. While Stafford's furniture was of an excellent quality, only a few pieces graced the interior. She also noted an abundance of windows, as well as French doors opening onto a terrace.

A plush prison. But it hadn't been made for a prison, no matter how closely they guarded her. She felt her spirits lighten. She would escape, just like all her heroines. Well, all save Lady Wilhemina. *Terror in the Abbey* was one of B. B. Wyndham's most popular works, even though it did not have the usual happy ending. After being ravaged by a lust-filled monk, Lady Wilhemina had died in his arms, thus driving him insane and exacting revenge from the grave.

"Once the highwayman is captured, he'll hang," Dorothea said smugly. "And I will watch from the front row."

Again, Elizabeth swallowed an angry retort. Instead, she glared at her stepmother. Dorothea made a regal sight, framed by the carved wooden mantel and a large painting of Westminster Bridge.

No prison hulks disturb that vista, Elizabeth thought, marveling at how the painting's rendering of a brilliant London sky precisely matched the blue of Dorothea's gown. Had she planned it, she couldn't have achieved a more flattering pose. No wonder she enjoyed wealth. It became her.

"I'll make certain your room is readied, dearest," Stafford said. He sounded so honey-tongued, a swarm of bees might very well have flown directly toward him. No denying that he was a first-rate actor.

Following his retreat, Dorothea's manner changed. "You fool," she spat. "You almost ruined everything."

"I don't know what you're talking about."

"All this." Her gesture encompassed the room. "You treat Lord Stafford like an idiot. If he chooses to believe your story, 'tis because it makes the game more interesting, not because he thinks it true. Don't push him too far, Elizabeth, lest his mask slip."

"His mask has already slipped."

"What does that mean?"

She shrugged.

"Lord Stafford will find your lover if he has to pursue him from here to China. Lord Stafford is relentless. Don't gamble on your highwayman, Elizabeth. He's already a dead man."

"I don't know what you're talking about. I was kidnapped. I didn't go willingly."

"Save that prattle for the others, you wagtail. Now that we have the right bait, we shall hook your blackguard soon enough. I had a terrible time convincing Lord Stafford of your innocence." Dorothea approached Elizabeth's chair. "But men can be such dolts when they're consumed by love."

"Lust."

"Whatever."

"I'm very tired, Dorothea. I'd like to go to my room now."

"Patience!" she shouted.

"No, now," Elizabeth said, as a squat, muscular woman with iron-gray hair surfaced from beyond the parlor. She wore a belly cheat over her somber gray gown. One of Walter's housemaids?

"You've been given your instructions, Patience," Dorothea said, nodding sharply toward Elizabeth. "Take my daughter to her room."

Blunt fingers dug painfully into Elizabeth's upper arms as Patience raised her from the chair and guided her, none too gently, toward the door. Elizabeth stumbled and would have fallen if not for the maid's relentless grip.

Should Rand try to rescue me, he'll have more to fear from the brutish Patience than the law, Elizabeth thought, her throat tightening.

"Lord Stafford is not so magnanimous as he pretends." Dorothea minced across the carpet while Patience halted Elizabeth's advance. "I haven't figured out which matters to him more. His regard for justice or his love for you."

"Hogwash! Lord Stafford doesn't possess enough character to care about justice. He's interested in criminals for the monetary compensation. And to use love in connection with me is absurd. Lord Stafford is merely a prideful man determined to have his own way. If you think otherwise, you're deluding yourself."

"You might ponder this, Elizabeth. One word from me to the proper authorities and you shall hang along with your lover. I'll tell them that you were a willing accomplice, that you conspired to rob Lord Stafford and me. I dislike warring with you, but I'll do what I have to do." She stroked her diamond necklace. "I enjoy the life Lord Stafford has shown me. I love London, and I have no intention of returning to the Dales as an innkeeper's wife."

"Ponder this, Dorothea. If I hang, you'll have no hold over Walter. Without me, he won't spend a shilling on you."

"I hope it will not come to that. I trust you'll realize the error of your ways and settle down. Respectable women do not rut with highwaymen, nor do they write books. You've never wanted to be what you should be, and therein lies your folly."

Dorothea nodded to Patience, who ushered Elizabeth out. Ascending a winding staircase, they were joined by two male servants. Upon reaching Elizabeth's room, the two servants took their places on either side of the entrance.

Once inside, Patience locked the door,

dropped the key between her copious breasts, then plopped down onto an upholstered armchair. "We can make this as easy or as toilsome as ye choose," she said. "I'm gettin' well paid t' make certain ye don't bugger off. I know all the tricks, so ye might as well save us both grief."

Elizabeth ignored her. Crossing to the window, she gazed out through its polished glass. Unfortunately, there was no roof jutting below. The shade trees, well-trimmed and at a distance, mocked her. The two-story drop was perilous, virtually impossible, even if the window had not been locked. Fog had crept over Westminster. Elizabeth could barely glimpse the other residences with their vertical lines, elegant doorways, fanlights and porches. Despite the sameness of the exteriors, Great George Street was a coveted address. At Beresford's drum, she had heard it mentioned in reference to a duke and three political figures.

"How far are we from St. James's Park?" she asked Patience.

"Why d'ye want t' know?"

Elizabeth shrugged. Shepherd's was near St. James's Park. Perhaps she could get a message to Rand through his cousin, Tom. It would be best, however, if Rand fled London without her, even though that might mean she'd never see him again.

She felt an intolerable anguish at the thought.

I will see him again. I must. I cannot live without him.

Trying to formulate a plan, trying to keep her fear at bay, Elizabeth stared down upon the yard, the mews, the coach house and stable area, until a thick cloud of foggy mist closed over the vista like a black flux.

Elizabeth sat up in bed. A rose-colored wrapper with lace cuffs discreetly covered her nightshift. Various pillows were plumped behind her. A velvet overspread warmed her legs. Weak sunlight trailed through the bedroom's white satin curtains with their pink ribbon bindings.

Walter had positioned himself on the left side of the bed. Occasionally, he interrupted his reading of the *Morning Herald* to stroke her hand or rearrange her pillows.

"Oh, look!" Walter's crow of delight included Dorothea, whose head had disappeared inside a cone designed to protect her clothes while a hairdresser powdered her latest coiffure.

"The press has finally mentioned the king's madness," Walter continued. "It says here that he has an unknown malady. His

Majesty was able to hold a levee for a brief time at St. James's Palace on Tuesday, October twenty-third, but the strain caused a bad reaction, and he is currently under the care of his physicians."

"Do tell!" Dorothea's voice echoed inside the cone.

"That is not the half of it. I know for a fact that after he returned to Windsor, George had a fit. He supposedly said to an equerry, 'I return to you a poor old man, weak in body and mind.' Then he developed a raging fever, just like yours, Elizabeth. Only, unlike yours, His Majesty's fever manifested itself through incessant talking. The prince's allies say that George is totally insane. Does that tale distress you, dearest?"

"No. Why should it?" Elizabeth shot a scathing glance toward her warder, Patience, who sat at her right, wrestling with a piece of embroidery. *If I lose my mind, Patience will be the cause.*

Following her "rescue" ten days ago, Elizabeth had managed one outing to the theatre, during which she had been politely but insistently flanked by Dorothea, Walter, and Grosley. Unable to endure further charades, she had pleaded illness. But confinement had proven a double-edged sword. While it spared her any harsh treatment from Walter, it isolated her from the outside world.

She knew Walter's men, including members of the Bow Street Runners, were combing London. Walter himself often came and went at a moment's notice, conferring with strangers, or leaving the house, only to return hours later. Each time, she feared he would disclose the news of Rand's capture. But Walter kept his own counsel, which meant Rand remained free.

I must decide upon a proper plan, Elizabeth thought. She had devised several and discarded them all. Sometimes her heroines languished for months in their dungeons or locked tower rooms, but that was designed to lengthen her novels. In real life she'd never endure weeks, let alone months.

Walter pushed aside the *Morning Herald.* "You've been in such a delicate state, my dear, we haven't had an opportunity to discuss, in detail, what happened after your abduction. Every time I mention it, you have the vapors. But today roses bloom in your cheeks."

"I believe I am now strong enough to discuss my ordeal," she said, even though she knew her cheeks were bleached rather than rosy. "Ask your questions, my lord."

"What exact route did you and Turpin take?"

"John took a circuitous route, sometimes backtracking, until he had me thoroughly confused."

"Did you sleep at any inns?"

"We usually hid within a dense forest. John said we must sleep during the day and ride at night."

"But you robbed the Duke of Newcastle in broad daylight."

"I didn't rob the duke. John did. How could I, a mere woman, stop him? In any case, the day was stormy, the afternoon dark and dismal. John said we'd be safe."

Walter fondled the froth of lace at his throat. "My men never found your residence near Covent Garden, nor any place resembling it. Do you have an explanation for that, Elizabeth?"

"I told you. I was confused and couldn't recall details, except for the abandoned baby near the gate. I swear on my life there was a baby."

A knock on the door mercifully interrupted. Walter's butler entered.

"A message just arrived, m'lord." The butler handed Walter a piece of paper. "Most important, I was told."

Walter unfolded the paper. After scanning

its contents, he laughed mirthlessly.

Dorothea had just finished inspecting her coiffure in the looking glass. "What is it?" She flicked her wrist at the hairdresser, dismissing him. "Good news, I trust."

Walter addressed the butler. "Who left this?"

"A street urchin, sir. He scampered away before I could question him."

Walter handed Dorothea the missive. She perused its contents, shot Elizabeth a triumphant look, then read it out loud.

" 'I demand a duel to the death, on sunrise of the morrow. I will meet you at the end of the Mall, near the entrance to St. James's Park. Mistress Wyndham is to be on the opposite end of the park, near the Horse Guards, where I can easily see her. If you do not comply precisely with my instructions, I will not appear.' "

"It's signed with the initial 'J,' " Walter stated.

Elizabeth kept her expression serene, as she tried to figure out what Rand had in mind. Under the circumstances, a duel was worse than reckless. It was stupid.

"You're not going to fight him, are you?" she asked Walter.

"Of course not. He's no gentleman. A duel would be impossible, even if I were so inclined. The whole idea of an officer of the law dueling with a criminal is completely absurd. Who the hell does he think he is?"

Dorothea bent her head and tapped her teeth with her finger. "There must be some way to turn this to our advantage." Raising her chin, she glared at Elizabeth. "How could the highwayman know where Lord Stafford lives? How could he know that Lord Stafford . . . redeemed you?"

"Dear Dorothea," Walter said, "my address is on the posters and handbills. I'm sure Turpin has connections who have informed him of Elizabeth's whereabouts. I didn't try to hide the fact. Actually, I did quite the opposite, to flush him out, which is precisely what happened."

"How clever. Then I assume you'll greet him with a welcoming party."

Walter reached for his snuffbox. "You assume correctly." He sniffed a pinch up each nostril. "I shall hunt the hunter."

"You are so wonderfully devious, my lord." Dorothea clapped her hands. "By this time tomorrow you'll have the fiend in Newgate, where he belongs."

"Or even better," Walter said, smiling at Elizabeth, "he'll be dead."

Walter's coach rattled through a street,

deserted save for a handful of laborers. St. James's Park was nearly adjacent to Great George Street, an easy stroll, but Dorothea had insisted on riding.

"We shall be safe inside the carriage," she had said. "No one can get in to cause mischief. And you —" she motioned toward Elizabeth "— cannot get out."

Squeezed between Dorothea and Patience, Elizabeth sat with her back pressed stiffly against the cushions. She wore a cream satin dress over paniers. Her hands were clasped tightly together, warmed by a white velvet muff, but she couldn't control the chattering of her teeth. Accompanied by two dozen men, Walter had already left for the Mall. As soon as dawn arrived and Rand finished his ride, he would be captured or killed.

And I am the bait that draws him to his doom. Not a willing betrayal, but just as bad.

Once the carriage entered the Mall, Elizabeth tried to grope back into the recesses of the past, to touch the emotion that Lady Jane had felt the moment she removed her necklace — the moment she knew she would betray Ranulf. If Elizabeth and Rand were not connected with Jane and Ranulf, why did she experience such panic at the very thought of that centuries-old betrayal? Panic, yes, and an overwhelming despair.

She yanked herself back to the nonce. She must not face that abyss or she might splinter and become trapped forever between the past and the present. She might even become as mad as His Majesty, babbling incessantly, making no sense at all.

The Mall was little more than a grand alley, wherein royalty had played the game of pall mall. Elizabeth couldn't see Lord Stafford's men, but she knew they were stationed behind the trees that flanked both sides of the road — four towering columns of trees, their spidery branches tangled against the horizon.

When Rand appeared, Walter would allow him to ride all the way to the entrance of St. James's, where Walter himself waited. Then he and his henchmen would surround Rand.

The highwayman comes riding, Elizabeth thought. *Death comes riding.* She could scarce believe that Rand had picked such a vulnerable place to rendezvous. Couldn't he have anticipated Walter's treachery? Suddenly, for no apparent reason, a man who lived by his wits had shown himself uncharacteristically witless. "I'm not Zak," Rand had said atop Westminster Bridge. But he was just as reckless. Rand planned a duel with Death, not Stafford, and Death must always win.

Dorothea rapped her gloved knuckles against the carriage window. "Yonder lies St. James's Palace." She pointed toward a red brick building with pale stone edgings. In the uncertain light, the gate-tower was a chiaroscuro of smoke and charcoal.

"I wonder if the king is in residence," she continued, when Elizabeth failed to comment. "Perhaps, at this very moment, he is drooling about the halls or shouting obscenities at some buffle-headed maid."

They passed Green Park, whose flower beds provided wisps of darkness against the spacious lawns. The carriage turned into St. James's Park. Opposite the park was Buckingham House, but for once Elizabeth didn't care about history. Her fingernails bit into her palms as she pictured Rand's body being shattered by a dozen lead balls. She tried to imagine a life without her beloved. Lady Jane had carted Ranulf's body for five years, then willed herself to die so that she could lie alongside him. Could "Bonny Bess" do the same?

St. James's Park was only a half-mile long. The sun had not yet risen, so the copses, statues, and grazing deer were indistinct blurs. A large lake, the color of graphite, rested in the park's center.

The Horse Guards — which housed the king's personal soldiers — was a tall building located at the park's southern edge. As they circled to a stop beside a stone wall, Elizabeth battled down a feeling of helplessness. Buffeted by Dorothea and Patience, she would not be able to alter the future by so much as a whisper.

Through the carriage window, she watched the sky lighten. Clouds swooped low, like hawks marking their prey. The air smelled of coal smoke and waste, and near the stone wall, of dampness bred too long in ancient places.

Dorothea removed and replaced her gloves, toyed with the window shade, and repeatedly cleared her throat. "I cannot tolerate this," she groaned, pushing open the door and stepping from the carriage.

Almost immediately, she addressed the coachman. "Go see what is happening."

The coachman dutifully set off toward the park's entrance.

Dorothea circled the carriage. She peered up at the Horse Guards, focusing on its distinctive clock turret. She walked along the park wall and kicked at a discarded budget. Then she stalked back to the carriage, yanked open the door, and glared at Elizabeth. "I'll wager your lover never even shows. He knows how badly we want him."

Elizabeth shed her muff and stood, her heart pounding. "Let us watch for him together." She stepped past Patience.

"Stay right where you are," Dorothea warned.

"But how will he know I'm here? If John cannot see my face, he'll get suspicious. He might even run away." Nonchalantly, Elizabeth extended her leg to the topmost step.

"I mistrust you in open spaces." Dorothea slammed the door, barely missing Elizabeth's shin.

Rather than give Patience the satisfaction of witnessing her distress, Elizabeth sank onto the seat and gazed out the window. A handful of exotic ducks dotted the lake. Otherwise, the park appeared deserted. Atop the rocks, a lone pelican rested. It looked as forlorn as Elizabeth felt.

Finally, the coachman returned. "Beggin' yer pardon," he said breathlessly, "but 'e's comin'. 'Tis the 'ighwayman fer certain, enterin' the Mall."

"Damn and blast! I'll miss all the excitement. Oh, I do hate not to see him." Turning, Dorothea surveyed the carriage as if weighing her options. "Patience! Don't let Miss Wyndham leave. I don't care how you restrain her, but if she escapes, it will go hard on you. Do we understand each other?"

Patience bobbed her head. Dorothea bounded across the lawn, escorted by the coachman.

How close is Rand now? Elizabeth wondered. *Halfway down the Mall? I must warn him.*

"Ye'd best behave. I'll obey me orders even if I have t' chop yer legs off." Intent upon her charge, Patience didn't see the carriage door swing open.

"Good morrow to you, Bess." Rand saluted her with the muzzle of his pistol.

Patience wasn't the least bit intimidated. She let loose with a stream of obscenities.

"Stop it," Rand ordered. "If you'll shut up, I'll not hurt you."

Patience inhaled, preparing to scream her bloody head off.

Rand knocked her across the chin with his fist. She grunted and collapsed against Elizabeth's shoulder.

"Damn! I dislike hitting a woman, but I warned her." Rand held out his hand. "Come along, Bess. We haven't much time."

Elizabeth stood. Patience drifted to the floor.

"What if she awakens?" Lifting her skirts, Elizabeth stepped over the inert form.

"Shouldn't we tie her up?"

"Not enough time." Rand swung Elizabeth down, then pulled her through a door cut into the park wall.

While running past the Horse Guards, following the curve in the wall, she peppered him with questions. "How did you get here? Lord Stafford's coachman said he saw you. How did you slip Walter's trap? How can you be in two places at once?"

"Shepherd's is close by. My cousin Tom is on a business errand. If you recall, Tom looks like me. Any moment now, Stafford will discover he's made a dreadful mistake and will be forced to apologize profusely to my cousin."

They reached Birdcage Walk, which skirted the park, before they heard an ear-splitting scream.

"Patience," Elizabeth cried. "The woman you clobbered," she explained.

"Impossible. I hit her hard enough to keep an ordinary person unconscious for hours."

"Patience is anything but ordinary."

"True enough. She looked as bluff as bull beef. Never fear, Bess. The horses are close by, just beyond the gate."

Halfway up Birdcage, they veered out Queen Anne's Gate. The maid's screams followed them.

"Christ," Rand swore. "She'll wake all of London." He hoisted Elizabeth atop Greylag, then mounted Prancer.

" 'Tis a difficult seating," Elizabeth murmured, squirming in the saddle and catching up the reins. "I wish I had my boots and breeches."

"Damn me for a bird-wit! I should have brought them." He looked doubtfully at her petticoats and voluminous skirts. "If we should become separated, we'll meet in Dover. On the beach, below the castle. Do you understand?"

"Yes."

"If Stafford catches me, I'll hang. If *you're* captured, you must say that I forced you to flee at gunpoint, that I threatened to shoot if you did not comply."

"All right. Walter might not believe me, but he does not like to be made the fool."

Rand dug his heels into his stallion's flanks and began galloping along the narrow streets.

Elizabeth raced after him. Sparks flew from Prancer's iron-shod hooves. They clattered past Westminster Abbey and along the Thames. Custom houses loomed dark and silent. Upon the Thames itself, boats stirred and groaned and slipped into the current. The river's scent filled Elizabeth's nose.

Above the water, patches of fog hovered like hesitant ghosts. To the east, the sun burned a crimson hole through the clouds.

Suddenly, the clatter of other hooves mingled with their own. Elizabeth glanced over her shoulder and saw several riders galloping toward her, their arms upraised, their hands brandishing pistols.

Rand pulled farther ahead. Elizabeth crouched over her mare. "Faster, Greylag, faster!" she urged.

A musket ball whizzed past her ear. Greylag's mane lashed her face and stung her eyes. From the various docks, dogs yapped. Elizabeth dared not look back. The entire world might be chasing her.

Rand swiveled in his saddle. "I love you," he said, the wind whipping at his words. "I always have and I always will."

Elizabeth slammed her heels into her mare, who responded with a powerful surge. The Thames lapped at the embankments. A patch of sunrise splintered the clouds and flashed scarlet upon the water.

A milkmaid at a crossroads leapt out of the way. Milk splashed from her pails onto the cobblestones. "Cork head!" she screeched. "Clod pate! The devil take ye!"

The devil shall not take me, Elizabeth thought desperately. She would not let Walter or his fellow vermin capture her.

She tried to keep up with Rand, whose trail resembled that of a serpent's. The river disappeared, reappeared. Greylag skittered round a corner, then raced on. Through blurry eyes, Elizabeth saw occasional fields and orchards . . . fewer houses . . . they were leaving the city. Escape actually seemed possible —

Greylag stumbled over a loose cobblestone. Elizabeth tilted sideways. Dropping the reins, she grabbed at Greylag's neck, which was slick with perspiration. *No! Please, God, no!*

Desperate, Elizabeth kicked the stirrups free, hoping to better grip the horse's barrel with her legs. Then she felt her feet tangle in her billowing skirts.

Greylag, still game, kept on going. Elizabeth did not.

CHAPTER 24

"I've had all manner of interesting patients, some of them quite mad."

Through the pounding of her head, Elizabeth recognized the sonorous voice of Doctor Arthur Purefoy.

"Some years ago I treated a prominent lord who believed himself to be a turkey hen. He made a nest of straw in his coach. Except for a brief luncheon and the evacuation of his bowels, he sat there, atop a veritable dozen of eggs."

"I trust the gentleman didn't lay the eggs himself." Walter sounded sardonic.

"What happened to the prominent lord, Dr. Purefoy?" Dorothea's voice. "Did you cure him?"

"No, Mrs. Wyndham. Eventually his wife, an accommodating woman, removed the eggs and replaced them with chicks, whereupon his lordship strutted about, clucking delightedly."

"I wonder if His Majesty thinks he's a chicken. Have you attended *him,* Dr. Purefoy? Is he as clapper-clawed as they say?"

"Ah, Mrs. Wyndham, the stories I could tell."

Elizabeth opened her eyes to discreet slits. Judging by the shadows, it was late afternoon, though it was impossible to be certain since the sky was obliterated by a dreary rain. Incense pots burned pastilles, saturating the room with a strong, pleasant scent. Dorothea, Walter and Dr. Purefoy were seated at a table. The physician was middle-aged and corpulent, his nose broken-veined, his complexion marked by either venereal disease or smallpox.

"Did I tell you about the time at Windsor when His Majesty, dressed in a nightshirt, happened upon the Prince of Wales and his younger brother?"

"No, Dr. Purefoy, but I'm breathless with anticipation," Dorothea said, pouring coffee from a silver urn.

Even the weak light was painful, thought Elizabeth. During her fall from Greylag, she had struck her head on the cobblestones, and she wished Dr. Purefoy would not speak so loudly. Every word was a hammer blow to her brain.

But he had already launched into a spirited account of the incident. "Old George said to young Frederick, 'Oh, my boy! I wish to God I might die, for I am going mad.' "

Flourishing his gold-knobbed cane, which along with his black wig and pompous expression were necessary accouterments of his profession, Purefoy continued. "One of the king's physicians, Dr. Baker, tried to lead His Majesty from the sitting room. Whereupon, the king grabbed Dr. Baker by the throat and pinned him against the wall. Nearly strangled the poor chap."

"Mercy!" Dorothea exclaimed.

"His Majesty's actions bring to mind an interesting dilemma," said Walter. "Whether force can be used on a king, or whether you must allow him to kill you if it pleases him, rather than commit treason by restraining his illustrious person."

Elizabeth's eyelids drooped. She knew Dr. Purefoy had bled her, but she remembered little else, save that Rand had escaped. Even through her haze of pain, she had heard Walter bellowing his rage and frustration.

"Many physicians treat His Majesty," Purefoy said, "but some of their remedies are nonsensical. One physician insists on immersing the king in hot baths when everyone knows how unhealthful water is. I recommended shaving the top of His Majesty's head and blistering it to remove the poison in his brain. And indeed, when that remedy was applied, His Majesty immediately improved."

Elizabeth struggled to stay awake. The potion Purefoy had earlier administered made her feel so drowsy.

I must escape, she thought. *Must. Find. Rand.*

"Two o'clock and a fine clear night, and all's well."

Elizabeth heard the call of the watch outside her window. Save for the sound of coal shifting in the fire grate, her room was silent. An oil lamp burned, illuminating Patience asleep at the table, her face resting on her arms.

Head spinning, Elizabeth inched upwards. Gritting her teeth, she touched the dressing Purefoy had applied to the side of her head. Pray to God the doctor didn't recommend shaving and blistering for anyone other than the king. A lock of hair, tangled but securely fastened to her scalp, reassured her.

"All right, Bess," she whispered. "Think." She knew that she had fallen from Greylag and hit her head. She didn't know how she had been returned to Great George Street, but that wasn't important. Rand was important. His whereabouts. He had said they'd meet in Dover. Had he said it this morning? Yesterday? Three days ago? Perhaps at this very moment he waited for her on the sands below Dover Castle.

I must escape!

The maid's sudden snores provided an excellent opportunity, as did the lack of guards at the doorway. Since her debilitating injury, Walter had dismissed them.

In *Castles of Doom,* quiet but determined Lady Guinevere had given lust-crazed King John the slip by climbing out of a tower window. By comparison, Elizabeth's escape would be effortless.

She edged her calves over the side of the bed. Her legs felt remarkably leaden, but she eased herself successfully off the mattress. Overcome by a wave of dizziness, she slouched back until the spell passed.

From outside drifted the sound of an off-key baritone, struggling through a ballad. Patience snorted and sputtered, but didn't awaken. Elizabeth tiptoed past the table. Her balance was awkward, and while she tried to be stealthy, her legs responded erratically. One foot left the softness of carpet for bare wood. A board creaked. Heart in her throat, she froze and stared at Patience.

Lamplight played across the maid's small eye socket while yet another snore wheezed through her lips.

At long last, Elizabeth reached the door. The knob felt cold in her hand. She turned and pulled. Nothing happened. Desperate, she tried to yank the door open.

"Damme," she breathed. "Locked." She should have known. If her mind hadn't been so fogged, she would have known.

What now? Think! Patience carries the key between her breasts. I don't want to grope around in there!

Trying to conjure up an alternative solution, Elizabeth slumped against the door. She spied the poker beside the fireplace, near a stack of wood, and sighed with relief. She would whack Patience over the head, rend her bodice, then extract the key.

Once again Elizabeth tiptoed past the table. Reaching the fireplace, she grasped the poker.

"What're ye doin'?"

Elizabeth whirled. Face thrust forward like an angry bull, Patience was on her feet.

"Give me the key!" Elizabeth hoisted the poker.

Flexing her fingers, Patience approached. "Get back in bed 'fore I throw ye in."

Elizabeth swung the poker. Patience

grabbed it and wrenched it from Elizabeth's hands. Off balance, she staggered and fell. Scrambling to her feet, she scooped up one of the logs.

Weapons in hand, the two women circled each other.

"I'm not giving up and you don't dare hurt me," Elizabeth said. "Lord Stafford will pike your head if you do."

"When ye buggered off last time, I took the scold. This time I'll make certain ye stay put."

"The only way you can stop me is to kill me, and if you kill me you'll be dismissed."

" 'Tis worth the price!" Patience shouted, swinging the poker at the log.

The shock of impact reverberated along Elizabeth's arms. Pain stabbed her brain so suddenly and powerfully, she was momentarily blinded. Dropping the log, she stumbled toward the table, hoisted the coffee urn, and threw it. The urn bounced harmlessly off the far wall. She hurled the cups and saucers, even the tray, but Patience dodged them all.

Walter bolted into the room, followed by Dr. Purefoy.

"What's going on here?" Walter demanded, dropping his ring of keys into the pocket of his silken dressing gown. In lieu of a wig, his shaven head was covered by a turban.

"She tried t' kill me!" Patience screeched. "I was only per'tectin' meself."

Walter's eyes narrowed. "Do you have an explanation for your behavior, Elizabeth?"

"I should not be kept prisoner, especially since I am innocent of the first abduction and did not instigate the second. John threatened us with a pistol, which *she* can verify." Elizabeth pointed at Patience. "When John was far ahead and I could have halted, your men shot at me, forcing me to continue my ride. I am not at fault and should be allowed to come and go as I please."

Dorothea swept inside, while a half dozen servants peeked through the door. "What has happened?" she cried.

"Your daughter was trying to escape," Walter replied, his gaze still fixed on Elizabeth.

"Surely not! Why would she do such a thing?"

"I could administer another sleeping potion," Purefoy offered. His wig, hastily donned, was off-center. His head bobbed and the cascading curls brushed one shoulder. "Her actions prove how sick she is, how irrational —"

"Nonsense!" Walter scowled at the physician. "She knows precisely what she's doing!"

"Are you questioning my expertise, sir?" Purefoy assumed his most authoritative stance. "Need I remind you that I have a degree of Doctor of Medicine from Marischal College, Aberdeen? Furthermore, I am a member of the Royal College of Phys—"

"I don't care if you're a member of the Royal College of Asses, and I don't require a list of your bloody credentials. All of you! Get out!"

Dorothea hesitated at the doorway. "Elizabeth isn't herself, my lord. Her head suffered a nasty crack. Please don't judge her too harshly."

"Out now!"

Once they were alone, Elizabeth faced him. His breathing sounded as loud and uneven as her own. To support her body, shaking from fear and fatigue, she sagged against the table.

"You bitch! How dare you humiliate me?"

"I didn't mean to. I merely wanted —"

"Shut up! Ever since our first meeting, you've treated me like a bug. I didn't mind. Challenges always intrigue me, but this time you've gone too far." His face contorted. "I won't be made to look the fool."

"That was not my intention." She inched away from the table. The poker remained in the middle of the room. If Walter became violent, she might be able to protect herself. "Even you must admit I've never led you on. From the very beginning I was truthful about my feelings."

"I don't give a damn about your bloody feelings. You should have thanked God that I even deigned to look at you. No money! No prospects! What did you ever have to offer except a pretty face and body?"

"That's what I despise about men like you." She felt her temper flare. "Why should I have to bow and scrape just because your private parts are a different shape than mine?"

"What about your highwayman?" Walter grabbed her wrists. "You were happy enough with *his* private parts. That's the ultimate insult, the one thing I cannot tolerate. To prefer a common criminal's cods to mine."

"I didn't prefer —"

"Shut up!" He jerked her to him. "You've driven me to distraction. I don't desire anyone but you, and I hate it. You've ruined everything." He pinioned her against his chest. "I was willing to marry you, even after I knew you were despoiled for honest wedlock. That's how far I've fallen. A

422

magistrate who lusts after the mistress of a highwayman!"

"I'm not his mistress."

"Whore, then."

"I'm not his whore." *I'm his love, his only love.* "It wasn't my fault. John threat—" She swallowed the rest of her words as terror stabbed through her.

Walter was *smiling!* His eyes sparked, but a smile that could only have been cast by the Lord of Vermin himself twisted his lips.

"You'll not have a shred of pride left when I'm done with you," he said, pushing her to her knees.

Her gaze skimmed the edge of his dressing gown. Walter was wrong. Her pride ran deep and left no room for begging. In any case, she had a feeling his lust fed on rebellion. Swallowing bitter bile, she prayed she could endure.

"No resistance, dearest?" Walter crossed his arms over his chest. "I thought you were filled with contumacy. Remember our discourse? Lady Guinevere?"

"Yes. Outside the White Hart, in the fog, the night you were robbed. That was when you first said you enjoyed a challenge." She touched her fingers to her bandage. "In my weakened state, I am no challenge."

"We shall see. Lie on your back and raise

up your shift."

"Go to hell," she said softly.

"Do you prefer the bed?"

"I prefer death, my lord."

"I think not." A chuckle rumbled in his throat as he grabbed her wrists, pulled her from the floor, and crushed her against his chest.

She reacted instinctively. Situated beneath the canopy of the forest, waiting for nightfall, Rand had taught her several methods of defense. Now, she yanked her knee up hard into Walter's groin.

His smile finally disappeared. His eyes bulged. Doubling over, he groped beneath his gown, below his stomach.

Elizabeth froze, torn between the urge to flee and the urge to whack Walter with the poker. That indecision, brief though it was, cost her the advantage she had gained.

Only partially recovered, he was on her in an instant, toppling them both with the momentum of his body. The hard floor rose up to meet her back. Pain exploded in her rump and legs, as well as her head. Her arms felt numb.

Still grunting, Walter ripped apart her shift, his nails leaving small gashes across her naked flesh. His hand squeezed her breast and she let out a piercing wail. Then, with the greatest effort in her life, she bit back a second scream.

Walter appeared disappointed, but that didn't prevent his lustful gaze from scouring her body.

Elizabeth shut her eyes. Footsteps sounded in the hallway, soon muffled by the loud beat of her heart. She felt her thighs wrenched apart, felt Walter grind his hips into position.

Suddenly, his hardness diminished. His weight abruptly left her body. Taking one deep breath, then another, Elizabeth opened her eyes.

Dressing gown askew, Walter loomed above her, facing a man who stood less than three feet away.

Billy! Rand's cousin, Billy Turnbull.

The Stafford livery barely contained Billy's chest, a prizefighter's chest. Beneath the livery, his muscles rippled menacingly. His gaze imparted anger and sympathy, just before he challenged Walter's glare.

"Get gone from this room!" Walter shouted, his face red with fury.

"The lady's hurt," Billy said, his fists clenched.

"That's none of your concern!"

"I heard her scream, m'lord. I sent a servant for the doctor an' her mum."

"How dare you! I'll have you killed, you witless scum!"

"For wot?"

Elizabeth struggled to a sitting position. A fierce stab of joy coursed through her. Rand wasn't in Dover. He had planted Billy in Lord Stafford's employ so that Billy could watch over her, protect her. If her pride had not prevented her from screaming at the very start, Billy would have put a stop to the rape much sooner.

Walter's mouth opened and closed like a fish, and Elizabeth realized that Billy was in no immediate danger. Walter couldn't kill him. What explanation would serve to justify such an action? Interrupting the rape of a gentlewoman would never suffice, and Walter might even find himself gaoled with the same felons he had captured — a fate worse than death.

"You're sacked, dismissed!" Walter roared.

"In that case, m'lord, I have nothin' t' lose."

Billy's fist snaked out so quickly Elizabeth couldn't believe her eyes. She heard Walter hit the floor with a teeth-jarring thud. Billy tossed her a blanket from the bed, then grabbed Walter's ankles and dragged him toward the door.

"His lordship won't come 'round till mornin', Miss Wyndham," Billy said, his taut muscles rending the seams of his livery. Dead to the world, Walter's weight was considerable. "And me cousin will have brewed up some new scheme by then, never fear."

"Where is . . . ?" Elizabeth clamped her mouth shut. Dr. Purefoy, Dorothea and Patience had entered the room.

Dropping Walter's ankles, Billy bolted through the confused maze of bodies.

Nobody tried to halt his flight, and Elizabeth silently wished him Godspeed.

Everything was gray, as if viewed through a fog. She saw herself from a position directly above the bed where she lay. Her pale hair spread across the pillows, dwarfing the delicate features of her face. She had wasted to little more than a shadow. Finally, she was dying. Upon Ranulf's death, she had willed herself to die, but it had taken far too long. She welcomed Death. More than welcomed him. Hungrily embraced him.

But Death had proven himself a capricious lover, just like Ranulf. She wanted Ranulf so badly. She missed him more than the children she'd never borne. Without Ranulf, her life had lost all meaning, like a summer without sun. Life would be forever gray and black and white, without the green of tree leaves, the red of roses, the pinwheel colors of excitement and laughter. Soon she and Ranulf would be reunited. In hell, most assuredly, for their sins had been great.

Her soul floated upwards, beyond the canopied bed, past the shadows hiding the ceiling rafters, into a blackness pricked with stars . . .

Elizabeth's eyes snapped open. Her world was dark, too. No matter how hard she tried, she couldn't escape. Her head still ached but it was a dull pain, akin to the pain in her heart.

I feel like Janey.

Lady Jane had lost Ranulf and she had lost Rand. Without Rand, the flowers were gray, the trees white, the sun black.

Why struggle anymore?

CHAPTER 25

The next day Walter, Elizabeth and Dorothea visited the Tower of London. Elizabeth saw the celebrated statue of Henry the Eighth. Walter pressed a piece of floor and Henry's overstuffed codpiece, lined in red velvet, rose in a lewd fashion. Believing it to be a protection against barrenness, several women stuck pins into the codpiece. Handing Elizabeth a pin, Walter insisted she do the same. She complied.

Why struggle anymore?

Inside the tower's armory, Elizabeth happened upon Ranulf Navarre's broadsword, displayed in a case that contained relics from the thirteenth century. "Used in the treacherous uprising against Henry III," the inscription stated.

Ranulf's sword had been ravaged by the centuries, but a sliver from the true cross of Christ had once rested inside its pommel. Janey had belted the sword across Ranulf's hips before he went into battle. Elizabeth could see it all so clearly, yet it didn't seem to matter anymore. Lady Jane was dead and Rand's Bonny Bess might as well be dead, too.

Damn your soul, Walter Stafford, she raged inwardly, a momentary spark of fury tempering her weariness. *Save for your stubborn greed and blasted pride, Rand and I would have spent the rest of our lives together.*

Following their Tower visit, Elizabeth accompanied Walter and Dorothea through the gardens of Ranelagh. She vaguely noted that Walter had covered his bruised cheek with heavy white makeup. Despite his mustache and goatee, the bright sunshine made him look like the man in the moon.

Moon! Dear God, what would happen tonight when Billy was not in residence? Pray God that Rand had "brewed up some new scheme" to thwart Walter's pending assault.

Ranelagh possessed an enormous rotunda with a huge central fireplace, and — in Walter's words — was *the* place to take tea and be seen. Rather than tea, Elizabeth sipped a punch that smelled of lemons and oranges and was so loaded with sugar she could scarce taste the brandy.

Portions of Ranelagh's spacious lawns had

recently been cut. Inhaling the scent of new-mown grass, Elizabeth was reminded of the White Hart gardens. She missed her father, who was administering the renovations on Wyndham Manor. She missed the Dales, too. The moors would be cold and wind-blown now, the trees shed of their leaves, the sheep and cattle huddled in their rock barns. Perhaps the hills would be blanketed with snow, the streams overlain with a layer of ice.

She wished she could go home, but dismissed the notion as whimsical. And impractical. Rand was in London. Even if he had fled, he wouldn't have headed north.

A fragment from the poem she'd written after Zak Turnbull's execution teased her memory:

I have been here before,
But where or how I cannot tell;
I know the grass beyond the door,
The sweet, keen smell,
The sighing sound, the lights around the
    shore.
You have been mine before,
How long ago I may not know;
But just when at the swallow's soar
Your neck turned so,
Some veil did fall — I knew it all of yore.

Tears threatened to overflow. She had lost her only love, possibly forever. Only remnants remained, like shredded dreams.

Dorothea leaned across the table. "Did Lord Stafford tell you? We're going to visit Shepherd's tonight."

Perhaps Tom would be there and she could ferret out news of Rand, thought Elizabeth. She would have to be very careful. Surely the aborted ambush had revealed Tom's kinship to Rand. Perhaps not. After all, Walter knew Rand as John Turpin.

"You look pensive, dearest," Walter said. "Don't you want to visit Shepherd's?"

"I don't care where we go." Most likely Tom wouldn't be there. Even if he was, Walter would surely stick as close to her as the rowel on a spur.

"The Prince of Wales is scheduled to put in an appearance." Walter sipped his drink, awkwardly crooking his little finger. "Prince George is a dedicated gambler. How would you like to meet a real prince, Elizabeth?"

She studied her punch. If she tilted the glass just so, she could see her reflection in its depths. Or at least one eye and a portion of her nose.

"Mind your manners and answer Lord Stafford," Dorothea said sharply.

Elizabeth stared blankly at Walter.

"Oh! I nearly forgot!" Reaching into his pocket, he retrieved a folded sheet of paper. "Look at this."

Elizabeth gazed down at a sketch of Rand's face. The poster appeared identical to all the others she had seen, save for the bold headline: 2,000 GUINEAS REWARD

The vast amount jolted her from her apathy. "Two thousand guineas! God's teeth!"

Walter looked pleased with himself. "I finally persuaded the Duke of Newcastle to increase his reward. The duke is still incensed over the brutal treatment of his lovely wife."

Brutal treatment? Elizabeth stifled a snort.

"It is merely a matter of time before someone turns the thieving bastard in," Walter said.

"Saint Peter himself would sell his soul for two thousand guineas," Dorothea gushed.

Walter laughed. "Fortunately for us, the world contains far more Judases than saints."

Lord Stafford's carriage halted in front of Shepherd's. Descending, Elizabeth felt her ankle begin to twist. But her stepmother's handsome escort, Anthony Harrod, swiftly reached out and set her securely on her feet. Father had insisted that he and he alone orchestrate the renovations on Wyndham Manor, thus Anthony was Dorothea's current "Cicisbeo" — the euphemism for a man who escorted married women.

Elizabeth heaved a deep sigh. She suspected the manor's repairs had less to do with Father's absence than his daughter's despicable behavior. Father had always lived in a world of illusions. If he wasn't present, it couldn't be happening.

Once her illusions had been her whole world. Not anymore. She would give anything she possessed, including her writing career, to be held by Rand, kissed by Rand, caressed by Rand. Only he would never expect her to give up what Walter called her "scribblings." Rand admired her intellect.

And my courage, she reminded herself, raising both her chin and the hem of her skirt.

Shepherd's interior included heavy velvet and brocade drapery, inlaid floors of polished wood, hand-painted Chinese wallpaper, Chippendale chairs and upholstered settees. A magnificent staircase led to game rooms on the second floor, while the first floor contained two rooms devoted primarily to faro and hazard. As Anthony escorted Dorothea to the ladies' water closet, Walter explored every nook and cranny. "Very nice," he said repeatedly. "Very expensive."

"You've never been here before?" Elizabeth asked, surprised.

"This lovely home was once owned by a Miss Angel Cipriani, who opened it for public entertainments. Well known leaders of the town attended her parties and masquerades, including the Duchess of Hamilton and the Duke of Gloucester . . ."

His calculated pause hinted that Elizabeth should express the appropriate awe, but she couldn't have cared less if the Devil himself had attended.

"Miss Cipriani's galas hid all kinds of illegal doings," Walter continued, "and the attention of my mentor, John Fielding, was eventually drawn to them. She was brought before the justices, convicted and fined. Afterwards, she sold her home."

"To Mr. Shepherd?"

"No. Richard Shepherd bought it three years ago, changed its name, and made it quite respectable."

"Then I don't understand why —"

"Miss Cipriani sold it to one of her lovers. I wasn't welcome. You see, I was somewhat responsible for the lady's downfall. Now that I'm a business partner in my own gambling establishment, I've become honorable, even praiseworthy, an irony you should appreciate. I've waited twenty years to enter these doors. On my oath, I'll never again abstain from what I deserve or desire."

"Why do you believe you deserve me?"

"I'd be the first to admit that I deserve better. You are nothing more than a landlord's daughter. But I *desire* you, my dear."

Her tranquil expression never faltered, never betrayed the terror that grew with every word he spoke. Tonight he would become dishonorable and there was nothing she could do about it.

Before she could respond, Dorothea returned. A servant took their wraps and they entered the second room, where a mahogany hazard table dominated. An overhead lamp shone down upon its green playing field, illuminating the dice boxes.

"Every evening gamblers are given three new pairs of ivory dice," Walter said. "An expense that annually sets Mr. Shepherd back two thousand pounds. But it's a pittance compared to the food and drink, which is free to all players."

"Free?" Dorothea squealed. "Goodness!"

" 'Tis not so magnanimous," said Elizabeth. "The longer one remains at the table, the more likely the odds will turn against him."

"That is correct, dearest." Walter smiled, although she suspected he had a different meaning in mind — her capitulation. "You are very wise for a woman."

They passed a tray heaped with culinary delights. "Peacock steaks, lobster and salmon!" Dorothea exclaimed, snatching a cluster of grapes.

"Shepherd's has a divine French chef," Anthony said. "Even if he is a bit difficult, as all Frenchmen are."

Elizabeth surreptitiously sought Tom among the croupiers, but any anticipatory hope had waned. If she spotted Tom, what difference would it make? She might slip him a note, but what if Walter, hound-like, sniffed out her ploy and questioned Tom?

For the moment, it was safer to do as she was told.

"Look at those cunning little cakes," Dorothea gushed. "Oh, Anthony, do get me several. I believe I can play much better on a full stomach."

Anthony dutifully followed the waiter. Elizabeth wondered if her stepmother's escort would spend the night in Dorothea's bed. Probably. Ciscibei enjoyed being part of the entourage of beautiful or high born women and satisfied their every desire. Anthony had been hired by Walter, of course, but Elizabeth was no longer certain of anything regarding her father's marriage. She only knew that Dorothea's face had the look of a satiated lover — a look Elizabeth would never have recognized had she not met Rand.

"Would you like some cakes?" Walter asked. He surveyed Elizabeth's gown, a blue silk decorated with flowers, ribbons, lace and ruching. It had been sewn by a dressmaker who emulated the French designer, Rose Bertin. Rose Bertin serviced Queen Marie Antoinette. "In truth, you are a mere shadow of your former self."

"Who is that man?" Elizabeth discreetly gestured toward the far end of the room, thinking to change the subject since Walter knew very well why she had lost so much weight. Her trepidation over Rand's capture contributed, as did her reluctance to consume one morsel unless it was served from a shared platter. She suspected Walter was not above drugging her again. "The man seated behind the large desk," she clarified.

"That's Richard Shepherd, entering private wagers into a betting book. He also metes out loans on drafts and pays off successful claims."

Dorothea jabbed Elizabeth with her fan. "There he is! The prince himself!"

Elizabeth followed Dorothea's impolite finger. The Prince of Wales was the most striking of the gentlemen clustered around Mr. Shepherd. Not much older than Elizabeth, George was tall and even more handsome than she'd heard. Gossips maintained he pursued women as passionately as he gambled — as passionately as he collected mansions, fine paintings, and racehorses.

Many patrons stood a prudent distance away, ogling England's heir apparent, who was well aware that he was playing to a wide audience. Repeatedly, his gaze found Elizabeth's and his grin seemed to intimate all manner of sensual delights.

"Ladies and gentlemen, you've all heard my wager." George's gesture, surprisingly graceful in one so intoxicated, included Elizabeth and her entourage. "I am certain that by November, 1789, I shall be King of England. My good friend here disagrees." George's arm encompassed the shoulder of a shorter man with a pleasant, intelligent face. "Charles declares that I shall be king much sooner."

From behind her fan, Dorothea said, "Who is that young man with the prince?"

"Charles James Fox," Walter replied. "He's

the son of Lord Holland, an enemy to King George and one of Parliament's most brilliant orators. Fox is a Whig, always in direct opposition to His Majesty's policies, which, I suspect, is the primary reason why the prince chose him for a friend."

George's wager shattered Elizabeth's favorable impression. To become king, George would have to issue a *coup d'etat,* force his father to abdicate, or assume the throne upon His Majesty's death. How could such a sweet smile mask such treachery?

"Recently my father carried on a conversation with an oak tree." George's voice was both masculine and melodious. "The conversation was rather one-sided. Thinking the tree to be the king of Prussia, Father engaged in a rather spirited discussion on the divine rights of kings." George's padded shoulders lifted in a delicate gesture of revulsion. "Unfortunately, Father never paused long enough to allow the poor tree a chance to respond."

"I believe I prefer a mad monarch to a disloyal brat," Elizabeth murmured.

"Many people agree with you, dearest." Walter stroked her bare shoulder.

Shrugging off his hand, Elizabeth walked away, and was pleasantly surprised when he did not follow. Upon entering the front gaming room, she immediately spied Tom. They stared at each other for a long moment before he leaned over and, using a small wooden rake, swept the losers' counters across the table.

Walter grasped her by the elbow; he had followed after all. "There's a handsome young man," he said, staring at Tom. "The lad looks familiar to me. Does he to you?"

Elizabeth's mind raced. Tom had taken Rand's place at the duel. Unless Walter was totally absentminded, which he wasn't, he damn well remembered where he'd seen Tom.

"If you mean that young croupier, he resembles John Turpin." She feigned a shudder. "He frightens me, my lord."

"Don't fret, dearest. Your highwayman will not despoil you again, and that's a promise."

A promise you'll never keep, she vowed.

At the faro table, Tom swiftly turned over several cards. Then, unaccountably, he dropped the deck, which scattered on the table and floor.

"What a nervous lad," Stafford scoffed.

Once again, Elizabeth retreated. The very sight of Tom was too painful, and with Walter shadowing her, too dangerous.

Inside the second room, amid much

441

laughter, wine and bantering, the prince and his friends were playing faro. All of them had turned their coats inside out in a ritual designed to generate good luck, but tonight the ritual had proven worthless. The prince, especially, had racked up heavy losses.

Walter took his place at the hazard table, while Elizabeth stood numbly by his side. Suddenly, she realized that she was surrounded by dozens of people. What was to prevent her from just walking away? It might be feasible, especially since Walter appeared increasingly distracted. Sometimes he left her alone and disappeared into the adjoining room for long periods of time. His indifference was unsettling. Elizabeth wondered if she dare take advantage of his preoccupation, but concluded that Walter was conducting some sort of test. Should she call his bluff, he might spring an appropriately diabolical trap.

What could be more diabolical than the rape that awaited her? She didn't know, but she didn't care to find out. Passivity was the answer. Passivity before, during, and after. She would endure because she had no choice. She would survive because Rand would want her to survive. *I love you, Bess. I always have and I always will.*

Aye. This time she would survive.

This time? The familiar fist knotted inside her belly, then rose to her throat. Lady Jane was invading her mind again.

While Walter continued his erratic behavior, George played faro. Occasionally, he stared at Elizabeth. Although she didn't dare ignore him, she returned his attention with a distant smile.

"My dear!" George beckoned. "Would you assist me? You look like the piece of luck I so desperately need."

Obeying, Elizabeth wondered whether an opportunity had just presented itself. Perhaps she could figure out a way to exploit the prince's weakness for women.

"What is your name, my pet?" he asked.

"Elizabeth Wyndham, sire." She curtsied low, giving George an eyeful of her décolletage.

"Why have I not seen you about London before? Such a lovely lady should not be kept hidden."

At that moment, Walter returned. Looking both pleased and alarmed by George's attention, he edged over to Elizabeth's side.

In a flash, she conceived her plan. Would it work? It had to. "I don't go out very much, sire. Lord Stafford keeps me busy at home. 'Tis a full job being a man's mistress."

Walter's face turned puce. Several ladies tittered behind their fans. George's eyes widened in surprise, but he recovered quickly. "I trust it is a full-time job, if done laudably. May I say, Mistress Wyndham, that Lord Stafford is a very lucky man."

"I surmise that you are also lucky." She felt Walter's anger, battering her in invisible waves. "I could bring you luck, sire, not only at the gaming table but in other areas as well."

His eyes appraised her. "I'm sure you could, my pet."

She leaned closer. "I wouldn't require much. I'm a daughter of the quill, an authoress. If I had a small house in the country and a meager allowance until I sell my next novel . . . well, all I ask is that you do not beat me."

"I would never harm one so lovely as you, my beauty."

"Let us discover whether I can bring you luck at faro," Elizabeth said, as she placed her hand atop George's and helped him push all his counters to the center of the table. Purposefully, she allowed her breast to touch his chest, a strand of perfumed hair to brush his chin.

Walter mopped his brow with his handkerchief, then clenched his fist as if to strike her. Surrounded as she was, however, Elizabeth knew he wouldn't make a violent scene.

Several turns had already been taken until only three cards remained under the winning one. Around the table, bets were placed on the order in which the three would appear. Twice, George called the turn correctly, his arm snaking around Elizabeth's waist, his warm hand squeezing her stays after each successful call. When the croupier turned over the final card — a nine of spades, just as George had predicted — the table erupted with delighted shouts.

The prince cradled Elizabeth's chin and kissed her on the lips. "You did bring me luck, my sweet," he exalted.

"I could bring you something better than luck," she said softly. "If you take me home with you tonight, I'll initiate you into delights you cannot imagine." Delights she could not imagine either, though she included Charles James Fox in her provocative smile. "Both you and My Lord Fox, if 'twould please you."

George exchanged glances with Fox, who grinned and nodded.

"It would please us both mightily. Why don't we leave right now? We might even begin our delights inside my carriage. Does that please *you,* my pet?"

"It does, sire. I'll retrieve my cloak." She walked past Walter, who glared helplessly after her.

Elizabeth almost floated from the room. In a few moments she'd stroll out of Shepherd's under the protection of the Prince of Wales. Somehow, before she had to deliver her "delights," she'd shed herself of both George and Fox. Then, after pawning the jewels she wore, she'd maintain a furtive existence until she could contact Billy Turnbull, who'd know Rand's whereabouts.

She had traveled the deserted hallway only a short distance before somebody behind her said, "Don't turn around."

She made an about-face. Dressed as a croupier in makeup, wig, white neck cloth and velvet jacket, Rand looked nearly identical to his cousin.

"As obedient as ever, aren't you Bess?" His voice teased, but his expression was deadly serious. "Listen to me carefully, we don't have much time. After we enter the front room, we simply walk to the swinging doors located at the far end. On the other side of the doors, a narrow hall leads to the kitchen, but there's a side door, unlocked, which leads to an alley."

"How . . . ?"

"Tom gave over his table to another, met me outside, and we traded places. By the way, I just witnessed your performance."

"I was so frightened, but it was the only method I could think of to extricate myself from Walter. Was I good? Did you believe me? Did I miss my calling as an actress?"

"You were wise to stick to writing." Rand hurried her along the hallway. "I detected a note of insincerity, at least I hope I did."

"You did. Fortunately, the prince and Walter did not." Rand's hand around her waist felt both familiar and safe. How had she ever endured without him? "Every day I expected Walter to crow about your capture, Rand. I was afraid you'd try to rescue me, and even more afraid you'd fled London, and I would nev . . . never see you again." She forced back her tears. Later she'd have a good cry.

Rand escorted her through the room, then the swinging doors. "Tom's outside in the alley with two horses," he said, halting momentarily to hug her. "I can't wait to get you alone so that you can exhibit all the *delights* you promised the prince."

"How on earth did you know I'd be here tonight?"

"Stafford isn't the only one who has spies."

"Of course." She pictured Billy, his muscles rending his livery.

"Come along, Bess. Here's the door."

Elizabeth followed Rand outside. Surrounded by tall buildings, the alley was especially dark, and stank to high heaven from the numerous heaps of garbage.

Tom waited with the horses. "I must get back to the tables before I'm missed," he said, handing Rand the reins.

Rand helped Elizabeth mount, not an easy task considering the bulk of her skirts. Then he leaped atop a somewhat skittish horse, whose hooves scattered the trash and a pair of white cats. "Thank you," Rand said, glancing over his shoulder. "I swear you'll be rewarded well."

"Never mind that, cousin." Tom hesitated in the doorway. "We all do what we have to do."

Tom's expression was hidden, but Elizabeth caught the strain in his voice. He had risked much by helping them. If their plan was discovered, Tom himself might face the hangman. She remembered her original feeling of distrust when they had conversed atop Westminster Bridge. She had misjudged him, and someday, when she had more time, she'd apologize.

Leading the way, Rand trailed the cats'

path. Clouds had obliterated the moon and they were surrounded by darkness — a darkness that was not unlike the watchers who had surrounded Barbara Wyndham's corpse. Elizabeth experienced an almost palpable disquietude. Was the somber darkness a haven or an omen?

Their horses' hooves rustled the garbage, intensifying the odor, while the cold night air cloaked her bare shoulders and penetrated the silk material of her gown.

From out of the gloom, a rider materialized, blocking the alley's exit. "Hold, sir!" he shouted, his pistol extended.

"Damn," Rand swore. "Another bounty hunter."

"John Randolph Remington, alias John Turpin, you are under arrest, by order of the crown!"

Elizabeth gasped. The armed man was no ordinary thief taker, but a magistrate. The area behind him teemed with other men, holding aloft torches that illuminated their weapons.

Walter, who had exited the alley door, approached from behind. "You bloody bastard, I've got you now!" He leveled his pistol at Rand. "I've waited a long time for this moment. You were smarter than Zak Turnbull, but not smart enough. With his generous

449

reward, your cousin will be able to buy into a first-rate gaming establishment."

"I don't believe you, Stafford. Tom would never betray me."

"Your first mistake was in allowing your cousin to take your place at the duel. Once we became acquainted, I conceived the plan to flush you out, then persuaded the Duke of Newcastle to increase the reward. The rest was simple. Money can make whores of the most sanctified. Remember Ranelagh, Elizabeth? I told you there were more Judases than saints."

His jaunty attitude abruptly altered. "I hate you," he said, his voice shaking. "You nearly ruined my life, you bitch, and most certainly my reputation. Thanks to your performance with the prince, I'll be the butt of hundreds of jokes."

"You've always been the butt of mine, and you could never loathe me as much as I loathe you," she replied.

"Bess, hush!"

"No, Rand." The defeat of their escape overwhelmed her fear. Chin raised high, she gave Walter a rebellious glare. "I'd rather face the gallows than spend one more moment in your company. The mere thought of being your wife . . ." She clenched her fist. "God's teeth, I'd rather hang!"

"Good. Because that's precisely what's going to happen to you." Stafford nodded toward the magistrate. "Take them both to Newgate Prison."

CHAPTER 26

December 1787–March 1788

From her research, Elizabeth was aware that Newgate Prison had been built on a site dating back to the twelfth century. During the Gordon Riots of 1780, much of Newgate had been burned down, and while the recently completed prison looked outwardly impressive, she had read that conditions inside remained as appalling as ever. Since its present-day status didn't affect her Gothic romances, she hadn't analyzed particulars.

Now she wished she had.

Upon stepping from their iron-barred carriage, she and Rand were met by Newgate's Keeper, William Huggins.

"My, aren't we privileged," Rand muttered. He appeared to have regained some of his equanimity, shaken by Tom's betrayal.

"Lord Stafford bade me to personally make you feel at home," Huggins said,

452

seemingly without sarcasm. He was a short fellow whose girth implied a prodigious appetite, and whose left eye contained a cast. His wigless head, which seemed lodged on his shoulders without benefit of a neck, had been shaved. That, along with his eye, added to his unsavory appearance. If he had worn a cowl or cassock, thought Elizabeth, he'd have resembled every lusty, avaricious clergyman she had ever penned.

"I'll escort you to your quarters." Ignoring Rand, Huggins spoke directly to Elizabeth. "You'll be housed in the Castle, which is reserved for our most influential guests. I hope your stay will prove as enjoyable as circumstances allow." He either winked or blinked, she couldn't tell which. "You're to be tried in York, not here. However, so long as you're with us, you need but ask and I'll do my best to accommodate you."

"How kind of you, sir." She attempted a smile. Her heart felt as if it had been subjected to repeated blows, yet the Keeper's loquacious manner provided at least one small measure of comfort.

Raising his lantern high, Huggins led them across the cobblestones to Newgate's entrance. "Lord Stafford gave very explicit instructions regarding your welfare. I've known him from his time as a Bow Street

Runner, and one of the best he was. Relent-less. I wasn't a bit surprised when he switched to the more rewarding aspects of the criminal business and became a first-rate prig napper."

"The criminal business can indeed be lucrative, Bess," Rand muttered. "Keepers pay a large fee to become head of a prison, which is an unpaid position. But they derive enormous profits from the sale of gin and other spirits. Prisoners pay for candles, food, water, even their ineffective sea-coal fires. Add to that various other fees, fines and bribes, and keepers inevitably become wealthy men."

"Just like first-rate bounty hunters," she said. "Wouldn't it be a fine jest if Walter was ever gaoled alongside the very felons he's captured?"

"A fine jest indeed. He wouldn't live long. Remember the carrion crows at Shotover Hill? Picture the birds as prisoners —"

"Ripping apart Walter's flesh," she finished, a shudder coursing through her.

Inside Newgate proper, Huggins's lantern jolted the darkness, casting bizarre patterns. The light bobbed and shadows leapt as they maneuvered the first set of stairs.

"The Castle is located on the third floor," said Huggins. "Tread carefully, Miss

454

Wyndham. I don't want anything to happen to you."

What else could happen? Why not just hang me and get it over with?

Elizabeth knew that incarceration would be torture. Until she had foolishly allowed Walter to court her, her freedom had never been curtailed. She remembered her wild rides across the moors and swallowed a sob. Even her restrictive bedroom, with Patience as her gaoler, had been lavish. There, she had food, drink, light, warmth . . . and hope.

Newgate was asleep, silent as a church, but Elizabeth sensed the pain and suffering, the centuries of horror swirling beyond the stairway. The darkness that camouflaged Newgate's evil was as tangible as its stone walls. Newgate's stench was also unmistakable. Before they reached the first landing, she choked on the fumes which seemed to thicken the very air. Her struggles for breath, hindered by her corset, only drew the dampness deeper into her lungs and fueled her panic. To steady herself, she grabbed Rand's arm.

Behind her, the guards halted, waiting until she regained her composure.

Huggins turned. Shadows swooped from his lantern like bats deserting their perches. "Are you all right?" His voice echoed.

"Don't worry. You'll soon get used to the smell. 'Tis not near so bad as during the times of gaol fever when even I can't stand it. Once we reach the Castle, the air should be kinder."

"No need to be afraid, Bess," Rand soothed, swinging his arm around her waist. "We've been through worse."

"We have?"

"I managed to bribe a guard. In a few short hours, Billy should be here with enough money to provide us with everything we need. At Newgate, money is the ultimate king."

"Put yer 'ands back where they belong, Captain Queernabs," a turnkey jeered. "Unless ye'd 'ave me cuff ye."

"Captain Queernabs?" Elizabeth raised her eyebrows. "Whatever does he mean?"

"My croupier's garb," Rand explained, withdrawing his arm. "I don't imagine many prisoners show up clothed in blue velvet coats and pristine white neck bands. Do you feel better now, love?"

"Yes." She pretended to be consoled, even though she considered Rand's faith in his cousin absurd.

With some difficulty, they continued the climb. Elizabeth was tempted to hike up her cumbersome skirts but she didn't want the guards to glimpse her petticoats, or even worse, her ankles. She almost laughed out loud at her sudden modesty. Trapped inside Newgate, wearing a gown whose décolletage was daring to say the least, why was she fretting over a bit of exposed ankle?

Beyond the lantern light, the darkness pooled upon the stairs so that Elizabeth had to grope her way. She recalled her careful descent down the Beresford staircase when the world had been vibrant, alive. No, it hadn't. She had been consumed with thoughts of her black-haired knight, and she hadn't met Rand.

Never forget, Bess! Without Rand, the world is bleak and you feel more dead than alive, just like Janey without her Ranulf. Keep that in mind and you can endure.

"Newgate is divided into sections," Huggins said, his voice still echoing. "The Master Debtors' side, the Common Debtors' side, and the Master Felons'. You'll be lodged in a place all your own, across from the Master Debtors, which is a stroke of luck. Newgate's always overcrowded, and if you haven't got the money to pay the garnish, it will go hard on you." He twisted around and stared at Elizabeth. "That's a fine sapphire bracelet, Miss Wyndham. I've always been partial to sapphires."

"Which means he intends to have your bracelet before the night's out," Rand whispered.

"My Aunt Lilith gave it to me," she whispered back, touching in turn her sapphire bracelet, necklace, earbobs, and her diamond tiara. "But then, I planned to pawn all my jewels, so what's the bloody difference? Anyway, I'll soon kick the bucket, just like your aunt Franny."

"Have faith, Bess. We'll be out of here in no time."

They began the final flight of stairs.

"What was I saying? Oh, yes, garnish." Huggins puffed from the exertion of simultaneously talking and climbing. "Penniless arrivals are stripped of their clothes and booted into a common ward."

If Huggins was trying to scare her, he was succeeding. Had Walter given explicit instructions about that, too? His *I hate you* reverberated off the walls and pounded inside Elizabeth's head.

"The Stone Hold, for example. Since it's belowground, there's no natural light." Huggins might have been discussing the weather. " 'Tis paved with stone, but prisoners sleep on straw, if they can get it."

"The poorest of the poor are relegated to Stone Hold, where the mice become their closest companions." Rand's voice possessed the same sad, acrimonious tone he had used while talking about Zak and the prison ship.

"How do you know so much about Newgate?" she asked.

"This isn't my first visit."

Elizabeth managed to control her gasp. Why was she surprised by Rand's revelation? After all this time, she should know better.

"A wench'll sell her body for a scrap of bread," Huggins continued cheerfully. "A condemned wench'll do the same for naught. Should the creature have the good fortune to become with child, she'll escape the gallows, at least temporarily."

Having delivered this last pertinent information, Huggins escorted them into a moderately large room. With equal portions of dismay and relief, Elizabeth saw a partition, wooden floors, a fireplace, one chair and two beds.

The turnkeys prodded Rand toward an iron plate, bolted to the floor. Chains were attached to a thick ring located at the center of the plate. "I want to pay for easement of my chains," Rand said.

Huggins shook his bald pate. "Can't do it. Orders from Lord Stafford. You're not allowed the privilege. No matter how much you offer, he'll give me double to keep you fettered."

Rand shrugged, as if being chained was a matter of minor importance. Watching the turnkeys remove his coat and padlock him, Elizabeth blinked back tears. *We've brought ourselves to a sorry pass and we've only ourselves to blame.*

Newgate's darkness was momentarily broken by her vivid image of snaking torch lights and the monks who marched down Green Hill — the monks who carried their grisly trophy. There had been no turning back from that act of betrayal, but perhaps history would not repeat itself. Perhaps she and Rand still had a future to chart, although she couldn't fathom how a future was possible. She only knew that Rand had said they would get out and she trusted him implicitly. He could have been free, safe, yet his undying love for her had led to his capture.

Undying love. She would clutch at those two words like a talisman.

Huggins approached her. "You will not be subjected to the indignity of irons, Miss Wyndham. Your sapphire bracelet should cover all customary fees. I'm not greedy, my dear. You may keep your other jewels until such time as they are needed."

The lantern oscillated, casting the keeper's bull-like head in half light, half shadow, and Elizabeth imagined Huggins as one of the devil's minions.

"I'll have a proper fire laid," he continued, "and you'll be allowed to move freely about the prison, which is a privilege afforded a lucky few."

About to ask why Lord Stafford allowed the privilege, she held her tongue. Perhaps Huggins himself had stretched the rules. Perhaps he felt compassion for a woman who would soon have her neck stretched. Unfastening the clasp, Elizabeth handed him Lilith's bracelet.

"For your diamond tiara, I'll throw in two, no, three blankets, and some fresh bread and water on the morrow."

"Cheap at twice, no, three times the price," she said, fumbling at her tiara.

After Huggins left, Elizabeth listened to the crack of the outer door as it locked, the scraping of the exterior bolts, and the clink of Rand's chains when he shifted position. She unfolded the three thin blankets and shook them vigorously, as if to redeem them from their foulness. Then she stretched out on one of the reed-thin mattresses and stared at a patch of night, framed in the barred window opposite the bed.

When Walter took her to trial, it would be as an accessory. He had never alluded to the bounty hunter's death, which meant he didn't know anything about it. Or the bounty hunter hadn't died. *I should not have embarrassed Walter in front of the prince,* she thought. *If I had not punctured Walter's vanity, he might have spared me Newgate.*

I wish I could have punctured more than his vanity!

She squeezed her eyes shut. She had once considered Walter a trifling fiddle-faddle of a man. She had even prevented Rand from shooting him. And yet, had she been spared Newgate, her reward would have been rape, a brutal, almost unimaginable violation of her body and her mind.

"I prefer Newgate," she whispered fiercely, trying to bolster her courage and control the unbidden tears that trickled warmly down her cheeks, veered toward her icy ears, and dampened her tangled hair.

According to Huggins, Stafford had orchestrated her incarceration. She wondered why he had gaoled her with Rand.

She contemplated joining Rand, but she needed time to regain her emotional strength. She must show him that she could be as brave as he, as brave as Zak, as brave as a man.

Finally, with the dawn, she rose from the bed and walked toward him.

"Such a dismal countenance," he chided.

"Please don't tease."

"If I don't tease, I'll weep. For you."

"If you weep, I'll weep."

"Then I won't shed one tear." He stared up at her. "You must be damned uncomfortable, my love. If I'm Captain Queernabs, you're Mistress Tight Corset."

"I'm Mistress Can't Breathe. Are the guards watching us?"

Rand shook his head.

"Are you certain?"

"Yes."

"I didn't know if they had apertures, or something equally odious."

"Bess, we are located above the prison gate. By Newgate's standards, we have luxurious quarters, but the Castle is also the most impregnable so the guards have no need to watch us."

"All right." She threw off her gown, unfastened the tapes of her whalebone pannier, and dropped it to the floor. Feeling exposed in her chemise and petticoat, she reached behind her for the laces on her corset.

"I wish I could play ladies' maid," Rand

said, rattling his chains.

"No need. If I can just manage this damn knot." Her arms and shoulders began to ache from her twisted position. "Why the bloody hell don't they make corsets that tie in front? There! I've done it!" She took one deep breath, then another. Finally, she divested herself of the corset and shrugged her gown back on. "A long time ago, a lifetime ago, someone told me that wigs were the biggest fashion nuisances ever created, but I disagree."

"Come here, my pretty little prison mouse."

Rand extended his arms, and she could see that his wrists were already chafed from the irons. Situating herself across his lap, she kissed each wrist in turn.

"Maybe I should get you with child, Bess. According to our esteemed keeper, 'tis one way to escape the gallows."

"Always you jest! Always you tease! Is there nothing that frightens you?"

"Yes. Your estrangement. I cannot live without you."

"Nor I, you." She sighed. "If we hang, we hang together."

"We won't hang."

She snuggled against him until the prison ordinary arrived, bearing a Bible and an irritatingly unctuous manner. Elizabeth found the Rev. Mr. Warren's interminable smile particularly annoying. Whether discussing damnation, sins of the flesh, or London's abominable fog, Warren's smile never wavered.

Rand retreated to the ends of his chains, where he made a great show of examining the fireplace bricks. Elizabeth answered Warren's questions in monosyllables. Should she be condemned to hang, he would write the pamphlet that would be sold to the masses, and she didn't want to supply him with pertinent details. Not that the *truth* made any difference.

After the Rev. Mr. Warren departed, the turnkey opened the door to visitors, and Billy Turnbull burst in. "I'll kill Tom!" he bellowed. "Pox-ridden bastard! He's disgraced the family name and I'm shamed t' call him kin."

Tossing a full purse of coins toward Rand, Billy walked over to Elizabeth and handed her the morning paper. "Me cousin Rand's already something of a bigwig, Miss Wyndham, but you're not even mentioned, which is probably yer beak's doin'."

"Mayhaps Stafford means to free you, Bess."

"And mayhaps we'll have hasty pudding

for breakfast on the morrow." She scanned the columns and saw that she was referred to as "an accomplice." Handing the paper to Rand, she addressed Billy. "I don't know how to thank you for your timely arrival the night before last."

He blushed to the roots of his hair, and Elizabeth remembered that he had seen her naked, her shift ripped by Stafford's avid hands.

"No need t' thank me, Miss Wynd—"

"Bess. Please." She gestured toward the purse. "Where did you get so much money on such short notice? Not at pistol point from some unsuspecting lord, I trust?"

"How'd you guess?"

"Damn! You're as dense as your cousin. Haven't you figured out cause and effect? Robberies cause you to be locked up. The effect is that you'll hang."

"My cousin made his money boxing," said Rand.

Her cheeks flamed. "I'm sorry, Billy."

Picking up Warren's Bible, Billy flipped through its pages. "Revelation might have some proper words of redemption, cousin." Closing the book, he handed it to Rand, then left the room.

"What was that all about?" Kneeling, Elizabeth retrieved the Bible from Rand. "I

466

surmise Billy hasn't suddenly acquired religion." The book opened to a page in Revelation, marked by a small watchmaker's file.

Rand snapped shut the bible. "We'll read scripture together later, Bess."

"What are you going to do?" she whispered. "Hold Newgate hostage with a file? I don't think Huggins will be impressed."

Rand grinned. "Oh, ye of little faith. Trust me, sweetheart. This might even be fun."

"Fun?" She shook her head. "Everything's an adventure with you, isn't it?"

"I enjoy a dare. So do you. Admit it."

"Not recently. What is your plan, my love?"

"I don't have one. But I'm working on it."

"That makes me feel *so* much better."

"Good. As soon as I come up with something, you'll be the first to know."

That afternoon they were visited by the Duchess of Newcastle, accompanied by a bevy of beautiful court ladies.

"Is he not as handsome as I told you?" Katherine swept toward Rand, her skirts billowing, her large fur muff resting against her stomach. Her green eyes sparkled and her cheeks were flushed.

Elizabeth hated her.

Withdrawing her right hand from her muff, Katherine extended it toward Rand. The ladies fluttered their fans and giggled while a turnkey watched from beyond the door.

"I'm delighted you dropped by for a chat, my lady," Rand said, sitting back on his heels. Despite the chains, his movements were graceful.

"I do apologize for that outrageously high reward my husband offered. Charles has no sense of humor. Neither does Lord Stafford, for that matter. I, on the other hand, would enjoy being accosted by you at any time."

Katherine's friends whispered behind their fans.

"Actually," said Rand, "I was flattered by the size of the reward. I would hate to be undervalued. If I'm to hang, I don't want to hang cheaply."

"I don't want you to hang at all, Sir Highwayman."

"Neither do I, my lady. Nor do I intend to."

"You are frightfully dangerous, aren't you?" Katherine moved so close, her skirts billowed against Rand's legs. "I like that in a man." Leaning forward, she kissed him.

Rand lost his balance and made a grab for the muff. Then his hands sought the floor behind him.

Katherine's friends giggled and poked each other while Elizabeth retreated to the fireplace. Imagining Katherine's neck in her hands, she twisted her fingers.

"I have dreamed of you every night since we met." Rising, Katherine stepped away from Rand. Her gaze touched upon Elizabeth's discarded underclothes, whereupon her delicate brows arched.

"My sister," Rand explained. "She's called Mouse."

"Mouse. Aye. 'Tis apt." Katherine crinkled her exquisite nose. "I'm going to be in London until the first of the year, Sir Highwayman. If you are ever in Westminster, I do hope you'll contact me."

After Katherine and her entourage had departed, Rand beckoned Elizabeth to join him.

She shook her head. "If I had a pistol, *Sir Highwayman,* I'd shoot you, most probably between your legs."

"I thought we were beyond jealousy. I'm as faithful as an old dog and you know it."

Elizabeth heard the turnkey close and bolt the door against further visitors. She felt an almost monastic isolation until she focused on Rand. He patted his lap. "Come here, mouse. I've something to show you."

"I've seen what you have to show me and I'm not interested. Save it for the Katherine."

"Don't be difficult. I'd rather spar with you than fight."

Reluctantly, she approached him. "You're not nearly as irresistible as you and your duchess think you are."

"Speaking of Katherine . . ." He reached beneath his rump and retrieved a long nail, a small hammer and a chisel.

Elizabeth felt her eyes widen. "But how did she pass them? I didn't see anything."

"The tools were hidden inside her muff. For a writer you aren't very observant."

"I was busy watching your mating ritual."

Once again, he patted his lap. "I've robbed Stafford twice, challenged him to a duel, and played a damnfool croupier. Would I do that for any other woman, including the Duchess of Newcastle? When will you believe how much I love you?"

Sinking to her knees, Elizabeth buried her face against his shoulder. "I do believe, Rand, truly I do." *Most of the time.*

Walter Stafford entered the room. His eyes were red-rimmed and puffy from drink, his face taunt and lined, as if he had aged a decade in three weeks.

Elizabeth had been stretched out upon her bed, awaiting Rand's return from an interrogation. London's lawmakers were convinced that Rand had hidden his booty and he toyed with them, refuting their allegations with a wink and a jest. By that method, he secured a brief respite from his heavy chains.

Now Elizabeth rose and retreated to the fireplace, which flickered and smoked. Beyond the barred window, fat snowflakes drifted and the sky was as gray as ashes.

"I've changed my mind," Walter said.

Elizabeth didn't respond. She felt like the mouse Rand had taken to calling her, insisting that she was his favorite companion, just like the mice who befriended the men trapped below. What trap did *Walter* have in mind? What kind of cheese would he use to bait the trap?

"I cannot stand you in this hell-hole anymore, Elizabeth. Robbers. Murderers. Pickpockets. Underworld scum, all coming and going precisely as they please, all on the lookout for vulnerable women to ravage. That's one of the reasons why I locked you up with Remington. I thought he might afford you some protection."

Walter's explanation didn't ring true, thought Elizabeth. How much protection could a chained man offer?

"One reason, my lord? Do you have others?" The room was so cold, her breath plumed in front of her face.

"By now you must hate your blasted highwayman," he spat. "Even your jewels are gone. I assumed he had you under some kind of spell, which would be broken by the tribulations of your close quarters."

Elizabeth regarded Walter warily. He appeared sincere. However, once again he had overplayed his hand. He might have a keen knowledge of the male species, but he tended to underestimate women, especially a woman in love.

She had been about to retort that close quarters only made them stronger, more certain of their love for each other. But if she said that, Walter might very well separate them.

"Rand and I fight day and night," she admitted, her voice deceptively low. "You have achieved your purpose, my lord, so you might consider removing him from the Castle."

Elizabeth held her breath, dreading Walter's reply. Had she gone too far?

"I'd rather remove you," he said.

"To what? Stone Hold?"

"No. The Dales. Come home, Elizabeth.

There's no real evidence that you were anything but an unwilling accessory, and I don't want you to suffer any longer. I need but say the word and you'll be freed."

Astonished, she took a few steps backwards. "And what is the price for your generosity?"

"I plan to take a wife, the wealthy widow I once told you about. You will become my mistress. It won't be the prolific existence you could have enjoyed, but I'll set you up in your own cottage. I expect you'll birth a few bastards, unless I tire of you quickly. It's your job to see that I do not. You might even call it your life's work. With all those bastards, a lack of servants, and the anticipation of my visits, I doubt you'll have much time for scribbling."

"Dear God, you want to break my spirit. If you think I'll agree, you're sadly mistaken."

"I'm a graceless loser, my dear, especially since I've had so little practice at it." Walter paced back and forth, as if he wore Rand's chains. "You *will* succumb."

"Never! I'll stay here and take my chances in court."

"If you do, you'll hang. They'll put you in a cart, most likely along with several other felons. You'll be forced to ride backwards, a rope around your neck. The cart will set out from Newgate, but you'll stop outside St. Sepulchre's to hear the bellman's final proclamation. Then he'll hand you and the other condemned souls a floral wreath, which you will clutch in your hands — your shaking hands — as the cart wends its way down Snow Hill, up High Holborn, past St. Giles, up to Oxford Road. 'Tis a long route, Elizabeth, agonizingly slow, and the street will be lined with people, all anticipating your death."

"I'm to be tried in York, not London."

"That doesn't matter. The final result will be the same."

"Rand won't testify against me, and I'll plead my case eloquently," she said with far more conviction than she felt. "I work with words, I'm not unknown, and the courts, especially up north, don't like to hang women."

"They do it all the time."

"Not on such flimsy evidence. How can you tie any of Rand's robberies to me?"

"I can't. But I know you murdered Robert Whitney."

Elizabeth blinked. So the corpse had a name. "Who on earth is Robert Whitney?"

"Don't play innocent with me. Whitney is the man you shot. I've kept my peace because he was vermin, but if you stubbornly persist, I'll unleash Peter Skully. Skully saw your face and heard Remington shout your name, and Skully will testify that you killed his partner."

"It was self-defense and I can prove it. Was Robert Whitney not found with a gun in his hand?"

"Of course. But he wasn't a threat to *you,* Elizabeth."

"How can you say that? He was sneaking furtively into my room and —"

"Your *highwayman's* room. If you were not Remington's accomplice, you would have helped in his capture. Instead, you primed your pistol. You cannot have it both ways, my dear."

For a moment she fumed silently. Then she said, "Do you honestly believe I could become your mistress, you —" she remembered Billy's epithet for Tom "— pox-ridden bastard!"

Walter dug his fingers into her arms, his fingers pinching. "You told the prince not to beat you. He said he would never harm anyone so lovely, but I don't embrace George's scruples, and I can beat you where it doesn't show. Since your beauty is your main asset, it is mine as well."

Releasing her, he withdrew his silver

pocket watch from his waistcoat, and she envisioned the jeweled watch Rand had stolen, the one that still lay hidden beneath the dirt and stones at the peel tower. "Whatever assets I possess are my own," she said, resisting the urge to scratch at his face. "Not yours. Nor any man's."

"Nevertheless, I shall give you time to think about my offer."

Walter appeared jumpy. He kept glancing over his left shoulder, then his right, as if he expected someone or something to pounce upon him. Elizabeth recalled Rand's comment about the carrion crows and wished with all her heart that she and Walter could trade places.

"Tomorrow is Christmas Eve," he continued. "I'll be back Christmas morning for your answer."

When Rand returned, Elizabeth sobbed out a garbled account of Walter's threat.

Rand pressed her face against his shoulder. "Have a good cry now, my love, for tomorrow we make our escape."

CHAPTER 27

"Even Newgate celebrates Christmas Eve," said Rand. "Both guards and prisoners alike. What do you say we spend Christmas Day across the channel in Calais?"

"Have you not forgotten something?" Elizabeth lifted his chains a few inches from the floor. "I do admire your optimism, my love, but there's the small matter of your irons. Huggins inconveniently forgot to leave us any keys. And since we're not ghosts, we cannot walk through walls."

"Newgate's layout isn't unfamiliar to me. Katherine and Billy's generous gifts should help. I've wrestled with more than my share of irons, Bess. Zak and I grew impatient if we stayed inside a gaol longer than three hours. This time it's taken me a few weeks, but I think I've conceived the perfect plan."

"The perfect plan," she echoed, noting that his dark blue eyes gleamed. *He's teasing me, but why?*

"After I free myself from these chains, we shall escape up the chimney."

"Don't be silly. Not even smoke escapes up that chimney."

"The Red Room is directly overhead. From there we'll have a clear path to the roof."

"Odd's bones! You're *not* teasing!" She glanced doubtfully toward the fireplace. "Did I ever tell you that I have an aversion to tight places?"

"The window is too narrow and if we broke through the door we'd still be on the same floor, which wouldn't accomplish much at all. The chimney seems our best bet."

"Not to me! I'd rather take my chances with the hangman."

"The turnkey brings our dinner at two o'clock and removes our tray at three. After that, we'll have two hours of daylight left, which should give us a good start."

Elizabeth didn't respond. Arguing with Rand was always an exercise in futility. But if he couldn't think of a better method to facilitate their escape, she would.

Dinner consisted of thin gruel and reasonably fresh bread. When the turnkey returned for the tray, he said, "If ye need water or sea-coal, tell me now. I'll soon be busy in the Lodge below." He winked at Rand.

"Hoist one for me, mate."

"That I will, sir. Merry Christmas."

Snow hurled past the barred window. Elizabeth kneaded her icy fingers, then bunched the ends of her thin blanket around her neck. Rand had refused to pay for a fire, so their room was even colder than usual. If he truly meant to escape up the chimney, a cold hearth made sense, which was the only part of his scheme that did. While Rand was forever concocting foolhardy plans, this one approached lunacy. They'd never successfully break out. Worse, they might be killed in the process.

"Are you ready, Bess?"

"I don't think —"

"You can use Billy's file to open the damn padlock. Meanwhile, I'll remove my hand irons."

"But 'tis a *horse* padlock!" She heaved a deep sigh. "Oh, all right. I'll go along with you, though this is your most preposterous idea yet." Retrieving the watchmaker's file, she turned it over in her palm. "What the deuce am I supposed to do with this?"

"Pick the lock."

Somewhat gingerly, she approached the horse padlock, an immense affair which secured the chains around Rand's ankles to the staple in the floor. Wishing Tim the Ostler was present, she dug around in the keyhole. Her numb fingers made her movements that much more clumsy. "In *Castles of Doom,* Guinevere was thrown into the dungeon by King John," Elizabeth mumbled. "She escaped by picking half a dozen locks. It was so much simpler when she did it."

Holding Katherine's nail between his teeth, Rand bent over his irons. Before long he'd freed his right hand.

"You're even more skilled than Guinevere," Elizabeth said admiringly. Maybe Rand was right and they would escape. If the rest was as easy as the beginning, they'd soon be strolling down Newgate Street. "How did you do that?"

"Keep working. I'll explain some other time."

While she attacked the padlock to no avail, Rand worked free his other cuff. Then he gently pried Billy's file from her hands. "Stand watch at the door, Bess. Make certain we're not interrupted."

"Make certain *you're* not interrupted. I'm useless." She peered out through the barred window cut into their door. The Master Debtors' side was directly opposite their room, and prisoners often left the area for the taproom below. Other than Rand's frequent curses and the occasional whisper of a rat running across the floor, everything was silent.

"Are you making any progress?" she asked.

"Not much."

The day was waning fast. A guard appeared to light the lone torch positioned beside the Debtors' door, but he ignored their room. Elizabeth had no idea how long Rand had been at work. Maybe he'd never get free of the padlock, which meant, come tomorrow morning, they'd have a lot of explaining to do.

"Got it!" Rand struggled to his feet, the leg irons still attached.

Elizabeth hurried toward him. "Now what?"

"We must remove this chain linking my ankles together."

She bent over the chain, but in the dim light she could see very little. Running her fingers across the links, she tried to discern some sort of imperfection or weakness. "Damn! Guinevere picked *locks.* She never had to worry about chains."

"Some of the links are rusted. If you twist the chain back and forth, you should be able to break the weakest link."

"Weakest link. There's a lesson to be learned in that, I suppose, but I can't think straight right now."

Rand spread his legs until the chains tightened while she knelt and twisted the links.

"Harder, Bess!"

"I don't want to hurt your ankles."

"Never mind that."

She alternated between twisting the chain and using Katherine's hammer and chisel midst the links, but the chain seemed as impervious as ever. Wiping the perspiration from her face, she said, "This isn't going to work."

"It has to. Just keep at it."

When she was certain the chain would never break, one of the links snapped.

"Good!" Rand tied the links around each leg in order to keep the chains from dragging on the ground.

"Did I hurt your bad leg?"

He pulled her upright. "I've suffered worse. Now, the fireplace."

"Is there not some other way? I truly don't want to attempt the chimney."

Rand poked his head up the flue, then thrust his arm inside. "There's a thick square iron bar across the opening. The ends seem to be buried between the brickwork. Obviously, we're not the first prisoners to contemplate an escape up the chimney."

Relieved, she said, "I guess we have no other choice. We'll have to try the door."

Rand continued to probe the flue. "Too risky."

"But you said there's a bar across the open —"

"We'll have to pull down the chimney, brick by brick, until we can remove the bar."

"That's ridiculous!"

"Are we sparring or fighting?"

"Neither." Grabbing up the nail, she scratched away at the mortar joints. Rand chiseled between the bricks. "I'm glad you know what you're doing. If it were left to me, I'd still be here by next Christmastide."

"No, you wouldn't. Don't forget Stafford."

Grimly, Elizabeth scratched harder.

Rand finally pried loose a brick. Tossing it to the floor, he said, "The rest should be easier. Bring me the horse padlock and I'll use it as a sledgehammer. You can keep watch again."

Elizabeth took up her previous position at the door. With each slam of the padlock against the bricks, she winced, fully expecting a dozen warders with drawn pistols to rush upstairs. But nothing disturbed them save the off-key singing that emanated from the taproom and Lodge.

By the time Rand finished, bricks were strewn all around his feet. Dust from the mortar drifted downward like settling fog, and Elizabeth watched helplessly while he suffered a lengthy coughing fit. The bar had crumpled loose along with the bricks. After retrieving it, Rand said, "I'm going up the chimney now. I'll use the bar to batter my way through the floor above. Once I've broken through, follow me."

"I can't. I'll panic. I know I will."

"Please, sweetheart, we don't have time to deal with your doubts." Bar in hand, Rand disappeared up the chimney.

Debris plummeted to the hearth and raised puffs of ashes. Coal dust mixed with the choking particles of mortar. Trying to figure out some other exit, Elizabeth looked around the room. "I can't do it," she whispered. "No matter what the consequences."

She heard Rand smashing his way through to what she assumed was the Red Room. Finally he called, "All right, Bess. Your turn."

Desperate, she tried to gain control over her racing heart. Every minute she dawdled only increased their danger, and with his chains, bad leg, and larger body, Rand had suffered far more than she would. But *he* wasn't afraid of anything. The greater the risk, the steeper the odds, the more he enjoyed the challenge. And, unlike Stafford, Rand played fair.

If you were going to back out, you should have done so at the very beginning. Climb the cursed chimney! Climb, dammit!

She took a deep breath and peered up the flue. While the darkness obliterated its dimensions, she could discern a lighter shadow far above, where Rand had battered the hole. She felt around the flue's perimeter. Impossibly narrow.

"Hurry, Bess!"

She tied her gown between her legs. The removal of the bricks had left a hole at least five feet high and two feet in diameter, so she would be totally enclosed for only a short distance. Positioning her arms on either side of the flue, she began edging her way up. Her mouth soon tasted of coal dust. Ashes fell upon her hair like polluted rain. She closed her eyes, but that was worse, so she opened them. Panic gripped her like a vise. The flue squeezed her arms and legs. Her body broke out in a cold sweat. Images of rats and spiders consumed her mind. Her limbs were dead weights, refusing to move.

"You can do it, Bess," Rand called. "Think

of something beautiful, something peaceful."

"I can't," she whispered. Then, louder, "What should I think about?"

"Us. Think about us free. Or think about the first lines from your novels. Can you remember them?"

"I can't remember *anything!*"

"Start with your first book. What did you say about William the Conqueror?"

As she searched her memory, she began to edge upwards again. How had her first novel begun? She had written something about William's illegitimacy. Yes. Something like, "People called him William the Bastard because he was one." Not a beautifully crafted sentiment, but interesting. What had she written in her second book, the one about William's son, William Rufus? Rufus had made a wonderful villain. How had she begun *The King Who Hated Women?* Something about her heroine wandering in the forest, accosted by the king's henchmen.

By the time Elizabeth had advanced to *Richard of the Lion's Heart,* Rand pulled her through the shattered wood. Sprawled on the floor, she gasped for breath.

"Are you sure you've never done this before? You're rather good at it." Helping her to her feet, Rand hugged her. "This is just the first step, love. We have a long way to go. How do you feel?"

"Winded. Triumphant. Exhausted."

"Good. I didn't hear the word 'defeated.' "

The Red Room measured twenty feet by ten. Judging from the thick dust on the floor, the stagnant air, and the cobwebs spun between the corners, it had not been entered for years. Standing on tiptoe, Elizabeth peered out through the barred window. The snow had stopped, but nightfall had arrived with a vengeance. "We won't be able to see anything, Rand. How the bloody hell are we going to figure out where we're going?"

"Darkness is our cloak, my pretty mouse." Crossing to the Red Room's door, he retrieved the hammer and chisel from his pocket, then bent aside the plate covering the lock box. "Do you still have Billy's small file?"

With a curt nod, she removed it from her bodice and handed it to him.

In a surprisingly short time, he had picked the lock and forced back the bolt. The door opened, its rusty hinges protesting loudly. Rand stepped into the passageway. Turning, he took Elizabeth's hand and drew her forth, as if leading her toward the center of a dance floor.

"You're amazing!" Suddenly, she was exhilarated by the whole affair. They were escaping from the most notorious prison in London. When she and Rand were old and settled, she would write a book about it, her best ever.

He pulled her along behind him. They turned left, past a staircase, then came to another locked door. "I believe this is the door to the chapel," Rand said, running his fingertips around the edges. "No lock, which means it's bolted on the far side. We can break through if we must, but I'm going to search out an easier exit."

After Rand had retreated, the chill of Newgate's walls and the stillness of the passageway dampened Elizabeth's previous exhilaration. Newgate's darkness seemed a living thing, teeming with eyes.

Upon his return, Rand shrugged and said, "We'll have to go through the chapel. I'll batter a hole in the brickwork beside the door."

"Won't that be awfully noisy?"

"Who is going to hear us? The chapel is three stories above the taproom and Lodge, where all of Newgate should be." He retrieved the iron bar from the waistband of his breeches. "There's a door inside the chapel. It leads to a passage that opens onto the roof. Once we break through, the rest should be easy, even fun, just as I promised."

He began ramming the wall. The noise was frightful. Surely they could be heard all the way to Westminster. Elizabeth watched him batter a hole large enough for his arm. Thrusting his hand through, he fumbled at the bolt.

She shivered violently when they entered the Condemned Hold, reserved for prisoners sentenced to death. Fun, indeed! The Hold was topped by a row of iron spikes, which Rand knocked off with his bar. Ironic to think that the flue bar, a deterrent, could prove so useful.

Balancing on a coffin, they climbed atop the spiked partition, then jumped into the nave. From the chapel, they made their way to the door of the passageway. Rand levered the lock box far enough aside so that he could pick the lock. At long last, they hurried along the passageway to the final door. Nothing more separated them from the roof — and freedom.

"Almost there!" Elizabeth exalted, as Rand explored the door's surface.

"Don't celebrate yet, Bess."

"What's wrong?"

"Feel for yourself."

She ran her hands across the door and

peered at the various devices attached to its surface. An immense iron-plated lock box was clamped to the door by means of iron hoops. Beneath the box, an enormous bolt was fastened into its socket by a hasp, secured by a large padlock. Overall, the door was strengthened by four vast metal fillets.

" 'Tis rather . . . forbidding."

"To say the least." Rand leaned against the wall and massaged his bad leg.

"But you had little trouble with the other doors. You'll break through this one in no time."

He continued rubbing his leg. "I'm tired, Bess. This door's heavier and better secured than all the others combined. I can't see a damned thing, we have shit for tools, my leg is giving out on me, and any moment now someone will discover our absence."

From beyond the prison, the clock bells of St. Sepulchre's Church chimed. Elizabeth counted. " 'Tis ten o'clock, Rand. That means we've only been working seven hours and we have the whole night ahead of us. Give me your bar. I'll break through."

"You're not strong enough to do it alone." With a sigh, he faced the door. "I suppose the best way is to remove the metal fillet. That's where the lock and bolt are attached. Should I work a hundred years, I'd never be able to force the bolt, so I'll take the top of the fillet while you take the bottom."

Elizabeth tried unsuccessfully to wedge the hammer and chisel between the fillet and lock. The head of the hammer snapped off. Feeling helpless, she could only stand back and watch Rand wrestle with the fillet. Apparently, her tenacity had infused him with a new, even stronger determination. Using the iron bar as a lever, he gouged the wood, then forced the bar between the fillet and the door. Muscles straining, he wrenched the fillet free. The lock and bolt tore away with it. Slumping to the floor, he rested his head upon his arms.

"Are you all right? Rand, answer me!"

He nodded, but remained in the same slumped position for several minutes. When he finally stood, his leg buckled. He reached for her shoulder to steady himself, but waved aside her expressions of concern. "Remember what Zak said when he robbed your coach? 'If I'm not dead now, I should live forever.' "

Now was not the time to remind him that Zak hadn't lived forever!

Rand pulled open the massive door and they walked along the corridor to the roof.

"Oh, no." Elizabeth felt all the color drain from her face. "Another door!"

"Easy, mouse, 'tis locked with a bolt." Rand easily shot back the bolt, opened the door, and they emerged onto a portion of roof surrounded by high walls.

Cold air pummeled them, an invigorating contrast to the fetid atmosphere inside. Elizabeth drank in the sight of brittle stars and a night sky washed clean by the snow.

"I never thought anything could look so lovely," she said, crossing to the stone wall. Her thin-soled slippers crunched on the crust of snow and the wind cut through the silk of her gown. Already the air was passing from invigorating to icy. She turned and faced Rand. "Where do we go from here?"

He climbed atop the door through which they'd just emerged. Balancing on it, he reached to the wall above and swung up. Elizabeth followed. They jumped down on the other side, then crawled across a tiled roof. She gouged her nails into the slates, fingers aching from the cold. Inching along the steep-pitched roof, she tried to ignore the tiles scraping against her legs and the fact that one misstep would send her tumbling to her doom.

After what seemed an eternity, they reached the parapet wall of the gateway. For the first time, they could see below.

The sharp outline of a quarter moon

hovered above the sea of London's chimneys and the steeples of her churches. Moonlight caught on the snowy peaks, causing individual flakes to glitter like scattered diamonds.

The houses below were tall and narrow. Pale patches of light spilled outward, onto the streets. A lighted carriage rumbled past, providing the only noise. A linkboy, carrying a torch for his customers, wound his way along the narrow lanes, his light winking like a fallen star. Elizabeth tried to estimate the distance from their position to the highest roof — at least twenty-five feet.

Rand voiced what she was thinking. "It's too far to jump."

"What are we going to do?"

"I'll return to our cell, get our blankets, and collect a spike from the chapel. Then we'll simply tie the blankets together and climb down."

"You wait here. I'll fetch the blankets."

"No!"

"Yes! Your leg might give out altogether. I'm more agile."

"What about the chimney? You can't —"

"Yes, I can. This time I'll think about *us*."

Swiftly, Elizabeth retraced her steps. Alone, she found she was terrified. But she couldn't give in to her fear, especially since she had to concentrate, probe the stifling blackness, and reconstruct their previous route.

She began her descent down the chimney. Halfway down, she lost her foothold and crashed into the hearth. Picking herself up, she headed for the bed and tripped over the scattered bricks. Cursing, she finally grabbed the blankets and headed back toward the chimney. Then she froze. Did she hear footsteps beyond the door? Yes. The steps were moving closer. Holding her breath, she silently prayed for whomever to pass. Keys clanked. Light from the turnkey's lantern pierced the door's barred window and bounced off the cell's interior.

"Damn," she breathed.

The guard fit the key into the lock.

Elizabeth stood there, paralyzed with fear. She must do something, but what? She could escape up the chimney before she was discovered, but then the turnkey would alert the others. If he just glanced inside, he might not see anything amiss. More than a cursory inspection, however, and their escape would be revealed. All their tribulations would be for naught.

That thought, and that thought alone, tempered her panic. Dropping the blankets, she picked up a brick and stumbled toward the door. As it swung open and the guard stepped inside, she bashed him over the head. Still holding the lantern, he plummeted to the floor. The light immediately extinguished, baptizing them both with darkness, but Elizabeth could discern the guard's form as he struggled on all fours. She hit him again. Then she groped for his keys and locked the door.

Keys in her bodice, blankets round her neck, she quickly navigated the chimney. Tossing the keys into the corner of the Red Room, she squeezed through doorways, raced along passageways, climbed the coffin, and retrieved the spike. Not taking time to think or feel, she crawled along the steep-pitched roof until she dropped down, next to Rand.

"The turnkey . . ." she panted. "He entered our room. I hit him over the head . . . with a brick . . . but I didn't kill him . . . so we don't have much time."

Rand nodded sharply. Sitting upon the parapet wall, he bound the blankets together, drove the broken spike into the wall with the chisel's handle, tied one of the blankets round the spike, then climbed down onto the roof below.

Elizabeth followed. Her cheeks stung with the freezing night air. Her breath plumed before her like the puffs of smoke frozen above London's chimney pots. Her hands grasped the rough woolen blankets, but her slippers were soaked and provided less protection than bare feet. Resolutely, she kept her eyes on her hands, agonizingly slow in their descent.

"Almost there," Rand said, disentangling her hands and helping her through an attic window. "We have three flights of stairs to navigate, then we'll be able to walk right out onto Newgate Street. Be steadfast a little longer, my brave little mouse."

"I will. I must."

Rand edged the door open, grasped her hand, and hurried them down two flights of stairs, onto the first floor landing. As they moved toward the last flight of stairs, Newgate erupted. Shouts echoed from all directions. So did running feet.

"They've discovered the turnkey," Rand said. "Run, Bess. Follow me."

She bolted down the steps, stumbling in the dark. Suddenly, the staircase was awash with light.

Someone shouted, "Halt!"

Elizabeth kept running. Ahead, Rand's leg collapsed and he slammed to the ground. A pistol cracked, the shot ricocheting off the stone wall.

"Keep going, Bess!" he shouted.

She veered around him. From the corner of her eye, she saw him grope at the wall for support. Then he lurched to his feet.

Ahead was Newgate's front door, only scant yards away.

She reached the bottom of the stairs and spun around. One man held a lantern. A second held a pistol to Rand's head. The passageway swarmed with prison guards.

I can't help Rand now, she thought with despair, *and I certainly can't help him if I'm captured.*

Yanking open the door, she burst outside, onto Newgate Street.

CHAPTER 28

Elizabeth raced through London's streets. This part of the city contained an incoherent mix of buildings, haphazardly constructed, leaning like blowsy lovers into each other.

She saw a rubble-filled alleyway. Picking her way over the remains of a fallen tenement, she searched for a comparatively sheltered spot and tried to ignore the biting cold.

A pair of guards hurried past, their complaints audible. Even in her terrified state, Elizabeth realized that their search was more perfunctory than committed. Had Rand escaped, the area would have been teeming with lawmen, and she vaguely wondered if she should be insulted by the guards' indifference.

The last time she had considered the hour, it had been ten o'clock. Now it must be close to one, and yet the poorest Londoners were already stirring from their tenements. A clear-starcher passed, then a washerwoman who carried dirty laundry. Scrambling from the alley, Elizabeth approached the washerwoman.

"I need something warm to wear. I have nothing to trade except this gown, which was once very costly. If you're handy with a needle, the fal-lals can be sewn back on. The silk can be laundered . . ." Elizabeth faltered when yet another pair of guards came into view. Quickly, she grabbed one end of the washerwoman's tub. "Here, let me help you."

The woman watched the guards march toward Newgate. She stared at Elizabeth, then rummaged through her laundry and pulled out a threadbare greatcoat. " 'Ere, Miss, an' good luck t' ye."

"Thank you, oh, thank you." After hugging the startled washerwoman, Elizabeth continued on her way.

She passed a watch-house and bade a sleepy watchman good night. She navigated Holborn Hill by way of Snow Hill and Fleet Bridge, then headed for the open country beyond Gray's Inn Lane. Her feet were so cold, each step was agony.

By dawn she reached the village of Tottenham and found a cow shed where she could hide. She crawled atop a pile of hay, removed her sodden slippers, rubbed her icy feet, and blanketed herself with the straw. Taking several deep breaths to calm her beleaguered heart, she drifted into an exhausted sleep.

She awakened to a growling belly and a glowering sky, and pondered her next move. First, she must get away from London — specifically, north to York. Rand's trial would take place there and surely she could find shelter with her Aunt Lilith, who lived there. Once safe, she would send word of her general whereabouts to Billy Turnbull.

York was over one hundred and ninety miles from London. She might be able to walk that distance, even with sore feet, but it would take an eternity, so she'd have to "borrow" a horse.

In fact, if she set her mind to it, she could be at Aunt Lilith's by this time tomorrow. In Daniel Defoe's book, *Tour Through the Whole Island of Great Britain,* he had penned a tale about a robber named Swift Nicks. Needing an alibi, Swift Nicks had ridden from London to York in fifteen hours.

Fifteen hours! Lord Stafford and his fellow bounty hunters would still be searching London. Walter would never believe a woman capable of devising such a scheme, let alone implementing it.

She found a white stallion tied to a fence, then galloped across the county of Essex, through Tilbury, Horndon and Bilerecay, all the way to Chelmsford, where she stopped to rest.

Following the general route of Swift Nicks, she rode through Braintree and Wethersfield, then over the Downs to Cambridge. Upon reaching Huntingdon, she rested again. Finally, striking onto the North Road, she raced toward Middlethorpe Manor.

Aunt Lilith immediately ordered a couple of servants to feed and rub down the white stallion. Afterwards, they would return him to his fence.

Exhausted, hovering between awareness and oblivion, Elizabeth told her aunt everything that had occurred since the Harvest Ball. She ended her lengthy account with Walter's proposition and her escape from Newgate.

Lilith's eyes widened, but she merely said, "I knew something terrible would happen."

"No, Aunt, something wonderful happened. Despite all the hardships, including Newgate, I still love Rand with all my heart."

Lilith ensconced Elizabeth inside a storage room, located near the servants' quarters. Its window overlooked the drive so that she could survey all departures and arrivals. The storage room also possessed the entrance to one of the several secret passageways that honeycombed Middlethorpe, dating from the religious wars of the Reformation.

During the next few weeks, Elizabeth stayed in her snug room. To the servants she remained little more than a noise heard in the passageway, a figure glimpsed in the darkness, and she rather enjoyed the air of mystery that surrounded her presence. She imagined a gardener pausing in his work long enough to wipe his brow and gaze up at the third story window of her supposedly empty room. After spying her, he would mistake her for a ghost and spread all sorts of frightening tales. "I'm a legend in the making," Elizabeth told Lilith, a rare smile tugging at the corners of her lips.

Lilith's husband was in London, tending to business. Elizabeth murmured a grateful prayer. Uncle Raymond could be sweet, but when he was in his cups his behavior was unpredictable.

A fortnight later, Walter, accompanied by Rand, arrived in York. After incarcerating his prisoner in York Castle, Walter posted a hundred guinea reward for Elizabeth's safe return, then began a systematic search to find her.

"I don't mean to harm your niece," he informed Lilith during his third visit. "In fact, I've dropped all charges against her. I just want to make certain she's unharmed, I swear. You pretend ignorance, but my instincts tell me you're evading the truth. I know she's somewhere in York."

Lilith invariably responded with metaphysical ramblings, which frustrated Walter as much as they delighted Elizabeth, listening from her secret place behind the wall.

After Lord Stafford posted his reward, Lilith called together her entire domestic staff and countered with a sum of two hundred guineas, so long as Elizabeth remained undetected and unharmed.

Other than worrying about Rand, Elizabeth found her stay at Middlethorpe pleasant. The atmosphere was peaceful, her room warm, the food delicious.

She began penning a fictionalized account of her life as a land pirate. She had read such books as *Jackson's Recantation* and *The Recantations of an Ill-Led Life*. There were no books about female highwaymen, of course, since highway robbery was not a profession employed by the gentler sex.

Only men possessed the necessary strength, cruelty, marksmanship and horsemanship.

If men are so superior, why do they always get caught?

She decided to embellish her own admittedly meager exploits and transform herself into a celebrity on a par with Claude Duvall and the dashing Captain Hind — an ardent royalist who specialized in robbing Puritans.

During the next six weeks, Elizabeth's imagination took flight. She robbed the Prince of Wales, engaged in a pistol fight with a gang of smugglers, divested the Duchess of Newcastle of a second diamond ring, and successfully dueled against a duke. Elizabeth enjoyed her exploits, especially since she could control the outcome. In the end, she and Rand would flee to America. A shame one could not rearrange one's life as easily as one could one's plots.

Naturally, she kept abreast of events with Rand, whose trial was scheduled for the tenth of March. Lilith sent a servant to one of Billy Turnbull's pugilist events. The servant passed Billy a carefully worded note, and several times Elizabeth managed to meet with him in Middlethorpe's garden. He assured her that Rand was well. Billy was trying to figure out a legal way to get his cousin released, especially since another escape attempt seemed virtually impossible.

"We need money," Billy said bluntly, two weeks before the trial. "We might have t' bribe some witnesses, or if the judge rules against us, the hangman."

Silently, she cursed Charles Beresford for absconding with her funds.

"Wait, Billy, I nearly forgot. I *did* forget! There's a buried coin purse . . . the peel tower . . . two hundred pounds."

"Where's the peel tower?"

"You've not been to the Dales and you'll never find the blasted purse. I'll have to do it."

" 'Tis far too risky, Bess."

"If I ride at night, I should be safe."

Billy nodded. As he readied to leave the garden, he said, "I hate t' be a Job's comforter, but what do ye know 'bout the murder o' Robert Whitney?"

"Whitney," Elizabeth echoed. She hadn't forgotten the bounty hunter, but Walter had said that all charges against her had been dropped, the lying bastard!

"Me cousin's been charged with Whitney's murder," Billy said. "Did Rand kill 'im? *He* won't say nothin'."

"Odd's bones! How can they blame Rand? What proof do they have?"

"There's a witness, Peter Skully. He's stayin' in York, at the Cock and Bottle."

Skully! The skeleton man!

"Don't worry," Elizabeth said with more confidence than she felt. "Skully's a thief-catcher. He'd sell his own mother for fiddler's money. Rand didn't kill Robert Whitney, and that's a fact. Keep working for your cousin's release while I ferret out Peter Skully. There must be some way to rid ourselves of that bloody liar."

Skully succeeded in ruining Elizabeth's writing, her appetite, and her sleep. She couldn't think of anything save him. Walter knew she had shot Whitney, so why had he charged Rand with the murder? The judge was supposed to serve Rand's interests. Under severe questioning, Skully might very well arse-about, which would exonerate Rand and implicate Elizabeth. Once accused, her efforts to free Rand would be severely curtailed. Even if those efforts were successful, she might be caught and hanged, an irony beyond belief.

I must do something, she thought, *but what?* Maybe she'd obtain a witness who'd testify that somebody else shot Robert Whitney. Such witnesses could be found around any courtroom. They were called Straw Men because they made known their services by sticking straw into their shoe buckles.

After I visit the peel tower, I'll send Skully a note. I'll say something like: If you want money, meet me tomorrow at midnight, inside the Church of St. Crux.

Elizabeth only hoped the blasted bounty hunter could read.

Before riding out on one of Aunt Lilith's horses, Elizabeth removed a pistol from Uncle Raymond's gun cabinet. Over and over she played a possible scenario in her mind. As soon as Skully entered the church, she would step out from the shadows and threaten him. Then she would bribe him.

I don't want to kill him, she thought, as she entered York through Bootham Bar, one of its ancient gates. *Robert Whitney was a big mistake, a mistake I'll have to live with for the rest of my life.*

She wondered if she'd ever use her quill to kill anybody again. On paper her murders had always been motivated by forces beyond the hero or heroine's control, but she'd never considered the consequences. Since her villains deserved to die, the matter of a guilty conscience had never been probed.

If I hadn't shot Robert Whitney, he would have shot Rand. And me. It was self-defense, no matter what Walter says. Walter wasn't there. I would have been killed, I know it. Whitney deserved to die.

Justification achieved, at least temporarily, Elizabeth rode along Low Petergate toward the Church of St. Crux, located at the end of the Shambles. The Shambles was a street filled with inns and shops, medieval in nature. It possessed upper stories that leaned so far into the street, locals maintained one could shake hands with somebody from across the way.

She paid for an inn with a view overlooking St. Crux, and stayed there throughout the day, watching to see if Walter had uncovered her plot. As ambiguous as she had made her note, should Skully show it to Walter, he'd figure it out.

Elizabeth saw servants clothed in a variety of colorful liveries. She saw ladies who wore drooping hats and spreading skirts. She saw merchants. She saw governesses with their charges in tow. They all passed the Norman-style church, or entered, or paused on its steps to chat, but no unusual activity took place. Nor did anyone vaguely resembling Walter put in an appearance.

Before leaving Middlethorpe, Elizabeth had donned boots, breeches, shirt, vest and coat, unknowingly donated by Raymond.

Thank the good Lord her uncle possessed an insignificant stature.

Scarcely breathing, Elizabeth entered the church through a side door. Save for some cheap lights smelling of whale oil, the building was dark and still — not even a whisper.

She hid behind one of the church's stone tombs. It was ice cold, as was the tomb upon which she braced her feet, and the stone wall where she rested her back.

Two ghosts inhabited St. Crux, but they weren't particularly frightening. One was said to be a tall, bold-looking man who could be seen in the wee hours of the morning, gazing through a window. He never appeared outside the church.

The second was a beautiful lady, dressed in white. She always emerged from the church yard when the Waits of York passed. The lady followed the Waits, who wore scarlet livery and silver badges and played musical instruments. Whenever they stopped, she stopped. When they moved, she moved. The Waits, who acted as watchmen and speaking clocks, were said to look forward to the beautiful lady's visits.

But there was one person who would not. Lord Stafford.

Elizabeth recalled his agitation during their long-ago ghost discussion. If Walter planned a surprise visit and the church ghosts appeared, he might very well suffer an apoplectic stroke.

What a stroke of luck that would be!

The hours dragged past. Finally, Elizabeth heard footsteps. Standing upright, she peered around the edge of the tomb and saw a lance-thin figure hesitate at the entrance to the nave. "Be ye 'ere?" Skully removed his hat and walked forward. His elongated shadow preceded him.

Elizabeth waited, but he was alone. She prayed he would listen to reason and give in to his greed. She didn't want to pull her gun.

Nobody followed Skully. Stepping out from behind the tomb, Elizabeth blurted, "Are you planning to tell the truth about Robert Whitney's murder?"

"What d'ya mean?"

She rephrased her question. "Who killed Robert Whitney?"

"That depends on who's askin'."

"*I'm* asking. I'm the highwayman's chosen pell, his partner, and I want to know how you're going to testify at his trial."

"Depends."

"What does it depend on?"

Skully shrugged his bony shoulders.

Elizabeth tried again. "Lord Stafford has

questioned you about that night, has he not?"

"Aye. Over an' over."

"What did you say? What do you remember?"

"Enough."

She heaved a deep sigh. Perhaps now was the time to mention money. If Skully refused her bribe, perhaps the mere *threat* of death would be enough. He had seen her shoot Whitney, so he realized full well that she was capable of murder. Except Skully had no idea who she was. For all he knew, she might be the Prince of Wales. "Rand Remington has been charged with Robert Whitney's murder," she said, trying to keep her voice gruff. "Are you going to testify that Remington shot him?"

Skully grunted.

Tossing her coin purse from hand to hand, Elizabeth stepped toward him. "If you testify that someone else shot Whitney, I'll reward you generously."

" 'Ow generous?"

"Seventy-five guineas, more if you leave York. Should you swear under oath that Rand Remington shot Whitney, you'll be murdered in your sleep. Horribly, painfully murdered. Is that quite clear?"

"Aye. Give over yer seventy-five guineas. I

know wot t' say."

Elizabeth placed the coins in his hand. Her fingers brushed his knobby joints and his nearly fleshless palm, which was as cold as the tomb stones. Quickly, she withdrew. "Remember, Skully, I'll be watching." Eager to flee from him, she retreated toward the church's side door.

"Miss Wyndham," he said in a voice that creaked like the hinges on a coffin.

Slowly, Elizabeth turned around.

"Ye forgot t' hide all that pretty black hair 'neath a hat, so 'tis clear ye're the 'ighwayman's lady, the one what shot me partner."

Her mouth dropped open, but she quickly regained her composure. "That does not matter. I have friends —"

" 'Lord Stafford promised me one hundred guineas t' say yer 'ighwayman did the killin'."

Stunned, she blurted, "Rand will hang for highway robbery so why would Stafford need a murder charge?"

Skully shrugged, then thrust the coins inside his pocket.

"Wait! If you plan to testify for Stafford, give me back my money!"

Skully spit an obscenity, one Elizabeth had never heard before, one she could add to her growing list of underworld cant. Before she could pull her pistol, his long shanks found the door, and she could only watch him disappear.

Elizabeth shivered in the cold March air. Her brocade slippers crunched on the hard crust of snow, her toes were chips of ice, and she fervently wished she had borrowed her uncle's boots again. "Where are you, Billy?" she whispered, glancing up at the stars that pockmarked the sky. "I can't wait here all night. I'll probably die from hoarfrost."

Her breath plumed in front of her face. Why was Billy so late? What if something bad had happened in court today? The Assize Judge only came twice a year and was hearing several cases besides Rand's, but Rand's was the most serious. Rand's crime was a crime against property and the natural order of things. To take a man's property was more serious than murder, or at least murder among the poor, which meant that Rand was doubly doomed. And yet so much depended upon the judge's interpretation of the law, his mood, his prejudices and sensibilities, not to mention the jury's opinion of events. Those opinions could oft be changed with bribes.

Which is why we need money, Elizabeth

thought, pacing the garden path. *We never have enough.*

Aunt Lilith refused to throw a sop to a criminal. The contents of the stolen coin purse had been spent. Billy had pawned Walter's watch and ring, but that money had been spent as well. After all, Rand must eat, bathe, exercise, stay warm.

At long last, Elizabeth spied Billy's stocky figure, swathed in a black cloak. Almost stumbling, she hurried toward him. "How is the trial going? How is Rand?"

"Fine enough on both counts." Billy affectionately mussed her hair and kissed her cheek. "Judge Herriott's a blustery fellow, full of himself, but he seems a fair man."

"Is there any chance Rand might be freed? How strong is the case against him?"

"The murder's not yet been brought up. There's someone here who might help us, Bess. Please don't piss on a nettle."

"Why would I be upset? If someone can help . . ." She paused when Tom Turnbull stepped from the shadows. "You! How dare you show your face anywhere near me?"

"I felt the same," Billy said, his voice calm, "but Tom thinks he can help us free Rand."

Elizabeth shook her head in disgust. "What will you do now, Judas? Tell Lord

Stafford where I am? Collect another reward?"

"I'm sorry matters turned out as they did, Miss Wyndham."

Tom wore his own hair, which strengthened his resemblance to Rand. Tom also wore an exquisitely tailored greatcoat. He had gained weight, and Elizabeth thought he sounded every bit as unctuous as Walter ever had. Chewing her bottom lip, she regarded him both angrily and warily.

"With my reward, I bought into Shepherd's and have already tripled my original sum," Tom continued. "I'll not apologize for that. I found a way out of poverty, and I'll not apologize for that either."

"But you betrayed your own flesh and blood!"

"I love my cousin, despite what you might believe, and I plan to spend a portion of my money to free him."

"Your generosity overwhelms me, Thomas Turnbull! Without you, Rand wouldn't be in need of funds. He'd be a free man."

"Sooner or later, Rand would have been caught. Better now when we might exercise some control."

"How can I trust you?"

"I must come first, Miss Wyndham. Since I no longer have to worry about money, I can help my cousin."

Turning toward Billy, she said, "This is absurd. Get him out of here."

"Tom's been talkin' with some barristers, Bess, and it looks promisin'. We could get Rand off on a . . . what's it called, Tom?"

"Meaningful detail. Two, in fact. There were two minor errors. My cousin's name was listed as Randolph Remington, rather than *John* Randolph Remington, and his date of capture as Saturday, December first, when it was actually Sunday, December second."

"That's ridiculous," Elizabeth fumed. "No court would free Rand over some minor mistake."

"It happens all the time, Miss Wyndham. I stood up today and informed Judge Herriott of the errors, as is my right. He took my objections seriously, and is presently considering whether he should throw the whole case out."

"Can that be possible?" Elizabeth tried to decipher Tom's expression. What treachery lay behind his glib facade? "Are you planning to tell Lord Stafford my whereabouts? Is that your real reason for coming here?"

"Tom knows what will happen if we're betrayed again, don't you, Tom?" Billy's tone remained matter of fact, but the implied threat was obvious.

"Of course. I didn't have to offer any help at all, did I?"

"Yes, you did," Elizabeth said. "If Rand dies, you won't enjoy your profits, for I shall haunt you. Or kill you."

Tom drew himself up to his full height. Despite his youth, he looked like a father about to scold a recalcitrant child. "Should my meaningful detail scheme fail and Rand be convicted, he could still cheat the hangman. We can always ask for a royal pardon."

"What are the odds of that being granted?" she asked.

"Much depends on Rand. If he acts properly contrite at the sentencing, he has a good chance of being transported. I have several friends of influence who have agreed to plead for him."

"I'm sure you do. And what are the odds that Rand will act properly contrite?"

"Has he ever expressed regret over his misdeeds?"

She considered the question. "Not since I've known him. It was obvious to me that he didn't care for his actions, but he blamed them on events that occurred five hundred years ago. Oh, 'tis all so complicated." She glared at Tom. "Had we left England, Rand would have changed. He might still crave excitement, but I truly believe he would have used his wits and strength to carve out a better life for us, a *profitable* existence, one that wasn't achieved at the expense of others, especially his own family."

"Then if all else fails," Tom said, ignoring Elizabeth's outburst, "Rand could ultimately decide whether he lives or dies."

CHAPTER 29

On the final day of the trial, after Rand had been found guilty of both murder and robbery, Elizabeth decided to attend the sentencing. Not surprisingly, Tom's ploy had resulted in nothing more than a short postponement, so the next step was to plead for a royal pardon. Elizabeth had written Rand an eloquent speech in which he begged that his life be spared, and Billy swore up and down that Rand had memorized it. Tom was right about one thing. Royal pardons were frequently granted.

Head bent, Elizabeth approached York's Assize Courts. Law officials were everywhere, but she hadn't seen Rand since her escape from Newgate ten weeks ago, and she hungered to glimpse him again, if only from a distance.

This time she had invaded Lilith's wardrobe. Over three panniers, Elizabeth wore an elaborate polonaise, its fitted waist and draped cutaway overskirt partially hidden by a fur-lined cardinal. Beneath the hood of the cardinal, her hair was arranged in side curls, powdered white.

Not a comprehensive disguise, she thought. *But if Skully attends, my man's garb might spark a dim memory. Hoping to collect the reward, he could point me out to Walter.*

The Assize Courts was a two-story structure of smoke-colored stone, topped by a statue of Justice bearing scales and a spear. While taking her place at the end of a line snaking down the broad stone steps, Elizabeth noticed the two guards who stood on either side of the entrance, watching the crowd. She hoped they weren't looking for her, but feared they were. Had Walter surmised she'd attend?

Of course he had. Never again would she underestimate the bloody lawman's talents, nor his obsession for her.

Gaze fastened upon her heeled slippers, chin sinking to her neck, Elizabeth grabbed the arm of a nearby gentleman and scooted past the guards. The wigged whip kept his silence, intrigued by her air of mystery. Once safely inside the Crown Court, she murmured an apology, then hurried upstairs to the gallery, which flanked three sides of the room. Weaving her way among the spectators, she finally positioned herself at an angle where she could see both the bench and Rand.

Crown Court was not as large as Elizabeth had imagined, but it was more bedazzling. She had expected a place of death to be somber, its architecture as weighted as its sentences. Instead, she observed a beautifully painted ornamental dome, topped by a circular window. A feeble wheel of sunshine, emanating from the window, illuminated the oak paneling and yellow marble columns that supported the first story.

She spied several familiar faces in the benches below, including Walter's and Dorothea's. Although he conferred with a steady stream of people, Walter continually craned his neck. When he scanned the gallery, Elizabeth pretended to adjust her panniers.

A collective sigh, like waves against the sand, brought her attention back to the scene below. Judge Herriott had entered. He wore a scarlet robe, lined with ermine, and a full-bottomed wig, not unlike those in fashion a century past. Trials were designed to compel righteousness in the multitudes, so the judge made a purposefully impressive figure.

Several men and one woman were led into

the prisoner's box. Judge Herriott would sentence them in order of the severity of their crimes, with the least serious first.

Rand was the last to enter. Irons were customarily knocked off before passing into the courtroom, but Rand's remained in place. He wore an iron band around his waist to which shackles were attached, and Elizabeth was reminded of the Newgate door with its hasps and fillet. Not that Rand's girdle resembled a door. However, it looked strong and unyielding. No wonder Billy had sworn that escape was impossible.

Shears were attached to Rand's legs. He walked as if used to them, but the length of iron affixed to his ankles must particularly pain his bad leg.

After Judge Herriott dispensed with the lesser crimes, he put on his black cap of judgment to signify that he was about to pronounce a sentence of death, which meant that John Randolph Remington's turn had come. The courtroom stilled.

While the prosecution was allowed to question witnesses during a trial, a defendant had no one to look out for his interests save the judge. Listening to Herriott give a lecture on proper morality, Elizabeth forgot the people packed around her, the unpleasant smells exuding from too many bodies in too tight a space, and the ache in her feet from her hours of standing. She could only think that in a few moments the man she loved would officially be sentenced to death.

Rand was brought forward. He stood before the judge, who transformed his expression into one of profound sorrow. "You have strayed from the path of righteousness," Herriott stated solemnly. "From a respectable family and an honorable record in the American War, to a life of lawlessness."

Elizabeth saw Rand raise his head. His gaze swept the gallery. Could he sense her presence?

"England is a country of laws, and the most sacred laws concern the right of a man to own property without threat from anyone." Herriott paused to adjust his black cap. The room was so quiet Elizabeth could hear the ragged sound of her own breath. "It is King George's earnest desire and intent that all his subjects be easy and happy. But without order, without the preservation of the laws of the kingdom, how miserable must be all the king's children!" As if to embrace the entire courtroom, Herriott spread his arms. "Look, all of you, where crime leads you. Only to Death!"

The dreadful sentence was imminent. The gallows was the terrible threat around which England's entire social system revolved. Without it, the British empire would crumble, or so most wise men believed. Elizabeth swallowed hard, knowing what the judge's next words would bring.

"One week hence, on March 20, 1788, you will be transported to Tyburn and hanged by the neck until dead." Was she mistaken, or did Herriott's eyes glisten with tears? Leaning forward, he eyed Rand. "You still have an immortal soul, and in these few remaining days you must seek salvation. Have you anything to say before you're taken to the Condemned Cell?"

Elizabeth held her breath. This was the moment she had been waiting for, the moment that might yet spare Rand the gallows, the moment when he would deliver *the speech.* Before pleading for clemency, Rand would lament his past misdeeds as well as his debauched life. According to Tom, judges loved such speeches, which provided powerful moral lessons and allowed the law to temper justice with mercy. Often, if the prisoner sounded eloquent and remorseful enough, the judge would recommend a royal pardon on the spot.

As Rand made ready to speak, Elizabeth's

lips formed the familiar words. She had labored for hours over the opening line: "What a low creature I am, lower than the worms wiggling at my feet."

"I don't mind going to my death," Rand said.

Obviously, he was improvising. Perhaps she shouldn't have used the words "low creature."

"I've known thirty-five good years," Rand continued. "I've known some fun, much excitement, and a measure of sadness. I've also known the love of a beautiful woman. What more could any man want?"

Did Elizabeth fancy it, or did he raise his eyes to her? She was so shaken she couldn't be certain, for with his defiant gesture Rand had effectively placed the noose around his own neck. Yet even while she abhorred his act, she admired his refusal to conform, his insistence on remaining true to himself no matter what the price.

Several ladies fainted. An angry murmur, like a hot wind, swept through the room. Prisoners were supposed to beg for mercy, to tremble and be carried weeping from the court. This devilish man was not behaving like a proper criminal!

"If it were possible," Rand said, "I'd return England to a time when the wealthy felt a moral obligation to care for and protect the poor, not blame them for their poverty and work them into an early grave."

The crowd murmured again, but this time Elizabeth heard a vague undertone of assent.

"I won't miss England, sir. On the contrary, I'll be glad to be shed of her."

Judge Herriott bellowed for Rand to be removed from the premises.

Elizabeth stared at her slippers. It was over. Rand would die as splendidly as he had lived, but he'd die nonetheless.

Lifting her head, she spotted Billy's stricken face among the spectators. Even Tom had lost his usual aplomb. Dorothea coiled a curl of hair around her finger, while Walter looked as satisfied as if he'd just completed a ten-course dinner.

How different the result might have been without the murder charge, thought Elizabeth, digging her fingernails into the flesh of her palms. Juries sometimes reduced the value of stolen goods in order to lessen a crime and spare a defendant the gallows, but they wouldn't mitigate murder.

Melancholia gripped her. If only she hadn't shot and killed Robert Whitney.

'Tis I, not the judge, who sentenced Rand to die!

■ ■ ■ ■

Five days later, Elizabeth and Billy entered the exercise yard leading to the Debtors Prison. Mud sucked at the wooden-soled pattens which elevated her feet and increased her height. As she struggled across the yard, she gripped Billy's arm with one hand, her basket of food with the other. Angry clouds swarmed around the cupola topping the clock turret and nearly obliterated its weathervane. To Elizabeth, the enormous prison appeared as forbidding as the gathering clouds, and all her instincts screamed that she turn back. But Rand was locked inside the Condemned Cell — or "Pompeii's Parlor," as the locals called it.

"These damnable shoes," she muttered. "Maybe we should have devised a more practical disguise."

She, Tom and Billy had long pondered the best way to sneak her inside. Should she dress as a cleric? A law clerk? Doctor? Barrister? Rand's sister? Mother? Grandmother? Ultimately, they had decided that the safest strategy was simply to blend with all the others who daily viewed the condemned man. To that end, Elizabeth was clothed as a servant. She wore a plain wool dress, white apron, and a frilly mob cap above one of Lilith's old wigs, powdered gray.

Now she ran her hands across the padding she'd added to increase her girth. She had also powdered her lashes and brows, so that they faded into her face. She no longer cared if she looked pretty. On the day of Rand's execution, she would look her most stunning, and Walter Stafford could bite his codpiece!

When they finally reached the front steps, Billy said, "I'll enter after ye do, Bess. That way, ye won't be suspect."

The Debtors Prison contained two stories, as well as a basement level located above ground. Rand's cell was in the southeast corner of the basement.

"Once inside, you'll see the line," Tom had told her last night during their solemn meeting in Middlethorpe's garden. "The place is swarming with Stafford's men, but they shouldn't pay you any heed. Rand's expecting you, and the guards usually allow you more time when you bring food. Even so, you'll only have a few minutes."

Elizabeth waved good-bye to Billy, just before entering the cold, cheerless prison day room. She felt vulnerable, terrified, but if she wanted to visit Rand, she must brazen it out.

Odd's bones! There are as many guards as spectators!

She spotted Lord Stafford's London servant, Grosley, who had positioned himself so that he could see anybody enter or leave. Grosley inspected her, but judging from his bored expression he didn't recognize her.

The line inched forward. Two warders guarded Rand. One stood in front of the metal-studded cell door, a second against the opposite wall. The door was open only wide enough to allow one person at a time access, and the guards often questioned or searched individuals.

I hope to God they don't search me. I'm wearing more stuffing than a mattress.

Repeatedly, Elizabeth had imagined her meeting with the warders, how she would speak and act, how easily she would slip past them into the cell. Guards were supposed to be notoriously stupid. She shook her head. If guards were stupid, all highwaymen were chivalrous and all women ached to marry wealthy men. These guards didn't look stupid. They looked vigilant.

She could see Rand, seated on a bed frame supported by stone blocks. He was reading the last volume of *Castles of Doom*. Generally, after a perfunctory glance at those entering, he returned to the novel, though Elizabeth noticed with annoyance that he smiled at the most beautiful women.

When she finally reached the warder, she paid the customary four-shilling fee. "I've brought the prisoner food, sir."

Elizabeth held up her basket, which the guard promptly yanked from her hand. The second warder eyed her suspiciously. "Where do ye know the prisoner from?" he asked.

"I used to work at the Silent Woman, sir." Elizabeth had concocted an entire fictional background, should the need arise. "Master Turpin came in sometimes. He always tipped me well for services performed, and I found him right handsome."

The guard snorted. "You and half the wimmen o' York!"

" 'Tis Master *Remington*," the first warder corrected, returning her basket.

Reaching in, Elizabeth removed a mince pie. "Would you like this, sir? I'm a fine cook. All the gents say so."

The warder took the pie and waved her inside.

Rand looked up from his book, then down again. *No smile for me,* Elizabeth thought.

Aloud she said, "I've brought you food, Master Remington." Then, lower, "I have long imagined someone like you in my novels."

Rand's head jerked up. Rising, he walked toward her.

"You're very thin, sir," she said fretfully, even though her pulse quickened and her head spun. "I want t' fatten you up."

"And you look like the lass who could do it." Whispering, he added, "You look dreadful, Bess. I'd never have recognized you."

"That's reassuring," she whispered back. "I think."

He led her to the bed and she sat beside him. A thin mattress covered the iron frame. Rand shouted that he wanted more time with her, then removed the contents of her basket — Umble Pie, an apple, a hunk of cheese, bread and butter pudding.

"I couldn't hide a file. Tom said I might be searched." Elizabeth looked around the small cell. A stone table possessed a circular central hole, which served as a stove. In addition to a window covered with bars, a hanging iron lantern shed light upon the whitewashed brick ceiling and stone walls. A corner fireplace provided a smoky blaze and a flicker of warmth.

Now that she was finally close to Rand,

531

she had difficulty meeting his gaze. It wasn't only shyness due to their many weeks of separation. It was shame.

Following her failure to bribe Skully, she should have confessed her guilt. Instead, she had rationalized — and validated — her actions. One, she could better serve Rand if she was free. Two, he might hang anyway and she'd only swing by his side. But she knew now that, save for the murder charge, he might very well have been pardoned.

"I'm sorry," she whispered.

"For what, Bess?"

"Whitney. If I had confessed —"

"Don't be ridiculous. If you had confessed, I would have disallowed your divulgence. I was there, remember? I could conjure up more details than your writer's mind could ever possibly conceive."

"Not true," she retorted, uncertain as to whether she should be reassured or irritated by the slur on her talent.

"We haven't much time." Rand covered her hand with his, then positioned her skirt so the guards wouldn't detect this minor intimacy. "Has Billy informed you of our latest plan?"

"No," she said, surprised. Did Billy believe she might betray Rand? "I think we can rule out a royal pardon," she added sarcastically.

Rand grinned. "Rebellious to the end, the chapbooks will say. The only thing that makes better copy than a penitent highwayman is an arrogant one." Lowering his voice even more, he said, "Billy slipped me a fine sharp knife, which I'll hide behind the buttons of my waistcoat. Before they put the prisoner in the cart, they usually remove his irons and bind his wrists with a cord. While heading for Tyburn, I'll force the blade against the cord. Once I leap from the cart, I may be able to lose myself in the crowd."

"God's breath, Rand! They didn't remove your chains for the sentencing. The iron band about your waist possessed more tentacles than an octopus."

His hand tightened in hers. "I don't want you to attend the execution, Bess. Stay at Middlethorpe. Should I fail to escape, or should I die on the gallows, Billy will contact you. Otherwise, we need a place to meet afterwards."

Should I die. He said it so casually, as if he were discussing a character in one of her novels.

"We could meet at the peel tower," she said. "All the charges have been dropped against me, so after the —" she swallowed "— after the hanging, I can return to the White Hart. Aunt Lilith said Father spends most of his time at Wyndham Manor. The inn is run by a caretaker now. He won't bother me."

"I'll come to you at the peel tower, or the inn, though I can't say when. If my escape from the cart is thwarted, we shall have to rely on the hangman. But even if we successfully bribe Master Hodges, my neck will be stretched. Once I'm resurrected, I don't know how long it will take to recover and —"

"What if you hang, Rand? I mean, really hang?"

"Tom and Billy have repeatedly informed Master Hodges that, should I fail to be resurrected, his life will be cut short. All the money in the world won't help Hodges if he's dead."

"Are you absolutely certain you can trust Tom?"

"I don't trust anyone save you."

Elizabeth winced. Was Rand being sarcastic? Or did his words mean that he was giving her a second chance, a chance to wipe out the betrayal against Ranulf, spawned by Lady Jane?

"Tom played Judas once," she said. "He could do it again."

"If he does, I'll be dead and unable to regret my mistake."

"Stop treating death as a joke!"

One of the warders poked his head inside. "Time's up."

Reluctantly, Elizabeth stood. She stared into Rand's mesmerizing blue eyes and longed to stroke his beard.

The guard yelled, "Hurry it along!"

"Midnight, Bess," Rand whispered urgently. "Wait by your window, or at the peel tower, every night. Until I come for you."

Fighting back tears, she stumbled from the cell into the hallway.

"You!" the guard called.

Heart in her throat, Elizabeth turned.

He held up her basket. "You forgot this."

Forcing a smile, she retrieved the basket and hurried toward the entrance.

She was so upset she didn't look for Billy in the day room, but rather plunged outside into a vicious storm. Sleet slashed the courtyard. Mud exploded in angry bursts. Dropping her basket, Elizabeth sped down the prison steps. Suddenly she halted, as if stopped by an invisible wall. From the corner of her eye, she saw a tall man standing beneath a black umbrella.

Half a dozen lawmen immediately surrounded her.

"Damn," Elizabeth breathed, waiting for the tall man to reach her. Water streamed from his umbrella, obscuring his face, but she'd stake her life on his identity.

"I knew you'd show," Walter said.

"How did you know it was me?"

"Your walk. I've been watching from a side room every day, freezing my arse off. And while I must compliment you on a rather successful disguise, I have made it my business to study mannerisms. How could I ever forget yours when I run everything about you over and over in my mind?"

Sleet drummed upon the fabric of Walter's umbrella. Despite the frozen rain that slanted sideways and stung her eyes, Elizabeth saw his face spasm.

"Where did you hide? At your aunt's? At Wyndham Manor? Here in York, under my very nose? That seems most like you, my dear, and I both detest and admire you for it. Who would have thought that a woman could have such a lively, determined intellect?"

Raising her chin, she faced him defiantly. "You can't hold me against my will. You've dropped all charges. I'm free to go as I please."

"You're free to do as *I* please. Charges can be reinstated."

"That's absurd! Rand was already found guilty of Whitney's murder. You once told me that I couldn't have it both ways. Well, you can't either."

"Charges can also be falsified."

"I've talked to my barristers," Elizabeth lied. "They told me the accomplice accusations would never hold up in court."

"Perhaps. But I can charge you with stealing."

"What have I stolen?"

"My pocket watch and my ruby ring. There are many who will swear they saw both items in your possession."

Silently cursing Walter, Elizabeth took off her mob cap and wig, both impossibly soaked by the downpour. "Even I can figure out that you don't want me to hang," she said, thinking she could be as brave as Rand. "Which means your threats are just bluster."

Walter's eyes narrowed. "Why do you insist on goading me?" Handing his umbrella to a lawman, he reached out as if to touch her, then abruptly dropped his hand. "You've been a worthy adversary, Elizabeth, I will admit. For a woman you have a good mind, though you've driven me to distraction."

"*You* pursued me from the very beginning. I merely wanted to be left alone."

"Enough talk! You've been like a sickness

with me, but not anymore." Grabbing her arm, he dug his fingers into her flesh.

At that moment, Billy bounded down the steps. "What're ye doin'? Get yer hands off her, ye bloody bastard!"

Billy rushed toward them, but Walter nodded to his men, one of whom slammed Billy on the side of the head with his pistol. Knees collapsing, Billy fell face down in the mud.

"Turnbull threatened me and will be gaoled until after the execution," Walter proclaimed, his voice triumphant. "That way I can make certain he doesn't ruin my plans. And you, my dear Elizabeth, are going to be caged again."

Temper beyond control, she swung wildly, hitting Walter's nose. One of the lawmen pinned her flailing arms behind her. Sleet slashed her cheeks as she faced an enraged Walter.

"You're going to pay for this," he said, dabbing at his bloody nose with his handkerchief.

"You don't frighten me," she said with false bravado.

Squeezing her nape with his fingers, Walter propelled her across the exercise yard. "I want one thing from you, Elizabeth, and one thing only. I want you to witness your highwayman's execution. I want to savor your expression as you watch him hang. After that, I'll count it among my greatest joys if I never set eyes on you again."

CHAPTER 30

Behind the grimy panes of the inn's window, York Minster rose like a mountain, so close Elizabeth could barely see the top of its spire. In a few short hours, Rand would be executed.

Unable to sleep, she had watched the Minster's stones change from dove-gray to cream. Stained-glass windows sparkled in the sunrise. *Like a woman in the bloom of youth and just as short-lived,* she thought, as the bright colors abruptly faded.

Her fingers picked at the peeling paint on the window ledge. Whatever youth she had left was passing, her life was passing, and without Rand nothing remained except desolation and the threat of Walter. In truth, Walter was like the mistletoe that clung so prettily to a tree while sucking the life from it.

Slouched in a chair before the room's lone door, Grosley stretched his shanks. His mission was to make certain Elizabeth did not leave this nameless inn, located on some nameless side street. Turning her back to him, she tried for the hundredth time to reason her way through this present predicament. If he failed to escape from the death cart, Rand would expect the resurrection plan to proceed. But what if Walter had tortured Billy and learned details? Elizabeth knew all about torture from her research on *The Dreadful Secret of Good King Stephen.* The rack. The Iron Maiden. The Scavenger's Daughter. Billy might be tough, yet even hardened knights had sung like nightingales at the very sight of such torture devices.

Thumbscrews would be less elaborate but just as effective.

Fortunately, *she* had been spared any torture device. Walter didn't believe that a man would confide in a woman, and he was very nearly right. Hadn't Billy kept his silence? Rand, however, had always regarded her as an equal, which was one of the reasons she loved him.

Billy had disappeared a mere two days ago, so Rand might not remark upon his absence. Even when Billy had been free, Rand's plan had contained far too many flaws. Now it was doomed.

"Doomed," she whispered.

A bolt slid back on the door. Dorothea minced into the room, her skirts swaying. She was followed by two servants, clothed in the Stafford livery, bearing a virtual cornucopia of food. Rather than the usual breakfast of bread, butter and tea, Elizabeth inhaled the scent of ham, pastries and sausages.

By way of greeting, Dorothea said, "You look simply dreadful, my dear. So thin. Lord Stafford sent for me. He says you haven't eaten in two days and he wants you strong so that you may attend the festivities."

"Walter may think to keep me prisoner inside this flea-infected hovel," Elizabeth said, glaring at her stepmother, "but nothing will induce me to watch Rand's execution. I won't give his lordship the satisfaction."

"Yes, you will."

The servants and Grosley withdrew. Dorothea eased herself onto the bed, then reached for a plate. Between bites of stewed tomatoes and ham, she mumbled, "I've been spending most of my time at Wyndham Manor. 'Tis a lovely place now, cozy and prosperous, so much more peaceful than the White Hart." Lifting a silver lid, she inspected a rice pudding dotted with raisins.

"How is Father? Is it true that Horace Exe is running the White Hart when he has a reputation for cheeseparing?"

"The White Hart turns a small profit." Dorothea stuck her finger into the pudding. "Your father and I have shut one door and opened a new one." She licked her finger, made a *moue* of disgust, sliced a portion of ham, chewed it, then spit a piece of gristle into her napkin. "After the execution, you really should visit Wyndham Manor, Elizabeth. Perhaps you might rearrange your life."

"Without my highwayman I have no life," she stated. "Where, may I ask, is Billy Turnbull?"

Dorothea picked up a sausage and sucked it through her lips. "Lord Stafford plans to keep Turnbull occupied until after the hanging."

Elizabeth peered out through the window again. With Billy gone, nobody would make certain Master Hodges followed instructions, and it was disastrous to rely on Tom.

The sunrise had faded completely, leaving the morning dun-colored, with a dreary feel to it. Perhaps it was only the time following dawn, where the sun seemed to hesitate before taking hold. Perhaps it was a harbinger of a forthcoming storm.

'Tis so hard to predict how the weather will unfold, or even our fates, she thought, blinking back tears.

As if she had read Elizabeth's mind, Dorothea said, "I married your father, knowing full well his gambling problems, thinking I could change him. I couldn't, and you can't change your highwayman. I learned long ago that we always dig our own graves. You made your choice when you decided to fall in love, and please don't fool yourself, Elizabeth. Love is a conscious choice. Now you must suffer the natural consequences of your ill-fated decision."

"But all I have ever wanted was to be left alone and live with Rand. Happily. Peacefully."

"Is that what *he* wants? To live peacefully?"

"I don't know," Elizabeth confessed, almost inaudibly.

Wiping her mouth with a linen napkin, Dorothea tossed it on the bed, then stood. "Lord Stafford has selected a gown he wants you to wear, a festive gown, not unlike the blue silk you wore at Shepherd's. Do as he says, Elizabeth. You must stop fighting, for you cannot win, and in the process you shall only be destroyed."

As she swept through the doorway into

the hall, Dorothea's last words seemed to echo. *You shall only be destroyed.*

Walter led Elizabeth up the stairs of an inn situated along the execution route. He had bound her hands and held one end of the rope.

"This room has a perfect view of the Minster," he said, "which will be the first stop on the thieving bastard's journey."

Entering, he jerked her over to the window. Below, the streets were packed with bodies. Atop the surrounding roofs, spectators perched like brightly colored birds. Leaning from the windows, people laughed and waved and shouted to one another, enjoying the public holiday and the joyous atmosphere.

The Minster bells tolled. Through the inn walls, Elizabeth could feel their reverberations and the excitement of the city. She heard the noise increase as a contingent of peace officers came into view, followed by the City Marshall, the Under Sheriff, and a posse of constables.

"Look, Elizabeth!" Walter pressed against her back, his belly denting her tightly corseted waist. "Here he comes!"

The prison chaplain stood at the rear of the cart. Rand had been placed in front, forced to squat atop his own coffin. He was clothed in a coat of claret velvet, a white shirt fronted with lace, brown doeskin breeches and high boots.

"My, doesn't he look the gentleman? Plain yet elegant," Walter said sarcastically. "Listen to them cheer, Elizabeth. The crowd loves him, though not as much as you do."

The cart inched past. Elizabeth prayed that Rand had managed to smuggle the knife inside his shirt, that even now he was severing the ropes around his wrists. Once they reached Tyburn, it would be too late.

A troop of soldiers followed the cart. Their coats were scarlet, like blood.

Walter continued pressing against her. Elizabeth struggled for breath, struggled for control, struggled to keep from screaming.

The procession stopped at York Minster. Rand stood up. His coat was more purple than the coats of the soldiers, the color of a bruise rather than blood. While the Minster bells continued tolling, a bellman intoned a prayer.

"All good people pray heartily unto God," Stafford mouthed against Elizabeth's ear, "for this poor sinner who is now going to his death, for whom this great bell doth toll—"

"Stop it!" she cried, trying to maneuver

away from him.

Walter laughed. "I've been to more executions than I can count, but I've never enjoyed myself as much as today." He tapped the window pane. "Look at the young women throwing your lover nosegays and kisses. Don't they know they're making love to a corpse?"

Below, the spectators showered Rand with flowers, petals, ribbons and confetti. He acknowledged their attention by raising his arms over his head. His manacles glinted in the feeble rays of the sun, and it took Elizabeth several moments to realize that Rand had not been allowed the customary rope. If he had smuggled a knife inside his shirt, it wouldn't do him any good.

"And now our little procession will be making its way toward Tadcaster and the gallows. Shall we follow?" When Elizabeth didn't respond, Stafford jerked her as he would a dog. "Come along, dearest. I've a carriage waiting, and a special place roped off for us at the site of the wooden mare."

"I won't go."

"Yes, you will." Stafford yanked the rope.

"I won't watch."

"Yes, you will."

Walter's carriage lurched along, following a

human stream. Elizabeth sat next to him, her voluminous skirts crushed against his thigh. She felt as if she were the one traveling to the gallows. She felt as if she were viewing somebody else's dream. She felt as if she would soon start screaming and never stop. She felt nothing at all.

"Almost there." Walter squeezed her knee. "We're moving a bit slower than the death cart, but we haven't missed much."

The carriage finally halted.

"A perfect view," Walter exalted.

The gallows dominated the area. Grandstand seats, reserved for the wealthiest people, surrounded the scaffold on three sides. Constables and soldiers had formed a ring around it to force back the crowd, which undulated for what seemed like miles.

Rand was already on the gallows. A breeze ruffled his black hair and the lace at his throat. From the carriage window, Elizabeth looked at that handsome face, a face she loved with all her heart. She stared at the arms that would never more hold her, and the hands that would never more caress her. She would never again hear the sound of his laughter, nor see the flash of his teeth against the darkness of his beard. She and Janey had both betrayed the men they loved.

"God!" The sound was torn out of her

before she even knew it. Her fingernails dug into her palm as she began to shake. "I killed Robert Whitney," she whispered. "Rand only kept silent because of me, as you well know. Tell them to stop the hanging, my lord. I want to confess."

"You're too late, Elizabeth. Nobody wants to hear."

The minister opened his Bible and read several passages. Then, as he began the Fifty-First Psalm, the crowd joined in.

"Have mercy upon me, O God . . ." the hanging song began ". . . Behold, I was shapen in inequity and in sin . . ."

Elizabeth's teeth chattered. "Stop them, I beg of you. You can do it. Stop the execution."

"Join in, Elizabeth. Pray for your lover."

She turned her face away. "I'll take his place. If the crowd wants to see someone hang, let it be me."

"Watch, Elizabeth. You're not watching."

She shook her head.

"The sacrifices of God are a broken spirit," sang the crowd, "a broken and a contrite heart, O God, thou wilt not despise . . ."

"I despise you," Elizabeth hissed.

"I told you to watch." Walter pushed her face against the window. When she turned her head aside, he grabbed her cheeks between his palms and forced her head straight.

"No!" She struggled wildly, her arms flailing, but Walter grabbed a handful of hair and pulled her head back until she thought her neck would snap.

"Look, damn you, look!"

Her eyes watered with pain. Through her tears, she saw Master Hodges tie the noose around Rand's neck, then fasten a handkerchief around Rand's forehead. One corner hung down. When Rand was ready, he would signal by grasping the corner and pulling the handkerchief over his face.

She stopped struggling and Walter released her. Mesmerized with horror, she couldn't look away. She couldn't even close her eyes.

As if moving through water, Rand's hand slowly drifted upward, toward the handkerchief.

Elizabeth began to scream. She screamed until she could no longer feel the pain which had imbedded itself like a spear point in her brain, until she could no longer hear Walter's curses or feel him shaking her and slapping her, until she could no longer see or hear or feel anything at all.

They were back at the inn before Walter

successfully revived her.

As he splashed brandy on her face, then tried to force it down her throat, Elizabeth made an effort to maintain her state of darkness.

"Wake up, you little fool," Walter muttered, kneeling beside her.

Elizabeth turned away from the sound of his voice. She wanted to shut out Walter. And reality. As long as nobody mentioned what had just happened, she wouldn't have to face the fact that Rand was dead.

Walter pressed his lips against her ear. "You should have seen it. My, but he was slow to die. I watched every jerk of the rope, every agonized contortion. But I shouldn't have to *tell* you. You should have seen it for yourself. Damn you and your woman's constitution. You managed to cheat me out of my ultimate revenge, Elizabeth, and I am not pleased."

Opening her eyes, she rolled away from him. She must gather her wits about her and clear the numbness from her brain. But then she would have to face the truth.

Walter placed his hands beneath her armpits and pulled her to a sitting position. Thrusting his face in front of her, he said, "Not only did they hang him, but afterwards they covered his body with tallow and fat, dressed him in a tarred sheet weighted with iron bands, and hung him in chains. Then they returned him to the gallows, and there he shall remain until he falls into dust."

As if to negate Walter's words, Elizabeth shook her tangled curls. "He never had a chance, did he?"

"What do you mean?"

"You conspired with Thomas Turnbull from the very start, didn't you? There was never any hope of resurrection, was there? You directed the entire scenario from beginning to end, even provided all the money Tom so generously donated to the cause. I'll wager Master Hodges was never even approached with a bribe."

Walter's features contorted until he looked more like one of the Minster's stone gargoyles than human flesh. "I don't care what you say, you scheming bitch. Your lover is a ghost. Try laying with him now!"

CHAPTER 31

Through the carriage window, Elizabeth glimpsed a second coach, coming up fast on the outside. The coachman and guard, all bundled against the weather, perched like gnomes atop the coach box. Lamps pierced the darkness like dragon eyes. As the coach flew past, Elizabeth heard the creak of springs, the thud of wheels, and the snap of the driver's whip. She saw sparks spray from the horses' hooves, like fireflies on a summer night.

A motion inside the carriage caught her eye. Across from her, Walter's snuff-stained fingers raised a flask of whiskey to his lips.

Knees tightly clenched together, she stared out the window again, but this time the view was as dark and formless as her thoughts. What was today? She struggled to remember. The days blurred together, so it was difficult to believe that Rand had only been dead three . . . nay, four days.

"There's a hound called Padfoot that haunts the wilds of Yorkshire," she said. "He has fiery eyes and appears on nights like this, on country lanes and lonely roads. He lopes alongside solitary travelers who should be at home. I wonder if Padfoot might be out there, watching us."

"Don't be so macabre." Walter sneezed luxuriously. "I'm not in the mood for it."

The coach began the steep climb up the hill to the White Hart. In a few more minutes she would be rid of Walter forever, but Elizabeth couldn't even muster the appropriate relief.

Opening his snuffbox, Walter removed yet another pinch. He sniffed, leaned back, and closed his eyes. In a quiet voice, he said, "I still envy him."

"Who?"

"Your highwayman. I'm jealous that he could arouse such devotion in you. I wanted to make you appreciate me, perhaps even love me. I never meant you any harm."

Elizabeth winced.

"I feel old," Walter continued, "old and tired. So tired . . ." His voice faded. "I've battled criminals for more years than I can count, lived by my wits so long I've forgotten how to relax. I've fought my way to prosperity, but I've done things for which

I'm ashamed, especially concerning you."

Unaccountably, Elizabeth's eyes misted. It was so easy to apologize, but how could Walter take back all the humiliations? How could he take back Rand's strangulation?

Not that Walter alone was to blame, she reminded herself, feeling once again the dread that had kept her from confessing her guilt. Yet she knew that Rand had entered into a love affair with Death long before she — or even Walter Stafford — happened along.

"What will you do now?" Walter asked.

She rubbed a hand across her forehead. "I don't know."

"I received the customary forty pounds for Remington's capture, Elizabeth. I'll give it to you."

She was too exhausted to feel insulted. "I don't need money. And even if I did —"

"I'll bring the money by tomorrow."

"Please don't."

They approached the White Hart. A lamp burned inside the stable, its light spilling into the yard. The coach that had earlier passed them was parked nearby. A pre-occupied Tim was leading the fatigued horses toward the stable, conversing with them in a soothing manner. Tim's footprints and the horses' hooves disturbed the dusting of snow upon the cobblestones.

Elizabeth quickly stepped down from the carriage before Walter had a chance to help her. Leaning out the window, he said, "Until tomorrow."

"No!" she cried, but her voice was lost in the clatter of hooves and the scrape of wheels.

Once alone, she allowed the feel of the inn to settle upon her. A chill wind off the moors whipped her cloak, unbound her neat club of hair, and stung her cheeks. It had been a long time since she'd smelled such a wind. The scent, fresh and familiar and brimming with memories, brought tears to her eyes as she stared into the darkness. Out there was the peel tower. She longed to run her hands across its crumbling stones, lie upon its dirt floor, and wait for her highwayman to come riding, riding —

"Mistress Wyndham!" Tim stood at the barn door. "Blessed Mary and the saints! Is it truly ye, come back t' us?"

" 'Tis me, Tim." A tired smile tugged at her lips as she walked toward the stable. Her ostler's fiery blush and gap-toothed smile warmed her. She even knew how he would smell — like the barn, like solid animal things that were simple and good. "How does Rhiannon fare?"

"She's missed ye, but I told her every day ye'd come back."

He led Elizabeth past the largely empty stalls, while she tried to still her questions concerning the White Hart's obvious demise. Only one other stable boy was there, rubbing salve into the neck of an off-wheeler. Reaching Rhiannon, Elizabeth swung her arms around the mare's neck. "He's dead," she murmured, pressing her face against Rhiannon's throatlatch. "Rand is dead."

"Yer friend?" Reaching out as if to comfort Elizabeth, Tim hesitated, then brushed back the mare's forelock. "I saw ye ride with him months ago, an' the next thing ye're in London."

"They hanged him." Elizabeth's voice broke. She felt safe here with Tim and Rhiannon, but even a snug harbor could not soften reality. "Then they tarred him."

"An' that makes ye sad, eh?"

Tears spilled down her cheeks. "Very."

"I thought o' yer friend last night, Mistress. 'Twas late an' I seen . . ." With an embarrassed cough, Tim retrieved a curry comb from the shelf and began combing Rhiannon's tail. " 'Tis lonesome here when no one comes."

"The White Hart looks like a ruin." She

sniffed and lifted her head.

"Mail coaches stop, Mistress, an' from time t' time a carriage. The rest just died away. They have a new inn at Horsehouse. But now ye're home, so the lights'll come on, the coaches'll be back, an' things'll be like always. Better."

Elizabeth stroked Rhiannon's velvety nose. "Oh, Tim, I wish that were true."

Before she could start weeping again, she said good night to her ostler, left the stable, then crossed the yard. The coach guard blew his horn, signaling his passengers. Soon Tim would have to re-harness the horses, a chore he wouldn't relish. Not because he was lazy, but because he thought the horses required a longer rest, which they probably did.

Inside the hallway, Elizabeth removed her gloves and cloak.

A coachman buttoned his second great-coat atop his first, all the while loudly urging his passengers to finish their meals. "We're be'ind schedule an' must 'urry along!" he shouted.

The four passengers vociferously protested being rushed.

"I can't help it if the service 'ere is slow," the coachman fumed, wrapping his neck cloth around his throat. "We've a way yet ter go an' I mislike drivin' at night."

Elizabeth walked past them into the common room. Save for a couple playing draughts and a lone man nursing a pint at the bar, the room was empty.

Grace, her old maidservant, appeared. She wore a spotted apron and a badly frayed mob cap. Eyes downcast, she carried a broom, and, as she walked, she made a halfhearted attempt to sweep the floor.

Elizabeth saw that the windows were streaked. Dust layered the pianoforte and grandfather clock. The fire barely flickered and the poker was absent. A poker would have allowed the guests to stir the ashes.

Looking up, Grace dropped her broom. "Mistress! Ye've come back!"

"Odd's bones, lass! What's happened here?"

"He's a mean man, that Horace Exe. 'Tis like workin' for the devil and a miserly devil at that."

As if Grace had summoned him, Exe scurried past, chasing the departing passengers. Hand outstretched, he yelled, "One moment now! That'll be three and six-pence."

"But we haven't had time to eat," a portly passenger protested. He began to wrap one of the fatty steaks in his handkerchief.

"Is it my fault you're slow eaters?" Exe snapped. "And it's against the rules to take food from the inn. Some would call it stealing."

"See, Mistress?" Grace pouted. "That's what I put up with. Can ye imagine my 'umble disgrace? I'm thinkin' of other employ, I can tell ye that!"

"He's a bad one," Elizabeth agreed. She knew exactly what Horace Exe was up to. It was an old trick, one used by many unscrupulous innkeepers, one her father would have died before employing. The same food would be set out for the next round of passengers. No wonder so few frequented the White Hart.

Grace balled her hands in her apron. "I can hardly keep from speakin' me mind to that old skinflint. Oh, but wouldn't I love to tell him what I think of him."

At any other time Elizabeth would have questioned Grace about her unaccustomed reticence, but now she simply retreated to her room. So the White Hart had come to this. A cheerless inn with a miserly keeper who cheated his customers of their rightful due.

I don't care. Just let me be.

Her bedroom possessed an unused, musty smell. Elizabeth fumbled for the tinder box beside the candle, struck the flint and steel, caught the linen tinder on fire, then inserted a match tipped with brimstone. Raising the lit candle, she inspected her room. It looked the same, yet not the same. For one thing, dust decorated her writing table, bureau and washstand.

She sat heavily upon the bed and ran her fingers across her mother's quilt. The top layer of material was smooth and thin from years of use. Her warming pan, which had heated her covers on thousands of winter nights, rested at the foot of the bed. It felt as relentlessly cold as the rest of the room.

"Everything's wrong," she whispered. Rising and replacing the candle upon the table, she watched shadows flicker across the wall. All the lights and laughter were gone. Gone were the tantalizing kitchen smells, the purposeful bustle of servants, the feeling of home.

She had once believed that without Rand all the colors of excitement and laughter would disappear. She had once thought that without Rand the flowers would turn gray, the trees white, the sun black. But that had been an abstract summation, formed when Rand had been very much alive. Now, with his death, her worst fears had been realized.

Elizabeth thrust her hands beneath her skirts in an effort to warm them. She felt cold outside and hollow within. *I have noth-*

ing left to live for. If only I could will myself to die like Janey. Perhaps I'm already dead. My mind and heart feel that way. Perhaps 'tis only my body that does not yet realize it is a cover for a corpse.

Suddenly, she heard Rand's voice, loud and clear: "Where is your courage, Bess? I love you for your sense of adventure."

The voice was inside her head, of course, but she understood that Rand wouldn't want her to admit defeat. Rand wouldn't want her to lie down and die. What *would* Rand want? What had he told her during her all too brief prison visit?

Something about how the only thing that made better copy than a penitent highwayman was an arrogant one. Something about how the chapbooks would say that he was rebellious to the end.

But Elizabeth could say it much better than the chapbooks.

Charles Beresford was gone, but there were other publishers. They would appreciate her established reputation, not to mention the profits her novels generated. Suppose she wrote a fictional account of a highwayman whose courage and convictions defied all reason? The tale would be told by the heroine, and not one of her vaporous, timid heroines either.

No, by God! This heroine would love her highwayman to distraction, give up her inheritance, perhaps even her virtue . . .

Three hours later, Elizabeth put down her quill, rubbed her neck, and stretched her sore shoulders. She had written a beginning, just a beginning, but already she felt warmer, less hollow. She would call her book *A Highwayman Comes Riding*, and through her prose Rand Remington would live forever.

The shutters rattled unexpectedly, as if disturbed by an unseen hand. Remembering Rand's promise, Elizabeth's heart leapt. Perhaps he had waited for her at the peel tower. Then, when she didn't appear, he had decided to visit the inn.

Absurd! Rand was dead. A sudden thought made her bite her lower lip. Could Walter have lied about the tarring? The press accounts hadn't continued beyond the execution itself. If Rand had not been tarred, he might conceivably have survived the hanging.

Stumbling to the window, she swung open the shutters. Wind swirled the powdery snow above the cobblestones and caused bits of debris to jerk across the courtyard like drunken dancers. Only the lonely light from the stables disturbed the darkness.

Elizabeth glimpsed Tim, standing in the lantern's glow, maintaining a vigil for the coaches that no longer came.

The next day Elizabeth felt fatigued, both in body and spirit. Glancing toward her pen and ink pot, she decided that her sense of emptiness could best be assuaged by riding.

The next chapter could wait.

Tim saddled Rhiannon and Elizabeth rode to Great Whernside. She crossed fields dotted with sheep and passed cattle huddled close to their barns. She galloped across bleak moors and barrows, then followed icy streams into dark, secret valleys. She halted occasionally to uncap a silver flask and sip lemonade baptized with brandy. The brandy lit a fire inside her belly, but her extremities still felt numb. Near the peel tower she reined in Rhiannon. A flood of memories overwhelmed her and she quietly wept.

She remembered Rand as he'd stood framed by the rubble, his hair blowing in the wind. She remembered the feel of him as he'd swept her from his stallion and she pressed against a chest that rippled with finely hewn muscles. And yet that same rock-hard chest had adapted, yielded, enticed and protected her.

Elizabeth gazed at the spot where they had

lain, when the night had swirled around them and the moon had raced overhead. She could taste Rand's tongue and smell his sandalwood scent. She could feel the hardness of his body, the urgent suck of his mouth, and the tease of his lips against her breasts. Most of all, she remembered the tender touch of his hands, slowly bringing her to a peak of ecstasy she had never known before, nor would ever know again.

When she returned to the White Hart, Tim said, "Lord Stafford hisself rode in a while ago. He asked fer ye, Mistress."

"Damn! He said he would visit, but I forgot."

"He's still inside, waitin'."

Elizabeth sighed. She had raced Rhiannon across the moors for hours and the mare was tired. Another ride was out of the question, so she'd just have to face Walter and make it very clear that his presence was unwelcome.

What would he threaten her with this time? Dorothea had said something about the prosperity of Wyndham Manor. "Cozy and prosperous," she had said.

But Elizabeth had not wed Walter. Did he hold the deed to the manor? Would he now hold it over her head?

Nonsense. He had sworn he hated her,

not once but many times. And yet last night he had said that he was old and tired and meant her no harm. What new tricks did he have up his sleeve?

With trepidation, she neared the inn's garden. A flock of ravens stampeded up from the hedges. Startled, Elizabeth followed their dark flight above the roof.

From a window on the second floor, a movement caught her attention. Two faces hovered there. One belonged to a woman with pale, unbound hair. The other face, bearded, was framed by curly hair, black as the ravens that dotted the sky. The bearded man was looking up, but the mournful woman seemed to be staring at Elizabeth.

In an attempt to better examine the faces, Elizabeth shaded her eyes. She was too far away and the slant from the sun precluded seeing every feature clearly, yet the woman's unbound hair distressed her. The White Hart employed four maids and they all wore their hair tucked inside mob caps.

Elizabeth gathered up her skirts and ran for the inn. She stumbled up the stairs and flung open the door.

The room was empty. It wasn't large enough to hide anyone and nothing appeared disturbed.

Elizabeth shook her head. " 'Tis the

brandy," she whispered.

Yes . . . perhaps the brandy had caused her to envision faces that weren't there.

With a start, she realized that the air inside the bedroom was cold enough to make her bones ache. Racing downstairs, she headed for the front door.

Walter grasped her by the arm, halting her flight.

"Elizabeth! What ails you? You ran down those steps as if pursued by demons."

"I swear I saw someone upstairs, but the room is empty. Did you see a fair-haired woman with a delicate, oval face? She had a haunted look to her."

"I've seen nobody matching that description."

"Did you send someone to spy on me? A woman? Perhaps a man, as well?"

"Why would I do such a thing?"

Her gaze skimmed his body and face, looking for any sign of pretense. His feet didn't shuffle. Above his goatee, his mouth was drawn, rather than set in a taunting sneer. His eyes remained impassive, nary one trace of the hypocritical piety she'd come to recognize so well.

She drew a calming breath. "Forgive me, my lord. I know 'tis rude, but I feel ill and must retire."

Walter glanced at his pocket watch. " 'Tis eventide, Elizabeth. Perhaps a glass of wine?"

"No, thank you." Wine was the last thing she needed. "Good night, my lord. I mean, good afternoon. In truth, I don't know what I mean."

Eyes blurred by sudden tears, she turned away from him, stumbled down the hallway, entered her bedroom, and swiftly locked the door.

Then she stretched out on the bed and for the first time in months slept deeply, dreamlessly, without any fear at all.

Chapter 32

Ranulf and Janey!

Ranulf and Janey had been the faces at the window.

Had she been less fatigued, less fuddled by brandy, she would have recognized them immediately.

Rising from her bed, Elizabeth removed her crumpled riding attire and donned a wrapper. So, two ghosts now inhabited the White Hart.

Strange. The thought did not disturb her. On the contrary, it comforted her. With Rand gone, Ranulf and Janey had come to watch over her, protect her, and she now understood that Janey had been trying to convey an urgent message.

Nonsense. Ghosts often appeared, and sometimes they moved from place to place, but they never spoke.

Even Padfoot didn't bark.

Elizabeth had no idea what time it was.

Perhaps she'd slept ten hours, perhaps five. When had she sought the sanctuary of her bedroom? Three o'clock? Four? "Eventide," Walter had said.

Now it was night. She had missed dinner but she wasn't hungry, and she wondered if she'd ever be hungry again.

The wind prowled outside her room and slammed her shutters against the walls. Walking over to the window and peering through, she saw Tim's shadow when he passed what he called "the barn's winnock." Beyond the stables, the silver highway wended its way across purple moors, as if spun from moonbeams.

Hedges shook while trees waved their bony branches at the sky's tattered clouds. Moonlight spilled upon the clouds, which crested, swirled, and changed shapes. *Death and his huntsmen,* she thought. *Death and his hellhounds galloping across the face of the moon.*

She had heard such tales as a child. How Death sat astride his mighty horse, blasting his horn to mark the hunt. How Death and his sky-riders scavenged the night, seeking yet another harvest of victims.

Elizabeth shivered. Seated at her dressing table, she brushed her hair. "One, two, three," she whispered. It was impossible to think and count strokes at the same time. "Seven, eight, nine . . ." Perhaps it *was* possible, for she could not dismiss the deadly sky-riders. "Twelve, thirteen . . . damn!"

The wind rapped at her window pane. Its cries swirled around the White Hart's corners and crevices like the shrill of a banshee. She imagined a banshee, a bone-thin woman with long hair and eyes streaming blood, drifting in the air beyond the window, searching for the inhabitant whose death was imminent.

"God's breath! Banshees and sky-riders. I must stop this."

A whistle pierced the room. Elizabeth dropped her brush. *The wind,* she thought, *screeching like a banshee, and now whistling like Rand.* She rose, then sank back onto her chair.

A second whistle.

"Don't do this to yourself," she admonished. "Don't respond to every gust of wind, every strange noise."

The whistle sounded a third time.

Slowly, as if sleepwalking, Elizabeth rose from her chair and approached the window. Opening it, she leaned far out over the casement.

Rand was below, astride his black stallion. She blinked several times. The wind skittered shadows across the rider's face. She rubbed her eyes. The moon dipped behind a cloud. When it reappeared, he was still there. "Rand?"

"None but, my love."

Oh God, *this* ghost spoke. "It cannot be you," she said calmly, rationally, even though every instinct urged her to scream or swoon. "You are dead. They tarred you, then raised you in chains."

"Who said so?"

"Walter. He swore —"

"He lied, Bess. Save for Billy's absence, everything went as planned." In the moonlight, Rand smiled. "But it takes a wee bit out of a man, coming back from the dead."

Yet uncertain, she gazed down at him. He might be a dream or he might be a vision. She mistrusted her senses, mistrusted the joy and relief racing inward.

"I waited for you, Bess, every night at the peel tower. I even rode into the courtyard once, thinking you might be at your bedroom window. Then I saw you return from York with Stafford." He darted a glance toward the highway. "I was most diligent at my post, sweetheart."

Rising in his stirrups, Rand caught a strand of her hair and kissed it. "Come to me now and welcome my return. We have some catching up to do."

He *sounded* like Rand. Still only half believing, Elizabeth climbed out through the window and dropped to the ground. "You look like Rand," she whispered.

Laughing, he lifted her up and settled her across his saddle. He didn't smell of the grave, nor was he cold. On the contrary, he was blessedly warm. She snaked her arms around his chest and snuggled her head beneath his coat of claret velvet.

"I can't believe it," she said, and even to her own ears, her voice sounded half soppy, half reverential. "After all my pain, to think you are truly alive."

Rand's arms tightened around her. "How could you doubt? I'll die when I'm ready and not one moment before."

At another time she might have argued, but now she merely raised her head to accept Rand's embrace. His lips brushed her eyelids, the tip of her nose, her cheeks and chin. *This is a dream,* she thought. Her fingers crept up beyond the lace at his throat, for she wanted to feel where the rope had scarred him.

Rand caught her hand. "Don't. Please. My neck is still sore. I have a welt as thick as my wrist."

"Does it pain you?"

"Much less than the alternative."

"Always you tease." She dotted his face with kisses.

The stallion snorted and danced.

"Dismount," Rand murmured against Elizabeth's mouth. "This was *not* one of my better ideas." He placed her bare feet upon the ground. "Your room —"

"Is cold. The fire's out and there's no wood. Horace Exe, the new innkeeper, is frightfully frugal."

"Together we shall light a new fire." Rand swung down from the saddle, shed his coat, tethered his stallion to a tree, then hoisted her through the window. Graceful as a cat, he followed her inside.

It was the first time he had ever entered her room and the sight of Rand dwarfing her furniture brought home the reality, as did the slant of his lips on hers. His kiss was feather-soft, but gradually he intensified the contact until her mouth opened and his tongue began to plunder. Dimly, she realized that she hovered between awareness and oblivion, ecstasy and torment.

Shuddering violently, she stumbled backwards and began to weep. Rand pulled her into his arms and pressed her face against his chest. His fingers rubbed the small of her back.

"You were d-dead," she sobbed, "and I wanted to d-die too, just like Janey."

"I know," he soothed. "I know, my love. I couldn't get word to you right away. I wanted to —"

"But Walter would have sensed my joy," she finished, lifting her face, the tears still coursing down her cheeks. "I'm not that good an actress." With a tremulous sigh, she reached for the tinder box.

Rand stilled her hand. "The moon shall be our lantern," he said. "Ah, Bess, I've been hungry for the sight of you."

"Just the sight?" she asked with mock indignation.

"No. I missed the sound of your laughter. I missed the taste of your breath. Most of all, I missed your body next to mine. I've always loved you, but I never realized how much until we were separated. 'Twas the lack of your closeness that made me a prisoner, not the bars on my cell." Removing her wrapper, he palmed her breasts.

She felt her body melt like the tallow on a candle. "Rand, I can't stand up."

His answer was to draw her against the unyielding wall of his chest. Easing her chin up, he began an assault on her lips. Elizabeth's frantic grasp captured his shoulders. The muscles rippling beneath her fingers felt warm and firm. And alive.

He encircled her waist, his fingers digging into her bottom. Then he brought her up hard, grinding their hips together. Once again, his mouth met hers in a kiss that left her breathless.

His kiss deepened as he scooped her up into his arms. Placing her on the bed, he followed her descent, until she was pinned beneath him. Her mother's quilt felt soft against her back. Her pillow cradled her head, its pliant down nuzzling her cheeks. The contrast of Rand's roughened palms and the feathery pillow, both pressing against her flushed face, brought forth a blissful moan.

He halted to divest himself of his boots and clothing. His body lifted and wriggled, as if he purposely timed his movements for the optimum impact.

Elizabeth savored each tantalizing inch of him. "You're cast from steel," she sighed, her legs spreading beneath the urgent press of his knee.

"Steel can be tempered by fire, my love."

"True," she murmured, aware that *she* was on fire. A torrid blaze traveled throughout her body, inciting an almost volcanic tremor between her legs. Her skin smoldered at Rand's every caress, and he never stopped, never rested.

Fondling, petting, stroking, he ignited flame after flame; a conflagration that was so intense, she wondered if she could possibly survive.

She felt his hand creep up her thighs, then cup her mons, and a sharp cry of pleasure broke from her lips. He swallowed that cry, then another, his mouth possessing hers so thoroughly, she couldn't tell where his breath left off and hers began.

Rand's lips moved lower, his tongue darting out every so often to lick the strained arch of her neck. He found the pulse that beat wildly at the base of her throat, and his lips pressed hard against the erratic throb.

Eyes shut, Elizabeth writhed beneath him, but he pinioned her wrists, holding her upper body motionless. His lips moved again, and this time he found her breasts. She felt his tongue sear, first one nipple, then the other. Her head thrashed from side to side, while whimpers of delight forced their way up her throat.

In the midst of her passion, a vise of fear clamped her heart. From somewhere deep inside, rage cut across her desire. She jerked one wrist free from his grip and lashed out with an angry sweep of her arm, pushing him away.

Letting go her other wrist, Rand pressed his palms against the mattress and raised himself up. "What's wrong?"

"This. You think to reward me for my days of anguish."

"I think to reward us both. Why does that pain you?"

"Afterwards you'll leave me," she cried, as she wondered who was speaking? Bess or Janey?

"I cannot promise to stay by your side like a faithful dog," Rand said, "nor would you want me thus. Perhaps you consider our lovemaking an atonement, Bess, but I consider it a rare gift."

At his words, desire once again clouded her mind. Drawing him down to her, Elizabeth licked his nipples, alternately circling and suckling the taut nubs.

Beginning anew, Rand caressed. *Dorothea's wrong,* thought Elizabeth, her head whirling. *Love isn't a conscious choice. 'Tis a rare gift.*

"Please! Now!" she cried.

At her urgent command, Rand penetrated. When she would have drawn her legs together, he kept them apart, rising slightly, pressing the heels of his hands gently but firmly against her inner thighs.

"Now," she pleaded.

Releasing her legs, Rand began to thrust.

Elizabeth recalled her earlier task, brushing her hair.

One, two, three.

Four, five, six.

Seven, eight, nine.

They would never reach twelve, she thought, as the rhythm of Rand's thrusts increased. She would die from ecstasy before they reached twelve.

She was right. They reached eleven.

Elizabeth ran her fingertips across Rand's face. "When I saw you on the gallows, I wished it could have been me."

"You saw the hanging? I told you to stay away."

"Directly after my prison visit, Walter captured me. Did Billy not tell you? Or is he still locked up?"

"No. He's free. But he didn't say one word about —"

"Perhaps he felt ashamed. He tried to come to my rescue, but was knocked unconscious for his efforts, poor lad."

"That must be it, then. My cousin yearns to play the hero."

"He doesn't have to *play* at being a hero. God knows what I would have done without his support during your trial. Billy has more strength of character than all my book heroes put together. I truly believe he would slay dragons for a damsel in distress . . . even if he didn't possess a sword."

"Billy loves you, Bess, at least a little."

"I cannot love a little, Rand. I must love wholeheartedly. 'Tis the way I am." His chest hair tantalized her breasts as she rubbed against him. "Walter was here this evening, determined to give me the forty pound reward for your capture. Life looked so utterly bleak. I imagined banshees and sky-riders and —"

"Stafford was here, at the inn? Did he hand over the forty pounds?"

"No. I would never accept his blood money, not even if —"

"When did he leave?"

Rolling sideways, sitting up, she shrugged. "I don't know. I retired to my room. My guess is that Walter waited to see if I would sup. The food here is dreadful, but I rode all day, and Walter would assume I'd be ravenous. Don't fret, my love, he's long gone."

"No, Bess. If Stafford tarried till seven, 'twas less than two hours ago. Was he alone?"

"Of course. He's killed every highwayman in England. Why should he fear the roads?"

"Stafford's out there by himself with my reward. God, what a stroke of luck!"

"Rand! Don't even think what you're thinking. You were just hanged for robbery, remember?"

"I was hanged for murder." Rising from the bed, he lit the candle. "I still have a score to settle with your bloody beak. He killed Zak, he nearly succeeded in killing me, and he kept you a prisoner." The candle's glow distorted Rand's eyes, causing them to shine more black than blue. "The world would be well rid of Walter Stafford and I, conscientious Englishman that I am, must not shirk my duty."

"Let it be!" Elizabeth watched him rapidly clothe himself. "We've been given more than our share of chances. Don't tempt fate again."

"But wouldn't it be a fine jest for us to spend the crown's reward? What say we return to London and invite King George over for forty pounds' worth of tea and crumpets? How can we pass up such an opportunity?"

"Very easily." Elizabeth balled her hands beneath the quilt. "Something will go wrong, I just know it."

"What could go wrong? Stafford thinks I'm dead. He'll believe I'm a ghost. I can't wait to see the look on his face. Perhaps I won't have to kill him. Perhaps he'll die of fright before I lay one hand on him."

Scooting from the bed, she buried her face against the lace of Rand's shirt. "Let us ride away from the Dales. Please?"

"You're so beautiful." Holding her at arm's length, he scrutinized her from head to toe. "I've seen you in brocade and silk and wool. I've seen you in breeches and stuffed like a scarecrow. But I think I prefer you with no clothes at all."

"I prefer *you* alive!"

"I'll return after it's finished, Bess."

"And if something should go amiss?"

"Look for me on the morrow. If things go amiss, I'll return tomorrow, by moonlight. 'Tis your turn to play the watcher, and I swear I'll not fail you."

"I knew you'd leave me." She gestured toward the bed. "I told you so."

"And I said I wasn't a faithful dog. If you want a dog —"

"I don't want a dog. I want you." Stepping away, she blinked back tears. "Do you know how much it hurt when I believed you dead? I felt as if my very heart had been ripped out. Don't do this to me. Please!"

The entire scenario would be played all over again, she thought. Once again, she'd wait and pray for her highwayman's safe return. She could understand how he felt about Stafford, truly she could, but Rand had taunted Death so long, thwarted him so many times. Wouldn't Death grow tired of the game and want compensation? The same way Rand wanted to pay Walter back in his own coin? Rand, however, was mortal, while Death was omnipotent. Furthermore, Elizabeth had a feeling that Death was rapidly running out of patience.

Rand cradled her chin. "One last kiss. For luck."

She clung to him until he removed her arms, then watched him climb through the window, still as graceful as a cat.

But a cat had nine lives. How many lives did Rand have left?

Chapter 33

Elizabeth bolted upright in her chair. From her position she could see out the casement window. She had kept vigil for endless hours, but Rand had not returned.

Had she been dreaming all along? No. She could not have dreamed the tender caress of his hands, nor the plunder of his tongue. She could not have dreamed the welt on his neck.

Even now Rand's scent lingered on her bedclothes. Even now her lips felt bruised from his kisses. Even now she felt a pleasant ache between her legs. Thankfully, that was not, nor ever could be, a dream.

Tim stood in front of the stables, speaking to a man on horseback. Tim's hair shone white-yellow in the early morning light, but it was impossible to identify the rider, although she knew it wasn't Rand. Her ostler waved his arms excitedly as the rider bent toward him. Abruptly, the rider wheeled his mount, dug his spurs into its flanks, and galloped from the yard.

Uneasy, Elizabeth watched Tim walk toward the barn. Might the scene she had just witnessed have something to do with Rand?

All day she tried to shake off her sense of doom. Feeling like a thief in her own house, she tiptoed into the kitchen for bread, cheese, fruit and tea. One of the maids retrieved her chamber pot, then brought it back empty, along with some clean towels. When Elizabeth tried to question the young girl about unexpected visitors, she blushed furiously, curtsied, and fled.

Perhaps the maid had a lover.

Elizabeth wondered if *she* still had a lover. By God, she had mourned Rand so many times, wept so many times, the idea merely numbed her.

She tried to write. Instead, she kept pondering the various reasons why Rand had not returned. Something must have gone amiss. But if Rand or Walter had been killed, surely one of the carriages would have brought the news. Perhaps Rand had never found Walter. Perhaps Rand planned to lay in wait tonight, then come for her afterwards.

If things go amiss, I'll return by moonlight.

Desperate, Elizabeth wanted to ride across the moors until she was exhausted, beyond thought, beyond fear.

'Tis your turn to play the watcher, and I swear I'll not fail you.

"I shall play the watcher," she said grimly, remembering how she had sat with the watchers during her mother's funeral, waiting for Barbara to come back to life.

But her mother had remained motionless, while Rand had truly come back from the dead. Pray God he hadn't abused the privilege.

Near sunset, Elizabeth heard the tramp of marching feet. A troop of soldiers entered the yard, their coats a scarlet stain against the gray of the cobblestones.

Why would soldiers be here? She studied the score of faces as if their expressions might provide the answer. A troop of redcoats was an uncommon sight at any time, so why would they suddenly decide to pay the White Hart a visit?

"There's only one way to find out," she murmured. After plaiting her unruly hair with a red love knot, she raced down the hallway. Then she skidded to a stop.

The soldiers are here because of Rand, you bird-wit.

No other explanation sufficed. Rand had somehow muddled his attempt to rob Walter and the furious magistrate had summoned the redcoats.

The White Hart had a back exit. She would sneak out that way and wait for Rand at the peel tower. But what if he rode directly toward the inn?

I'll wait for him on the road. Somehow, I'll head him off.

Grace stood by the front entrance, watching the soldiers through the door's misty pane. "Why are they here, Mistress?"

"I have no idea."

"I'm affrighted, Mistress." Grace twisted her apron. "Dear me. As soon as ye come home, strange things happen."

"Then I must disappear again." Just as Elizabeth turned toward the back rooms, the front door opened. Three soldiers entered. In their tri-cornered hats, bright coats, white breeches and high black boots, they appeared inhumanly tall.

The leader of the three, a lieutenant, breathed through his mouth, since his nose looked as if it had been broken more than once. "Elizabeth Wyndham?" he asked, his voice raspy.

Fear rose tight in her throat, but Elizabeth simply shook her head. "I'm the new maid, sir."

"Mistress, are ye mad?" Grace turned to the lieutenant. " 'Tis her, sir, Miss Wyndham, standin' right next t' ye."

"Damn you," Elizabeth fumed, as the soldiers surrounded her. "Why can't you keep your mouth shut?"

"But Mistress, that be your name, and I dare not lie t' the king's own soldiers."

Elizabeth faced the lieutenant. "I lied because I was frightened. What's this all about? What have I done?"

"I can't say, Miss Wyndham."

The lieutenant wore a military sash across his chest. A steel gorget hung from a chain around his neck. He looked like someone who would do as he was told.

"You'll have to wait for Lord Stafford," the lieutenant continued. "He will inform you of what you need to know."

Elizabeth muttered a profanity under her breath. Somehow Walter had outfoxed her again.

Walter strode into the common room, his face as white as the bandages that wimpled the crown of his head. "I was so distracted by your hysteria, Elizabeth, I did not stay to make certain your highwayman was properly disposed of. I was a fool to trust Master

Hodges. One can never trust the loyalty of a man who can be bribed."

She raised her chin. "I have no idea what you're talking about. Rand was hanged at Tyburn. I saw him lower the handkerchief and *you* told me he was tarred and chained."

Judging from Walter's appearance, Rand had indeed caught up with him. But if Rand had been captured or killed, there would be no need for the troops, which meant Rand was still out there, Elizabeth thought, and Walter planned to use her as bait.

The muskets, with their dark wood, gleaming barrels and bayonets, seemed to fill the room. One of the soldiers looked little older than eighteen. The tip of his nose glistened with sweat.

"You're a fine actress," Walter said angrily. A rusty stain darkened the bandages at the spot where blood had seeped through. "Your grieving act looked so genuine, I almost felt sorry for you. But you knew all along that he was still alive."

"You're insane. My distress *was* genuine. This I swear on my mother's grave."

"Now you've added sacrilege to your other sins." He made a disgusted sound. "Your bastard highwayman caught up with me right out of Horsehouse. I had just left the coaching inn there. He forced me to lie upon the ground and put a pistol to my head. Then he hesitated. I could have sworn he said 'Bess has made me soft. I cannot do this.' Sensing an advantage, I began to struggle. I don't know what happened next. Perhaps he moved his hand, or the gun misfired, but the bullet merely grazed me. After I regained consciousness, I told Grosley to ride here. Even then I didn't believe . . . your grief . . . how the hell could you fool me like that?"

Grosley! The unexpected visitor had been Walter's servant. Bundled against the cold, atop a horse, he had looked much smaller. No wonder she hadn't recognized him.

"When Grosley entered the yard," Walter continued, "your ostler was babbling. Grosley could scarce understand him. Something about a ghost riding through the night — a ghost come to claim you. When Grosley related the tale, *I* understood."

Elizabeth felt as if all the blood had drained from her face and body, but she managed to hold herself steady. "Tim saw two ghosts, my lord," she said. "They haunt the inn. I saw them myself. Yesterday. Don't you remember?"

"Yes. But you asked me if I had seen a lady, not a man."

"I swear! There was a man at the window,

right next to the lady. He . . . he looked nothing like . . . the highwayman."

Up until now Elizabeth had told the truth, but for the first time she faltered. Because Ranulf had looked very much like Rand. Ranulf's hair was curlier, his beard coarser, his smile more evil, yet the resemblance existed. Ranulf, however, wasn't the least bit soft. He'd have killed Walter without pause.

She didn't know whether to feel relieved or dismayed that Rand had not played the cold-blooded killer.

Relieved, she decided.

Until Walter said, "You conniving bitch, do you honestly think I'd believe one word you say?" He nodded sharply toward the lieutenant. "You've been given your orders. Proceed."

The soldiers all looked from Walter to Elizabeth. The lieutenant appeared uncomfortable. "Are you certain about this, sir?" he asked.

"I've never been more certain of anything in my life."

The hours crawled by, toward midnight. Clothed in a pure white gown, Elizabeth knelt at the foot of her bed, facing her casement window. On the floor, in front of her knees, two heavy marble bookends secured a flintlock musket whose barrel was bound beneath her breasts. Her wrists were roped together. She had repeatedly tried to twist her hands free, but the knots held.

Ironically, the musket was called a Brown Bess.

Her room was dim, lit by a small fire and the moon, so that Rand would not detect the soldiers underneath her casement. Flat on their bellies, they cradled their long-barreled muskets.

Other soldiers were positioned behind the inn's second-story windows.

Walter sprawled at her writing desk, drinking from a bottle of wine. He had read the first chapter of her book-in-progress. Then, in a snarling fit of fury, he had used the pages to fan the fire, watching their edges slowly blacken and burn.

It didn't matter. The words were indelibly printed on her brain. Rand was indelibly printed on her brain.

"If you should try and warn your lover, I'll pull the trigger," Walter said with a sneer. "I'm gambling you'll keep silent and let him ride into a trap. After all, you preferred to let your lover hang rather than admit to Robert Whitney's murder. When the moment comes, you'll choose your life over his."

Elizabeth's rump pressed against her bed. If only she could dissolve into its frame, into the wall.

You're wrong, my lord, she thought, working the ropes. *Now that I know what it's like to live without Rand, without hope, I would rather be dead than experience such pain again.*

"He won't come," she said. "He's far too smart for you. All you'll get is a sleepless night."

The lieutenant, situated halfway between Stafford and the window, stared intently outside. Walter continued drinking. Elizabeth continued working the ropes. Her hands and fingers were raw from the struggle. At the point where the musket barrel rubbed her chest, her gown was soaked.

Her entire being concentrated on two things: Rand's arrival and the musket. Despite her defiant words, she knew Rand would come. Which meant that, unless a miracle occurred, she would have to choose.

Death for Rand, or death for herself?

Walter rose and walked unsteadily toward her. Bending, he breathed wine fumes into her face. "I curse the day I first laid eyes on you," he said. "Why don't we end it now?"

Terrified, she could only stare at his face.

"If I pull the trigger, I'll be a free man," he said.

"Nay, my lord. If you pull the trigger, you'll be gaoled with the very felons you've captured. Robbers. Murderers. Pickpockets," she recited, remembering his words inside Newgate. "Underworld scum, all coming and going precisely as they please."

Walter's expression altered and she caught a hint of fear in his eyes. He squeezed her chin rather than the trigger. Spinning on his heels, he returned to the table and groped for his chair.

Elizabeth worked diligently at the knots. Her hands were slick with perspiration, or blood, she couldn't tell which. Sometimes it seemed the ropes might be looser, other times they felt even tighter.

Stafford took a long pull from the wine bottle, wiped his mouth with the back of his hand, then jerked his head toward the window. "Are you keeping good watch, *dearest?*"

She didn't answer. The barrel brutalized her rib cage. Her legs ached. Her arms and hands felt numb. She looked beyond the soldiers to the ribbon of road, visible in the moonlight. The night was as still as the inn, as if it too watched and waited.

Had she heard something? The trot of a

horse's hooves? Sound would carry far on such a quiet night. She thought she glimpsed a shadow on the road. But it was far away, of no more substance than a bat flitting across the mouth of a cave.

"Let me go," she pleaded. "If you do not and something happens to me, you'll hang for murder."

Walter laughed, a harsh sound. "You don't have the courage to warn your lover. You forget, Elizabeth, I've been obsessed with you. I know you better than you know yourself. You'll keep silent."

Abruptly, the lieutenant turned toward the desk. "He's coming, my lord!"

Walter lurched from his chair. "Are you certain? I don't see anything."

"Out there on the road." Turning, the lieutenant pointed.

Elizabeth heard the clock chime midnight. At that very moment, her ropes loosened. Her finger reached between the bookends until she found the musket's trigger.

It curved so smoothly and fit so easily. This was the moment of decision. If Rand's stallion's hoofbeats were distinct, the sound of a gunshot would surely shatter the night's eerie silence. Unlike Janey, Elizabeth had a second chance, a chance to set things right. One squeeze. The falling hammer would strike the frizzen, the priming powder would flash through a touchhole, and the resultant shot would alert Rand.

Is that why we were allowed to remember our previous lives? So that I might make the final choice?

She saw Janey framed in the White Hart's window, staring down at the yard. She heard Janey's voice inside her head: *Don't you remember? Don't you know?*

Yes, Elizabeth knew. She realized full well what Janey had been trying to tell her all these months. That life without Ranulf had been a living hell, a living death.

What Elizabeth didn't understand was why she had been chosen to redeem Janey. Perhaps it had something to do with Dorothea's words: "Respectable women do not rut with highwaymen, nor do they write books. You've never wanted to be what you should be and therein lies your folly."

It had all started with *Castles of Doom,* with her written account of Simon de Montfort's rebellion. Nay, it had started long before that. As a child, hadn't she oft dreamed of broadswords and chain mail? Hadn't she been discovered at Fountains Abbey when she was a mere ten years old? "We found you screaming among the ruins," her father had said outside Wyndham

Manor. "I thought we'd never calm you down." And the peel tower! Had she not dreamt of shadowy knights on horseback, engaged in some sort of battle?

Ranulf and Janey had always been on hand, orchestrating her every move.

Why should I atone for Janey's mistakes? Why?

Elizabeth knew why. Because life without Rand would be a living hell, a living death.

"Come on, you bastard," Walter urged, gazing avidly at the window.

Elizabeth heard the ringing of hooves against cobblestones. All at once, she knew what she must do, how she'd save Rand and destroy Walter at the same time.

Even as she destroyed herself.

The soldiers looked to their priming.

Elizabeth stared at Walter, holding his gaze, praying he wouldn't see her finger on the trigger.

The lieutenant had turned his attention to the window. If Elizabeth managed to get Walter close enough she could shout "Don't shoot me, my lord!" and pull the trigger.

Walter would be arrested, gaoled, possibly hanged. In the eyes of the law she had done nothing wrong — nothing to provoke his vengeful wrath. Even if Walter managed to convince a judge and jury that she had played the highwayman's accomplice, there were witnesses — the Crown's own soldiers, no less — to testify that she could not have escaped. Wasn't she tightly bound to a musket?

"Come here, my lord," she said.

Walter's face glistened with sweat. "Soon he'll be dead, Elizabeth. Just a few more minutes and —"

"Come to me."

Walter hesitated. Then, as if compelled, he obeyed.

"Closer, my lord." Her gaze was steady. "I have something I want to say, something I don't want the others to hear."

"What lies will you tell me now, bitch?"

Walter bent forward until the sleeve of his coat touched the musket barrel, until he and Elizabeth were cheek by jowl. She saw the gash of white upon his head. "What do you have to say?" he asked harshly. "Why can't the others hear your words?"

"You will hang," she whispered. "At the very least you will be gaoled with carrion crows. How I wish I could witness their feast."

"Carrion crows?"

"Prisoners. They will feed on every inch of your body." With a tight, triumphant smile, Elizabeth shouted, "Don't shoot me, my lord!"

Walter recoiled, a look of horror on his face. His gaze darted toward her finger on the trigger, but he had already grasped her meaning.

Elizabeth drew a calming breath. Her serene expression never faltered as she squeezed the trigger.

Walter's scream of rage and fear pierced the room. Just before the haze of smoke completely blinded her, Elizabeth saw him pull his pistol from his pocket and turn it on himself.

EPILOGUE

Rhiannon whinnied her displeasure. She didn't particularly care for the scent of sheep, and she was surrounded by the bothersome "woolbirds."

The day had dawned cold and bright. No clouds scuttled the sky. Death had feasted on Walter Stafford. Full to bursting, Death had apparently decided that Rand would be superfluous.

Tom and Billy Turnbull stood beneath a grove of distant trees.

In the sunlight, Elizabeth could clearly see the welt on Rand's neck, especially since he was once again clean-shaven.

"I should have come for you directly, after my attack on Stafford," he said. "But my leg . . . my endurance . . . was all used up."

"It takes a wee bit out of a man, returning from the dead," Elizabeth teased. "Rand, I've been meaning to ask you about your attack on Walter. Why did you not shoot?"

"Stafford saw me, believed me a ghost, and fell from his horse. I couldn't shoot, Bess. 'Twas too easy. I wasn't threatened. Then, when I hesitated, he jolted my hand."

"Walter said your gun might have misfired. Thank the Lord his musket did." She shuddered. "I guess you could say I came back from the dead, too."

"I didn't know about the musket." Momentarily, Rand's blue eyes looked bleak, haunted. "If I had —"

"Hush, my love. There was no way you could discern Walter's black-hearted scheme."

Glancing toward the fleecy sheep, the woolbirds that now populated Wyndham Manor, Elizabeth remembered last night. Nay, this morning. Had the clock not struck twelve? She remembered squeezing the musket's trigger and the subsequent flash of the pan.

Once, when she was only seven years old, she had wondered how it would feel to sleep evermore. *Now I shall find out,* she had thought.

But God had other plans for her. Perhaps the musket's priming had been wet or its flint had dulled. Whatever the reason, the gun had misfired, belching smoke rather than its deadly ball.

Ironically, it was Walter who had warned Rand away from the inn.

Believing Elizabeth dead, believing he would be gaoled with the felons he had captured, Walter had swiftly retrieved his pistol and placed the barrel between his terrified eyes. His pride had won out in the end, for he had preferred death to indignity; death to the thought of human carrion crows feasting on his flesh.

Or had he finally realized that Elizabeth was irrevocably lost to him?

Now, Rand lifted her hand toward his lips. Then he stopped short. "Your wrist, Bess! 'Tis every bit as swollen as my neck."

"It will heal, just like your neck."

Rand's misery was clearly visible. "Such a brave, foolish, *bonny* Bess. I'm not worth it."

"Yes, you are. You once told the Duchess of Newcastle you didn't want to be valued cheaply. I think you're worth much more than two thousand guineas."

"I can't even put a value on you, my love. The Crown Jewels? No. They pale, compared to your radiance." He kissed the back of her hand, above her bruise, then sighed. "Stafford oft said he knew me better than I knew myself, and he was right. Had I not heard his pistol, I would have ridden straight into his trap. I love you so much, I wasn't even thinking. Fortunately, Stafford miscalculated."

"He never believed I would pull the trigger."

"True. And there's something else. Had I known you were trussed up inside your room, a musket at your breast, I would have continued my ride regardless."

"Perhaps that's what I was supposed to learn from Janey."

"What, sweetheart?"

"Sacrifice. The ultimate sacrifice, dictated by love. Despite his neglect, Janey loved Ranulf more than life itself. Yet she saved her own life by conspiring against him, which she regretted to her dying day. I love you so much, Rand. I would never betray you."

"I know. I've always known. I think I learned from Ranulf that I must never take you for granted. That life is precious and I must protect what we have, perhaps even settle down."

"You'll never settle down, but I don't care. So long as we are law-abiding, you can tempt danger whenever you choose. Of course, I must go along for the ride." Hugging him hard, she felt a slight resistance, a tightening of his muscles. "What is it, Rand?

What aren't you telling me?"

"While imprisoned, I learned that Stafford was responsible for your mother's death. My uncle, Tom and Billy's father, visited the Dales and —"

"But why?" Elizabeth swallowed her anguish. "Why would Walter want my mother dead?"

"Having gambled recklessly, your father owed vast sums. Upon Barbara's death, he would inherit the White Hart. 'Tis as simple as that. Walter was hired to murder Barbara by the same man who accepted your father's wagers. Stafford, in turn, hired my uncle."

"No wonder Billy looked familiar, that day on the bridge. I must have seen your uncle prowling the grounds the night before the murder. God's teeth! Now I know why Walter gave my father the funds to restore Wyndham Manor. With age, he had begun to develop a conscience. Unfortunately, he was so blinded by his obsession with me and his hate for you that his purgation was short-lived."

Rand gently tucked an errant curl behind her ear. "Do you want to visit America, my love? At least until my evil deeds are forgotten?"

Before she could reply, Tom and Billy joined them.

"Did I hear ye say America, cousin?" Billy waved his hands exuberantly. "Could I go with ye? I'd fight me way t' a fortune there, and I'll get the passage money somehow."

"Not by robbing some unsuspecting lord, I trust," Elizabeth chided.

"How'd ye guess?"

"I'll pay your passage," said Tom.

"Will ye join us?" Billy asked his brother.

"No. I've just begun to amass my own fortune."

Elizabeth hesitated, then held out her hand. "I misjudged you, Tom. When Walter told me Rand had been tarred and chained, I thought you had betrayed us again."

"I must confess. 'Twas your words that brought me round."

"What words?"

"You said Rand would never achieve success at the expense of others, especially his own family. You said Rand would have changed." Tom's austere neck turned beet-red. "I would change my ways for a woman like you," he blurted, clasping her extended hand.

"I see I shall have to find American brides for both Turnbulls." Elizabeth extracted her hand. Tempted to count her fingers and see if she still possessed five, she added, "You'll join us one day, Tom, for I expect America has need of gambling establishments even more than London does."

Rand grasped her shoulders and stared into her eyes. "The thought of leaving England does not repel you, Bess?"

"On the contrary, it intrigues me. At the sentencing you told the judge you wanted to be shed of England, and I couldn't agree more. I can pen my novels once we reach America. In fact, I began a new book at Middlethorpe. When I bid Aunt Lilith good-bye, I shall fetch the pages."

"What is your book about, my love? Mad monks? Lusty half-brothers? Debauched kings?"

"No." Elizabeth flashed him a grin. " 'Tis about a female land pirate whose lover keeps telling her to reform and give up her wicked ways."

The woolbirds echoed their laughter.

AUTHOR'S NOTE

In telling the story of Bess and Rand, it has been my intention to use nothing but historical facts. I have tried not to distort time or place or characters to suit my convenience, and although it has sometimes been necessary to rely on my own interpretations, I trust they are legitimate and backed by probability.

Some might question Bess's success as a Gothic Romance novelist, while some might even wonder if the term "Gothic Romance" was in use during my book's time period.

It was.

Gothic fiction began in England with *The Castle of Otranto* (1764) by Horace Walpole. Prominent features of Gothic fiction included ghosts, castles, darkness, death, madness (especially mad women), secrets, hereditary curses and persecuted maidens.

The term "Gothic" was applied because the genre dealt with emotional extremes and dark themes, and because it found its most natural settings in the buildings of this style — castles, mansions and monasteries, often remote, crumbling and ruined.

It was, however, Ann Radcliffe (1764–1823) who created the Gothic Romance novel in its now-standard form. Among other elements, Radcliffe introduced the brooding figure of the Gothic villain, which developed into the Byronic hero. Unlike Walpole's novels, Radcliffe's novels were best-sellers and virtually everyone in English society was reading them.

The Tyburn gallows, known as "the three-legged mare" or "three-legged stool," really did exist. The gallows were last used on November 3, 1783, when highwayman John Austin was hanged. I have changed the date to fit the context of my story.

ABOUT THE AUTHOR

Mary Ellen Dennis developed a love for Alfred Noyes's poem "The Highwayman" when she was very young. She memorized all the verses, but changed the ending to a happy one. During a high school speech class, she recited her adaptation. Before she could finish, the bell rang, signaling the end of class, but none of the mesmerized students moved. At that moment in time, Mary Ellen decided two things: She'd be an actress and she'd write a novel inspired by her favorite poem. She has achieved both goals. Mary Ellen likes to hear from readers. Her email address is maryellen dennis@shaw.ca.

The employees of Thorndike Press hope you have enjoyed this Large Print book. All our Thorndike and Wheeler Large Print titles are designed for easy reading, and all our books are made to last. Other Thorndike Press Large Print books are available at your library, through selected bookstores, or directly from us.

For information about titles, please call:
  (800) 223-1244

or visit our Web site at:
  www.gale.com/thorndike
  www.gale.com/wheeler

To share your comments, please write:
  Publisher
  Thorndike Press
  295 Kennedy Memorial Drive
  Waterville, ME 04901